# WATCH WHAT
# YOU SAY

ALSO BY GEORGE W

*Hardscrabble Road* (SFK Press, 2018)

*Aftermath* (SFK Press, 2018)

*The Five Destinies of Carlos Moreno* (SFK Press, 2018)

*The Caretaker* (SFK Press, 2019)

# Praise for *Watch What You Say*

"George Weinstein tackles the complexities of modern life—including the exploitative power of new media—and entangles them in a thrilling tale of vengeance and suspense. Bo Riccardi is a popular radio and podcast host whose troubled marriage and past secrets, including a decades-old murder, make her vulnerable to a madman. Weinstein exposes the reader to the literally colorful and intriguing world of chromesthesia, which plays a role in Bo's relentless hunt for the killer. *Watch What You Say* is a cat-and-mouse chase, and race, to the pull-no-punches, take-no-prisoners finish."
—Jenny Milchman, *USA Today* best-selling author of *Cover of Snow* and *Wicked River*

"The reason a reader stays with a novel is because the novel stays with a reader. George Weinstein's *Watch What You Say* is such a book. Unique, tense, teasing, perplexing, made of twists and turns that only a creative writer could conjure, this is a story of a gifted radio personality tormented by a man who has kidnapped her husband and manipulates social media for the sake of vengeance, leaving injury in its wake. Weinstein's versatility as a writer—the ability to handle numerous genres—proves again that he understands his audience."
—Terry Kay, international best-selling author of *To Dance with the White Dog*, *The Book of Marie*, and *The King Who Made Paper Flowers*

"With *Watch What You Say*, author George Weinstein gives the mystery mayhem crowd a nerve-wracking tale with an inimitable twist to the genre's bread-and-butter ingredients of unbridled passion, murder, and revenge. Bo Riccardi, a tough-as-nails female Internet radio journalist, has gained national fame as "The Barracuda" due to her chew-'em-up-spit-'em-out on-air interviews of a long line of poseurs, hucksters, and narcissists. Her gift is chromesthesia, the ability to see sounds as well as hear them; I kid you not, this is a real neurological condition—in essence, she possesses a bona fide BS detector. She also is burdened with a dark, homicidal memory from two decades earlier. And when revenge finally comes a-callin' and her husband is kidnapped . . . well, I guarantee you'll have as tough a time putting *Watch What You Say* down as I did. This truly is a brilliant read."

—Jedwin Smith, author of *I Am Israel* and *Our Brother's Keeper*

"The suspenseful pacing and masterful use of description both work to make this a page-turner. Unique as its protagonist, a successful radio host with the astounding gift of chromesthesia and the terrifying responsibility of outsmarting the sociopath who has her husband's life in his hands, this story is full of twists, wonderfully unsettling, and will keep readers on the edge of their seats."

—Kimberly Brock, author of *The River Witch*

"Non-stop, pulse-pounding action with a protagonist who must use her gift of chromesthesia to see into the heart of a killer and save her family. This one is a heart-stopper!"

—Emily Carpenter, author of *Burying the Honeysuckle Girls*, *The Weight of Lies*, *Every Single Secret*

"George Weinstein weaves an ever-tightening web of suspense in this superb, page-turning thriller as a web radio show host attempts a desperate rescue of her husband from a sadistic kidnapper. The kidnapper demands to be the show's featured guest, thus giving him a platform from which to annihilate the host's reputation . . . and maybe her husband."
—H. W. "Buzz" Bernard, author of the EPIC eBook award-winning novel, *Cascadia*

"In this high-stakes game of cat-and-mouse, a shockingly cruel cat goes toe-to-toe with one very smart mouse possessed of a most unusual talent. The relentlessly rising tension kept me squirming all the way to the end."
—Roger Johns, award-winning author of the Wallace Hartman Mysteries

"Spellbinding. . . . Explosive. . . . Gifted storyteller George Weinstein keeps the dramatic tension as he takes readers on the ultimate thrill ride."
—Dana Ridenour, award-winning author of the Lexie Montgomery FBI undercover series

"No one does cat-and-mouse like George Weinstein, and his newest, *Watch What You Say*, proves he's at the top of his thriller game. Vividly cast and wholly atmospheric, Weinstein starts the clock of his suspenseful novel ticking from the first page and keeps the pace relentless—for both his imperiled characters and his reader—until the very end. A chilling, twisty tale of revenge!"
—Erika Marks, author of *The Guest House*

"*Watch What You Say* will grab you and not let go as Weinstein explores the minds of a psychotic killer, a brainwashed, kidnapped husband, and a woman who sees words as bursts of color. Unlikely heroes, unexpected traitors, and a twisty plot will keep his readers guessing up to the last page. A thrilling psychological read!"
—Susan Crawford, best-selling author of *The Pocket Wife* and *The Other Widow*

# Share Your Thoughts

Want to help make *Watch What You Say* a best-selling novel? Consider leaving an honest review on Goodreads, your personal author website or blog, and anywhere else readers go for recommendations. It's our priority at SFK Press to publish books for readers to enjoy, and our authors appreciate and value your feedback.

# Our Southern Fried Guarantee

If you wouldn't enthusiastically recommend one of our books with a 4- or 5-star rating to a friend, then the next story is on us. We believe that much in the stories we're telling. Simply email us at pr@sfkmultimedia.com.

SFK
PRESS

GEORGE WEINSTEIN

# WATCH WHAT
# YOU SAY

Published by
Southern Fried Karma, LLC
Atlanta, GA
www.sfkpress.com

Books are available in quantity for promotional or premium use. For information, email pr@sfkmultimedia.com.

ISBN: 978-1-970137-85-9
eISBN: 978-1-970137-86-6
Library of Congress Control Number: 2019942231

Cover design by Olivia M. Croom. Cover art: iStock.com/petekarici. Interior by April Ford.

Printed in the United States of America.

*For Kate, whose empathic abilities, steely resolve, and supreme badassery inspired this book.*

# Chapter 1

The calfskin driving gloves Deke Powell always wore stretched tight as he clenched and flexed his hands against the steering wheel. He had pulled back the left sleeve of his brown coveralls so his gaze could flick between the Swiss Army chronograph strapped to his wrist and the view of Bo Riccardi's home through the rain-beaded windshield.

He'd parked his anonymous SUV rental down the street from her two-story house before sunrise. Over the last few months, the ruler-straight road had provided many perfect stakeout spots. Renting a different vehicle every other week had taken a chunk out of his bank account, but that's what savings were for.

The front door opened, and Bo's seventeen-year-old daughter stepped into the drizzle. At five-foot-nine, Candace was two inches taller than Bo and much skinnier. No curves under her tight blouse and fashionably ripped jeans. Blond hair so pale and limp that it looked like tarnished tinsel.

Burdened by an overstuffed book bag, she scuffed to an old hatchback parked in front of the garage and slung the pack onto the shotgun seat. She set out toward the subdivision exit.

*On schedule*, he thought. *Just another boring start to another boring school week, poor kid.*

If Bo followed her own routine, the garage door would ratchet upward in an hour or so, and she would reverse her late-model Mercedes sedan down the drive. He had witnessed the family's patterns so often, he could visualize them.

A careful driver, she would always check both ways. He'd captured her with his long telephoto lens a few times when she had looked down the street in his direction. Over the months, he had accumulated hundreds more images and recorded every one of her video podcasts. Except for her last name and a few extra pounds, she hadn't changed much in twenty-five years: a more expensive hairstyle with blond highlights, laugh lines around her brown eyes, diamonds in her ears instead of the cheapo gold hoops she'd sported at Virginia Tech.

Once Bo departed for work, that would leave only her husband, Oscar Riccardi, at home.

Gloved hands back on the wheel, silent and still, Deke envisaged for a final time what he'd do, and when and how.

# CHAPTER 2

Thanks to chromesthesia, Bo Riccardi didn't just hear sounds, she saw them as well. The closer she listened, the more nuances she noticed in the colors and shapes and their movements across her mind's eye. On her mental canvas, each voice and noise appeared as distinctive as a fingerprint. Some even featured similar ovals and whorls—while others flared as spiky as barbed wire.

Every utterance conveyed the speaker's feelings. And their intent. She could literally watch what they said.

Not long ago, her husband Oscar's voice had created the most beautiful images she'd ever seen. But since his layoff, it had lost all its bright, smooth contours. Now the way he spoke to her looked gloomier than anything else in her world.

"Yes or no?" he demanded at the kitchen counter. "Should I get the rental car or not?"

On her mental canvas, in front of the backdrop of apricot that was unique to him, a row of graphite pyramids thrust up. Resentment, anger, and jealousy. Lashing out to mask the hurt inside.

She remembered how she had felt during the times when she'd been out of work: the loss of confidence, the fear that even her loved ones looked down on her. Beating herself up for something beyond her control while moodily punishing those around her.

Her phone vibrated against her palm. She paused in the kitchen doorway, replying to an ongoing text conversation with friends. Glancing up from the screen, she told him, "Do whatever you need to." She knew he would anyway, and she wanted to avoid another argument.

He grunted and scratched his cheek, which was dark with stubble. Still playing the tough Italian from South Philly. The swagger—that poise she'd always found so sexy—had left him, however, and she felt more pity than attraction lately.

With swift strokes of a chef's knife, he slashed through a half-dozen green onions, dividing them into tiny cylinders. The snick-snick of the blade against the cutting board produced crimson splashes in Bo's mind, while the wet slicing sound of the scallions sent forth mustard-yellow streamers.

Not a fan of knives, she gave it a wide berth. She tugged up her pencil skirt, sat at the kitchen table, and continued to thumb-type. Some of her besties had initiated their favorite "Can this marriage be saved?" game, speculating about whether an acquaintance's relationship could survive if the couple worked hard enough.

Bo made certain her own twenty-year marriage never warranted their scrutiny by always having positive things to say about it. An on-camera professional, she needed to be as good an actor as she was an interviewer. In truth, though, while she still loved Oscar, she didn't like him much lately—and didn't like herself for feeling that way. She also didn't know how much work she wanted to do to save their relationship, which made her feel guilty as hell.

Some of the green onions rolled off the board and scattered on the tile floor around Oscar's slippers. His robe and the pajamas underneath had begun to fray from daily wear since the layoff. He shifted his burgeoning weight and crushed the scallions underfoot as he scraped the remainder onto the scrambled eggs cooking in a skillet.

His slipper left a trail of green. It resembled the image that appeared in Bo's mind whenever their daughter Candace gave an aggravated sigh. Which was daily.

Oscar wiped up the mess with a paper towel. "I'm asking because you're always talking about money. Or the lack of it."

She'd seen a lot of black pyramids lately, too. "Well," she

replied, "do you really need a car this week? It's not like you have anywhere to go."

The only voice she couldn't visualize was her own, but her comment didn't require blended senses to interpret. She cringed at the bitterness that had slipped out while she'd been distracted. *So much for your acting skills*, she thought. As someone who talked for a living, she knew better than most how words could hurt.

As if in retaliation, he dropped the cutting board and knife into the deep steel sink. Bruised colors—muddy browns and greens—flared behind her eyes, overlaid by a streak of gray as the blade clattered against the metal sides. The detonation made her drop the phone. Her fingers curled into fists.

Oscar scraped the eggs onto two plates. More for him, but he stood six inches taller and outweighed her by at least eighty pounds. Probably closer to one hundred now.

She pushed her cellphone aside to make room for the plate and tried to rein in her emotions. His once-reliable sunny attitude and sense of humor would surely return as soon as he found work again. He'd been unlucky all the way around, even having had the misfortune last weekend to skid on an oily patch of road and bash his Corvette against a guardrail.

"Get the rental," she said. "Candace has a bunch of after-school things, so she can't give up her car."

He plopped into the chair opposite her. "You're sure we can afford it?"

As he spoke, aquamarine horsetails of apology and regret overlaid the apricot background of his voice, and scaly pink flecks showered down. He was afraid. She wondered if his ego would allow him to hear the fear in his voice as clearly as she saw it.

"Everything will be okay," she said, touching his hand. "Thanks for breakfast."

He shrugged and pulled up the food-stained sleeves of his robe. "No problem."

Melancholy colors and shapes contradicted his statement, but Bo also saw a narrow silver lining of love there. A slender thread on which to hang her wishes.

STEADY SPRING RAIN MADE the Monday morning rush-hour slog from the northern suburbs to midtown Atlanta even worse than usual. Bo tried to distract herself from the never-ending stop-and-go with a hypothetical list. If the actual answer to Oscar's "can we afford it" question changed from "just barely" to "hell no," what would they need to give up to save money? Her leased Mercedes would be the first thing, though she'd miss the superb insulation, which dampened the otherwise constant technicolor splatter of shapes caused by traffic noises. Occasional splurges—for nails, hair, and shoes—would go as well. And fans of her online show might notice when she began to wear the same outfits in tedious rotation.

Oscar's expensive networking lunches and dinners hadn't yielded any leads yet, but maybe they would soon—if not, that would be yet another discussion she'd need to manage. On the other hand, she would take a second job to ensure Candace got whatever she wanted, so nothing of their daughter's made the list.

In the basement garage, with forty floors of offices pressing down, Bo eased into one of the few slots set aside for On-Air Web Radio employees. It was a reserved space in a second respect as well: her producer Jeffrey Hays, who was also her director and sound engineer, had painted "Bo Riccardi: The Barracuda" on the concrete parking bumper. Though Jeff referred to each member of the small staff by a nickname, he hadn't singled out a parking spot for anybody but her.

His friendship was one of the things she loved about working at On-Air, along with the chance to interview such a broad range of professionals—from entertainers to entrepreneurs, soldiers to senators. It still amazed her that she got paid to speak with remarkable people. Of course, there were also those days when she earned her salary and then some by taking a bite out of those trying to put one over on the public. Despite her reputation, there seemed to be no end of poseurs, hucksters, and other narcissists who wanted to plunge into The Barracuda's tank for an hour and try to emerge unscathed. To date, none had succeeded.

After an elevator ride to the twenty-seventh floor, she pushed through the glass entrance of the company office. A two-note chime rang, which she saw as a light green diagonal heading upward and then becoming dark green and descending as the tone did.

No one called a greeting, but she welcomed the silence, a respite from the usual colorful shape-shifting her mind's eye had to filter.

Her cubicle sat closest to the door, so the task of welcoming any arrivals usually fell to her. As she was the only female employee, this ad hoc receptionist role had felt sexist since she'd started there years before. Most visitors were her interview guests, but still. . . .

She set her satchel on her desk and savored the aroma of fresh-brewed coffee from the breakroom, courtesy of Jeff. Before getting a cup, she noted the lit ON AIR sign that jutted above the studio door, and she crossed the carpet.

Peering through the small rectangle of glass set in the wood, she glimpsed Sean O'Shea in his usual blousy poet shirt. He cooed to his audience of lonely hearts from the small, soundproofed room of fuzzy gray walls and matching carpet. His mouth hovered just above the circular mesh "pop block" screen, which protected the microphone from sudden vocal spikes. Not that Sean needed a Popper Stopper: his on-air tone never rose above a soul singer's throaty purr. His pale fingers curved and swooped on either side of his mass of wavy black hair while he dispensed relationship advice. Unlike Bo, he seemed to relish the webcam on Jeff's console, which transmitted his image while the mic delivered his words.

Beyond the table where Sean held forth, Jeff sat at a long desk, the lenses in his gold-framed glasses reflecting two computer screens to his left—sound levels and the webcam feed—as he tweaked one of the dozens of sliders on the mixer board in front of him. His thick mustache quirked up on one side in a smirk, his default expression whenever he recorded "The Irish Teddy Pendergrass," or "ITP," as Jeff had dubbed him. ITP was also Atlanta slang for those who lived Inside the Perimeter of the city, which Sean did. Given the number of panties he boasted about taking from his groupies, ITP was actually a triple entendre.

She caught Jeff's eye through the window and waved. With one hand, he pantomimed long-toothed jaws snapping back at her while holding up a laminated "30 SEC TIL BREAK" card to Sean with the other. Jeff had given her the "Barracuda" nickname after she'd torn into a congressman whose vocal shapes and colors revealed the lies behind his spoken promises. The On-Air Web Radio president had loved the new moniker and plastered "Home of the Barracuda" all over the station website and social media.

Though it was too melodramatic for her taste, she couldn't deny that the nickname brought her a higher salary and more endorsement deals. And those had certainly come in handy since Oscar's layoff. If she still prayed, she would've given thanks for The Barracuda.

Sean glanced her way as he continued his usual sensual discourse that probably made some of his fans disrobe. In the On-Air lineup, only his show challenged hers for live-broadcast ratings and subsequent podcast downloads. But she trusted her audience kept their clothes on.

Stroking his denim-clad thighs, he winked at her. As usual, edging up to the border of harassment but never quite venturing inside *that* perimeter.

Bo typically ignored him, but her tense breakfast with Oscar had put her on edge. She smoothed one eyebrow with her extended middle finger. Retaliation delivered, she headed to the breakroom for Jeff's custom-blended, high-octane java.

Steaming cup in hand, she returned to her cubicle in time to hear "That's Amore" blare from her satchel. Sparkles and bright swaths of warm colors. Oscar obviously had reprogrammed the ringtone after his previous selection, "Sexual Healing," embarrassed her during a staff meeting the previous week. That had been a doubly cruel joke—they hadn't made love in months—and the new one seemed to be a dig as well. She let him go to voicemail.

# CHAPTER 3

Deke parked the rented SUV close to the Riccardis' garage door. He didn't worry about Bo's husband exiting after her; the idiot's wrecked Corvette was in the body shop. Thanks to spyware Oscar had unwittingly downloaded to his phone months before—courtesy of a fake job-postings email—Deke could see each mundane text and hear every boring conversation the man had, including this morning's call to the rental car company to request pickup service.

If Bo was worried the fuckup was cheating on her instead of looking for work, there was no need. The guy never did anything interesting. Even his porn choices were dull.

Deke snugged the calfskin gloves over his fingers, tugged his ball cap down to his eyebrows, and checked the coverall pockets for his gear. The only way the operation could hit a snag was if they had nosy neighbors, but this was typical Atlanta suburbia: houses set far apart, busy people with no interest in the folks next door. See no evil, hear no evil. Still, he waited for a car to go by before stepping from the vehicle. No point in tempting fate.

At the pebble-glass front door, he removed the black and yellow Taser from his right pocket and hid it behind him. He knuckled the doorbell. Getting into character, he dipped his face, pretended to focus on the phone in his left glove—just another working stiff on the clock, nothing threatening here.

A full minute elapsed before a large silhouette appeared on the other side of the door. Deke watched Oscar try to peer out, hesitate, and lift a hand to his ear. On his phone, Deke saw Oscar's call to Bo's number and heard the automated reply in his wireless earpiece, with a generic female voice repeating the number dialed and inviting Oscar to leave a message, which he didn't.

Bo had always been a careful girl: didn't use her name or voice on her recording, wouldn't open any of the fake texts or emails he'd created to launch spyware on her phone or computer, never fell for any of his lines in college. So goddamn careful.

After another moment, the deadbolt lock clicked open, and Oscar pulled the door inward. Tall, thickset, and olive-skinned, clad in rumpled chino pants and an untucked polo shirt. He frowned and said, "Can I help—"

Deke slowly tucked his phone in a left pocket, drawing attention that way as he brought the Taser around from the right and shot Oscar in the stomach, scoring hits with both darts. Two slender copper wires leading back to the stun gun delivered its high-voltage load. The unit cycled, clicking rapidly. A bitter ozone-like odor accompanied the noise.

Joints locked, face frozen in a rictus of pain, Oscar moaned and began to topple forward.

Deke was ready, stepping inside the foyer as he stopped Oscar from falling. He kicked the door closed. Letting go of the Taser, he slipped behind the larger man and lowered him to the wood floor. With his arm wrapped around Oscar's neck, elbow under the chin, Deke applied a sleeper hold and counted as the electrical paralysis wore off and Oscar started to struggle. Seven, eight, nine, ten.

The man now hung limp against his arm. Steady pulse, deep breaths, but unconscious.

From the zippered breast pocket of his coverall, Deke removed a hard-shell case containing several syringes of barbiturates. He injected Oscar with a dose to keep him down for hours and returned the case and the Taser to his pockets.

Dragging the big, heavy man through the dining room and kitchen and into the garage was a pain in the ass. Deke grunted as he dumped Oscar onto the oil-stained concrete.

He drove the SUV under cover, slung Oscar across the backseat, and secured him using thick zip ties. After he concealed him with a tarp, he reversed the SUV outside again. Back in the garage, he hit the button to lower the door a final time and sprinted toward the shrinking gap. He hurdled the electric eye at ankle-level to avoid sending the door up again and swung into the driver seat.

As he shut his door, another car drove past without pause. See no evil, hear no evil.

The whole thing had taken less than fifteen minutes according to his chronograph. He raised his ball cap and allowed himself a satisfied sigh.

From the time he was a kid, people had remarked on his eye for detail, his ability to plan. Those skills had always served him well.

# CHAPTER 4

Following a salad lunch she'd brought from home to save money, and a brisk tooth-brushing so the webcam wouldn't find any spinach in her smile, Bo reviewed her notes for the daily live interview. She'd be speaking with the author of a memoir about growing up in an abandoned Kentucky coal mine. It should be a cakewalk; though people in the arts could be provocative, they rarely instigated the full-on Barracuda treatment.

She consulted the clock on her phone just as "That's Amore" played again. This time she answered Oscar's call. "I'm on-air soon. What's up?"

A deep, robotic voice said, "I have your husband." Spikes of mottled brown hate and red flame tips of passion appeared against a rust-colored background.

"Quit screwing around. I don't have time for this."

Even as she spoke, though, she knew there was no way to fake the malice and desire she saw. Not even the best actors could fool her color-hearing synesthesia. Her heart began to beat double-time, as if she were running wind-sprints.

"He's right here." The distorted voice no longer spoke directly into Oscar's phone as it commanded, "Say hello."

"Bo, it's me. I'm fine." He sounded only a little like Oscar now, his voice warped and its apricot backdrop dimmed by whatever electronics the other man was using. Scaly pinks and splattered purples overlapped her vision: fear and panic.

Breath caught in her chest. She wanted this to be a sick joke he and some friend were playing on her, something to make her angry, not frightened.

"I told you," the rust voice cut in from a distance, "to say hello."

Oscar gasped, an arrow of brick red. "Hurts, it hurts. Okay, okay, hello."

His pain made the horror show undeniable. "Stop it," she shouted. "Please." Somebody had abducted him. This was really happening.

"Bo, do whatever he says. I'm taped down, blindfold—" His sentence was cut off by the slamming of a door, as if the kidnapper had sealed him in a cell as soundproofed as the On-Air studio.

She fumbled with phone apps, finally launching one to record the call. "Who are you?"

"A friend." The red flames remained, but pale blue streamers replaced the cruel spikes. He spoke with utter conviction.

"What?" It was such an insane response she nearly dropped the device. "How do I get Oscar back? What do you want?"

He said, "I want you to interview me live in thirty minutes." Pulses of ochre and teal: ego, ambition.

She shut her eyes. The madness of the situation felt like a giant snake constricting her body, squeezing tighter and tighter. "That's not possible," she told him. "The president of the station has to approve every guest."

"Maybe Oscar didn't scream loud enough before. Or, maybe I need to snatch Candace from school."

"No, no, please don't. Let me think." She wiped at the sweat that glazed her face.

The door to the office suite opened with its two-note chime. Either someone returning from lunch, or the author arriving early for his interview.

"Well?" the distorted voice demanded, and copper lightning forked behind Bo's eyes.

Chills made her tremble. "Okay, we'll, um, set up the studio for a call-in and d-d-dial Oscar's cellphone with Skype."

"Call this one instead." He recited ten digits. "And no video."

She scribbled the number. "Audio only. We'll call, uh, about ten minutes before airtime to check sound levels and everything."

"In the meantime," he said, "don't call the police, the FBI, anybody. If you do, Oscar will die. Very slowly and very painfully, with my knife."

As if he knew her greatest fear. "Oh, God."

"Prayer is fine. Talk to Him all you want. Just not the law."

"Hello?" a man said from the entrance. Twangy Appalachian accent, mossy backdrop, flat, ice-blue disks of uncertainty. Palming the mic, Bo shouted, "I need a minute." Jeff jogged past her cube, coming to her rescue by greeting the author. She uncovered the phone and said, "After we talk on-air, you'll let him go, right?"

"I promise, after I'm finished with you."

The red flame tips had returned, but this time a perfect pearl accompanied them. Truth. When she analyzed it for flaws, she couldn't see any. This made the conversation seem even crazier. Like living through a nightmare.

Even more horrible than that. This had become the second-worst day of her life.

*But it could become the very worst.*

She snatched up a pen. "Uh, what will we talk about?"

"This, that, and the other." Golden swirls of amusement, like thin, curly ribbons.

"But I need to know what questions to ask you."

"Start with your favorite one." His tone rose mockingly, a cruel imitation of a squeaky girl, made shriller by his synthesizer. "'Could you tell our audience a little bit about yourself?' And then improvise like crazy—as if your husband's life depends on it."

"Wha . . . what name do I call you?"

"Call me Oscar." The passion again, but also graphite pyramids of jealousy, resentment, and anger.

She dropped the pen and squeezed the phone tighter. "No, I can't."

He said, "You will. Or else." Copper lightning.

Her eyes burned with tears, and her nose tingled, but she refused to let him hear her cry. She had no control over the situation, but that was one thing she could do.

Poor Oscar, trapped somewhere, terrified. Last week, he'd even told her about seeing the same car numerous times, as if somebody were following him. A paranoid delusion she'd dismissed out of hand.

Bo apologized silently to him for every spiteful thought she'd harbored, every angry thing she'd said at home and in their counseling sessions. Blaming his deepening depression on weakness, as if it were a personal failing, something he could overcome with a little willpower. Not loving him enough, not showing it more often.

She vowed to do whatever was needed to free him and then rekindle that affection. Make it burn brighter than it ever had, even during their first years together. This lunatic would not ruin their lives.

"Fine," she said. "Oscar. Last name?"

"Your choice."

Before she could think about the repercussions, she spat, "Asshole, maybe? Bast—"

Someone cleared his throat behind her while the voice laughed derisively in her ear with starbursts of white, like a window being chipped by stones. She spun her seat around. Jeff frowned at her, nose and mustache twitching. Beside him stood a tall man, pale and wide-eyed, his mouth open as he clutched a hardback book to his chest.

Jeff adjusted his gold-framed glasses and said, "I'll just get Mr. Wilcox comfortable in the studio." His vocal background was always the green of a leaf backlit by the sun, but she saw a muddy overlay of concern. He gave her a final worried look before leading their guest away.

"It's Internet radio," the rust voice was saying. "No FCC to worry about, no six-second delay to avoid offense, so use whatever name you want. But your listeners will expect better from their Barracuda. Didn't *The Wall Street Journal* applaud you for 'eviscerating with panache'?"

She read the gentler shapes and colors, indigo swirled in crème, and said, "You've gotten your way so now you're making nice, to put me more at ease. You don't want me to act hostile on-air and detract from your broadcast debut."

After a pause, he replied, "The reporter also complimented your . . . 'remarkable intuition and startlingly profound insights.'" Despite his sneering tone, his words were infused with the same flat, pale blue disks of uncertainty she'd heard in the author's voice. Probably the only kind of victory she could score against him.

Bo glanced at the phone screen to note the time. Ten minutes to pull herself together. She talked for a living, but she'd never talked to save a life.

*Run away,* a small, scared part of her urged: *you've done it before.*

A massive weight seemed to settle across her shoulders, and hot tears came. Voice cracking, she said, "We'll call you in ten," and severed the connection on the second try with a shaky jab of her finger.

# CHAPTER 5

As Bo washed and dried her face in the restroom, she felt so desperate that she considered praying. It would've been the first time in decades. Because of that, a plea to God for Oscar's protection seemed hypocritical. She could imagine Him saying, "Oh, *now* you need Me. What's it been, twenty-five years?"

Instead, she redid her makeup with the studio webcam in mind—bolder eyes, cheeks, and lips—while giving herself a pep talk. *You can do this.* The maniac just wants some attention, he wants to feel as if the world is listening to whatever crackpot things he plans to say. Give him an hour in the spotlight, pump up his ego, and he'll let Oscar go. He'd promised, and he said it truthfully.

She remembered that pearl as she stowed the cosmetics in her satchel. One day, she promised herself, this would be just a strange little episode they'd rehash over dinner with friends: *Remember when Oscar got kidnapped for a few hours so that nut job could pretend to be a star?*

A toilet flushed and a stall door opened. Bo greeted Kathryn Robertson, the tall, regal-looking redhead who worked for a media company down the hall. After once joking about their bladders being on the same schedule, they had become casual friends, sometimes getting lunch together at the ground-floor food court.

Kathy brushed some wrinkles out of her slacks, nodded to Bo's reflection, and said in an impressed tone, "That's one serious beat face."

Bo saw a purple carnation bloom over Kathy's background color of denim blue.

"It better be," she replied, slinging the bag onto her shoulder. "This interview's important."

Kathy began to wash her hands. "A celebrity?"

"He thinks he is anyway."

"Well, tomorrow's chicken tortilla soup day downstairs. You can tell me all about the jerk."

"I can't make any plans. Sorry."

The woman studied Bo. "Give this guy the full Barracuda treatment, okay?"

Her words produced a ball of morning sunshine that momentarily filled Bo with confidence. She thanked her but, as soon as she exited, morose thoughts began to assert themselves again.

Would the madman really kill Oscar if she couldn't go through with the interview, or would he just let him go and try another way to get attention? What if someone stopped her before they got started? Maybe Jeff wouldn't be able to connect to Oscar's phone by Skype. Maybe the On-Air president would put a halt to it when he realized she'd gone rogue with a mystery guest—Harry Pinzer hated surprises.

Oscar didn't leave a message when he'd dialed her earlier. Why had she been so petty about not answering? Was he calling to ask about a man outside? Tell her about the same car he'd seen earlier, now parked in front of the house? Maybe she would've had some intuition of danger and warned him.

Ahead, the hallway telescoped away; the On-Air Web Radio suite seemed to have receded by a mile. Her legs felt thick and heavy as she pushed against her suddenly leaden skirt, her shoes feeling like wedges of concrete.

She clomped along, gaze straying to the elevator and stairwell. So many escape routes, so many ways to flee from this terrible situation. Except she knew the only real escape would be to see the nightmare through this time and come out on the other side. Nut job appeased. Oscar freed. Guilt vanquished—the ledger set right. Maybe her soul redeemed.

Behind her, the bathroom door opened. Kathy called, "You

good? Sort of scuffing like my ten-year-old when she doesn't want to go to school."

Bo turned and sighed. "I'm good, I guess."

"Hunh. Sounds to me like you've already lost the battle. Surrendered, more like."

Kathy was right. Bo tried to shake off her dread by standing taller and squaring her shoulders. "No, just overthinking," she said.

"That'll get you in trouble every time." Kathy pounded her sternum. "Don't think. Feel."

The ball of sunshine was back. Bo imagined wrapping her arms around it, taking the heat inside. "Thanks again. Sorry, I've got to go."

"Go forth and win." Kathy raised her fist and headed in the opposite direction, toward an office at the other end of the hall.

Bo turned on a heel and strode into the quiet On-Air suite. Thinking clearer, she remembered the people tracker app she'd installed on Oscar's phone, Candace's, and her own. She opened it, and the screen showed Oscar on I-75, south of Atlanta, heading toward Florida. Was his abductor moving him to another spot? Would the man do the interview from the road? At least she could trace their movements. The app displayed Candace's phone at the high school, so that was a relief.

When Bo heaved open the heavy studio door, she heard the murmur of a preprogrammed show from the overhead speakers, which produced an orange EKG wave traveling across her mental canvas. She halted. In the guest chair sat the tall, pale author, clutching his coalfield memoir.

He cleared his throat and began to speak, but she interrupted with, "Um, I'm really sorry, Mr. Wilcox, but I need to bring you back another time."

While he gaped at her, Jeff said from behind his mixer board and screens, "Do what?"

She continued to focus on her guest. Holding the door open, she said, "Something's come up, and there's another interview

I need to do today." She checked the time on her phone. "We have to set up for it now. Please."

"I drove all the way down from Ashland for this." He rose to his full height, cheeks coloring. As he spoke, his voice had gone from cobalt ripples of worry to salmon barbs of indignation. Nervous about doing something, and then angry when that terrifying opportunity was snatched away.

Now that Bo finally felt ready to do battle, she wondered whether she'd react the same way—for a second anyhow—if the lunatic cancelled the interview and let Oscar go. "I'll make it a two-parter," she promised. "You'll get double the time. Twice the exposure for your book."

Jeff said, "Speaking of time, we're kinda pressed for it. What the hell's going on?"

"Boot up Skype," she told him, and let the door shut behind her with a thump that unfurled like a tawny fan. She noted Wilcox's sullen pout. "You can even do the sessions from home."

"After coming so far, I just hate leaving empty-handed."

She glanced around and seized a coffee mug with the On-Air logo, which Sean had left on the table, brown ring in the bottom. "Here."

"Would you sign it, ma'am?"

She felt like screaming, but said, "Sure." Anticipating Jeff's toss, she whirled and snatched a Sharpie from the air, flicked off its cap with a thumbnail, and autographed the mug. After pushing it into his free hand, she marched him out of the studio. "Exit's to the left," she called to his back. "I'll reschedule you soon."

Locking the door, which lit the "On Air" sign outside, she remembered that Oscar had also been sealed in a similarly soundproofed room. Now she needed to somehow free him from his confinement while cloistered in her own cell. The insanity of the situation made her throw the Sharpie against one of the fuzzy gray walls and screech like a madwoman.

"Yeah, no kidding." Jeff said. "That ink's gonna totally smear when he touches it."

A bark of laughter burst from her, sounding even more hysterical than her shriek. "Thanks, I needed that."

"Skype's up. What kind of deviltry are you embroiling your devoted sidekick in?"

The red flame tips in his voice were even more pronounced than usual. From the first time they'd worked together, Jeff struck her as the kind of guy who crushed hard on every woman he met. He never acted on his feelings, so she always gave his flirty banter a pass.

"All I can say is there's another guy I have to interview. We were supposed to call him a couple minutes ago. Audio only, no video." She handed Jeff the sheet of paper she'd yanked from her writing pad.

"Uh, did you loop in Harry and just kinda sorta forgot to tell your aforementioned devoted sidekick?" He typed in the number. The Skype boop-boop rhythm and electronic ringing followed. "Of course, I'm up for anything that doesn't get me fired along with you."

"Harry doesn't know about this."

"Oooh, curiouser and curiouser. I'm totally on bo—"

"You're late," the synthesized voice interrupted from the computer speaker.

"Holy shit," Jeff said, "you're interviewing Darth Vader?"

"Who's that?" Suspicion like a burst of violet shrapnel.

Bo said, "Jeffrey Hays. He's my producer, director, and engineer."

"At your service, Lord Vader."

"Stop calling me that. Why is he there?"

"He runs the show." She settled into her favorite chair: whichever one Sean hadn't just been sitting in. "Monitors sound levels, makes sure the connection is solid, watches the time. Did you think all that happened automatically?"

Jeff said, "So what do I call you?"

The maniac and Bo both replied, "Oscar." His voice sounded—and looked—triumphant. Now that they were about to go head-to-head, she felt anything but.

# CHAPTER 6

Bo swept her index finger across her throat to silence Jeff before he started to riff again.

She wondered again why the lunatic wanted to make it even more personal by adopting Oscar's name. If his intention was to get on the air and rant about how the world had wronged him all his life or whatever, why bother to abuse her further?

In a rare show of obedience, Jeff closed his mouth and got to work, patching Skype with the studio sound system. He muted the overhead speaker, cutting off the murmur of the current program in its final few minutes.

They both pulled on headphones, which would now be the only way to hear the kidnapper. Their cords snaked into the snarl at the back of the sound mixer. As soon as the padded ovals cupped her ears, they created a claustrophobic vacuum that always made her feel as if she'd been submerged in an aquarium where the glass walls, floor, and ceiling were all painted gray.

"Tell me what's happening," the rust voice demanded. It seemed close enough to imagine sour breath on her face.

"Gotta check the levels," Jeff said into the mic connected with his headset. "Say something for about thirty seconds."

"I'm looking forward to a mutually rewarding conversation with Ms. Riccardi. I think she'll agree that we both have a lot riding on this."

Though his tone sounded as convivial as the synthesizer would allow, it couldn't disguise the crimson thorns of his threat. She caught Jeff looking at her, but he showed no signs of the revulsion she felt. He nodded with satisfaction, apparently fooled by the madman.

She leaned closer to the circular mesh pop-screen that covered the mic. "My goal, when this is over, is for both of us to get what we want. How did we sound, Jeff?"

"Mister, um, Oscar? Whatever voice synthesizer you're using produces some weird distortions, but nothing I can't handle. Bo, you sound like an angel, as usual. Let's see if the webcam can catch a glimpse of your wings."

Ignoring his silliness, she checked the phone tracker again and saw that Oscar and his kidnapper remained on I-75, now below Macon. What the hell? She should've heard road noises as the kidnapper spoke.

Then she realized the phone was heading south while Oscar and his abductor stayed in place. Apparently, the bastard had some means of faking Oscar's number and caller ID using another phone. Maybe he knew she'd consult the tracker and was trying to screw with her.

She would usually turn off her cell to prevent an interruption during the interview, but this time she merely muted its speaker and then initiated the recording app. Pulling over one of the two spare headsets on the table, she placed it around the phone so that its mic would pick up the interview. When she listened to it afterward, perhaps she would hear—and *see*—something that would identify the man who'd turned their lives upside down and tell her where he was. After he set Oscar free, she'd call the police.

Glancing around, she realized she had come in empty-handed: no folder of questions, no summary of research spread out on the woodgrain table. For the first time ever, she had not prepared for an interview. Could not. And it'd be the most important one she ever conducted.

The studio lock opened with a faint click. Only Jeff and one other person possessed a key. She swiveled in her seat to look at the On-Air president.

Harry Pinzer was a short, perpetually red-faced man in shirtsleeves he always rolled up past his elbows. His pants strained to contain an expansive gut. When he'd recruited her from an AM talk-radio station, she had expected him to be a Napoleon-wannabe who bellowed incessant commands. However, though he could indeed be dictatorial, she appreciated that he never yelled. An increase in volume made the shapes and colors more pronounced, but she could see the same emotions and intentions in a whisper as easily as a shout.

His pleasant tenor voice was conversational and created its usual background in her mind—the gray-brown of tree bark—but now it literally dripped with marbled magenta sarcasm as he asked, "Why did I just run into today's guest in the toilet trying to scrub ink off his hands, instead of sitting here, cowering before our mighty Barracuda?"

She'd pulled away one ear cover to hear him clearly. Jeff had done the same and quipped to Bo, "Told you it would smear."

"Now who's in the room?" the maniac asked in her still-covered ear, showing his aggravation and a trace of panic in roiling green and purple.

Good to see the man could be thrown off his game by a minor disruption. What she needed to do was keep the pressure on without causing him to lash out at Oscar—watch for weakness, loss of bravado. "It's the president of our company," she said into the mic and then addressed Harry. "I'll reschedule Mr. Wilcox. We have . . . a special guest who became available on, uh, very short notice and can only do this today."

Harry pulled on the only unused headset. Still standing, he projected his voice toward the table mics like the stage actor he used to be. "Who am I speaking to?"

"You can call me Oscar."

Harry frowned at Bo and then at Jeff. "What's with the computer voice, mister?"

"I have many enemies."

"Uh-huh. And why should I allow you to go on one of our award-winning programs without being vetted by me?"

Although this would prove to the abductor that she'd followed his orders not to tell anyone, she knew the charade would unravel if Harry persisted. She envisioned the maniac taking out his frustrations on Oscar, imagined her husband dying in agony. Her only option sickened her: she had to go to bat for the kidnapper.

"It's my fault," Bo forced herself to say. "I've been, um, working on this opportunity for months. He's surfaced at my request . . . and will go back into hiding after the interview's over. This is our one shot." She studied Harry, who chewed the inside of one cheek. Maybe giving him back some power would help. "If you don't like what happens in the next hour, you can fire me—or order me to resign. Your choice."

Jeff said, "Only a minute thirty till air time."

The nudge from Jeff seemed to make up their boss's mind. "Okay." he said. "I'll be listening. Come to my office afterward. Both of you." He dropped the headset on the table.

They watched him depart. She removed her listening gear, locked the door behind him, and blew Jeff a grateful kiss.

Blushing, he adjusted his gold-framed glasses and murmured, "Where were we? Oh yeah—webcam."

She clamped on the headphones again, descending once more into her personal fishbowl. Then she resettled in the chair so that the mic, Popper Stopper, and stand hid most of her face.

He shook his head. "Why not just do your interviews under a blanket?"

"I hate that thing."

"Your fans want the whole package."

The rust voice said, "We have a deal, so cut the bullshit and get on with it."

To hide her growing anxiety, she put some bluster into her tone. "Welcome to the wonderful world of live entertainment. Everything we do is at the mercy of the clock."

Educating him gave her a morale boost. He wasn't all-powerful—it was good to remind herself that time imposed more control over the situation than he did. All she had to do was survive the next hour, and then he'd be done with her. "You might get revved up and want to monologue for forty minutes, but you'll get interrupted every twelve for a commercial break—that's how we pay the bills."

Jeff announced, "Thirty seconds."

"Nervous?" she said into the microphone with more false gusto. "You're about to be heard by tens of thousands of people. Every sound you utter. And another quarter-million will watch or listen to the podcast." Maybe her little speech would throw the man off his stride while using up every moment he could've taunted her.

He began to speak, but Jeff overrode him. "Going live in three, two—" He raised an index finger and then pointed at her.

# CHAPTER 7

Deke stopped pacing outside the basement room he had dubbed the Vault, where he'd strapped Oscar Riccardi, blindfolded, to a bunk.

He yanked the base of each calfskin glove to tighten the fit. In seconds, he'd be live on the Internet, heard by Bo's legion of fans—who would become his fans instead. He had left his script upstairs, but he didn't need it anymore. The next hour was about hanging in there with Bo, moment by moment, adjusting to her as she did the same with him.

Like a dance. Like fucking.

What had the Jeff guy called her? *Angel.* A more perfect description than that asshole could ever know. Ethereal . . . unattainable . . . untouchable. Until now.

In Deke's wireless earpiece, Bo said, "Welcome to a special edition of The Barracuda, brought to you by On-Air Web Radio, your home for the best interviews, advice, music, and more." She paused, probably collecting herself. Maybe folding her tanned arms on the tabletop and blocking the view of her tits, which had become fuller with motherhood and age—no longer the perky pair that mesmerized him beneath her maroon lacrosse jersey, but still captivating. He'd savor his recording of the website stream later. Right now, it was best not to get distracted.

Back in their Virginia Tech days, she could tongue-tie him by her mere presence, freeze him with a glance. And her uncanny ability to see right through him, no matter how hard he tried to sound casual and be her friend, had made him feel unworthy. This time, though, he was ready for her.

She announced, "I'm Bo Riccardi, and my guest today, via Skype, has chosen to use a synthesizer to mask his voice and to go by one name only . . . Oscar."

Had she choked up a little? He grinned and pumped his fist. Damn fine plan—it was working already. Get some transference flowing, keep her conflicted and off-balance.

She asked, "Why are you going to these efforts to disguise your identity?"

He'd expected Bo to use her usual opener, but she had gotten down to business immediately. Husband's life on the line, not screwing around. Clever girl.

In his regular speech, he said, "I've made a lot of enemies over the years." The mic conveyed his words, tone, and volume to his computer upstairs, which synthesized them and outputted the carefully crafted new voice through a burner cellphone that spoofed Oscar's ID.

Darth Vader? Please. Maybe Jeff needed to keep Oscar company for a while in the Vault and learn some manners. "If I didn't use these measures," he added, "the wrong people would recognize me and realize I'm still in the land of the living."

"Then what would happen?"

"They'd hunt me down and kill me, of course . . . Bo." Saying her name made him swallow hard and shiver, just like in the old days.

"And why is that?" she asked.

"Like I said, they're my enemies." He began to pace once more, passing the pegboards of tools and a neat line of lawncare equipment on his way to the Vault, and made a loop through a large alcove that housed the furnace and water heater. Then he strode by his gun cabinets, and the staircase leading up, and finally to the double doors that would open to the manicured yard and acres of woodland beyond. Another turn on his heel, and he trooped toward the Vault again like a soldier on sentry duty.

As he marched, he said, "I know too much for them to stay safe in their cushy Pentagon jobs and congressional offices."

The basement air still smelled of freshly sawn lumber and paint. His military surplus boots made firm *thunks* on the concrete slab, which sported a new coat of pearl gray—his month-long construction of the Vault had taken a toll on the owner's pristine floor. He didn't plan to seek the return of his security deposit, but a renter should be respectful of their landlord's property. As a bonus, the guy would even get a new, soundproofed room—the world's smallest mother-in-law suite—and about a dozen webcams ringing the house and grounds.

Bo said, "So, you wanted to come on our show to tell your secrets and settle scores?"

It was always "our" with her, never "my" show, as if she could fool anybody with her false modesty. Same as she would hide behind the studio mic, but keep revealing herself to the webcam in brief glimpses. She'd been subtle that way at Tech, too, Miss Prim and Proper, while her roommates had strutted around him in next to nothing.

"Even here I have to be careful," he replied. "I tell too many secrets, they'll be able to cross-reference the various assignments, narrow down their suspects to one."

Just like she'd be trying to corner him—but he was way ahead of her.

"Give our listeners a sample. Whet their appetites."

The phrase reminded him of how dry his mouth had become. He pulled a canteen from his belt, took a swig of water, and clipped it near his holstered Colt 1911 MKIV Series 70 Gold Cup.

"Okay, here's a good example." He recited his script from memory while he resumed pacing. "Stuff goes missing from Fort Bragg all the time. Arms, ammunition, ordinance, supplies, what have you. Also Jeeps, trucks, Humvees. Even tanks, choppers, and planes. Turns out there was a tight group of sergeants that had a sweet deal with a Mexican drug cartel. Done with the permission of some generals at the Pentagon, of course, and a certain Texas congressman. Those boys all got a regular payout. And here's how I put a stop to it." As he made the circuit around the basement—tools, Vault, alcove, guns, stairs, double doors—he spun out the first of a long list of stories he'd constructed, where he was the hero.

When he finished, Bo stammered, as if she had expected to be bored but was surprised to find herself interested instead. She finally said, "That's quite an adventure, but, um, what proof do you have?"

"Safe deposit boxes full of faked shipping manifests, receipts, orders from the generals, emails between the sergeants before I infiltrated and shut it all down."

Sounding back in control, she said, "These are serious charges you're making. In addition to coming on our show, how do you intend to get these tales to the public?"

"These aren't *tales*—this is the truth, pure and simple. And your audience recognizes facts when they hear them. They'll spread the news for me, using your podcast. Millions more pissed-off people will make it go viral."

He felt clammy patches in his armpits and realized he'd sweated through his woodland-pattern camo shirt. It was sort of funny, reacting to her the same way he'd done a quarter century ago. Back then, though, she'd held all the cards. Now, he controlled the key to *her* future happiness. Maybe even her sanity.

"We're just a minute from our first break," she said. "What do you have in store for us?"

As he reached the Vault again, he contemplated unlocking it and letting her and the audience listen as he gut-shot Oscar and let him bleed out in screaming anguish. How's that for *what's in store?* Payback of a kind, sure, but it would end this dance much too soon.

He said, "I'll tell how I stopped a team of mercenaries who attempted to assassinate a group of senators last year—at the direction of the Deep State, so they could curtail more of our civil liberties."

"Well, I'm sure it'll be a fantastic account, so stay tuned."

She'd pitched her voice to sound enthusiastic. However, he caught the snide insinuation in her word choice. "Fantastic," which originally meant unreal and unbelievable. Obviously, she thought he was too stupid to understand that but believed her audience would pick up the verbal wink.

So typical of Bo to underestimate him.

# CHAPTER 8

With the webcam paused and the first set of commercials murmuring through the studio speakers, Bo blew out a long breath. Arching her spine, she faced the ceiling and rolled her head from side to side to relieve the tension that had built up in her shoulders and neck. The cord connecting the headset to the mixer board waggled back and forth in response. Only three minutes to gather herself again for another twelve minutes of madness.

The fanatic said through the computer, "You think you're so smart, don't you?" Spikes of mottled brown, pure hate.

No pretense for Jeff's sake anymore. Maybe she'd pushed the kidnapper too hard. Maybe Oscar would die because of it . . . because of her. Glancing at Jeff, she saw displeasure but no fright. They'd hosted plenty of combative interviewees—apparently, he thought this was just another feisty guest. Bo told herself she was overreacting. All wasn't lost. At least, not yet.

"No," she replied. "But are we really going to spend the rest of the hour on more crackpot charges?"

"What I said is true. Every word."

From the moment he'd started telling his Fort Bragg story, she could see the knotted mosaic of lies, like a rainbow scarf tangled on itself. A steady barrage of other shapes and colors muddied the image, but his deception was obvious—at least to her. Critical thinking didn't seem to be a skill either prized or practiced by some people anymore. Still, she had to concede that he'd told the story well, which would make it credible to many of their listeners.

"Every word was bogus," she insisted. "Our audience will expect me to come after you if you can't do any better."

Jeff gave her a thumbs-up, lips and mustache raised in a double smile.

"What's this really about?" she asked, hoping she wouldn't pressure the man too much. "Why go to all this trouble to pose as just another conspiracy nut? The public will forget you even before the last commercial plays. Assuming they haven't already closed their browsers."

"It's about exactly what I said. Why are you attacking me like I'm a hostile witness? Aren't I an honored guest on your show?"

He was daring her to bring up the kidnapping in front of Jeff, like a test. "You can come off as ridiculous, but I can't. People will abandon me if I don't challenge you the way they expect."

"Just don't forget what's at stake."

How could she? Against her will, she conjured Oscar's words, and imagined him blindfolded and bound in a soundproof room. His life in her hands.

"Thirty seconds," Jeff muttered. His dislike of the man sent out a burst of violet shrapnel.

She let some time go by and finally said, "Let's get to know the real you."

Jeff said, "Coming to you, Bo." He clicked off the murmuring speaker at the five-second mark. "Three, two, one, fire."

"You're back with The Barracuda. This is Bo Riccardi, and if you just joined us, our special guest via Skype wants to be known only as Oscar. He's disguising his voice for reasons of personal safety. We spent the first segment on some of his adventures, but it's time to learn about the man behind the mask. Please tell us, where did you grow up?"

"Newport, Rhode Island." Another swirling tangle of falsehoods, but why pick there?

It was much easier to remember a lie if it included a kernel of truth. So, which was it—city or state? Playing a hunch, she said, "That's on the coast, right?"

"Yes."

It was *off* the mainland coastline, but she let that go. The sound picture showed truth, so the Newport where he really grew up was on the coast. She said, "I took a trip there once—so many marinas. Were your parents involved with fishing? Or something else to do with boats?"

"They ran fishing charters. My dad was ex-Navy, worked in shipbuilding after." He snorted, which created red sparks in her mind. "Mom actually was a better guide than he was." The statements were delivered with increasing self-assurance, and were all truthful: a string of perfect pearls, with sparkles of pride flashing across their surfaces. Something to build on.

Though she'd grown up in Roanoke, Virginia, on the other side of the state from Newport News, Bo knew about the sprawling shipyards there. A good bet that's where he'd come from. There was a Newport Beach in California, but would a West Coaster pick tiny Rhode Island, on the other side of the continent, for his lie? Testing her theory, she asked, "Did your parents ever let you pilot a boat on the river there?"

"Sure, but we didn't have much time for fun," he growled. "They worked hard to make a living, and I helped." Again, all true. The James River ran past Newport News, whereas Newport Beach had the Pacific Ocean, and bays and sounds surrounded Newport, Rhode Island. Rivers fed those, but confidence in her guess was growing.

She asked, "What sorts of things did y'all catch?"

"Flounder . . . striped bass, the usual."

Gotcha—no mention of lobsters. Anyone who'd made a living off the water way up in Newport, Rhode Island would talk about lobsters. So, he hailed from Virginia. Their mutual home state, she reflected grimly, could be for lunatics as well as lovers.

She wondered if she'd known him growing up, a friend from way back.

He said, "Enough about that. Let's get back to my military service."

Splattered purples of panic, as if he sensed she was onto him. "Okay, given those adventures you related, I assume you were in the army."

"Infantry to start with, then the Rangers. CIA recruited me after that."

All lies. Not only hadn't he made it to the CIA or Ranger school, even the infantry part was false. Maybe he'd been rejected before induction, or washed out during boot camp.

A pretender then. Based on others she'd interviewed— reenactors, survivalists, militia—a potential profile took shape: he probably favored a buzzcut, subscribed to gun magazines, and collected firearms. Maybe knives, too.

The image made her shudder.

Possibly he hung out at shooting ranges to be around real vets, to soak up their lingo and try to parrot them. A lot of such wannabes dressed in camo because they thought it made them look badass. No doubt he loved it when people mistakenly thanked him for his service.

Though it would yield more useless nonsense, she had to balance her need to drag real information from him with asking follow-up questions to his lies, so he wouldn't hurt Oscar. She settled for, "How long did you serve?"

"Twelve years, and then another dozen with the CIA."

"Did you go to college, either before or afterward?"

"After, on the GI Bill." A mix of truth and lie. Maybe he'd tried to enlist after college.

She said, "You were smart to take advantage of that veterans' benefit. Which school?"

"Brown. Comp sci."

The falsehood fit with the Rhode Island bio he'd manufactured. Smart.

To buy time to think and give him a chance to drop his guard again, she said, "What was it like, being a dozen years older than the other students, and having seen and done things they could never imagine?"

He launched into a song and dance that didn't provide any hints about his identity or whereabouts. The madman did have the storyteller's gift of almost hypnotic pacing, making his voice rise and fall and dropping in enough tangible details to entrance a listener. She wondered whether fans of the show were buying it.

Where to take this next? Probably impossible to trick him into blurting out his current location. Other than the steady footfalls she'd noticed since the start of the interview, no other noises penetrated whatever mic he used.

She would bring him into the present, she decided, and find more clues to help the police locate him once he'd released Oscar.

As the kidnapper finished talking about how he'd helped a struggling ROTC cadet get his act together, Jeff flashed the one-minute warning card. She said, "That was mighty noble of you. We have only a minute left in this segment, so let's move to the here and now. Can you give us a hint about what made you go underground?"

"The government decided I knew too much, and they began to suspect—correctly, it turns out—that I had the documents to back up my claims."

Acting with more confidence than she felt, she said, "Eat your heart out, Edward Snowden. We'll be back shortly, so please stay tuned."

# CHAPTER 9

B o waited until the first commercial of this segment burbled through the overhead speaker and then said, "Mister—"

"Call me Oscar. Though I like the Snowden reference. Nice ad lib."

Jeff flapped his lips up and down as he silently aped the kidnapper's synthesized words. Then he began reading from his cellphone, which made Bo wonder if Harry had texted commentary to him about the first half of the show.

She replied, "You gave me your word. You'll do what you said?"

"I told you I will, after I'm finished with you." Still the pearl, but his precise repetition of that ending phrase bothered her.

After sliding the headset off her own device, she confirmed that it was still recording and had plenty of battery life. She returned to the people tracker app. Oscar's phone continued its journey south toward Florida. Candace's phone still showed her at Roswell High.

Their daughter wouldn't stoop to responding to a text from her, but with jittery thumbs she sent a brief inquiry anyway about options for dinner. It felt good to do something—anything—normal.

At least Candace was where she was supposed to be. It was inconceivable she would've left the phone behind; she'd sooner forget her head. However, it was possible the maniac held her as a second trump card and had tossed the phone somewhere at the school to throw off a search for her, just as he'd done with Oscar.

*Better to knock off that line of thinking.* She knew from experience such paranoia could overwhelm her. Already she could feel it starting to immobilize her with fear.

She had more than two minutes before the next segment, so she cupped the headphone earpieces around her cell again, took off her own headset, and stood. "Jeff, I forgot my water bottle. Can I get you anything?"

"No, I'm good."

She unlocked the door and walked to her desk on wobbly legs. The paper tablet and pen still lay on the table, the blank sheet a reminder of how she'd abandoned her notetaking when the maniac demanded she call him Oscar.

Why make it so personal? None of the interview had anything to do with her—at least not so far—but the man had twice said, "After I'm through with you."

Yes, he was using her to give him a platform to spout his nonsense, but what was the point? There had to be something more. A connection that made him target her specifically, instead of someone else in the profession.

She'd read accounts of gunmen taking over television and radio stations so they could broadcast their delusions and make ransom demands. There had even been instances like hers, with an anonymous caller who abducted the spouse or child of an on-air personality. She couldn't recall any happy outcomes, only unsolved incidents where the hostages had died.

Bo would've given anything to go back in time to Oscar's initial call, that missed opportunity to save him from the horrors he was enduring. The kidnapper had phoned about three hours later, with Oscar imprisoned in a soundproofed room. So, that made his location less than three hours away from their Roswell home, assuming the abduction had occurred there. Maybe they were only two hours away, in northern or central Georgia, or even somewhere in town.

When the man let her husband go—not if, but *when*—he'd probably leave Oscar somewhere far from possible witnesses. She imagined Oscar being kicked out of an anonymous panel van, still blindfolded and bound, at midnight on a rural backroad. A fresh sheet of panic-sweat chilled her.

"Top o' the day to ye." The Irish brogue was fake, but the wounded pride was real. Bo saw the salmon-colored thorns overtop of Sean's usual background of butter-yellow. He blocked her cubicle exit. Dropping his affected on-air accent, he let his Jersey City upbringing burst out. "Why'd you give me the finger this morning?"

"You messed with me, I messed with you—we're even. Come on, I'm going live again in a minute."

"And what kind of bullshit interview is that, with the bogus voice? Harry's crazy to let it keep going on."

She drank from her water bottle and tried to settle her temper—but failed. "You've been doing your phony voice for years," she said, "and he hasn't shut you down. Now move."

Rather than retreat, he stepped in close. He seized Bo's wrists and stood on her shoe tops, immobilizing her. "I'm gonna go see him right now. Get him to pull the fucking plug before you ruin the reputation of the station and all our shows—including mine."

If he succeeded, he could end up getting Oscar killed. She struggled to back up, saying, "Let go."

He yanked her toward him and pressed his weight down on her toes. "I won't start over again someplace else. I've worked too goddamn hard building my audience here. You're not gonna piss all over that."

His comment gave her an idea. She made a fist with her hand holding the open bottle and squeezed hard. Water jetted against the crotch of his jeans.

He released his hold as he stumbled back. Cursing her, he tried to sweep the water from the denim before it soaked in, but that only spread it across the fabric, turning blue to black.

Bo grabbed her bag and scrambled past him. As she dashed toward the studio, she yelled over her shoulder, "Fix that bladder-control problem first. Harry's big on hygiene."

His vile insults followed her inside but were cut off as soon as the door shut. She flipped the lock. Good thing Harry had the only key. Assuming the president didn't fire her, she would demand he get rid of Sean, or she'd resign. Then she'd be looking for work along with Oscar. Before she could worry about a no-income household, though, she needed to get him back.

She dropped her satchel against the wall and guzzled the remaining water, but she couldn't relieve the dryness in her throat. What a day from hell.

*You've survived worse. Of course, that other time, you chose flight instead of a fight.*

And now, thanks to Sean, she had to do battle on two fronts. Rubbing her sore wrists, she felt even more shaky and exhausted than when she'd left the room—the inevitable crash that followed an adrenaline rush. Settling into her chair, she put on her headphones and perched behind the mic.

"You're cutting it close," Jeff said. "Who's screaming?"

"Sean had an accident."

"ITP is calling himself the C-word? Is that an Irish thing?"

"More of a Jersey thing. Is our guest still with us?"

The kidnapper's synthesized voice intoned, "Ready for the next round?"

As if she had a choice.

# CHAPTER 10

"We're back. I'm Bo Riccardi, and our guest today is a man of mystery. Calling himself Oscar, he has disguised his voice to protect his identity. We've learned so far that he's a military veteran who says he's been involved in some dark chapters in America's recent history. Born in Newport, Rhode Island, he grew up helping his parents with their fishing charter business. My next question is, now that you're in hiding, are you still able to get out on the water and do the other things you enjoyed as a boy?"

"Sometimes. Um, fake IDs allow me to rent boats . . . get a fishing license."

All lies. So, either he didn't live on a lake or river, or he did but never availed himself. To check the latter possibility, she said, "I guess that's one of the many sacrifices you've had to make, giving up the things you love. Do you at least get to see the water and boats every day?"

"No, but I'm not at liberty to answer specifics about where I live or what landmarks are nearby. Too dangerous."

Truth there, and there were lots of lakes and rivers in north and middle Georgia, so those locations were nixed. Maybe he was up in the mountains, or out in the country. Or just down the street from her and her family. Who knew what happened inside other people's homes?

Stalling for time so she could think of other leading questions, she went with her standard "feelings" inquiry: "I understand, but how does it make you feel, having given up so much because of what you know, and what you've been involved in during your service to our country?"

"It pisses me off, that's how I feel. I became a liability because I succeeded—not because I failed, but because I always came out on top, even when they didn't want me to. Finally, the chain of command decided they wanted a dead patriot, not a live hero." Her question had spun him up so much he launched into a story about foiling some senators' assassinations. She could tell he relished his fabrications, and he seemed relieved to have gotten back to the egotistical script he'd written for himself.

Wanting to gather more details to help the police, she waited for a pause in his tale and jumped in. "Let's get back to the present. How do you earn a living now?"

"At home, on the computer. I build and maintain websites for businesses." The first sentence was true, the second was a lie.

"How does your secretive lifestyle affect your ability to have romantic relationships?"

"I've had to give up on that. It's not fair to subject someone else to the security protocols I have to follow." Again, the former was correct, and the latter was not. Interesting.

Jeff displayed the one-minute-warning card.

Killing time and hoping Sean was still listening, Bo said, "That's very considerate—sweet actually. Maybe you'll end up doing the relationship program here if Sean O'Shea moves on. We only have about thirty seconds until our final break. I think you hit your stride when you get personal, so let's spend the last segment talking more about you. Stay tuned for that with The Barracuda, brought to you by On-Air Web Radio."

Jeff nodded to her and flicked the overhead speaker to life with its background mumble of commercials.

The kidnapper said, "You want me to get personal?" Spikes of mottled brown hate and red flame tips of passion, the same as when he'd first called.

"Personal about yourself. Why, do we know each other?"

"It's a one-way street. I know all about you, but you've never known me."

She studied the sound picture before it faded against the rust background: a pearl, but it was blurry, hidden behind waving yellow and amethyst tentacles. Hurt and shame. Had she ignored or rebuffed him at some point? Maybe he'd written some of the crude comments that had forced her to restrict her social media accounts and put extra security on the website where she endorsed products for a fee. Was the lunatic just another wounded soul with an emotional intelligence deficit and anger management issues? No, those types became trolls on the Internet. This was someone even worse.

"Never known you?" she replied. "Well, I'm starting to get a picture." She tried to recall an in-person encounter with a stranger where she'd felt threatened in some way. Nothing recent came to mind, and never any interactions where she'd seen such a mix of passion and menace in the person's speech.

Usually men showed simple emotions, either desire or anger, but not both so intertwined. Women tended to be more complex, but the kidnapper wasn't female. Oscar had begged her to "do whatever *he* says."

So, this was a man who harbored complicated feelings about her, but they had a relationship that existed only in his mind because he'd spoken the truth about her not knowing him.

Usually a synthesizer would be used to disguise a voice someone had heard before. In this case, maybe he was worried she'd be able to identify his voice if she heard it in the future. He could mask it all he wanted, though. While the rust background created by the voice synthesizer would be different from his real voice, she would never forget his unique blend of passion and hate.

She said, "Let's just get through the final twelve minutes. Then I'll have done my part, so you can do yours."

"No, you don't understand. I'll only do what I promised after I'm through with you." He paused, as if savoring a line he'd rehearsed many times. "We're not nearly there yet."

She shivered. Though she could see where this would go, she tried anyway, saying, "So, we're going to keep talking after the show's over? We'll disconnect Oscar's phone from Skype, and I'll call you back?"

"Not a chance. I'm your on-air guest tomorrow and Wednesday and so on, until I get what I want."

She glanced at Jeff, who stared back open-mouthed, his mustache drooping. The chill clawed deeper into her, penetrating her bones. As if it would lodge there forever. "What do you want? Tell me, and I'll give it to you now."

"That's not how this is going to work."

"But you don't understand how this place works. I'm not in charge. If the station president doesn't want you on tomorrow or the next day, you won't be. There's no way you can force him to do this."

"You'll have to convince him. Otherwise, what happens will be on you, not me."

The salad she'd eaten for lunch surged up in a sludgy mass. She choked it back down, nose running, eyes and throat burning.

Jeff murmured, "Thirty seconds." He looked at her with a mix of pity and dread, as if she'd stepped on a landmine that would detonate the instant her foot twitched.

She wiped her nose with the back of her hand. "One step at a time," she rasped. "Let's get through the next twelve minutes."

"Looking forward to it, Bo."

He just wants to talk, she reminded herself. It's what you do. You're lucky he's not asking you to strip for the webcam, or do something even worse that he could watch again and again.

Jeff flicked off the speaker. His countdown from five sounded like a reluctant judge delivering a death sentence.

# Chapter 11

As soon as they went live again, Deke resumed pacing. Vault, alcove, guns, stairs, double doors, tools, Vault. He pretended he was alone with Bo. No asshole techie there who could smell her perfume, who saw, along with the multitudes, how her body moved and her expressions changed as they listened to her no-bullshit delivery in that bedroom voice. If anything, being shaken up by his pronouncement made her natural huskiness even rougher. Sexier.

While she provided her summary of the interview so far—longer than ever, obviously trying to eat up their time together—he remembered standing behind her in a crowded elevator, disguised, in January. Breathing in the scent of her shampoo, gloved fingertips tingling as they lingered mere inches from her hips. Back in the early '90s, her dedication to lacrosse had given her the best legs and ass in Blacksburg; she'd lost some muscle tone, but at forty-five she could still rock a skirt.

She said, "My next question is, what are your plans for the future? Can you afford to stay hidden indefinitely?"

The future? He hadn't considered a future beyond executing his plan over the next week. And then watching afterward, to revel in how much he'd changed her. Payback's a bitch, honey.

Ever since a Facebook friend had posted a link to a different On-Air Web Radio program, and he'd seen the many promos for The Barracuda while perusing their website, he'd thought of little else. He would've glossed right over those ads except for the publicity shot of Bo in mid-interview, feisty and clearly having fun as she nailed some poor sucker. That image, and her podcasts, had kept him company when he hustled down from North Carolina. From a temporary command post in a suburban Atlanta apartment, he'd continued to run his businesses while he spent the better part of a year establishing a permanent Ops Center, surveilling Bo and her family, and deciding their fate.

Thank God for social media. He'd tried to track her after she'd left Blacksburg, but the early days of the Internet carried no trace of Bo by her maiden name. Her parents wouldn't tell him, no matter how many identities and stories he'd tried, and the university cited privacy restrictions. Without that innocuous post, he still would've been searching in vain for Bo Kroenke.

Focusing on her question, he said, "There's no future for me. More drones are in the air every day, more cameras all around us. Facial recognition software will ID me, and I'll be toast." Vault, alcove, guns, stairs, double doors, tools, Vault. "The black ops guys will break me under torture, and I'll tell them where I hid everything. After they find my stashes, I'll get the needle and a cremation. Probably end up in an urn on the president's bookshelf, like a trophy." He laughed. "Or some four-star will have my balls brass-plated to use as paperweights."

"That's so bleak," she said, sounding heartbroken. Should've been a goddamn actress in the movies. "Looking back, do you wish you'd gone into another line of work, or at least joined a different branch of the service?"

He kept pacing, watching his gloved hands curl and flex. "No, I was good at what I did, and what I did made me feel good. Necessary, valued. I was important to this country."

"You still are, it sounds like."

He snorted. "Just more valuable dead than alive."

"If you could change any event in your life, what would it be?"

He thought back to his mistake at Virginia Tech. But it was her mistake there he wanted to delve into. Not yet, though. Much too early for that. He replied, "I wish I'd never started to collect the evidence, just continued to be the uncaring, nonjudgmental asset at their disposal." Adlibbing based on her quip earlier, he said, "I like to think of myself as Jason Bourne, but I guess I've picked up a little bit of Snowden, too."

"Do you think a hero and a traitor are two sides of the same coin?" She sounded proud of herself, as if she'd just caught him in a trap. "The same thing viewed from different perspectives?"

"Maybe—just like someone who calls herself an innocent bystander might be seen by others as an accessory to a crime."

That shut her up. So much for the superior conversationalist. Just like at Tech, she was always trying to make others feel inadequate. Unworthy. It felt good to knock her on her pretty ass.

Finally, she said, "Does it bother you that the patriot you've modeled yourself after—the hero—is a fictional character, whereas the traitor is real? Aren't you much closer to being the villain? How does that make you feel?"

It made him feel like he'd just taken a fucking good combination of counterpunches. He shook them off and snarled, "Whistleblowers aren't villains."

"Bad guy or not, Snowden offered proof. So far, all you've done is talk. When will we see these mountains of facts you've supposedly hidden away?"

"When the time is right."

"Well, the time is running short for us here. What would you like our listeners to remember about you?"

He reached the Vault door again, fingered the deadbolt knob, and contemplated giving her—everybody—something to remember. "They won't be forgetting me anytime soon. We'll be chatting again tomorrow. Same bat time, same bat channel."

"From Bourne to Batman: evermore mythic but still in the land of make-believe. This has been an . . . interesting interview."

He launched into a retort, but she continued to speak, not shouting over him but at a conversational level. That fucker Jeff had muted him. "We need to make way for some important announcements, but we'll be back tomorrow for another edition of The Barracuda, brought to you by On-Air Web Radio, your home for the best interviews, advice, music, and more."

By the time she finished, he had flung open the Vault door

to remind her of the life she was jeopardizing. Now, he backed away, disgusted by the stink that enveloped him.

Oscar remained blindfolded and taped face-up on the bunk in the tiny gray room. His chinos were stained dark at the crotch and—given the odor—no doubt in the seat. The man breathed through his mouth, baring his teeth as if they could filter the air he'd fouled. He gasped, "Let me talk to my wife, you sonofabitch."

"You just did." Deke slammed the door and relocked it. He exhaled as hard as he could, emptying his lungs as he thought about the particles of shit and piss he'd inhaled.

In his earpiece, Bo shouted, "Leave him alone. I've done everything you asked."

The basement had decent circulation, but he opened all four windows to help exchange the stench that had seeped out of the Vault with the scent of grass clippings wet from the recent rain. He sucked in the smell of the mown yard and the sodden leaves, pine needles, and loam in the surrounding forest. "I'll call you at ten 'til one tomorrow, and we'll do this again. Remember what's at stake. You're getting awfully cocky for someone with so much to lose."

"What if I can't get Harry to agree?"

"Then Pinzer can listen to Oscar's screams with you. Remember my knife. There are so many ways to make him suffer. It can go on for weeks."

Recalling that asshole director was in the room with her, he took another deep breath of springtime air to focus his thoughts. "Now that our little secret is Jeff's, too, I'll repeat my rules: no police, no FBI, nobody. Bo and I talk on-air for as many days as I want until I'm done with her, and then Oscar goes free. If anybody else gets involved, Oscar dies in a horrible way, and you'll all get to hear it. Do you understand?"

"Yeah, I got it," Jeff said. "Did you notice how Bo had her middle finger up alongside her temple during the whole last segment? That goes double for me, pal."

"Thanks for the tip; I'll look for that later. Probably while I'm naked."

Jeff said, "*Fuckhead*, that's your official nickname."

"Maybe it's time for me to start collecting your family members and friends. The more the merrier down in my Vault."

"Please," Bo cried. "Stop it. We'll do as you say."

"I like you begging. You're a natural—and you're going to get even better at it."

# CHAPTER 12

Skype made a gulping sound: call terminated. Bo dropped the headset onto the table and shuddered as another frigid wave swept through her body. Her lips pressed tight together. She sucked them in and clamped down with her teeth to keep from screaming or sobbing or both.

Jeff put his headset aside and asked, "Why didn't you tell me he'd kidnapped Oscar?" Yellow tendrils of hurt curled and flexed under a scaly pink rain of fear—for her, her husband, or himself, she couldn't tell. Maybe all three.

Fists tight, nails digging into her palms, she tried to focus on breathing to calm her racing heart. *Pull yourself together. Losing control again won't help anybody.*

She choked back the agonized sounds she wanted to surrender to and croaked, "He ordered me to keep quiet. The slip-up is on him: he didn't want anybody to know about Oscar, except me."

"What a fucking nightmare. Why aren't you a nervous wreck?"

"I am, on the inside." Good to know Jeff hadn't noticed her panic—that meant the audience wouldn't either.

Oscar's pitiful shout continued to stab at her. Not only full of fear, it had also showed shame for some reason. And the victim-accessory comment made her wonder whether she'd met the lunatic at Tech. She had to have known him then. Somehow, he knew more about her than even Oscar did.

Jeff looked at his phone. "Harry wants us in his office." He clicked on the overhead speaker at low volume. It broadcast a prerecorded comedy show, which helped to fill out the daily On-Air lineup.

A reminder that life went on. People continued to talk and laugh. To love and raise children. But everything she thought of as most important in her own life was in jeopardy until she could save the man with whom she did all that.

"Tell him I need a few minutes." She freed her cell, turned off the recording, and checked Candace's phone: still at school. Oscar's phone continued southbound toward Florida. The app offered no way of locating him.

The stress that had built up like a tidal wave now crashed over her. She cupped her face but then remembered the webcam makeup. Rouge and foundation smeared her fingers and palms.

Wet wipes cleaned the mess from her hands. The blended colors coating the towelettes were the same as the pain and anguish she'd seen from Oscar. And the same as what she saw endlessly in dreams when her perverse memory cued up the soundtrack from a quarter-century ago.

To keep her emotions under wraps, she busied herself: blouse and skirt adjusted, phone put away in her leather satchel. Then she drifted from one gray corner to another, hugging her arms for warmth, feeling trapped.

Jeff walked around his desk, holding out a travel mug. "It's been sitting awhile, but coffee's coffee."

"No, thanks. Look, I'm sorry you're getting dragged into this, but I could tell he wasn't serious about doing the same to your family or friends." She leaned against the fuzzy wall, head down. So tired and cold and weak, heart triple-timing, that she felt as if she were going into shock.

"The joke's on Fuckhead. I don't have any family. And my friends only exist online."

"I know that last part's not true."

"Yeah, I can never get anything by you." The usual red flame tips had returned, but overlaid by concern in cobalt ripples. "Want me to tell Harry you need more time?"

"No, let's get this over with."

He set the mug on the interview table. "Then what?"

"I'll go home and wait for my daughter." She fluffed her hair where the headphone band had flattened it and flipped open the door lock.

"Cindy, right?"

"Candace."

"Damn, why can't I remember that?" He pushed open the door and held it for her. "You sure you're old enough to have a senior in high school?"

"Right now, I feel as old as the world."

Bo led the way to Harry's office but kept an eye out for Sean. Holding her breath, she passed his cubicle. No sign of him, and the company laptop wasn't there. Maybe he'd left to nurse his wounded ego and plot some juvenile revenge. It wouldn't surprise her if he keyed her car.

The president had the only space, other than the studio, with real walls and a door. "Shut it behind you," he said from his desk. His face looked even ruddier than usual. He steepled his stubby fingers and waited for them to sit in the two straight-back chairs facing him. "Bo, you told me if I didn't like what happened during your show, I should fire you or you'd resign." Uncharacteristically, ice-blue disks of uncertainty overlaid his usual bark-colored backdrop.

She nodded, stunned into silence. If she weren't employed here tomorrow, would the maniac murder Oscar immediately? Or would killing him become pointless? Losing her job could be the key to her husband's freedom—or his death sentence.

"Well," Harry continued, "I don't know if I liked it or not, because I don't understand what just played out. You said you'd been working on securing the interview for a long time. How'd you find that character in the first place?"

She considered and discarded some possible lies. The irony seemed cruel—nailing liars was her specialty. But confession would bring Harry into the fold as well. He was a law-and-order guy. Telling the authorities would be his first move, even if it meant going behind her back.

"I'm sorry," she murmured. "I don't know what to say."

Jeff jumped in. "It's bigger than you, Bo. There's no way you can keep this a secret."

Harry peered at her over his steepled fingers. "Tell me. I can't help you if I don't understand what the hell just happened."

For the second time that day, she considered prayer—for an answer, or at least guidance and strength. But she still felt unworthy.

"Well?" Harry asked.

Jeff blurted, "That guy kidnapped her husband and demanded to go on the air. Or else."

Bo hung her head, guilty with relief that Jeff had taken the decision out of her hands. Despite her reluctance to ask for help, had God just responded through her friend? Or was He still sitting on the sidelines with Satan, trading bets on how the situation would play out?

Harry said, "Why didn't you tell me earlier? We need to call the cops."

"Absolutely not." She forced herself to meet his eyes. "He ordered us not to tell the police or anybody else. Most of what he said on the air today was lies. I could tell. But he told the truth off-mic about murdering Oscar in a heartbeat if we bring in the law or anybody else. You guys aren't even supposed to know."

"Hmm." Harry moved an empty On-Air mug to the center of the desk blotter, hooked a finger in the top of the handle, and rotated it around the bottom rim, twirling it with increasing speed. An old deliberative habit, which Jeff called "getting on his Sit 'n Spin."

Finally, the president slapped his hand on the top to still it, creating a splatter of lavender in her mind. He said, "That asshole—"

"Fuckhead," Jeff interjected.

"Even better. He's holding the station hostage, along with Oscar. Pisses me off. I want to talk to him right now."

"No," she cried. "That'll tell him I violated his rules. He might kill Oscar immediately."

Harry said, "It's worth a try." When she shook her head in reply, he softened his voice. "Look, I'm not going to endanger Oscar. I just want to impose some rules of my own. Make it clear I refuse to be at the guy's mercy," he added, with pulses of ochre.

Now she felt even less in control than before. Unable to keep her fingers from shaking, she managed to dial the ten digits correctly on the third try.

The call went immediately to voicemail, but she didn't hear a message done in the lunatic's synthesized voice. Instead, he'd recorded the one from Oscar's phone. Her husband said, "You know the drill," sounding calm, almost bored—a placid sea-green pool—blissfully unaware of the horror to come. A nightmare from which she might not be able to rescue him.

Bo hung up and began to sob.

# CHAPTER 13

Ten more tries over the course of an hour, initially with Harry and Jeff, and then huddled in her cube, always with the same result: Oscar's voicemail message. By the fifth try, Bo had stopped groaning out loud when she saw that sea-green pool.

When she stuck her head inside Harry's office and reported her failure, he looked up from typing two-fingered on his laptop. "Too bad—I was looking forward to telling him what's what. Did you or Jeff reschedule the guests lined up for the rest of the week?"

"Not yet," she snapped. "I've been a little distracted."

He didn't flinch, but the red in his cheeks deepened. "One of you better see to it."

She read the traces of copper lightning and debated about whether to back down. He never minded a test of wills, so she said, "If the kidnapper bails out at the last minute, I'll still need to do a show."

"Tell Jeff to have a best-of recording standing by. He can do the rescheduling if you aren't up to it."

She started to counter, but he slammed down the laptop lid. "Goddammit, Bo, this isn't your station." He still hadn't raised his voice, but he projected so well he could've been standing toe to toe with her. "I know you feel the weight of the world on your shoulders, but I still call the shots around here."

Jeff's nickname for Harry was *Panzer*, for the play on his last name and his implacability. Either she could get crushed under his treads or move out of the way. The former wouldn't help Oscar. "Okay," she said. "For the rest of the week or just tomorrow?"

"Better make it the whole week. Might as well plan for

the worst." He swung open the laptop again and resumed his two-fingered typing.

Dismissed, she shuffled back to her cube, fired off promises to the interviewees to reschedule—blaming "personal exigencies"—and returned to the studio to relay Harry's orders.

Jeff made notes on his electronic calendar. "So, did Panzer ever talk to Fuckhead?"

"No, my calls went to voicemail every time."

He adjusted his glasses and peered more closely at her eyes. She wondered whether they were still as puffy and bloodshot as they felt. He said, "That must've been rough on you, hearing him over and over." Red flame tips as usual, but also an egg in rich turquoise.

Though she was surprised by his empathy, she didn't want a shoulder to cry on—she'd already wept enough for one afternoon. "I got numb to it," she fibbed.

He reverted to his usual banter. "Yeah, emotions are overrated. But speaking of deeply felt feelings, check this out." He swiveled one of his monitors around to face her. A screen capture from the webcam recording showed her in close-up: the semi-circle of her headphones, right side of her face propped against her hand—middle finger unintentionally extended and prominent along her temple. Her eyes looked fierce, and her teeth flashed white within blood-red lips.

Damn. She'd thought she had done a good job keeping her rage bottled up. "I look like I'm declaring war on the whole world," she said.

"Yeah, right? With those headphones jutting out, you're a pissed-off Princess Leia taking on the big, bad Empire. I forwarded it to Panzer, asking if he wants me to use that one as a global replacement on the website."

Thin, curly ribbons of gold swirled behind her eyes, but she didn't share his amusement. "No way. My contract says I control my image; I get to approve any likeness the station uses."

"Okay, okay."

As he pulled up alternative photos he'd saved from the recording, she remembered Oscar saying the same thing—but in pain and fear instead of good-natured defeat. *Hang on for another day*, she told him in her thoughts.

Then she tried to buck herself up with the same plea.

Jeff arrayed files in long rows across the screen, almost two dozen choices for the podcast link. The montage provided a distraction. She asked, "Do you spend all your free time playing with Photoshop?"

"They're just cropped and brightened a little. No need for gimmicks when you're the subject." He looked away and added in a rush, "For ITP, though, I have to pull out all the stops. The photos we use of him might as well be generated from scratch on the computer. Maybe I'll change his nickname to CGI."

Cobalt ripples overlaid everything he'd said: concern that he'd offended her with his overblown compliment.

Office relationships were such a minefield. Bo wasn't bothered—there'd even been times when she'd felt low and had welcomed his flattery—but she wished he'd direct that enthusiasm toward someone who could reciprocate it.

She studied the shots and pointed at a still that didn't exaggerate her appearance. "Make sure Harry doesn't use the other one, all right? Oh, and he said to have a 'Best of Barracuda' standing by tomorrow, in case the maniac doesn't call."

"Check and check."

"Thanks." She started for the door. "I'm heading home."

"Want me or somebody else to go with you? Fuckhead could be lying in wait."

"Meaning I should have a man there to protect me?"

"Stop bristling. I just mean there's strength in numbers."

Bo relaxed her shoulders and said, "No, I'll be fine."

"What are you going to tell Cath—uh, your daughter?"

"If I tell *Candace* the truth about her dad, all her friends will know within minutes and then the rest of the world will find out."

"Got a story ready for her?"

"Still working on that." She pushed open the studio door.

"Hey, not that The Barracuda herself could ever need anything, but if you just *want* to call someone, feel free to, uh, you know." He made a telephone symbol alongside his head with thumb and small finger. "Since you can't talk to any of your real friends about this."

She frowned at him. "You're one of my best real friends. And I'm grateful you do know, so I'm not dealing with this alone. I promise to call if I need a boost."

"Oh, okay, great." Red flame tips and actual fireworks of joy. "Well, have a good night . . . oh shit, sorry, I'm on autopilot." Just like that, amethyst fingers of shame crushed his happiness. "Um, what's the correct parting in this situation?"

"'See you tomorrow' works." She waved and exited, wondering whether he was such a hot mess around other women. Pondering that helped to distract her from anxious thoughts about Oscar and the question of what to tell their daughter.

The problem was, Candace had color-hearing, too, and detected every lie with ease. Bo grimaced. Like mother, like daughter.

# Chapter 14

Synesthesia often ran in families, but sometimes it skipped a generation—and then daughter was *unlike* mother. That irony ricocheted around Bo's mind as she drove home in the ongoing drizzle. Though her grandmother had chromesthesia, her mom hadn't exhibited the blending of any two senses; she'd passed that gift down without appreciating its wonders.

Bo was four years old the first time she began to perceive the world differently. Sitting with her dad at the breakfast table, she'd said, "Fridge is sick. It's like yellow sheets that are all—" She crumpled her napkin to show them. "Right before, it was blue. A yarn-ball going like this." She made an unwinding motion.

Her father lowered his newspaper enough to peer at her over the top edge. He frowned so deeply, his thick eyebrows met. "Mother Mary, I was really hoping we'd get an engineer, not an artist. Is that poetry you're spouting?"

Mom cut the remaining crust off Bo's buttered toast and set the plate in front of her with a square purple thump. "It's not poetry," Mom said. Hands on slender hips, the ever-present cross of white gold twinkling on its chain around her neck, she glowered down at Bo. "She's got that same thing Mother has, the color-hearing."

Dad nodded. "Chromesthesia. I remember her talking about it."

The refrigerator sputtered and wheezed. Its colors grew increasingly dark in Bo's mind, the shapes more convoluted. Then it died. Her father had looked from the fridge to her and back again. "Maybe you'll be an engineer after all—that little trick could come in handy."

Thanks to his prodding, she'd pursued the degree and discovered the trick had all sorts of handy applications, especially in communication and relationships. As Grandma had warned her, though, it was also something of a curse. The blend of sounds, shapes, and colors made memories indelible. A delightful benefit for sweet or sensual experiences—mica-like glitter when her lips separated from Oscar's at the end of their first deep kiss—but the bad ones abided as well.

Grandma had passed years before. Bo's parents now lived in an Arizona senior center. As with her friends, even if she could call them about Oscar's kidnapping, she couldn't imagine what possible advice they'd be able to give. Precious little in everyday life could prepare someone to deal with such a frightful crime.

Twenty-five years earlier, Mom and Dad had been equally ill-equipped. Their only help had been to pack up her stuff and move it from Blacksburg to their home in nearby Roanoke and then to Atlanta.

The garage door closed behind Bo. She switched off the engine. Safe and warm inside the cocoon of her Mercedes, which Sean hadn't keyed after all, she luxuriated in the silence. No colors and shapes projected across the blank expanse of her mind when she closed her eyes.

Did darkness and quiet surround Oscar as well? If so, were they soothing, or did they add to his terror? If—*when*—she managed to get her husband back, would he ever be whole? Could any survivors of trauma achieve that? She had certainly never recovered her peace of mind. After today, she didn't think she could feel safe, for her family or herself, ever again.

She glanced out the car windows—noting the bikes they hadn't ridden for months, the tools for a garden that needed tending—before she realized she'd stopped in her usual space. The other bay remained empty, with Oscar's beloved Corvette at the body shop. She envisioned that black beauty there again, looking like new; imagined Oscar in the house, healed from this trauma, slimmed down, and happy with a new job; pictured them playful and romantic like the old days. The concrete pad, empty except for dappled oil stains, seemed to mock her.

Maybe Candace, who was driving her dad's old car, should park in that spot until he came back.

The overhead light timed out, leaving only the narrow, rain-streaked windows in the garage door for illumination. Coping with his kidnapping and the overwhelming pressure of keeping him alive on a madman's whim had piled a mountain on top of her, and now here she sat, shrouded by near-darkness, suffocating inside a small box, within a bigger box.

Just like that, her cocoon had become a tomb. Desperate for breath, she clambered out and raced for the kitchen door. When she tried the deadbolt, the door opened without the need of her key. She'd told Oscar enough times to make sure it stayed locked that he always did so.

Someone must've been in her house. Maybe they were still there. Had the kidnapper returned to abduct her, too? Did he have an accomplice waiting inside? She should've brought Jeff. A chill started her shivering again.

The glass in the bank of kitchen windows appeared to melt as rain trickled down, casting the room in a gray light. On alert, she listened and categorized the sounds with their associated shapes and colors. Refrigerator humming, air blowing through the vents, the drip of a faucet in need of repair. All normal for her home. However, someone could've been hiding anywhere, silently waiting for her to turn a corner.

She told herself to stop being so afraid. With everything that had happened, though, this was exactly the right time for paranoia.

Self-defense options? Since Candace's birth, Bo hadn't wanted to own a gun, but she would've welcomed one now. Oscar kept all the knives shut away in a drawer at her insistence; they had weapons aplenty, but nothing she could bring herself to handle. From the laundry room, she hefted his aluminum baseball bat, which had collected dust and stray cobwebs along with the other neglected sporting goods.

Back in the kitchen, she glanced at the telltale signs of Oscar's earlier presence, as if he'd just stepped away. His tablet computer lay on the counter. Breakfast dishes and utensils sat in the sink.

She remembered their tense meal, her disloyal feelings. The guilt stabbed at her.

A creak from the floorboards, somewhere deeper in the house. Bo decided she'd defend their home to the death if necessary. She wouldn't run this time.

The neck of the bat wrapped with coarse tape reminded her of a lacrosse stick, except most of the weight was in the barrel. She kicked off her shoes, choked up on the handle for a faster swing, and eased across the hardwood floor into the dining room.

Pale light from the rain-washed windows revealed a china cabinet from Oscar's parents, a deco-style sideboard that was a wedding gift from her folks, and an oak table with six matching chairs they hadn't used in years. No sign of an intruder or any disturbance there.

In the same fashion—with stealthy movements, the bat cocked—she finished an anxious tour of the downstairs. And then the second floor.

No one lay in ambush; no madmen lurked behind doors.

Their home now seemed dead-quiet and turned her relief at being alone into a battle against desperate loneliness. Oscar was supposed to be driving her crazy by playing videogames instead of looking for work. They should've been arguing about stupid, meaningless things, their raised voices filling the house with life. Instead, she felt like a ghost haunting the silent rooms.

She put the bat away and poured herself a brimming shot of chilled Grey Goose to calm her nerves. As she sipped, she considered the items Oscar had left in the kitchen. Their breakfast flashed through her mind again.

Hard to believe they were the same couple who'd made love atop that kitchen table a few years ago. Hard to believe Oscar's freedom somehow depended on her, but she didn't know what she had to do to secure it. Hard to believe either of them would be sane after this ordeal.

The only thing she could do was stay busy. She downed the rest of the liquor, enjoying the burn and lightheadedness that dispelled her fears for a moment, then left the glass on the counter for refills and grabbed her satchel. Before Candace returned from school, Bo wanted to listen to the recordings she'd made for clues about the kidnapper's identity and whereabouts.

She entered the foyer, heading for the staircase, but halted. On her first pass, weapon poised, she'd overlooked Oscar's keys dangling from the front door deadbolt. She tried the door and found it unlocked, just like the one between the kitchen and garage. Maybe Oscar had been absentminded after all . . . or was she standing where his abductor had grabbed him?

A white rectangle stuck to the outside of the pebbled-glass front door caught her eye. Some kind of Post-It. A gust of wind made the bottom edge of the paper flutter.

She knew what it must've been: the maniac had left a note to torment her.

# Chapter 15

Staring at the back of the note, Bo pictured a shadowy figure ringing the bell and Oscar unlocking the deadbolt . . . and then what? Somehow he got knocked out. The kidnapper had probably dragged him into the garage and pulled his own vehicle inside so he could load up Oscar without any witnesses. That would explain the door leading into the kitchen being unlocked, too.

He'd probably worn gloves, but if not, his fingerprints would be on the paper. She pulled a tissue from her bag to avoid smearing any evidence. Wincing—as if narrowing her eyes could lessen the impact of his cruel words—she pulled open the door and read the sticky note.

A rental car company logo was printed across the top. Someone named Mike had written, "11:18. No answer to doorbell, knocking, cell. Call if you still need us."

The time could've been a red herring to throw her off. She retrieved Oscar's tablet from the kitchen counter and found the reservation confirmation email from the same rental car company. The message had to be legitimate.

Her theory still held water. Oscar had called her around 9:30, so at some point between then and Mike's arrival to drive him to the rental car office, the kidnapper probably appeared. The abduction could have occurred elsewhere, but doing it here would have ensured the fewest possible witnesses, so it was the wisest choice. Though evil, vicious, and insane, the man also showed a cunning intelligence.

Had the lunatic staked out the house this morning, to make sure she and Candace left at their usual times? Bo tried to picture the street as she backed out and drove away, but she couldn't remember anything unusual. Troubled thoughts had consumed her; she'd been unaware of her surroundings, driving automatically.

She didn't see scuff marks on the doorstep or any other clues, so she took the note and secured the deadbolt with Oscar's key. The pewter flash in her mind's eye reassured her, but she still double-checked the lock. And then triple-checked it. The thought of the fiend standing where she stood, exhaling air she now breathed, and touching the same things she did made her want to scrub herself with lye.

Once again, she wondered whether Oscar had sensed something wrong as he tried to look at the stranger through the thick, pebbled glass. If she'd answered his call, maybe they would've been standing here together now, with him saying how spooky it was that they'd shared a premonition about the man on the stoop—both of them clueless about the bullet they'd dodged. Perhaps, having been seen, the kidnapper could've decided to target a new victim elsewhere, leaving her and Oscar to continue their petty squabbles.

Given the choice, she would've welcomed fifty more years of discontent with him instead of this single day of terror and despair.

The rental car message remained pinched in the tissue between her fingers: a reminder to do something productive instead of torturing herself with woulda-coulda-shoulda. She dropped Oscar's keys into her satchel and climbed the stairs to her home office. There, she affixed the note to a sheet of copy paper. She wrote the current time below it, along with where she'd found the message.

Possible evidence for the madman's eventual trial, to help establish the chronology of his crimes. The thought of facing him in court one day thrilled and then scared her as she considered it further. Charges could range from kidnapping and assault . . . to Oscar's murder.

She cleared a space on her desk for a notepad, a box of tissues, and her cellphone with about eighty minutes of recordings she'd made. Thankfully, she hadn't brought up the vodka bottle from the freezer. Listening to a playback normally muted the shapes and colors, but alcohol could counter this effect and provide the vibrancy of a current event. It was going to be bad enough without that.

Taking a deep breath, she forced herself to relive the entire experience.

Shock. Fear. Anger. Anguish and frustration and guilt.

She could only see her own voice by listening to a recording of it. The images swirling through her mind made the emotional pummeling even worse. But she also saw her own strength and resolve. Her love for Oscar, and her determination to get him back.

Those feelings buoyed her until she remembered her contemptible, unworthy thoughts about him at breakfast.

"Forgive me," she moaned, over and over, rocking in the office chair.

By the end, dozens of tear-soaked tissues littered the floor and desk. Sweat chilled her and a vise had squeezed her ribs until they felt like a solid, suffocating mass.

Somehow, she'd managed to make notes about the madman's potential background and current whereabouts, flagging the truths he'd spoken as well as his lies. There were no dramatic insights, though. Not a single crucial lead.

The bastard had her over a barrel.

As she tried to pull herself together, yet another text made her phone vibrate across the desktop. In her mind, a lime-green coil compressed and expanded as it moved vertically out of sight, like a snake climbing a pole.

Texts had poured in all day, always friends wanting to share news, gossip, or make plans. The usual. Having let Oscar's possible call for help go unanswered, she'd begun to superstitiously check her cell each time. She was always both disappointed and relieved his kidnapper hadn't sent a message.

In her bubble of anxiety and dread, she couldn't focus on her friends' needs or interests, so she let their messages pile up. As much as she wanted to express her worries and terror to them, she needed to keep them in the dark for Oscar's sake.

That catty game of "Can this marriage be saved?" had become, for her, literal and deadly.

Another text, this one from Harry: "Call me ASAP. There's somebody I want you to talk to." Old school, he'd capitalized, punctuated, and spelled everything correctly.

She dialed him, and he answered after the first ring with, "I'm sending a guy over to your place tonight."

No inquiry about how she was holding up. Not even the basic courtesy of a greeting. She felt sorry for his current wife—and heaven help the woman if she were ever abducted; Harry would approach it like it was all a business deal. Forcing down a sarcastic reply, Bo asked, "Who is he?"

"A private detective named Gus Trumbull. Did good work on my third divorce, saved me a fortune. I figure he can get whatever info you have and then try to find the place Fuckhead is stashing your husband." He spoke with utter conviction—pale blue streamers flapped like pennants in a stiff breeze.

She'd misread Harry's character: yes, he was the law-and-order type, but only until circumstances affected him directly. Then he became a whacko vigilante. She said, "Absolutely not. The kidnapper told me no cops, feds, or others. That includes PIs. If we involve any of them, he won't hesitate to kill Oscar." She began to stalk around the office as her voice rose. "This is really about getting back control of your station, isn't it? At any price."

"I can tell you're upset. At least sleep on the idea. In the meantime, Gus can pull guard duty tonight. He'll make sure the asshole doesn't try to get at you or your daughter."

"No. I don't want some armed stranger in my house or parked out front."

"Why not?"

Groping for a reason, she said, "If word about Oscar's kidnapping leaks out, he'll die. It was supposed to be a secret I had to live with, but now you and Jeff are involved. That's too many already. The old saying goes, three people can keep a secret if two of them are dead. Now you want to add even more."

"Gus is as trustworthy and loyal and discreet as they come. He won't tell another soul."

"Then because . . . because—" Unable to think of another good argument, she yelled, "Shit, shit, shit," and kicked her chair, making it rebound off the desk in a flash of bronze.

"Hey, I understand. You want to be in control of the situation, too. Like Jeff said, though, it's bigger than you now. What I'm trying to do is give us an edge, or at least even the odds."

She fell into the chair and massaged her forehead. "I'm so scared for Oscar. There's no telling what he's going through. It's got to be an endless nightmare for him."

"Having Gus around might make it less of a nightmare for *you*. And for your kid."

Bo played her only other card. "I can't afford him."

"It's my party. I consider this an investment in my biggest star."

She realized she'd forgotten to tell him about her other battlefield. With a sigh, she said, "Your only star. You need to fire Sean." She described his assault on her in full detail.

To her boss' credit, he didn't curse or kick office furniture. Voice as rock-steady as ever, he said, "You should've said something earlier."

"I know. I don't want to press charges, but I can't come to work if he's there."

"Well that's the thing—if you quit, Oscar could suffer for it."

Startled upright, she said, "I didn't say I'd quit; I'll just work from home until he's gone. I have the full setup, even a cough button. Jeff can patch me in along with the kidnapper."

She thought he would fold but he replied, "You're fond of quoting from your employment contract. Take a look at, uh, page two, clause 9(b): 'Employee shall conduct her interviews in the station studio except with permission of the On-Air president.' That permission is hereby denied. And I'm not ready to get rid of my other star, either. We'll meet with Sean before his show and clear the air. In the meantime, you'll see Gus tonight. Understand?"

Stretched over two barrels now, she reluctantly agreed, and hung up before she said something that would get her fired.

# Chapter 16

Oscar Riccardi woke as the drug from the kidnapper's second injection wore off. He opened his eyes but couldn't see anything, and he couldn't remember where he was. Lying flat on his back, he tried to roll over but discovered his wrists were held down at his sides, secured by tight bands of duct tape to the aluminum frame of a narrow bed. His bare ankles were likewise fastened to cold, curved metal.

Same as the first time he'd awakened. That hadn't been just a bad dream.

The jam he was in crashed home again, igniting fear and anger. Sweat soaked his face. He couldn't catch his breath.

Still blindfolded by what felt like a sleep mask, he had to rely on other senses to get even a half-assed picture of his predicament. The ache in his shoulder from the needle remained. That made two times he'd been knocked out. Probably some kind of narcotic, highly addictive. Add it to the list of things to worry about.

There was nothing to do but worry.

A flowery air freshener scent had replaced the stink from his soiled chinos. Also, the cold oozing of bodily waste trapped in his underwear had vanished. His empty stomach groaned, the noise so loud in the otherwise silent room it sounded like shouting.

Though tape immobilized wrists and ankles, he could still wriggle his shoulders and hips. His outfit felt different: loose, soft, and warm, like a sweat suit. Also, his underwear seemed to be padded now, with elastic around his thighs and stomach. A fucking adult diaper.

The thought of having been cleaned and changed like a baby was even more humiliating than being overpowered by a runt in his own home. At six feet and 220 pounds, he'd assumed he could defend himself. The guy he remembered at the front door in brown coveralls had been a few inches shorter and fifty pounds lighter.

If Bo had answered his damn call so he could ask whether she'd scheduled work on the house, he probably wouldn't have opened the door to the stranger. Which meant he wouldn't have been tasered—the worst pain of his life, like a million fire ants biting his stomach—or choked out and drugged. Or now held somewhere like a goddamn prisoner.

This was all her fault.

With his luck, the sonofabitch was a sex freak, planning to rape him. Unless he'd already. . . .

Oscar bucked his hips and clenched his butt cheeks but didn't feel any soreness there or in his groin, so the guy probably hadn't messed with him yet. Still, the thought of being at the mercy of some psycho made him want to shout for help from Jesus and all the saints he'd ignored in Catholic school.

Thrashing around reminded him to keep taking inventory, to determine if anything else had changed. He slid the back of his head against what felt and sounded like the slick nylon of a bare mattress, instead of the sheets he'd no doubt stained. Besides the ache in his shoulder, his right nipple still throbbed where the maniac had pinched and twisted it until he'd said hello to Bo. Where did somebody learn to grab a man's nipple to torture him? Sex freak for sure.

The only good news was that the sleep mask remained in place: it must've meant the guy was planning to let him go and didn't want to be identified. If the blindfold ever came off, he'd probably be murdered soon after.

Unless the kidnapper wanted to kill him all along and was just fucking with his head.

That thought began to coil and twist through his mind until he told himself to knock it off. He didn't dare lose hope. If he stopped believing he would survive, he'd go crazy. Better to focus on other things, maybe a clue about where he was or what the guy really wanted.

When he had awakened the first time, he'd finally stopped fighting his restraints long enough to hear someone nearby, apparently pacing, given the steady back-and-forth sound of footsteps on carpet. Strides too long and heavy to be a woman's. Guessing the obvious who-when-where questions wouldn't be answered, he settled for, "Why'd you kidnap me?"

"To talk to your wife."

"Why not just fucking call her at work?"

Still pacing, the man said, "I will, but I need her undivided attention." The guy had a Southern accent, but Oscar couldn't place it—every redneck sounded alike to him.

He replied, "She'll tell you the same that I will: we don't have any money." The bastard didn't respond, and didn't stopped walking a trough into the floor either, so Oscar kept railing. "Yeah, I know, the house, the cars. Bo getting press and doing endorsements. It looks like we're rich, but what we've really got is a shitload of debt. And no relatives have any cash lying around either. So if you wanted a ransom, some big-ass payday, then you snatched the wrong guy."

The man didn't break stride. "What's your wife like nowadays?"

"What do you mean?"

"When I knew her, she was sharp, always on the ball."

"Still is. How'd you know her?"

"Is your wife still a good listener? I mean scary good?"

What was with the *your wife* crap the dude kept repeating? From the sneer in his voice, he made it sound like Bo had been stolen from him.

Something else in the guy's tone, a kind of wariness. Or was it respect? Fear? Who the hell knew—that was Bo's deal. She'd see his colors and shapes and shit and know instantly. All he could tell was that this dickhead was into her in a big way.

"Yeah," Oscar answered, "like she can read your fucking mind."

"That's exactly how I remember her. I'll bet she keeps you on the straight and narrow. No staying out late, saying you were only drinking with the boys. You go on a business trip and want to have a little fun but you don't dare. Because you know you'll get the third degree when you come home. She always was a major cock blocker."

In fact, that's exactly what being with her was like, especially when they'd dated and he fibbed once about keeping it exclusive. When he stayed honest and told the truth, she was—well, used to be—fun to be with and willing in the sack. Generous even.

Now she was hard as nails all the time. Zero interest in sex, her confidence in him shot to hell. And if she ever saw a photo of him diapered or trussed up this way, like some damned chick in a horror movie, she'd never think of him as a real man again.

A cellphone had rung then. The dude had stomped away and slammed a door, compressing the air enough that Oscar had felt the pressure in his ears.

Now, he decided he needed to be better prepared for the next time his kidnapper entered. Give that motherfucker the third degree.

Yeah, right. Diapered, taped down, blindfolded. No goddamn leverage at all.

Hopefully Bo would appease the nutcase soon, tell him whatever he wanted to hear so all this would be over. Obviously, something had gone on between them, but what? The woman wasn't much of an open book—she never talked about old boyfriends.

What secrets was she keeping?

# Chapter 17

Bo didn't receive a reply from Candace to her texts, but the tracker app showed when her daughter left school. Thirty minutes later, she heard the deadbolt open at the front door, pewter flashing behind her eyes. She blew out a relieved breath and unpackaged two French bread pizzas for the microwave.

Another flash when Candace relocked the door, and then an eggplant-colored whump announced she'd dropped her backpack on the carpeted stairs. Tall and lanky, scraggly bangs of ash-blond hair forever in need of trimming, the seventeen-year-old shuffled into the kitchen wearing a form-fitting blouse, shredded jeans, and vintage tennis shoes.

She scowled at Bo even deeper than usual. "Only two? How come Dad's not, like, eating with us?" Ever since she could talk, her voice carried a seafoam background. Cobalt ripples of worry roiled that picture.

"He's away," she replied as neutrally as she could. "Use his spot in the garage until he gets back or his car's repaired, whichever comes first."

"Your voice looks super-funny. Did you guys fight again?"

"Not really."

Candace made a harsh game show-buzzer sound, which opened a pretty scarlet rose in Bo's mind. The color and shape neutralized her annoyance at failing to get a lie past "The Human Polygraph," Oscar's nickname for their daughter since she was small. Santa Claus, the Easter Bunny, and the Tooth Fairy had never stood a chance.

"Just a little argument this morning," she clarified, "after you went to school."

"Well, I mean, where'd he go?"

Bo plated one French bread pizza, put it in the microwave, and set the timer. "Honestly, I don't know."

"So, he just sort of left us?" Her voice showed a mix of sorrow and fear in a flurry of yellow and pink.

"He didn't, I promise." She hit START, which produced a chromesthesia firestorm for them both.

No two people with the same kind of synesthesia ever experience it identically. Whereas Bo could endure the chaotic visuals in her mind, whatever Candace saw made her flee into the dining room. Bo allowed that it'd been a cowardly act. She did want to shield her daughter a little longer from the trauma, but she also stalled to put off a conversation she didn't know how to have.

Candace glowered from the next room, obviously anxious to pursue her interrogation. While the first pizza cooked, Bo took out the blender and threw in frozen blueberries, kale, protein powder, and coconut milk. She revved up the blades with a whining roar and a maelstrom of overlapping colors and shapes that reminded her of the only time she'd tried LSD, a bad trip.

Candace plugged fingers in her ears to mute her own audio-visual onslaught. When she returned to the doorway, Bo nuked the second pizza.

"Mom. . . ." The word came out as four syllables, rising in alarm.

Finally, short of taking out the mixer and whipping up a batch of brownies, Bo knew she'd made all the noise she could. She put their plates on the table in the breakfast nook, followed by the purple smoothies and utensils, and said, "Let's sit down."

Candace hugged herself, face and neck reddening. "Is he . . . I mean, did something bad happen?"

"Not what you're thinking—not the worst. Sit. Please."

"What then?" She collapsed into a chair as if suddenly boneless.

Chiding herself for still being a coward, Bo delayed for a final time by sipping a little of the berry smoothie. She didn't register any flavors, only a cold sludge in her mouth. Then she swallowed, took in a deep breath, and said, "Sometime this morning, a man abducted your dad."

A rush of tears dripped from her daughter's chin as she stammered, "What . . . who. . . ."

Bo pushed a wad of paper napkins into her daughter's fingers. "I know," she whispered and took Candace's free hand. "I know. It's terrible. But we'll get him back."

At last, Candace managed to ask, "Who did it? Where are they?"

"I don't know yet."

"Did it happen here?" Candace sniffled and wiped her nose again.

"I think so. The doors were unlocked when I got home."

"So the guy was, like, creeping our house?"

Before Bo could reply, Candace jerked her hand away. Her tone switched from scaly pink fear to a black sawblade of anger. "I'll bet he touched everything in my room. Pervert." She pulled the blouse higher against her neck.

"I'm sure he was focused on your dad, hon."

"But why would anybody even want to do this?"

As her voice continued to rise, Bo softened her own tone, hoping to calm things. "The man demanded I interview him on my show, so he could be famous for a while. He figured holding your dad would make me do it."

"Then this is totally your fault. You and your stupid show."

"Hey—"

"If you weren't always hustling for attention and literally selling out to those companies with their shitty products, the guy would've picked on somebody else."

"Settle down and listen. I don't know why he targeted me, but this is personal to him. Read my voice. You can see I'm telling the truth."

Candace slumped lower in her chair, as if no longer having a scapegoat had further deflated her. "So, you let him on the air, right? And now Dad's coming home?"

"I did let him go on, but he wants to do it again tomorrow. Then maybe he'll let your dad go."

"You don't believe that. I mean, what if he wants to do it every day forever?" She blotted more tears and twisted the wet napkin in her fists. "Or what if he grabs me next?"

Questions Bo had already asked herself a hundred times—questions without encouraging answers. Unable to meet her daughter's scared, accusatory stare any longer, she looked down at the so-called meal she'd fixed. The cheese had congealed and the bread had hardened as it cooled. She knew she wasn't going to win any prizes today as mother or wife.

"You're safe," she replied, something she knew she should've said much earlier. "In fact, my boss is sending over a detective tonight, an actual PI, to protect us and help find your father."

"What if he makes things worse? He might go, like, poking around and get Dad killed."

Though Bo had made the same protest to Harry, she needed to stay positive for Candace. "He won't. He'll make sure nothing happens to us, and he'll find out where your dad is and lead the police to him. Or, even better, when you come home tomorrow, your father will be sitting right here. Maybe he'll even cook dinner, so y'all can avoid another of my crappy meals."

She wanted to give her daughter a brave smile. Unfortunately, her acting skills failed her, too—she felt the corners of her mouth quiver as she fought to contain her own tears.

"This literally sucks," Candace said, rising from the table.

"You can't tell anybody. That's one of the kidnapper's conditions. If word leaks out, he'll hurt your father. Maybe worse than that."

"Okay, fine, Mom. I'm not an idiot."

"And use the lock on your door, if that'll help you sleep better."

She gave Bo an especially irritated sigh, producing a green smear across her mind's eye. On her way out of the kitchen, Candace groused, "You and your stupid locks. As if they did Dad any good."

# CHAPTER 18

Bo tossed their uneaten meals into the trashcan and took another gulp of purple smoothie before pouring the drinks down the drain. Unable to restrain the urge any longer, she hurried to the door leading to the garage and checked yet again to make sure she'd twisted the deadbolt into place. Jiggling the knob produced sparkler-like twinkles that always gratified her.

Oscar and Candace poked fun because she was a little obsessive about locks. Not just the outer doors and windows, but inner doors, too. The habit had exasperated Candace as a little girl because she couldn't barge into her parents' bedroom whenever she wanted.

A three-note series from the doorbell splashed deepening shades of blue over one another. Bo remembered Candace locking the front door when she'd come home, but there hadn't been a chance to double-check it. Eyeing the aluminum baseball bat in the laundry room, she decided she was better safe than sorry. Armed again, she eased to the front door.

She slipped her key into the deadbolt, confirmed it was locked, and tried to peer through the pebbled glass. All she could see was a large, looming silhouette: a giant of a man.

He must've noticed her movements, because he called out, loud enough to hear through the triple panes, "I'm Augustus Trumbull. Harry sent me."

The background color of his voice was that of French toast. Seeing the pearl of truth in his words, she leaned the bat in the corner, unlocked the door, and opened it wide. Augustus stood at parade-rest on the stoop in fading daylight. The huge guy wore a beige suit and maroon tie that complimented his coppery skin, and tan dress shoes that must've been size sixteen or bigger. His obvious strength and military bearing suggested a former soldier. The lines creasing his face told her he was at least sixty, maybe older.

"Bo Riccardi," she said, putting out her hand.

The softness of the hand that enveloped hers was a surprise, as was his soothing tenor voice. "Please call me Gus. You're to be commended for not opening the door until I identified myself."

Respect and friendliness in waves of green and gold told her she could finally relax a little. At least she wouldn't be dealing with a much larger version of Harry. She invited Gus inside and stepped back. Despite having enough clearance, he turned sideways and stooped as he entered the foyer—a lifetime habit, no doubt.

She shut and locked the door. Then double- and triple-checked the deadbolt. Not quite a lifetime habit in her case, but one she'd reinforced for twenty-five years.

With a glance at the bat, he said, "Of course, it's possible I intercepted your cellphone call with Harry and am posing as Gus for some nefarious reason. The only way you'd know for sure I'm who I say I am is to compare my biomarkers against a federal database—but computers can be hacked. Basically, then, we're left only with trust." He grinned, showing two rows of gold-capped teeth. The grillz gleamed.

That he could deliver such a long speech without pausing for breath made her wonder if he'd been an opera singer instead of a military man. She said, "And I could've broken in here and be posing as Bo Riccardi, so there you go. Trust."

She eyed the dining room chairs, glanced at his bulk again, and decided the living room sofa was the safest option. Leading him that way, she told him, "We can work in here, unless you want to go upstairs to my office."

"Here's fine. Given your circumstances and understandable state of mind—fraught with fear for your husband and anxious about the safety of your daughter and yourself, as you naturally should be—I won't stay long. Rest assured, though, I won't abandon you either. Per Harry's instructions, I'll spend the night on stakeout in my vehicle."

One hazard of interviewing people for a living was that she listened to everybody as if she might soon have to converse with them live on the air. Besides memorizing the background color of their voice, she always noticed the unique pattern with which each person spoke, their preferred cadences, catch phrases, and so on. Oscar spoke like the Italian tough-guy he'd learned to be in his South Philly neighborhood. Candace tried to protect her feelings with belligerence and wisecracks, much like her father. Bo knew how to respond to each of them, but Gus would've been a challenging interviewee.

Anticipating when he'd come up for air and in which direction he was headed reminded her of a long-ago family vacation to the Pacific Northwest. Every time she'd tried to photograph a humpback whale as it breached, she took the shot too soon or too late.

They went through the niceties of Gus declining the variety of beverages and snacks she offered. Then she excused herself to head upstairs. Not wanting to expose Candace to the recordings, she made sure her daughter's bedroom door was closed before grabbing the necessary gear.

Balancing notepad, cellphone, a Bluetooth speaker so Gus could hear the recordings, and her glass refilled with icy vodka to help her cope, she returned to find him on the sofa. Suit jacket unbuttoned, he faced forward with a placid expression, as still as a bronze Buddha.

She set up the electronics on a coffee table that appeared child-sized next to his enormous legs. "I'll play all the recordings I made, starting with his first call. Here goes," she said and pressed the PLAY button. Perched on a wingback chair that matched the sofa, she held her notepad in one hand while the other clutched her glass of cold, sloshing comfort.

It was a little easier this time to listen to her dialog with the kidnapper. Pausing often to give Gus her insights created some distance from the events as they unfolded. Still, when she heard the maniac torture Oscar, she had to drink steadily to keep from losing control again.

The PI captured every detail with his own phone app and also jotted items with an antique fountain pen in a reporter's notebook. Each shift of his weight made the wood frame of the sofa creak with whirling amber flower petals.

After she summarized the exchange with Harry that followed the interview, she took a break to refill her glass. Only water this time. The heat in her face and her unsteady balance warned that she'd hit the liquor too hard, too fast.

He flipped through his notes and said, "Quite a number of times, you stated categorically the man either spoke the truth or lied. I know you're a professional interviewer and highly acclaimed, but I too am in the business of communicating with people who can prevaricate and misrepresent as often as they take a breath. I'm at a loss to know how you derived such certainty without apparent evidence."

Bo wondered whether psychics also felt cornered when they were put on the spot. How could you explain that you *knew* because you knew? She couldn't fault Gus, though—he was testing every assumption, as a good investigator should.

Harry and Jeff incorrectly thought she excelled as an interviewer exclusively because of the skills she'd developed. Only her family knew about her gift. During their worst argument, Oscar told her that she owed all her success to the color-hearing; without it she would've been just another talking head. In her lowest moments, she feared he was right.

She sipped some water. "Well, um, have you ever heard of this thing called synesthesia?"

His expression brightened. "Indeed. I've read about sensory blending but never met anyone with it." He made another note on his miniscule pad. "Presumably yours has an auditory component?"

"Yes. It's called chromesthesia." He looked interested rather than skeptical. Some of the tension released its grip from her shoulders and neck. "Lots of creative types have experienced it, from Mary J. Blige and Tori Amos to Duke Ellington and Billy Joel. It might be how 'the blues' got its name. I'm not musical, but the gift does help me listen with my mind. Whenever I hear sounds, I see colors and shapes that move."

"Any sounds?"

"Voices, car horns, the clothes dryer, anything. My grand-mother had it, and Candace—that's my daughter—inherited it from me."

Pen poised, he asked, "What does my voice . . . *look* like to you?"

"Each person has a unique blend of color, which is like a consistent backdrop, but what I watch for is their intent when they speak. Other chromesthetes might not experience this. For me, though, purpose shows itself in moving, colorful shapes that overlay the background and change as emotions shift. Your voice has a nice French toast color, but I've focused on the fact that you haven't tried to deceive me. There's no manipulation or game playing, which I appreciate."

Gus screwed the cap onto his fountain pen and tapped it rapidly on his leg. "So—"

"Mint green ovals twirling like poker chips." He frowned at her, and she pointed at his hand. "The sound you're making with the pen against your leg. That's what I see."

He grinned, grillz flashing. "I haven't been this intrigued since I met a genuine mind-reader in New Orleans."

She made Candace's game show-buzzer noise. "That's your first lie . . . hmm, the location, right? You did that on purpose."

"Correct, and please forgive me. I know this isn't a magic trick you trot out to bedazzle guests, but I had to see it in action."

She shook her head. "It really is just a trick—it hasn't given us a single lead about who the kidnapper is or where he's holding Oscar."

Tumbling cubes of yellow accompanied her daughter's rapid footsteps down the carpeted stairs. She'd put her hair up in a ponytail and changed into a Peachtree Road Race tee.

She said, "Hey, you're like, the private eye? I'm Candace."

"Gus." With surprising agility, he stood and shook her hand. "Your mother and I were just speaking of her synesthetic prowess."

"I don't know about prowess, but I mean, she's not bad. Literally, I couldn't get away with anything as a little kid."

Bo said, "Now she keeps me and Oscar honest, too."

"True that. So, you're totally going to find my dad?"

"I hope to. However, my first priority is to keep you and your mother safe."

"Speaking of which," Bo told her, "you're coming with me to work tomorrow. I don't want you out of my sight until we get your dad back and the kidnapper's caught."

"No way. I can take care of myself. And there are like, a bunch of guards around school."

Bo turned to Gus. "Won't it be easier to protect us both if we're together?"

"It's the logical approach."

Candace folded her arms. "I've got a ton of things this week. I can't miss any of them."

Bo mirrored her gesture. "Sorry, you'll just have to. Your safety's more important."

"May I suggest a compromise?" Gus asked, showing the waves of green and gold she was coming to expect from his respectful, sincere demeanor. He turned to Candace, "Timely communication is key. Text your mother regularly while you're away from the house: when you arrive at school, after lunch, and when you're heading home. She'll do this as well, so you'll share the same burden. But you'll also benefit from the same peace of mind, knowing the other is safe."

He looked to Bo for agreement. Not a foolproof solution, but she'd been a combative teen like Candace, and she had even run away once when her parents became too controlling. She'd die if Candace did that, this week of all weeks. Reluctantly, she nodded, and Candace groaned.

Gus removed his cellphone from a jacket pocket. "Also, there are a number of free panic-button apps that send an instant text and email with your GPS coordinates. I'll give you my number so you can list me as well as your mother as your emergency contacts."

"Mom, would all of that chill your paranoia?"

"No, but nothing will."

"Tell me about it."

# Chapter 19

After Candace headed back upstairs, Bo talked Gus into a Diet Coke while she allowed herself another few fingers of Grey Goose. Taking a sip, she said, "Here's one thing we know for sure. Oscar called me at 9:30, and then the kidnapper used the same number about three hours later, so they've got to be someplace that's less than three hours from here."

Gus raised his eyebrows, so she explained herself. "If the man showed up here to do the kidnapping right at 9:30, he'd still need time to disable Oscar, move him to and from his truck or van or whatever, and confine him in that soundproofed room where we heard the door close. If we drew a circle on a map, the biggest possible radius of his whereabouts is less than three hours from here—and maybe much less. He could be just down the street. Maybe he's some neighbor who's been watching us for years."

"While I'm not seeking to challenge any of your conclusions, I think it best if we test each and every supposition, lest we make an error that results in serious consequences." He flipped through several pages of notes. "Given that you didn't answer your phone at 9:30, how do you know it was Oscar calling you rather than his abductor?"

Clammy perspiration prickled her scalp, and the vise squeezed her ribs again. Even her most basic assumptions were possibly wrong. And maybe those mistakes would doom Oscar.

"I, uh, don't know. Just a feeling, I guess. He'd sometimes call me about an hour after I leave for work."

"Well, thinking about your hypothetical map, is it not possible Oscar was seized just after 8:41—when he made the rental car reservation and requested a pick up—rather than 9:30? This would mean the maximum radius of travel is a somewhat less than four hours, rather than three."

She dragged her fingers through her now-sweaty hair. "Where else did I screw up in my thinking?"

He shook his head. "You mustn't flagellate yourself over potential, small errors of logic. You're under tremendous stress. I think you're doing very well to retain your composure and function at such a high level of calm and equanimity."

She envisioned Gus as a youngster—the size of three kids put together—reading a thesaurus at the kitchen table while his friends played kickball in the street. Translating his word-nerd vocabulary into everyday speech relaxed her a little. And the liquor helped even more. With a sigh, she replied, "I've lost my shit so many times today, I'm more numb than composed. If the lunatic starts shooting through our windows, I don't think I'll have the energy to duck."

"Oh, you'd be surprised what the body is capable of achieving in the urgency of a moment. But let's return to what we know and what we might infer. As you say, your husband and his abductor could be just down the street, or they could be three and three-quarter hours from here, or, most likely, somewhere in between. The maximum radius from your home could put them in Tennessee, Alabama, or either of the Carolinas, as well as most of Georgia. Crossing state lines would make this kidnapping an FBI matter."

"And you heard him say not to try calling the FBI specifically, like he'd know if we contacted them or the police."

"But how would he know such a thing? If he were so omniscient, so all-powerful, why dabble in a scheme to get attention where his name and voice are disguised and the stories he wants to tell the public are entirely without merit? Furthermore, why disguise his voice to you before he went on the air?"

"He thinks of himself as my friend, though he says I don't know him. Maybe he's trying to prevent me from recognizing him later, if I ever hear his real voice. Forcing me to call him Oscar and other things he said make this feel personal, like he's getting revenge for something I did to him. Except, I can't remember ever doing any harm to anyone."

True for sins of commission, but not for sins of omission—not helping someone when they needed her. She drank deeply and commanded herself not to think about Lori Lambo. With a sigh, she set her empty glass on the hardwood floor. "This is all so crazy."

"Perhaps that's by design. He wants you unsure, off-balance, so he retains control over the situation and has you reacting instead of being proactive. What he didn't plan on, however, is that your interviewing skills would yield some valuable intelligence about him: you two appear to have a Virginia connection."

"I grew up in Roanoke, though, way on the other side of the state from Newport News."

"Did you attend college in Virginia?"

"Virginia Tech." Not wanting to get into the Lori Lambo nightmare, she added quickly, "But I transferred after two years to Georgia Tech, where I met Oscar. We were both in enviro-engineering. He used his degree, but I stumbled into broadcasting."

"Did anything happen when you were in Blacksburg? There was that mass shooting—"

"That happened in 2007. I was there in the early '90s, so that's not what this is about." She looked at her glass and wished it held more vodka. "There must be something different that connects us."

"Someone in broadcasting who feels slighted?"

There was Sean, but he couldn't have been in two places at once. She searched her memory for others she'd worked with in radio and during a brief foray into local TV. "There were people who didn't like me," she said, "but no one crazy enough to do this for payback."

Gus nodded and sat back, making the wood frame of the sofa creak again, amber petals spinning in her mind. "We're dealing with a smart, motivated individual. He's left no substantive clues about who he is, where he is, or even what he wants. All we know is that he intends to maintain this charade until he's 'through with you,' whatever that means, and then let Oscar go."

"You think he'll get away with this?"

"He won't if you can trick him into revealing something vital."

That seemed like too tall an order, but she didn't want to sound pessimistic. She glanced down at her notes and asked something that'd been bugging her: "How can the guy use Oscar's number when my app showed that cellphone going down to Florida and ending up in Jacksonville?"

"With the right equipment, you can 'spoof' any cell number and caller ID and get away with it. That's why tracking is done with the IMSI number—the International Mobile Subscriber Identity is unique to each device. The tracker can use a cell-site simulator, a Stingray, to trick any nearby phones into connecting and then capture their IMSI numbers."

She anticipated good news, but he shook his head at her. "Sorry, but without knowing a general geographic location for the phone, though, a simulator isn't useful, and even IMSIs can be spoofed. Most likely, he shipped your husband's phone or hid it in some innocent driver's vehicle."

"So, all we can do is wait until show time tomorrow and trust that either I can get him to reveal something or he finishes his nonsense and lets Oscar go?"

Gus checked his watch and stood. The sofa seemed to groan with relief. "There's something I can do this evening. I'll knock on your neighbors' doors and ask whether they saw a stranger around here this morning or witnessed anything unusual. I won't reveal the real reason for asking, of course; I'll tell them

I'm doing security for the station because you received a threat there."

Bo stood, too. "Candace and I can help. Our lie-detecting ability will come in handy."

"Indeed, that would be an enviable skill for any PI to possess."

"Afterward, are you really going to watch the house all night from your car?"

"The stakeout is a hallowed part of the institution. It's one of the few things that hasn't changed much during my three decades in this line of work."

She shook her head at his stamina. "How do you get your rest?"

"I've trained myself to powernap with great effectiveness."

"Not me. I want to hibernate for a year, but I'll probably be too anxious to get any sleep."

He motioned to the front door. "Maybe a neighbor holds the key to your peace of mind."

# Chapter 20

Bo and Candace met some neighbors they'd never seen before. Overall, however, few people answered their doors, and no one who did had seen anything unusual. Gus didn't fare any better.

They all slouched back to the house in the dark. He declined to come in, choosing his black Ford Expedition instead so he could maintain a broader view of the street. A big SUV for a big man.

After her daughter shuffled off to bed, Bo checked the ground-floor doors and windows twice, armed the security system, and dragged herself upstairs as well.

As she'd predicted, mental and physical exhaustion didn't translate into the deep sleep she needed. Her eyes were open when the alarm clock on her cellphone chimed at 6:00. She checked again for texts and emails from the maniac, as she'd done nearly every hour throughout the night. However, she saw only the notes from her friends that she still hadn't bothered to read or answer yet, along with lots of social media traffic, which she ignored, and a surprising uptick in endorsement inquiries via her website, which she also disregarded.

Harry had sent a gleeful email around midnight, telling her and Jeff that the servers had crashed due to the number of people trying to view her podcast. A first for the company. He was so ecstatic he'd neglected to inquire about Gus or whether she'd heard from the kidnapper.

As she re-read his message at 6:00, her free hand strayed across Oscar's half of the bed, the fitted sheet as cold and smooth as a pane of glass. The stark physical reminder, and the thought of him possibly lying sleepless as well—but in much more terrifying circumstances—drove her from the bed. She parted two plantation blinds and peered through the gap at the Ford still parked across the street in the blue-gray predawn light.

Gus seemed as competent as he was congenial, so she couldn't be totally pissed at Harry for inserting himself into her crisis. Still, her boss's insistence that she "clear the air" with Sean kept her anger toward the On-Air president on simmer if not full boil.

She draped a light robe over her pajamas and unlocked the bedroom door, relieved it had remained bolted. Why that always came as a surprise, she really didn't know; she must've rattled the knob as often as she'd checked her phone overnight.

At Candace's door, she knocked until her daughter grumbled. Two more tries, with increasing threat levels, finally dislodged Candace from her burrow. She scuffed past without a glance or greeting and disappeared into the bathroom. Her revenge, no doubt, would be to use most of the hot water and enough towels to dry an entire lacrosse team.

Downstairs, Bo confirmed the doors and windows were still locked and the security alarm remained on. She'd probably made those rounds at least twice during the night, too. Safe in the knowledge that Norman Bates couldn't waltz inside and stab her to death, she trudged into the kitchen and considered what the most appropriate breakfast would be for Day Two in Hell.

Coffee. Lots of it. As it brewed, she pulled on jeans and a sweatshirt, and tucked her hair under an Atlanta Braves baseball cap. Then she filled a thermos, switched off the security system, and headed out front to bring some refreshments to Gus.

The sun hadn't breached the tree line yet, so a nearby streetlamp cast a long shadow beside her as she walked down the driveway. Gus lowered his driver window and flicked on the interior light. Between the vehicle height and his own size, Bo had to crane her neck. She asked, "Do you take your coffee black?"

"I do, and I appreciate your thoughtfulness." He took the thermos, set it on the console beside him, and studied her face.

"Anything more about Oscar?"

"No, but thank you for asking—and thanks again for your help. How'd it go out here?"

"The road was quiet all night. Were you able to sleep at least a little?"

"Maybe accidentally." She clamped her jaws together to stifle a yawn. "Is it that obvious?"

"Not at all," he lied. The twisted mosaic of his fib looked softer and paler than most, motivated by kindness rather than selfish interests. A car approached them, headlights on. She stepped closer to Gus' door so it could pass by with plenty of room. The driver tootled the horn despite the early hour. He probably thought he was being friendly, but the noise produced an explosion of browns and greens that obscured her vision for a moment.

Gus said, "My plan is to talk to nearby residents who didn't answer their doors last night. Based on our lack of success, perhaps I should've asked this sooner: do you know which neighbors might've been home at 8:30 or later yesterday morning?"

The question was an obvious one she should have considered, too, and the answer depressed her. She hardly knew any of her neighbors, and none well enough to be aware of their habits. One of them could hold the key to Oscar's freedom, but she had no idea who Gus should try.

She confessed her ignorance to him while yanking fretfully on a thread that poked from the cuff of her sweatshirt. Instead of snapping off, a foot of it unspooled from her sleeve. Wrapping the thread around her fingers, she tugged again but even more came loose. She wondered if this would be a metaphor for the day ahead.

When she looked up, Gus had produced a knife that appeared long even in his huge hand. "Hold steady." He reached through the window for her wrist, blade pointed at her.

She yelped and retreated into the path of another departing driver, forcing the car to swerve toward the opposite curb and then whip back onto his side of the street. He gestured as he zoomed away, maybe to reassure but more likely to flip her the bird.

Gus held out two now-empty hands. "Please accept my profound apologies. I certainly didn't mean to alarm you."

"It's fine—I'm just not a fan of knives." Faced with getting run over or putting herself in stabbing range, though, she returned to his door. "Um, do you store that thing under the seat?"

"It's called a fighting knife. I keep it in an ankle sheath." He beckoned her to step onto the running board and hold the doorsill. Moving with deliberate slowness, he demonstrated how he could pull up the cuff of his right pant leg, snag the ring-patterned handle of the weapon, and draw it clear in one smooth motion.

When he returned the stiletto to its hiding place, she eyed his suit jacket, "Are you carrying anything else?"

He moved his left lapel aside and rotated toward her to expose a pistol in a hip holster. "I have the Glock 19 on my person at all times, along with what's jokingly referred to as a 'New York reload.'" He reached into the right pocket of his slacks and revealed another pistol. "Because this is a bodyguard situation, I keep a third one on my left ankle."

"Jeez, when do you need that much firepower?"

"I've been in situations where their mere presence provided ample dissuasion."

Another car whipped past, too close and too fast, making her glad she was pressed against his door. "Have you ever shot anybody?"

"Once, but ironically not while I was working for a client. I'd filled my gas tank at a station in Atlanta, and the machine was out of receipt tape. Being somewhat rigid about confirming the charges on my credit card statement each month, I went inside to get a record of my purchase. I happened upon an armed robbery in progress."

"And you killed the gunman?"

"I did, but not before he shot me." He patted his stomach. "Apparently, my attempts to discourage him from his course of action were too verbose for his tastes. Since then, I've worn body armor under my clothes as part of my standard ensemble."

Bo shuddered. "Should I start wearing a bulletproof vest, too?"

"No. Harry hired me to be your shield. And in any case, your husband's abductor seems intent on something other than harming you."

"That's one of the reasons I didn't sleep—I can't figure out what he wants. He's holding all the cards, and I don't even know what game we're playing."

"Let's hope he reveals that today."

# Chapter 21

Deke opened the Vault mid-morning on Tuesday, snapped on the overhead light, and took a tentative sniff. The adult diaper seemed to have done its job—only a faint trace of urine in the air, along with the lingering floral scent from the air freshener he'd sprayed the day before.

On the bare mattress, Oscar turned his sleep-masked face in Deke's general direction. He gave a futile tug at the duct tape that secured his wrists and ankles to the metal bedframe. "Are you going to let me go today?"

"No. Are you going to eat anything today?"

"And lie here with shit in my pants until you decide to change me? Fuck you, no way. I'm on a hunger strike."

Who knew hostages could be such a pain in the ass? He'd figured the guy would be compliant the whole time—scared shitless, not shitless by his own choosing—and begging for his life. Maybe even come to sympathize with his abductor. But Bo's macho husband didn't seem to be a candidate for the Stockholm Syndrome.

"By the time I get done with your wife," he said, "she'll be a broken woman. She's going to need you strong and able. Unless, of course, she blames you for what I'm putting her through."

"She'd . . . uh, she'd never do that." Apparently, Oscar heard the uncertainty in his voice. He sharpened his tone, saying, "You still haven't said what the hell this is all about. What are you doing to her?"

With the leather gloves exchanged for latex, Deke rotated his hands as he peered at them, smooth and white and nearly featureless, like those of a mannequin. They looked kind of cool. Much better than the real things. "Just a little payback for what she did to me a lifetime ago."

"Which means?"

"It's between us."

"Were you together in high school? At Virginia Tech? She dump you for another dude?"

"No, she was never mine. Not for a second."

"So that's it. You got like, the worst case of blue balls in history?"

"You're way off."

"What then?"

Deke carried in a box he'd packed with replacement diapers, a towel, wipes, talcum powder, and trash bags. He set the container beside the metal bedframe and closed the door, to deny Oscar the cut-grass-and-gasoline smell of the mower, which on Monday he'd said he liked. "Last time I knocked you out to change you. Do I need to do that again?"

"No, I want to feel your strong, manly hands all over my junk."

Deke sighed. Time to accelerate the schedule again? Three more days with this asshole seemed like too much of a burden.

"No gas mask this time?" Oscar asked. "Getting used to the smell? Starting to like it even?"

"Forget it—you can piss yourself raw. Think how manly you'll feel when your wife has to treat you for diaper rash. She loved Hokie maroon, but it probably won't turn her on when your dick's that color."

Oscar cursed as he squirmed and bucked against the tape.

Deke waited for his captive's energy to flag before getting it over with. He yanked the waistband of the sweatpants down to the man's knees and shoved a towel under his backside. Then he ripped the tabs free at both hips, pulled the diaper out between Oscar's legs, and tossed it in the garbage bag. At least the hunger strike made cleanup easier.

He prided himself on his fitness, so it was strange to see a guy his own age who'd gone to fat. At the other extreme, his quadriplegic twin brother Billy's physique had shrunk and atrophied over the years. Thinking of all the times as a teenager when he'd bathed his twin—paralyzed in a motorcycle crash at age sixteen—Deke wiped Oscar and let him air-dry.

At least the man's vulnerable state had shut him up for the moment, made him turn his face away. No more Mr. Tough Guy when his package was exposed. Deke dusted him with talc, secured the new diaper in place, and removed the towel before pulling up the sweatpants.

Mouth clamped shut, tendons rigid in his neck, Oscar didn't stir. The same way Billy had found the baths so emasculating; he had never thanked Deke but only wanted him to vanish until he could recover some dignity. It was time to check in with Mama and Pop about his brother.

What would they say if they knew the things he'd done and planned to do?

He patted Oscar's shoulder. "Hey, buddy, it's all over. How about something to drink?" Averting his eyes from his hands, he stripped off the latex, tossed them into the trash bag, and yanked on the calfskin gloves he'd tucked into his belt beside the canteen and nickel-plated Colt. He pulled them snug over his palms and between his fingers and relaxed again.

No reply from Oscar, so he took the paraphernalia from the room and returned with an opened bottle of Ensure and a straw. He'd bought a couple of six packs of the stuff after Oscar's refusal to eat the night before. "Come on," he said and nudged the man's arm with the plastic bottle. "It's chocolate. I got vanilla for you, too."

Oscar turned his head just enough to face the ceiling. "Why are you doing this to me?"

"Like I said, it doesn't have anything to do with you. That's why I'm being so fucking nice."

The man grimaced, as if choking down a comeback. He swallowed and said, "Then why her?"

Seemingly on its own, Deke's gloved fist squeezed the bottle until Ensure nearly erupted from the top. He focused on his grip and relaxed it a little. "I told you that, too; it's between us. Now, come on and drink. You won't get another chance for hours."

Oscar turned his head the rest of the way toward Deke, who pushed the straw between the man's lips. Chalky-brown liquid rose up the tube, and Oscar's mouth and throat worked as he sucked in all eight ounces. When Deke heard the slurping vacuum inside the bottle, he pulled it away.

Back in the day, he'd held Coke cans for Billy and made sure he angled the straw to prevent his brother from getting every drop. Even now, jiggling a soda to hear sloshing in the bottom made him smile.

"Good job," he said. "I'll check on you later." He snorted, angry at himself. Who was acting like the real Stockholm Syndrome candidate?

After shutting off the light, he closed and locked the Vault door. He'd have to really hurt the poor bastard if Bo acted out or disobeyed. Fractures, slashes, puncture wounds—any of them would get her husband crying out good and loud. Guarantee her attention and respect.

As he climbed the stairs to the ground floor, heading for the master-on-main he'd converted into his Op Center, he thought back to the bedroom he'd shared with his twin. After Billy had been brought home following months in the hospital, helpless but in one piece, he'd apologized to Deke for bullying him so much while they were growing up.

Deke could've done anything he wanted, even put a pillow over Billy's face and ended him. He had settled for gagging Billy sometimes and occasionally raining down body blows as repayment for all the teasing and sucker punches his brother had delivered over the years.

As days turned to months, though, he'd discovered that promising to end Billy's suffering but then letting it go on and on was a better punishment.

# Chapter 22

Bo and Candace split a breakfast bar before she cleaned up with the remaining trickle of hot water her daughter had left her. Gus had promised he would come to the office and sit in on the next interview, after finishing his neighborhood inquiries and getting in one of his Zen Master powernaps.

Her thoughts remained focused on Oscar, but compartmentalizing had to be the order of the day. She still needed to deal with Sean, as well as all the minutiae of life, including getting dressed. Grabbing the first outfit at hand, she ended up in a blue pantsuit with a butter-yellow blouse and low heels.

Candace had texted her a checkmark: safe at school.

As soon as she reached the On-Air office, she replied with one of her own.

When she went to get her first cup of Jeff's finest, she found her friend and Sean facing off in the middle of the breakroom. Despite having more than an hour before his show went live, ITP had already given his wavy black hair a tousling and donned another poet shirt for the webcam, with pressed denims below. Jeff sported a grungy Def Leppard tee, board shorts that did nothing for his pale legs, and flipflops on his long, bony feet.

The contrasting outfits would've been funny except for the amount of testosterone on display. It pumped out of their pores almost as clearly as the graphite spikes jutting up from Jeff's angry voice. He was shouting, "—no idea what she's going through, so just leave her alone."

Sean glared at Bo and then back at him. "Your office wife's here," he sneered. "If you're nice, she'll take your balls out of her purse and let you play with them for a while."

She stepped aside as Sean strode out, but he still managed to clip her shoulder. Turning with the blow, she kept her balance as muscle memory kicked in. She'd received far worse body checks on the lacrosse field.

Too bad she hadn't filled a coffee cup already. She could've tossed its contents onto his retreating shirt and tight jeans. Pouring herself some of Jeff's steaming, aromatic goodness, she drawled, "You boys fightin' over little ol' me?"

"Panzer told me what you said to him last night about ITP. First that sonofabitch grabs and threatens you, and now he nearly knocks you flat."

"I'm like one of those kids' punching bags that pops up every time." She patted the seat of her pantsuit. "Too much sand back there to keep me down." Hopefully the joke masked her anger about Harry's indiscretion. As with the kidnapping, something that was supposed to have stayed private had gotten out—and now was beyond her control.

Jeff checked his phone. "Come on, he wants to see us."

The "us" surprised her. Why did he need to be included? She fumed, though it wasn't Jeff's fault Harry had pulled him into this. In fact, she was touched that Jeff cared enough to square off with Sean. Still, she grumbled, "You know nothing's going to happen to ITP, right? We're just supposed to *clear the air.* Start with a *clean slate.*"

"Yeah. I'd like to clean his clock instead."

"You're certainly dressed for it." Coffee in hand, she set off down the hall. Jeff's flipflops made an awful racket—and a splashy mural of colors—as he hustled to catch up. She asked, "You still going to be able to work with him?"

"Only if I get to keep working with you." The red flame tips as always, but they flickered around an opalescent pearl: passion and truth. He was willing to quit in solidarity.

She shoulder-bumped him with much more gentleness than Sean had shown her. "Thanks, office husband."

A blush spread from his face to his neck so fast she was surprised it didn't run down his pasty legs and across his exposed feet. "Welcome," he mumbled.

Sean had rolled an ergonomic chair over from his cube and sat glowering behind the president's pristine desk to Harry's right. Eddie Corrales, the bearded twenty-something who did marketing and social media for the station, slouched in his chair on Harry's left. The three men stopped their conversation and watched as she and Jeff entered and took the straight-back chairs on the opposite side of the desk.

All they lacked to have an all-hands meeting were the IT contractor named Pete and the part-timer who bought canned shows for On-Air.

Harry's usually ruddy complexion was paler than she'd ever seen. He'd even neglected to roll up his sleeves. Turning to Eddie, he said, "Tell them the latest." His voice radiated excitement in nearly erotic pulses of blue and gold. Now she understood the changes in his appearance: he'd hit the jackpot and was in a dazed delight. The horrible reason behind his sudden good fortune didn't seem to bother him.

"So," Eddie said to her, his vocal background the color of day-old oatmeal, "you're like, a thing."

"If she's Thing 1, can I be Thing 2?" Jeff said.

Eddie snorted. "Not like *The Cat in the Hat*. I mean she's totally trending, going on twelve hours now. Her show's lighting up Twitter and Facebook and everywhere else, and website traffic broke the servers twice. Pete doubled the rack space after we crashed at midnight and then had to reserve even more around four. He has the server farm on speed dial in case we need to keep adding."

As Eddie spoke, Sean stared down at his fists. Bo remembered the pain in her wrists when he'd grabbed her. He glanced up, and she switched her attention to Harry, saying, "You're complaining all the time about how much it costs to rent servers and how expensive IT contracting is. Can we afford so much success?"

"We're jacking up our ad rates, starting today." He nodded to Eddie. "Tripling them."

"I'm all over that. Cha-ching!" He pumped a pudgy fist. "The really awesome thing is that people are treating this like a TV show: dissecting the Oscar-dude's adventures, second-guessing his motives, wondering why Bo challenged him on such-and-such. Some have started writing fan fiction based on his stories. They're even debating if there's really gonna be a rematch today and, if so, who'll win it—there's a Round2 hashtag some guy started."

Jeff said, "Man, I always wanted to direct a TV show." He adjusted his glasses and cleared his throat. "Not that I'm in any way unhappy doing this job, Harry."

"Well," Bo said, "I'm not happy." Harry and Eddie's evident glee disgusted her, but the marketing guy couldn't know what was going on, and her boss didn't seem capable of shame, so she named another reason: "I thought this was going to be a private meeting."

"The situation is changing fast," Harry replied. "I wanted everybody to hear the news at once."

She set her coffee mug on the carpet, folded her arms, and leaned back. "I'm not comfortable with *everybody* hearing about everything we need to talk about."

"Eddie?" Harry indicated his door. "Text me if something big happens."

"No problem." Eddie looked at Bo and the men as if they were about to enjoy a banquet but he wouldn't even get a doggy bag. He wheeled his chair out of the room and closed the door behind him.

"Jeff, too," she said. "He's not part of the discussion we need to have." Peripherally, she saw him turn to face her, but she forced herself not to look and see whether she'd hurt his feelings.

Harry said, "No. He's the director for both shows."

"I don't care. This is a personnel matter—and a personal one."

"Overruled." Harry's volume rose a bit, his aggravation a grass-green slash. Her obstinacy also had brought the ruddy bloom back to his cheeks.

She couldn't appeal to a higher authority and resigning in protest could cost Oscar his life. "Fine," she muttered. She risked a glance toward Jeff—he stared at her as if she'd slapped him. Worse than getting shot down, she'd needlessly damaged her only work friendship.

Harry turned to Sean. "What's your side of the story?"

# Chapter 23

Jeff's presence proved useful after all. Harry listened to Sean's excuses and Bo's assertions without expression, his mind obviously made up to do nothing. However, Jeff provided an eyewitness account of the physical contact in the breakroom, which forced their boss's hand.

Harry turned back to Sean and stared at him with hooded eyes. "Where do you think you are, grade school?"

"It was an accident." He threw up his hands. "She was blocking the doorway, and we bumped. I even said I was sorry."

Instead of asking Bo to confirm, the president said, "Jeff?"

"That's bullshit. Bo moved, but he deliberately knocked into her anyway and kept going without a word." He looked at Sean. "That's how it went down, dude, and you know it."

"I'm being fucking railroaded by these two. Get Eddie back in here—maybe he saw what really happened." Graphite pyramids of resentment, anger, and jealousy.

Harry shook his head as he unbuttoned his shirt cuffs and started to roll the sleeves above his elbows. "Did you know that your podcasts are getting even more hits than usual, too? Bo's interview is the rising tide that floats all our boats. Unfortunately, yours has sprung a leak—you need some time in drydock."

"What the hell does all that mean?"

"It means you're on suspension without pay for the rest of the week. Come back on Monday with a new attitude, better manners, and respect for your colleagues." When Sean made no move to leave, the president added, "Besides seeing lots more web traffic, we're also getting quite a few resumés and links to audition videos. Some of those people even have talent—and a look they didn't steal from a Harlequin book cover. Now go."

Sean stomped out, leaving his chair behind. He also failed

to shut the door behind him. Jeff closed it with a gentle click and avoided eye contact with Bo as he returned to the straight-back seat by her side. Clearly, he hadn't forgiven her, but that didn't stop him from coming to her defense when she needed help. She owed him big time.

Harry said, "Jeff, queue up four of his old shows to get us through the week, and record an intro and outro about him returning live on Monday."

"Will he?" he asked.

"Meaning, do I think he'll quit? Not a chance. Besides resumés and the emails about Bo's show, we're also getting double the usual number of positive messages about his. He'll be asking me for a raise when all this blows over."

Bo picked up her coffee mug. "Can I get back to working on how to convince that madman to free my husband? Or should we string this out to maximize our ad revenue?"

Harry steepled his fingers as he regarded her across his spotless desk. "I told you yesterday, this situation is bigger than all of us combined. At no time since I launched this station in 2010 have . . . *we* . . . stood to gain so much. This growth in audience interest, though, can go away just like that." He snapped his fingers, a firecracker burst of tangerine. "People like it when The Barracuda strikes, because the target always deserves it. If you lose your cool, though, and lash out at the maniac for reasons the audience doesn't understand—and you're in no position to explain—you'll forfeit your credibility. People will turn their attention to other things. Or, worse, they'll tear us all down before they move on."

He softened his voice, a stage actor's trick that forced her to lean in and listen harder. "I know you didn't ask for this pressure, and that you'd give anything not to move up the celebrity ladder this way. It doesn't matter how you got this fame, though. What matters is how you handle it. And, right now, I'm not sure you're up for the challenge."

In the ensuing silence, Jeff clapped his hands a few times.

"Helluva pep talk. Go team!"

The president ignored the sarcasm. His eyes stayed locked on hers. She had to give Harry credit: he knew exactly how to motivate her, just as her parents had when she was growing up. A kick in the butt had always worked better than a compliment.

She said, "For the record, I know you can gain a lot from this, but let's keep in mind who has the most to lose." Before he could rebut, she held up her hand. "That said, I'm sorry. I'll try to do better under the circumstances."

"Apology accepted," he replied, and the pearl she saw told her he meant it. "Anything you need from me or Jeff until Fuckhead calls in?"

"No. I'll work on questions, and on my strategies for what to do if he wants to take the conversation in different directions." She sipped some now-tepid coffee from her mug. "Gus will be here before we go on the air."

"I know, he texted me."

Naturally. It was a good reminder that Gus answered to Harry; the PI was her ally, but he wasn't her friend. He'd do whatever their boss dictated, which wouldn't necessarily be what she wanted.

Her only real friend in this situation checked the time on his phone and headed for the door, saying to the president, "I've got to set up ITP's 'Best of' episode." He left without a backward glance at her, but she saw the bilious yellow tentacles of hurt.

Harry said, "Bo, before you go, could you return Sean's chair to his cube?"

He'd made it sound like an innocent request. However, his intent hung in her mind as golden ribbons interlaced with ripples of azure: amusement and hope. A test to see whether she would blow up again or had taken his speech to heart.

Though the man did know how to motivate her, he still pissed her off. With a sunny, "Sure," she retrieved the chair. She pushed it from the room left-handed while, with her right, she sloshed coffee out of the cup and onto the mesh seat. Most of the dark liquid drained through and dribbled onto neat-freak Harry's beige carpet. Meanwhile, what remained on the chair would stain Sean's butt next week. Two birds, one stone. For the moment, she had to be satisfied with passive aggression.

On her way to the breakroom for a warmup, Eddie called her name from his cubicle. He sounded like he had a mouth full of something. "Hey, what'd I miss?"

She walked over to see him. "It's not my place to say, but you probably heard Sean leave."

White streaks and dots flecked Eddie's beard and black tee. He pushed the rest of a donut between his lips. Before he spoke again, she stepped back, out of range of the powdered-sugar fusillade. "Yeah, he seemed kinda bummed, but I'll forward all the fan mail he's getting. That'll cheer him up."

"How nice of you." She took another step closer to the breakroom.

"You're receiving even more than him, of course, though Sean's still got you beat in offers to hook up." He grinned and shook his head, as if sharing a joke about a lovably incorrigible colleague, but she saw the twisted maroon branches of envy.

She said, "Keep deleting the ones meant for me."

"Totally. But you're also getting lots of legit kudos. And check your inbox—some people even claim to know who your mystery guest is."

# CHAPTER 24

Deke printed his favorite screenshots of Bo from the podcast of their Monday interview and taped them to the wall behind his computer. Then he sat back, gloved hands behind his head, and gazed at the collage: his Wall of Inspiration. He'd watched all her earlier shows numerous times during the long months of surveillance, planning, and trial runs, and had kept copies of her best stills, but this time she was talking to *him*.

In the eighteen or so months he'd known her at Virginia Tech, they'd never had as long a conversation as they'd had on Monday. And not one so intense, of course. Each of her expressions on his Wall was a reaction to something he'd said or the launch of one of her own salvos. Brown eyes flashing, lips parted to reveal pearly teeth: The Barracuda in mid-strike. Her uncanny instincts about when and how to pounce had kept him alert, and the thrill of stalking her even while she hunted for any weakness in him—being both predator and prey—was so damned sexy.

He especially loved the segment that asshole Jeff had gloated about, where her middle finger rested against her temple and she seemed to be snarling. That screengrab had a place of honor in the center of the Wall.

Her hands had always captivated him, the way they had clenched her lacrosse stick, slid along its length, and swiveled it to keep the ball trapped in the mesh pocket while she raced downfield. The perfect circles she made with a spoon while stirring honey into a mug of hot tea during those brutal winter days in Blacksburg. How she would put down her pencil and stretch and curl her slim fingers after working through the solution on an exam. Hands that had never touched him with affection, that would never do so.

During the three semesters he'd known Bo, he had contrived to pass her any number of items while at the university and in the house she and two friends rented off-campus: books, sports equipment, kitchen utensils, a cold beer. Often gripped in such a way that her fingers would have to brush his.

One time after a sophomore calculus lecture, they'd both stood and hauled their backpacks onto the L-shaped tabletops attached to the tubular chairs. Like most of the students shuffling toward the exit, they wore jeans and t-shirts, Pearl Jam for him and Janet Jackson for her, ponytail swishing against the suntanned nape of her neck. Aiming for polite curiosity, he said, "Hey, how are you and Nick doing?"

"Good days, bad days. You know how it goes." She jammed the textbook into her nylon bag, gripped the zippered sides, and shook it up and down to settle the contents and create more space.

"Definitely." He reached over, scooped up her spiral binder, and tried to fit it into the bulging sack she continued to jostle. "You've gotta lighten your load, girl."

"For real. Thanks, I've got it." She grasped the top of the notebook to stuff it down, and he didn't quite get his hand out of the way. A moment of contact, her fingertips cool and smooth against his. Pure electricity shot through him.

"Still," he said, "you guys are, uh, mostly good, right?"

Making his voice casual, he kept the small talk going—often to encourage her relationship with the lucky sonofabitch she was dating—so as not to call attention to the latest instance of her brief touch. He never let his gaze linger on her too long as they headed out of McBryde Hall and passed War Memorial Chapel on their way across the wind-swept Drillfield. The longer he walked alongside her, the more spellbound and excited he felt, and the harder he tried to hide it.

Somehow, she always knew how he felt about her, despite his purposefully laid-back attitude. He'd catch a side-eye, endure a hasty parting on campus, or note some nervous fidgeting if he appeared at her rental house later for a date with Susanna, one of her roommates. He'd gone for Suzie so he could stay close to Bo. If he had seduced the other one, Lori, everything would've turned out differently.

Ever suspicious, Suzie would grill him constantly about whether he had the hots for either of her roomies. On the plus side, reassuring her about his loyalty had meant lots of sex. She'd been cute and eager, but he never felt the same electric tingle—even doing the kinkiest things with her—that he did whenever he engineered a millisecond of contact with Bo.

Now, he studied his hands, encased in leather and capable of both marvels and murder. He would never know any more than that brief touch of hers. What the rest of her skin felt like, her hair. Her interior—how wet and how warm?

It was fucked up to have been on the periphery of her life, then to have tried and failed to become its focus, and now to finally force his way to the center of her world while knowing it couldn't last for even the span of a workweek.

Originally, he'd mapped out a five-day strategy, but the script he had envisioned was playing out faster than he thought it would. Battle plans never survived first contact with the enemy. No later than Thursday, then, he'd be done with her. But she would be finished.

With the next interview only a few hours away, he returned to his many social media accounts, none of which used his real name or photos. He posted new comments with pro-Bo hashtags and links to the podcast. In addition, he shared and retweeted other fans' messages to keep the excitement building about whether there would be another interview that afternoon—#Round2—and how it might go down.

He also utilized multiple IP addresses across a variety of devices in his workspace to send emails to the On-Air staff through their website. Each of these offered up a different theory about the identity of the interviewee; he listed the names and email addresses of real people who lived in Metro Atlanta.

Bo's fans around the country were probably filling the On-Air inbox, too, but fingering neighbors, ex-lovers, and relatives. He wanted to ensure that some red herrings would be within the most likely geographic area, to trip up any local cops, feds, or private help she'd involved despite his edict. Moreover, he needed to get one particular individual into the mix soon. And it had to appear as if that name was just another of a great many tips.

The Bourne/Batman comments had generated a ton of interest, so he returned to updating his draft for the Tuesday interview. He had to give his new fans what they craved. Then the conversation would need to turn in a different direction. When viewers realized the new revelations were about her, not him, and increasingly personal in nature, they'd pull in all their friends to listen and gawk.

Then, on Wednesday, with her largest audience ever looking on, The Barracuda would thrash helplessly on the end of his line as he revealed her secret shame. Even if the On-Air people didn't post that podcast, he would—and the audience size would go through the roof. Still more would watch live on Thursday, to witness the woman in ruins, laid bare on the dock. Gutted.

His Wall of Inspiration would celebrate each of those moments, from Bo's disgrace to her collapse. The multitude of epic screenshots would span the room. No longer just a collage, but an entire goddamned mural.

And if she quit before the end, he'd make sure the world learned the truth anyway. Along with how, in a vain attempt to save her reputation, she chose to let her husband die.

# Chapter 25

Bo scrolled back through each email Eddie had forwarded. Overnight, the On-Air website contact form had become a popular tip line. It also remained the usual place for people to critique her show—much more often than praise it—and comment on her looks, voice, skills, and so on. She focused on the emails that purported to identify her interview subject and, often, where he lived.

In every case, someone she never heard of named another person she didn't know. She deleted a few dozen who'd declared a woman was disguising her voice or a celebrity had punked The Barracuda, but nearly seventy potential leads remained. These were in addition to the list Eddie was compiling for her of men the public had suggested on various On-Air social media platforms.

She needed to find out whether any of these people could be the one holding Oscar. The kidnapper had called himself a friend, but one she'd never known. He had been sincere on both points—the guy had apparently convinced himself that they shared a personal relationship but at a distance. No sociopath she'd ever interviewed could pull off such a lie. Though they didn't have a conscience, their intent to deceive always showed itself in her mind's eye. However, the truly delusional *could* fool her. Maybe the abductor fit that profile. With luck, though, he'd been ratted out by someone who knew him.

When she checked her inbox again, it showed forty-seven new emails forwarded by Eddie. In seventeen of them, the tipster claimed to know the mystery man. Across the totality of these potential leads, no two tipsters ever named the same individual.

Even if someone fingered the lunatic here, it meant the others were nonsense. That made all those people delusional, too, unless they were really trying to be helpful and were just incorrect in their guesses. Or they were settling old scores. As she'd learned through her interviews and life experiences, an individual's motivations for everything from love to larceny often involved convoluted emotions rather than consistent logic.

She sent the tips to the printer and checked her phone again for any that might have been posted to her website and routed to her personal email. There, she discovered even more guesses about his identity along with a flood of endorsement proposals—doubtless the result of being a "thing," as Eddie had put it.

Heartless cynics such as Harry could argue Oscar's kidnapping had a lot of upsides, as would his death, which might increase her fame further and possibly lead to more riches, in addition to solving her marital woes. Well, she decided, those people could go screw themselves.

Nonetheless, she needed to remember that such pessimists existed and were taking notice of her, watching for blood in the water. Her daughter's college fund hadn't received an infusion of cash since Oscar lost his job, but she didn't dare risk a conflict-of-interest accusation by responding to the companies now dangling endorsement deals.

After she secured Oscar's freedom and got him back home, she could see if anybody remained interested in her. For now, though, the only thing she wanted to focus on was his safe return.

Ninety minutes until show time. Eighty minutes until the kidnapper would call and she'd demand to speak to Oscar. She needed to hear and see his voice again—if only for a moment, and regardless of however garbled by the synthesizer it would be.

Questions continued to plague her. What if I can't figure out the right things to say to satisfy the kidnapper? Would he change his mind and murder Oscar on-air? Would he grab Candace next?

Her daughter had continued to text checkmarks, but maybe he had gotten her and seen those on her phone and was spoofing—

The loop of anxiety sped up along with her heart rate and breathing. She knew if she didn't stop, her doubts and fears would spin out of control until she'd question her ability to form a single coherent sentence, let alone talk the maniac into releasing her husband.

Before she sunk even lower, she knew she needed to move. To do something. Anything.

She drained her mug and trotted to the bathroom down the hall. Kathy stood at the sink, washing her hands.

Welcoming the distraction from her ordeal, Bo said, "Hey, we're both early today."

The woman turned and smiled back at her. "More coffee than usual."

"Me, too."

"How'd that interview go down yesterday?"

"We fought to a draw." She sighed and added, "The rematch is today."

Kathy pulled paper towels from the nearby dispenser. "Mmm, sounds like you're not looking forward to it."

"Guilty as charged, but I've still got time to get pumped."

"Want me to come by later and motivate you? I have a ministry on the side, you know. I'll light a serious fire under that skinny backside of yours." She balled up the paper and threw it away.

"No thanks. I'll be fine."

"Okay." Her skepticism looked like a tumbling square of burnt toast. She passed Bo on the way to the door, but then stopped and turned. "Here's something that's worked for me: give yourself some genuine Cleopatra eyes. Make sure your opponent really sees the whites and those intelligent mocha-browns you've got."

"He paces when he talks, so I don't think he'll be watching."

"It doesn't matter. Pretend he is and that you can nail him to the wall with just a look. Make him wish he never heard of The Barracuda." She winked. "That's what I'd do."

Kathy left, but her assuredness remained with Bo. Opening her case of eye shadow, she began to psyche herself up.

When she returned to the office, she found Gus standing in her cube, filling half the space. He gave her an 18-carat grillz grin. She asked, "Any luck with the people on my street?"

The smile disappeared. "As with last night, I must confess to a complete failure in that regard. Few opened their doors, and none of them saw anything amiss. It's possible someone deceived me, of course, but I'm not easily taken in." He folded his arms across his massive chest. "Don't give up hope, though; we still have options."

Pale blue streamers of conviction glittered with sparkles of pride. She caught herself regarding him not merely as an ally but a literal godsend, as if a divine spirit had taken notice of Oscar's plight. Resorting to magical thinking—that meant she'd lost faith in herself, in her ability to handle the situation. Besides, God wouldn't come to her aid; He only bet on winners.

She talked fast, to disperse the freshening whirlwind of negativity. "We do have some potential leads, about a hundred of them. They're from people who think they know the kidnapper's name." She led him to the printer near the breakroom and hefted the stack of emails.

Gus took the pages from her. "Are these all of them?"

"Eddie, our marketing guy, is copying down the IDs people suggested on social media, too. He'll also forward new emails to me as they come in. Is there anything we can do with this?"

"Certainly—I have access to public record sites, and some that are not so public. Based on a maximum four-hour's drive from your house, I'll be able to identify those outside that circle. Not that we can eliminate them entirely—someone with a New York address could have Oscar in a rental in South Carolina— but we must start somewhere. For the ones inside the circle,

I'll narrow the possibilities further using likely demographics. I can prioritize those who remain based on proximity to your home and then work from the center outward."

"And if he's in that rental in South Carolina? Or if he moved Oscar to another hiding place?"

"A personal visit to the prime suspects' address will be required, so it's logical to try the closer leads first." He'd clearly read her anxious mood, because he added, "The soundproof room where he's holding your husband would've been built at considerable expense and effort—it's not something he would create and then abandon after an hour of use. In addition, moving Oscar again increases the odds of a police encounter or a witness. As for the contiguous states, Harry's funds aren't unlimited, but he might have enough to bring in some other resources."

She eyed the papers in his hand. "You really think this could help us find the guy?"

"Let's hope we won't have to. Perhaps you'll get Oscar back after today's interview." He ruffled the stack of paper. "Then we can simply turn this material over to the police."

# Chapter 26

Bo entered the all-gray studio ten minutes before the kidnapper was supposed to call. Ready for battle, with Cleopatra eyes and all.

Gus followed her through the door. The laptop he cradled seemed no bigger than a cellphone in his hand. By listening in, they hoped he could detect some clues about the madman or his location, which would let her focus on the interview itself. In addition, she was counting on his presence to diffuse the tension she'd created earlier with Jeff.

After she made the introductions, Jeff adjusted his glasses and offered a cautious hello. His wariness looked like pink feelers probing for a trap. As the sole producer, director, and engineer at On-Air, he ruled the studio and seemed to regard unexpected visitors as trespassers.

He lowered the volume of the talk show in progress, which lightened her view of the orange EKG-like peaks and valleys. Nodding to her, he asked, "How are you holding up?"

Though he tried to make the question sound solicitous and friendly, she saw the yellow fingers of hurt that remained. Her fault for being playful one minute and then trying to boot him from Harry's office the next, after he'd served his purpose.

Matching his intended tone, she said, "As well as can be expected, thanks." She put her cell, notepad, and water bottle on the table and took a seat near the mic.

He turned his focus to Gus. "I named her, you know."

She rolled her eyes but didn't say anything. He also told the same story to every one of her interviewees within a minute of their entrance into his domain.

Gus said, "Can you elaborate?"

"I'm talking about The Barracuda. It was 'The Bo Riccardi Show' at first, but then she tore apart this lying jerk on-air, and—boom—the show practically renamed itself. But it didn't. I did."

She hoped he was done, but he added, "Of course, if she went by her given name, I never would've gotten that brainstorm."

Stepping on his punchline, she told Gus, "My parents gave me three names: Boise State College. Weird, right? Dad knocked up Mom there in the early seventies, and that's how they commemorated the event." She shrugged. "What can I say? They were hippies before they got religion. If it'd happened any later in the decade, I would've been named Boise State University."

Gus gave her another golden grin. "There's a long tradition of that. I was conceived when my parents were living in Augusta, Georgia. They were hoping for a girl, so I count myself lucky they masculinized it. How about you, Jeff?"

He snorted. "Named after my mom's favorite brand of peanut butter. Her spelling sucked." A lie, but a funny one. Hopefully his mood was lifting.

She said, "Well, Skippy, if the guy doesn't call, we'll do a 'Best of' show, right?"

"Got it queued up just in case, with an intro and outro."

Her phone rang with the sound of windchimes—overlapping, lime-green hexagons—and Oscar's name appeared onscreen. She'd changed "That's Amore" back to the ringtone she had set before he started messing with it. Either the lunatic thought she was naïve enough to believe he was calling from Jacksonville, where the people tracker app still showed the phone, or he knew what seeing "Oscar" on the screen would do to her.

And, on cue, the desperate, magical-thinking part of her took over. She half-convinced herself it really was Oscar, calling to tell her he'd been set free and where she needed to pick him up. Adrenaline poured into her bloodstream as her heartrate tripled.

She answered the call. "H-hello?"

"Miss me?" The synthesized, rust-colored voice radiated the lunatic's signature blend of passion and hatred.

Her spirits crashed among those red flame tips and brown spikes. She hung her head for a moment. When she looked up, Jeff and Gus glanced away. She demanded, "Put Oscar on."

"No."

"Then we're done here. I'm hanging up."

"You'd really risk his life by pulling that stunt?"

They'd both begun to dig inside each other's psyches—probing for vulnerabilities, exploiting weaknesses—while trying to defend against the same. She counted on his desire to talk to her as being more important to him than anything else.

With a quivering finger, she ended the call.

Jeff gasped, sending a ginger-colored comet streaking across her vision.

She started counting. Three . . . four . . . five. The phone rang again: Oscar. She exhaled. Before the madman could speak, she said, "Put him on."

A jostling sound and then a rasp, as if he'd dragged the mic across something scratchy. Oscar's cheek maybe? He needed to shave every twelve hours to keep his facial hair under control. After a day of confinement, he probably sported the makings of a full beard already. He said, "Bo?" Though the synthesizer still warped his voice, she saw the fear blended with relief.

"It's me. I love you. Are you okay?"

Bo heard wet snapping noises, saw the overlapping ruby streaks. He yelled out in sudden agony.

The arrow of pain split her skull. His awful cry should've been brick-red and sharply defined. Instead, it looked grayed out and blurry, almost pixelated. That'd happened to her only once before, with Lori Lambo.

She screamed, "Don't hurt him. I'm sorry."

Oscar's cries were silenced along with any other sound. Nothing for a few seconds. Then the maniac said in his electronic speech, "Two fingers broken: there's your proof of life." The background of his voice flickered from rust to slate, and the ribbon-like swirls of amusement swam in and out of focus as they vacillated between gold and steel.

No background noises: the Vault door had shut, trapping Oscar alone with his anguish. The man said, "Call this new number, and no more fucking around." He recited ten digits.

She scribbled them on her pad, her jittery hand barely able to write. "If you touch him again, I swear I won't talk to you anymore."

"Then I'll fetch my knife. You might choose not to listen, but that won't stop him from feeling every second of it." Rubber-soled boots thunked concrete. The triangles changed from charcoal-dark one moment to auburn the next. "Like I said before, pain can go on for a long, long time. He'll end up begging me to kill him. But I won't. Not for weeks. Maybe months if I'm enjoying myself."

She squeezed her eyes shut and fought for control. The weight resettled on her shoulders and neck.

He whispered, filled with his lust and hate, which once again looked crisp and clear and awful, "Still think you have some leverage over me?"

# CHAPTER 27

The bastard disconnected.

Bo needed a full minute to collect herself. It's all your fault, she told herself. Oscar's suffering even more now because of you. This was all on your head already, and you've made it worse.

Jeff and Gus looked too nervous to ask the obvious question, so she finally cleared her throat and told them what had happened. To escape their pitying eyes, she concentrated on the pad with her nervous handwriting. A new phone number scrawled in terror.

She hadn't even started the interview, and she was already a wreck. He'd already won.

*Get it under control—focus on the now.*

She put on the headphones and felt the aquarium-like isolation close in. Leaning toward the mesh-covered mic, she read the number to Jeff. Her voice sounded the way her throat felt: like she'd gargled glass.

The kidnapper answered their Skype call on the first ring. Jeff patched him into the mixing console.

Their voices produced well-defined, technicolor shapes— her synesthetic short-circuit had apparently fixed itself. She motioned for Gus to put on the headphones near him, and she cupped the final pair around her phone with the recording app running.

Jeff said, "One minute." He silenced the overhead speaker and led them through a sound test.

The maniac seemed happy with himself, though the fluttering golden banner Bo saw didn't tell her whether his delight had come from hurting Oscar or his threats afterward. Probably both.

She asked, "Will you be done with me after today?"

The synthesizer warped his laugh into a jangle of discordant noise and produced white starbursts in her mind again, the window being battered by stones. "Depends on how cooperative you are, Bo. If you try to rake me over the coals again, we could be doing this every day forever. I've stocked up on Ensure and Depends for Oscar."

Against her will, she conjured an image of the sadist infantilizing her poor husband. Telling herself not to think about it instead burned the picture into her mind. He clearly wanted her to grovel again. Instead, she said, "One threat at a time, please. Otherwise, I can't keep up."

He chuckled, but clearly she'd annoyed him by not taking the bait.

Jeff checked one of his screens. "You're looking fine on the webcam, Bo. Better than fine. Maybe the best you ever have."

A ludicrous exaggeration and totally inappropriate. She didn't get upset, though, because she saw his intent: distraction. To get the lunatic to think about her instead of focusing on whatever he'd planned for the next hour. Her friend had joined the game of high-stakes manipulation. If their side won, Oscar would go free, but she still didn't know what prize the kidnapper wanted.

Jeff acknowledged her nod of thanks with a wave and started his countdown.

She gripped the table edge with both hands to stop them from trembling. Sweat soaked her armpits. Hopefully he had the webcam zoomed in so tight the viewers couldn't see any of that.

"Welcome to another special edition of The Barracuda, brought to you by On-Air Web Radio, your home for the best interviews, advice, music, and more." She took a ragged breath. "Joining us again today is the man who goes only by Oscar and is disguising his voice to protect his identity from apparent enemies. Yesterday he detailed several conspiracies he claims to have disrupted and documented while serving in the army, and we learned a little about his childhood and life following his discharge. He considers himself to be a combination of Jason Bourne and Edward Snowden."

She wanted to use up all of the first twelve minutes with a summary but knew the lunatic would take revenge on Oscar again. "We have a loyal audience," she said, glancing at the questions she'd jotted, "but nowhere as big as you could've found with a TV network or mainstream talk radio, so why did you come to us with this exclusive?"

"The truth is, I came to you personally, Bo. If you did this job for a different station, I would've contacted you there."

Her chest tightened as the vise compressed her ribs again. "Um, and why's that?"

"I like your interviewing style. I've been a fan of your show from the beginning, and I thought you were the only one who could do my story justice."

His typical assortment of lies and flattery, nothing she could work with. "We seldom do two-parters, but, thanks to the response to yesterday's program, we've agreed to have you back on The Barracuda. My colleagues here tell me your audience today might be about triple the usual number, and maybe millions more will watch the podca—"

"That's right. I'm responsible for your biggest jump in audience size ever. You're welcome. I'll bet you guys are making a fortune in ad revenue now thanks to me."

"Well, what else about your story does the public need to know, for you to feel like we've given it the justice it deserves?"

"For all my new friends out there, here's another true-life story that would do Bourne—and even Batman—proud." As he launched into the adventure, she forced herself not to pay attention to his storytelling skills but to listen instead for some clue about where he was calling from. Only his footfalls, in crisp triangles of auburn, sounded in the background. No help there.

To her left, Gus returned his focus to his laptop and databases. Three piles of emails grew as he evaluated each sheet: one stack where the pages accumulated quickly, on which he didn't write anything, and two much smaller groups that received either a quickly swirled question mark or a series of notations with his fountain pen.

Meanwhile, all she needed to do was murmur an occasional "Uh huh" or make a similar noise to keep the madman going. On the positive side, he was burning through the first quarter of the show. However, she hadn't elicited any helpful intel from him. Further, the outside world expected her to do a decent job, and she was failing the most basic requirement of an interviewer: to stay in charge. Her core audience was no doubt yelling at her through their computers and lighting up social media with their frustration about her passivity.

Jeff held up five fingers. The sight made her think of poor Oscar's hand. All her fault.

Did the sadist really want to recite a few more of these stories and then call it a day? No, she sensed something else was coming. This reminded her of a stall-ball lacrosse strategy that opponents had sometimes tried: lull her and the other Hokies to sleep with monotonous passing and then blast through their defenses the instant she or her teammates showed signs of fatigue. She told herself to stay on her toes and not get complacent.

At last Jeff flashed her a peace sign.

She interrupted him with, "We only have two minutes before some commercials. Can you skip to the finale?"

"Of course." He wrapped up with gusto: heroic acts of bravery and derring-do. Total BS but delivered well. He at least was entertaining the audience, while she felt more depressed and sluggish than ever.

Jeff held up the laminated "30 SEC TIL BREAK" card. She tried to do the outro but the kidnapper talked over her: "When we get back, Bo Riccardi, your Barracuda, will answer some questions I have for *her*, so stay with us." His excitement pulsed in blue and gold.

No more stall-ball. He was making his move.

# Chapter 28

Blindfolded and immobilized, Oscar found it impossible to keep track of time. Because of his hunger strike, he couldn't judge day from night by normal differences in meals. Being presented with an occasional bottle of Ensure or water didn't tell him squat.

Only when he could talk to Bo again would he know it was a little before 1:00 p.m. on . . . Tuesday? Yeah, he'd been snatched on Monday morning. The fucker had made a joke about Bo wanting proof-of-life "to get her juices flowing before showtime." Until he heard her voice again, he'd remain lost in the timeless dark, with only fitful sleep to break up the long stretches of too much thinking.

Talking and singing and cursing and shouting had left him hoarse, but he remained desperate for sounds. Even the growls from his empty stomach were welcome.

His jaw itched from beard growth—the only real indicator that many hours had passed—so he tried tilting his chin down and sliding it from one shoulder to the other in an arc across his collarbones, listening to the scrape of hair against cloth. The sound soothed him until the repetitive motion began to hurt his neck.

Everything else hurt, too. His back and arms ached from being locked in place by the thick tape that manacled his wrists to the cold metal bedframe near his hips. He'd bruised his fingertips by tapping out every song he could remember. Cramps seized his thigh and calf muscles whenever he strained to lift his taped ankles and bang his heels on the frame to create a rhythm that could distract him for a while. Periodically, the kidnapper would come in to change him, which provided both relief and humiliation, but his skin still chafed from the diaper and from lying in place for what felt like ages.

His nightmares had begun to incorporate peeing in bed—always to the disgust of Bo or various women he'd slept with before her. In other dreams, urine flowed down his legs during engineering presentations for clients and at staff meetings. Even if he escaped and finally got home, he knew these nightmares would haunt him for a long time.

Time. What hour was it? Were people sleeping, working, fucking, eating, checking their phones, watching TV, killing each other, rioting, or burning up the whole goddamn world? All of the above, probably, while he was blindfolded, strapped down, and trapped who-knew-where.

The scent of air freshener was a distant memory. With the aromas unvaried for so long, he couldn't smell anything but the stink of his armpits and his stale, warm breath.

A faint breeze from what was probably an overhead vent kept the room cool but never cold. He tilted his head back to feel a fresh wave of air pass over his face. The wide blindfold blocked any relief from reaching his cheeks and forehead. No odors came with it either. The sound of inhaling echoed in the center of his head, however, and consoled him.

If he and Bo traded places, what would she see with those sounds? Would she lie here wondering what he was doing to free her? Would she wonder if he was trying his best to get her home?

He wished he could remember what she smelled like. She seldom wore perfume unless they'd planned a date night or a romantic evening at home. Those things hadn't happened in so long he'd reverted to self-service with porn to remind himself he wasn't a eunuch.

When had they at least kissed? The previous week, before he'd wrecked the Vette. She'd given him a quick peck when she got home from work, a meaningless bump of her mouth against his. No emotion, no kind of passion. Just going through the motions before her usual interrogation about the number of job leads he'd pursued and how many resumés he'd sent.

The last time he'd seen her naked? That was when he had barged in on her while she sat on the toilet texting some friend. Talk about sexy.

No wonder he'd busted up his car, driving fast to meet some buddies and hit the bars, hoping to escape for an evening.

He remembered Bo and Candace as the tow truck flashers lit them with yellow strobes. Bo had looked even more pissed than usual, but Candy stared at him as if she didn't recognize his face, and on the tense drive home and all that weekend, she'd acted skittish around him.

Now, he would've given anything to hear her say, "Dad," or for Bo to whisper that she still loved him. As it was, the best sound he could hope for was the ear-popping, sucking whoosh of the door opening.

He'd made the mistake of telling his abductor he enjoyed the yardwork aromas that had first drifted inside with the man. Grass clippings, gasoline. The smells of weekends at home. After that, the asshole closed the door behind him whenever he entered.

Still, he couldn't deny his relief whenever the man came in, bringing with him the novelty of new conversation, noises, odors, and actions—even if that meant getting wiped down, powdered, and re-diapered like a helpless baby.

The air pressure changed in his ears now as the door scraped open, and again when it clunked shut. Heavy, rubber-soled steps on carpet. The smell of clothes that had been laundered with a detergent probably advertised as springtime fresh, almond-scented bath soap, wood-spice shampoo, the tarry wax of boot polish, and always something else, a tangy aroma like machine oil. Maybe from a gun?

Despite the blindfold, he turned his head in the direction of the sounds and smells. He imagined the man looking down at him, hopefully seeing a fellow human being. Someone with a history and a future.

He caught himself smiling as he anticipated the novelty of a new conversation. Grinning like an idiot wasn't the look he wanted to convey, though. Gotta stay tough and command the dude's respect. He sucked in his lips and clamped his teeth over them to conceal his joy at the interruption of monotony.

The man said, "Today's the day. If your wife finally does what she's supposed to do, you get to go home."

"Really?" He winced at the kid-like enthusiasm in his voice.

"Yeah, but that's a big *if*—she's not cooperating. I guess she doesn't really love you. I mean, if she did, you'd be home already, right?"

The man got the cleanup and diaper-changing business over with quickly as he talked about Bo's obstinacy, her incomprehensible reluctance to say a few words on the air, make a small, inconsequential announcement for him. It was her fault Oscar had to remain a hostage.

All the while, he tried not to believe the guy. Why wouldn't Bo do whatever it took to win his freedom? There had to be more to it.

"You're full of shit. You want her to do something illegal, right? Maybe even kinky?"

"I don't, I swear. So you're kind of screwed until she gets off her high horse. Sorry."

Oscar was still chasing his thoughts when the door opened sometime later with another ear-popping whoosh. Stone-faced, he reminded himself—don't act so goddamn happy.

He heard two rapid footsteps coming toward him and felt the same plastic microphone from yesterday slide across his bearded cheek. It settled near his mouth. Almost 1:00 p.m. then, on Tuesday. Maybe he'd be going home soon. He said, "Bo?"

The speaker lay against his cheekbone, not his ear. He couldn't understand her faint words.

As she spoke, the dude seized the pinky and ring fingers on Oscar's right hand in a leather-covered grip. In one fast, stomach-churning motion, he twisted, bent, and yanked. Bones snapped like chicken wings.

Oscar cried out and tried to pull his hand against his body for protection. The tape held his wrist tight against the bedframe, and his hand could only spasm limply against the metal, which produced more pain. Tears soaked the inside of his blindfold.

Long after the door slammed shut, he screamed curses until the ache in his throat forced him to stop.

Bo must've heard what he was going through. When would she get him out of here?

# Chapter 29

As soon as they went to the first commercial break, the sadist said, "Kind of passive, Barracuda. Lost your fangs?"

Bo didn't want to sit there and take his abuse. Anything she said that would feel good in the moment could get Oscar hurt even worse; any appeasement would feed the lunatic's ego and make her feel even more powerless. She dropped her headphones on the table with an ochre clunk and nodded to Gus, who continued to work through the pile of leads.

He pointed at the smallest stack and held up three fingers. She assumed that meant three people so far whose addresses put them inside the likely circumference. The question-mark stack—probably people with common names and no indication from the tipster about geographic location—had grown as tall as the longshots.

"I'll watch the time," she told Jeff. At least she didn't have to worry about a repeat encounter with Sean. That was a good thing, because she'd left her water bottle near the mic stand.

The psycho had promised to direct questions at her. Either that meant they shared some history, or he just wanted to probe for possible weaknesses.

She found herself pacing. They did have that in common.

During her circuit around the suite, she walked past Eddie's cubicle. He called out, and she returned to his entrance. Powdered sugar still flecked his black tee.

"I know," she told him. "I'm going to win Lamest Interview of the Year."

"Yeah, no, there are some WTFs about you, but mostly people are talking about the Oscar guy."

"You mean they're giving him the Lamest Award?"

He scratched at his thick beard, releasing a flurry of more sugar onto his shirt. "Just the opposite. They think he's supercool—James Bond come to life."

"You're kidding. Everything he's saying is complete crap."

"Really? It all sounds totally plausible to me."

Rather than pursue that, she asked, "How many more tips did we get?"

"They've fallen off since the show started, but you and Gus have twelve new emails waiting for you." His computer chimed, and he swiveled to face it, making a robotic whir that stretched a grape-colored rubber band in her mind. Then he completed the rotation, with sci-fi sound effect, to tell her, "That's lucky thirteen."

Even though she'd seen the sincerity in his voice, she had to say, "I know this guy's an impressive storyteller, but do people honestly believe he's credible?"

"Oh yeah, they should make a movie about him. Great catch, Barracuda."

Either she was missing something, or people had lost their critical thinking abilities. She'd always prided herself on the intelligence of her audience's discourse. Even when she held opposing opinions from some of them, their ability to write whole paragraphs of well-reasoned arguments—expressed with eloquence and even properly punctuated—had contented her.

Maybe any skepticism expressed by her core fans was being drowned out by the mob of new listeners that now filled the arena.

Still in a daze, she scuffed back to the studio and locked the door behind her. Gus had pulled off his earphones. He ducked his head when she sat near the mic. Jeff seemed to look everywhere but at her. Thinking they'd had an argument, she whispered, "What happened?"

Jeff blushed. At his normal volume, he said, "He's on mute and so are we." Amethyst shame quivered.

"Come on, tell me."

"He, uh, gave us a different . . . meaning for 'barracuda.' In explicit detail."

"The sex act, right? Fingers and thumb?" She looked between them as they both fidgeted. "Seriously? With everything he's done, that's what finally struck a nerve? Ever since we renamed the show, guys online have been offering to 'barracuda' me. Get over it."

They shrugged in unison, but still looked embarrassed. Men.

Jeff cut the overhead speaker as the final commercial played. "Sorry, we, um—" He looked to Gus for help.

"We are uncomfortable on your behalf."

"I can only hope he'll switch his focus to the sex stuff. That I could handle."

The lock opened with a pewter flash. Harry stepped in and clicked the bolt home again. Sleeves rolled up, cheeks ruddy, he asked, "How much time?"

"Fifty-seven seconds." Jeff seemed to be able to do that without checking his screen.

Bo settled the headphones in place and checked that the other pair was still clam-shelled around her phone. The device had plenty of juice, and the app continued to record. She made a mental note to skip the pornographic how-to when she listened later.

The On-Air president approached the table on Gus' side. "Our servers just crashed again because of audience volume. Pete's on it. I didn't want to miss anything."

That meant the audience wouldn't hear anything live; they'd have to watch the podcast later. She glanced at the men. Only they and the kidnapper would know what was about to happen in real time.

While Harry spoke, Gus piled his email stacks on his laptop keyboard, brought down the lid to sandwich them in, and hopped up with an ease that still surprised her. He turned to Harry, who looked child-sized next to him, "I'll work in Bo's cube."

Without a word of thanks, their boss sat in the chair Gus had occupied and pulled on his headset. The PI gave Bo a nod of encouragement on his way out.

Jeff clicked a button and said, "Okay, you there?"

"I am," came the computerized, rust-colored reply in my headphones. "Good thing for Oscar you didn't forget about me."

"Bo," Jeff said, "we're going live in three . . . two . . . one."

The madman had promised to make this personal; now Harry studied her from only a few feet away. Despite her nerves, she showed her game-face to the webcam. "You're back with The Barracuda. If you just joined us, our guest wants to be known only as Oscar. His voice—"

"That's right. Before the break, I mentioned I had some questions of my own. You were curious about my childhood. Let's hear a story about yours."

"My audience knows all about me. Let's get back to you. What—"

"A lot's at stake, Bo." He paused and then hit her with the same lines she'd used on him: "Give our listeners a sample. Whet their appetites."

At least the website had crashed—Jeff could edit out anything she didn't like. Plus, she could control the clock this way, burn through some time while she lost herself in a story.

A favorite one from childhood came to mind. Pretending she was addressing diehard fans instead of the kidnapper, she said, "My parents met as hippies in the late sixties but, after I came along, they got serious about starting careers and creating a stable homelife. They also became devout Christians—we went to our local Baptist church whenever they opened the doors, as the saying goes. One time, when I was thirteen, we had a guest speaker, a missionary talking about the religious fervor of the recently converted in a foreign land. He said, 'For one man, wearing a hair-shirt didn't make him feel that he suffered as our Savior had done, so, for days on end, he flatulated himself . . . I mean flagellated.' Everybody including the minister lost it.

I couldn't go up to take Communion because I'd peed through my dress from laughing so hard."

Jeff gave her a smile. His encouragement and the silly memory lifted her spirits for a moment. Then she thought about how much she missed her parents. She knew she should've called them last night; it would've been nice to hear their voices even if she couldn't have told them the reason she needed comforting.

"And that was in Roanoke, Virginia," the sadist said. "Now you live north of Atlanta?"

Warning bells began to go off in her head. "Just as you don't want to discuss your current whereabouts, I've found it best to follow the same policy."

"36 Meadowlark Drive in Roswe—"

Jeff muted him, but then checked his other screen. "Aw shit, the website's back up."

# CHAPTER 30

Bo looked at Jeff, who had just shared his profane comment with perhaps a million or more people, and then she remembered the webcam, which was transmitting her panicked, gaping silence. The madman hadn't gotten the chance to finish naming the city, but a quick web search would show only one possibility.

Probably nobody cared where she lived, but she still imagined Candace getting home from school in a few hours and being mobbed by gawkers and the press.

She grabbed the pad and pen and scribbled "Tell Gus" on a blank sheet. To hell with how that must've looked on camera. She pushed the note at Harry, who hadn't budged.

He considered it for far too long. It took her murderous glare and a hissed, "Do it," to get him to set the headphones on the table and abandon his chair. He took his time exiting the studio.

Finally, she cleared her throat and moved closer to the pop-screen and mic. "We, um, appear to be having some technical problems. Can we get our caller back?"

Jeff tapped a button.

"—Goddamn, fucking assholes. I swear to—"

Bo shouted over him, "You're live again." In a normal tone, she added, "Sorry for the glitch, but please watch your language. While there's no FCC for web-radio, I ask you to respect our audience. Now, let's get back to you. What—"

"No, we're going to keep the spotlight on you, Bo, until the end of this."

A trickle of frigid sweat wormed its way down her breastbone. Her armpits were still wet with it, and she could feel a damp tingle across her scalp. "How, um, how much longer until the end?"

"I dunno, two more days, maybe three. Maybe another week. As I told you offline, some things can continue for a long, long time if need be."

He'd been telling the truth until he threatened another week. She didn't want to talk to him for two more minutes, let alone two or three days. Trying not to think about the tortures Oscar could suffer in that span, she said, "There's nothing to cover after today."

"I have plenty I want to talk about. You gave us that delightful story about public urination earlier. Let's hear another tale from your youth."

She wondered about telling their audience what this was all about. Although she'd get public sympathy on her side, she might not gain any real advantages. Oscar would still be at his mercy, and maybe the sadist would drop the whole action hero pretense in favor of abusing Oscar on-air. The maniac also could start giving out Candace's information, her cell number, the high school she went to, and everything else he might have discovered about her.

No choice but to play along.

This had become a twisted version of *The Arabian Nights*, with her as Scheherazade. But telling stories to save her husband's life instead of her own.

Jeff held up five fingers.

She said, "Well, um, my dad always wanted me to be an engineer, so I graduated from Georgia Tech in environmental engineering along with my husband-to-be, who shared the same major."

Poor Oscar, injured and terrified in a soundproof cell. And Candace, maybe going home to a trap. Worry and guilt stabbed at her.

Clearing her throat, she tried to push her fears aside and think of Scheherazade and storytelling that could save a life. "Uh, he found employment immediately in his field, but I struggled to get work. Maybe the hiring managers were all sexist, but I think it was mostly me—my heart wasn't in the interviews or the profession and it showed. One day I was on the MARTA train, riding home in my stiff new business clothes after another poor showing. A painfully thin and bearded man got on at the next stop and sat across from me.

"He wore dirty clothes, a castoff coat, and mismatched shoes, and dropped a battered knapsack at his feet that might've held everything he owned. A terrible smell clung to him. Clearly, he hadn't bathed in a long time, but he'd also been forced to live and maybe sleep in nasty conditions, probably on the street. A police officer who'd been standing at the opposite end of the car strolled up and stood near the newcomer, holding onto a pole and looking down at him with an expression that said, 'Just go ahead and try something.'

"The man glanced up at the officer, tried a smile with rotten teeth, and then dug in his bag until he pulled out a small, plastic American flag on a stick, the cheap kind given out to kids to wave at parades. He fluttered it frantically at the cop, who continued to glower at him. The man grew increasingly agitated, looking at me and the other passengers and then back up at the policeman.

"Stress overwhelmed the guy. He took the pretzel-thin flagstick in both hands and nervously snapped it into smaller and smaller pieces and stuffed all of it back into his sack. Something had snapped inside him as well. He focused on me and snarled, 'Coming down to my town in your fancy clothes, money in your pockets. Think you're something? You ain't nothing. None of us ain't nothing.'"

Her eyes misted as she remembered those words. "The *us* comment flipped something inside *me*. The man went from being just some label—derelict, mentally ill—to a human being with a history I wanted to know. Even while the cop was telling him to settle down and stop bothering people, I said, 'Why do you feel like you're nothing?'

"The officer told me, 'Ma'am, please stay out of this,' but I persisted. The fellow said, 'Why you care?' and I replied, 'Because I do—because we all do.'

"It took a little more urging, with the cop getting more annoyed at me than the man he was standing over, but finally the gentleman started to tell me his story, with me coaxing more and more from him."

Bo had forgotten how much the encounter had meant, how it had changed everything. "No exceptional tragedy had sent him down this path—it could've been the story of ten thousand other people—but he made it unique with the words he used and with his emotions. His train stop came before mine. He grabbed his pack and stood, and I opened my purse, asking if I could give him something. The man said, 'You did. I'm Richard.' I told him my name, and he smiled at me with those pitiful teeth like it was the best thing he'd heard all day and said, 'Bo knows.'

"The officer watched him exit and then looked me over. He asked, 'Are you a psychologist?' I said I didn't have a job, that I was looking. Before he strolled back to the other end of the car, he said, 'Check out the talking professions.'"

She sniffled and quickly wiped her nose. "A woman in the seat behind me tapped me on the shoulder. She said she was a producer for the local NPR affiliate, and we chatted all the way to the end of the line. My casual interview with Richard turned into a formal interview for a job. Goodbye engineering, hello radio."

Jeff gave her a thumbs-up and held out the "30 SEC TIL BREAK" card. His eyes looked wet behind his glasses.

"We only have a few seconds before our break," she said. "Then let's get back to you. I'm sure our audience will find you much more interesting."

"No, the spotlight is just where it needs to be."

Inwardly, she groaned. "We'll, um, return with more on The Barracuda."

When Jeff switched on the overhead speaker to monitor the commercials, she didn't wait for the kidnapper's latest potshots. She dropped the headphones on the table and raced from the studio to her cubicle. Gus wasn't there, but he'd left a message in flowing black script on the back of the page Harry had delivered to him: "I have sent a cautionary text to Candace and am going to your home to provide security. Don't let this distract you from your mission."

His note heartened her, but he couldn't do guard duty there 24/7. Though only a few curiosity seekers or journalists might show up initially, trolls could spread her address across the Internet and incite vandals and deviants for days or weeks to come.

She couldn't afford to hire more security, and she couldn't ask Harry to pay for it. For the first time in twenty-five years, she was afraid to go home.

# CHAPTER 31

Bo checked her laptop and saw seven more tipster emails forwarded by Eddie along with a list of another sixty or so IDs suggested through social media. Any one of them could hold the key to Oscar's freedom.

When she returned to the studio, Jeff gave her the up-from-under look of a guilty child. He said, "On mute again. Sorry I didn't do it faster when he was blabbing your address." The stress was clearly tying him in knots, too.

"It's not your fault—he blindsided us. Gus will keep Candace and the house safe."

She took a seat near the pop-block screen and mic and drank some water. The curl of her fingers around the bottle made her imagine Oscar's broken ones, and how much it would hurt him to do such a simple thing.

He suffered because of her gamesmanship. She recalled her own broken fingers in college and how they'd hurt like hell. A girl had whacked her with a lacrosse stick after she intercepted a pass. The blow had fractured the index and middle fingers on her left hand. If she hadn't been in so much pain, she would've returned the favor.

"It's almost time," Jeff said. "Are you okay?"

"Just reliving something awful."

"Sorry I have to unmute him. I wish we could keep him in limbo forever."

"No, better to get it over with."

"If you say so." He shut off the speaker and tapped a button. "Here we go again. You there?"

"Ready for action," came the synthesized reply.

Jeff counted down as she looked at the webcam and readied herself. "You're back with The Barracuda. Our returning guest calls himself Oscar and is disguising his voice for personal safety following stints in the Army Rangers and CIA. We were about to discuss what you do now."

"Nice try, but we're still talking about you. What you're trying to pull is a tactic we call Survival, Evasion, Resistance, and Escape, or SERE. You probably think I love to talk about myself so much, you can SERE me and I won't even notice. Not so." His boots kept up a steady triangular auburn rhythm as he spoke. "We've heard about you peeing in public and showing empathy to the indigent. What else do you have for us?"

Though she didn't dare put Oscar at risk again, she needed to reassert some power.

Maybe she could scare him. Make him think twice about what he'd revealed and what he was planning. If he no longer thought he held all the cards, he might go easier on her husband or free him sooner. She would take a risk, and she'd just have to deal with the blowback. Her fans might dismiss *her* as delusional. And her friends could disown her or, at best, would become self-conscious talking around her.

She took a breath and plunged in. "I've gotten some nice press over the years about my interviewing skills. What those reporters didn't realize—and what only my family knows—is that I, along with a small percentage of the world's population, have a gift. It's called synesthesia, the blending of senses. In my case, I see colors and shapes in every sound, from voices to violins. This is called chromesthesia, or color-hearing."

From his comments, she knew he didn't watch her on the live stream, but she fixed her gaze on the webcam so he'd get the message loud and clear when he watched the podcast. "My personal version of this gift shows me the intent of any speaker: sincerity, manipulation, avoidance. Lies big and small. I've been able to do this since I was little. It's been especially handy for conducting interviews—and dealing with boys. I literally watch what you say."

He didn't reply, but he stopped walking. Was he thinking back over the past few days? Wondering whether he'd inadvertently offered some insights into who he was and where he could be found? Second-guessing what to do next?

She charged ahead. "It might sound like witchcraft or psychic powers, but it's not. Lots of musicians and other creative types have different degrees of chromesthesia. I'm not hearing something that's unavailable for others to pick out, but I filter the fakery and verbal misdirection that fool most people."

The madman still hadn't uttered a sound or moved. Score one for self-disclosure. Feeling emboldened, she said, "Therefore, when I hear unsubstantiated saving-the-world stories and I see nothing but lies, I get concerned that somebody is trying to pull a fast one on my audience. And I'm never wrong. Never." An exaggeration, but there was no way she'd tell a delusional person that she couldn't see through the false things he thought were true.

Still no reply. Instead of this, maybe she should've played the recordings of Oscar's torture and his abductor's threats to turn public opinion against him. Without his fandom, perhaps he'd leave her husband alive on some deserted road tonight and vanish from their lives.

However, the man could be just as likely to murder Oscar, bury his body where no one would find it, and disappear. Every choice she made was a gamble with Oscar's life.

"Want to test me?" she asked, pushing down her fear again.

The man hesitated a moment longer, hopefully feeling off-balance and flustered. He finally said, "No need for magic tricks. Turns out I can tell truth from fiction, too. Are you up for a test?" His voice shot sky-blue contrails of confidence across her mind.

Given the chance to trap him with his own arrogance, she said, "Sure."

"Maiden name?"

"I prefer birth name. It's Kroenke."

"Correct. I was rudely interrupted earlier while giving out your address." While he started to recite it, Jeff lunged for the mute button. Picturing Oscar's broken fingers, though, she waved him off as the madman continued to speak. "Everybody needs to visit Bo and her hot daughter, Candace. Your cell numbers?"

The trap had been his, the arrogance hers. She couldn't breathe.

While she scrambled to think of a reply, he said, "Oh, you don't want to play after all?"

She snapped, "No more personal information—no more nothing right now. We're going to an early break." Before he could reply, she swept off the headphones and ran from the studio.

# CHAPTER 32

Cursing herself for playing into his hands, Bo raced to the bathroom and dry-heaved over a sink. She needed Kathy and another of her pep talks more than ever. So far, though, she had the facilities to herself.

One problem with being alone with a big mirror two feet away was that critical self-evaluation was impossible to avoid. Perspiration slicked her forehead, the makeup on her eyes and lips was smeared, and her hair was a mess from the headphones. Though she'd hardly eaten since the ordeal had begun, stress made her look and feel bloated.

Someone rapped on the outer restroom door. Only a man would do that.

She called, "Jeff?"

"Naw, it's Eddie. Can you see that I'm telling the truth? I mean, if you didn't already know my voi—"

"What do you want?"

"Something's happening in the studio, and Jeff told me to get you quick."

The only important thing that could occur during a break would involve the kidnapper and Oscar. She flung open the two doors and barreled into the hall. Pushing Eddie aside, she sped to the office.

In the gray studio, Jeff's headset and glasses were at his elbow, and he'd planted his face in his open hands. The overhead speaker played a commercial at low volume.

From the headphones at the interview table, she heard a faint racket, an undulating tone she couldn't quite make out.

In her mind, however, she saw brick-red arrows firing through showers of scaly pink. Pain and fear. The images, coupled with the muffled quality of the sounds, opened a trapdoor under her feet and dropped her into the hell she'd fled a quarter-century earlier.

She fell back against the studio door and grasped the knob for support. The din coming from the headphones hadn't changed, and the commercial continued to murmur, but all the images wavered and grayed again. This time, though, they didn't snap back into colored focus.

Jeff scrambled for his headset and shouted into the end of the stalk near his mouth, "She's here. Stop, you motherfucker, stop." He flipped the switch to kill the overhead speaker. Closing his fist around the black foam egg encasing the microphone, he told Bo, "He wants to talk to you." The disgust in his voice should've looked like an earth-tone stack of pancakes. Instead it was warped, fuzzy, and as ashen as weatherworn granite.

The cries of agony coming from the headphones ended abruptly.

Was Oscar dead? Or had his tormenter just stepped outside the torture chamber and shut the door?

She forced her feet and legs to move. They felt disconnected from her, mechanical, as they conveyed her to the chair. Clamping the headphones around her ears, she leaned toward the mic. "What did you do to him?"

The man's soundproofed door opened with a whoosh. She heard Oscar keen as he fought to master the pain the maniac had inflicted. Between high-pitched whines, her husband cursed and gasped in dun-colored smears. The sadist said, "Here, tell your wife what my hammer did to your right hand."

Over the bump and rustle of the mic, Oscar moaned and gasped. "Oh Christ, the sonofabitch broke every bone. It's like goddamn pulp. Help me!"

She yelled, "I'm trying," but the mic had moved again. The door closed once more on Oscar's wailing.

Spit had flown from her lips and peppered the mesh pop-screen like dozens of soap bubbles. "Take me instead," she said. "Tell me where to meet you. You can do anything you want to me. Just let him go—he doesn't deserve this."

"It's all your fault." The computer voice sounded amused. Charred curls like bedsprings after a housefire faded in and out. They should've looked like golden swirls of ribbon.

This must've been how it felt to go insane—for the things you counted on as constants to distort before your eyes. For them to become perverted imitations that made you wonder if they'd been that way all along, concealed under a daub of paint, hiding beneath a veneer of gilt.

Jeff said, "Forty seconds. Give her a chance to get her shit together."

"Clearly you people aren't taking me seriously. Next, I'm going to get Candace and try out the *barracuda* on her with her dad watching. Maybe force Dad to do it to her with his one good hand." Flickering gray flame tips. "You can watch the video."

A chill juddered through her. She felt utterly helpless. Every time she'd managed to create the slightest shift in control, he knocked her flat with an even worse reminder of his power over her. She should've expected the escalation of threats, the increasing perversions to keep her in line. In fact, she'd instigated it by asserting herself, dueling with him both in private and on the air.

Her fate had become clear. The only way Oscar would survive—and the only way she could keep Candace safe—was by sacrificing herself. She needed to be totally compliant. Submit to all his demands.

It didn't matter what happened to her, she decided. She deserved it. Her family didn't.

Jeff flashed five fingers with his right hand and began to lower them one by one.

A dozen questions assailed her during the longest five-second countdown of her life.

Finally, Jeff pointed to her, and she gave herself up to whatever cruelties the kidnapper had planned.

# CHAPTER 33

Deke rubbed at the leather of his right glove with a rag. Streaks of red persisted. That last blow to the back of Oscar's hand with the framing hammer had done it. A little too much force in the swing. His enthusiasm had gotten the better of him, and now Oscar's blood had ruined the glove. He considered taking it off, but the sight of his naked, waxy hand would sicken him more. The glove was a regrettable loss, but a good soldier accepted casualties as a reality of war.

In his ear, Bo's voice was full of submissiveness, the fight gone out of her. "Here we are at the last segment. We've both revealed some . . . unusual things about ourselves. Do you, um, have anything new you want to share?"

He'd been trying to imagine her color-hearing thing, what it would be like not only to see a voice but understand the speaker—maybe more than he understood himself. All those times at Tech when he'd thought he was being smooth, always encouraging her relationship with Nick, maneuvering toward some incidental contact and then acting so casual afterward. Her aversion made sense now: she'd known his intensions all along, seen right into the center of his soul, and just been too fucking polite to call him on it. Instead, she had apparently told everybody else.

It explained why Suzie had cross-examined him so often, why Nick had treated him like a punk. And also why Lori had liked to flirt when no one else was around—she'd always been in competition with her two roommates for men, grades, everything. A caution from Bo would've been like catnip to Lori.

He started to pace again. "Absolutely, so I encourage our listeners to stay with us to the end. First, though, some background. Before you finished your engineering degree at Georgia Tech, you studied at Virginia Tech. Why'd you choose to be a Hokie?" Vault, furnace room, gun cabinets, stairs, doors, tools, Vault.

"Because I grew up close by in Roanoke." She sounded wary, probably seeing his intended path toward the minefield. "It allowed me to go to a great school and still get home on weekends if I wanted."

"You didn't live on campus the whole time you were there, did you?"

"Uh, no. I . . . I rented a house my sophomore year."

"Pricey—how'd an undergrad afford that?"

She hesitated but at last said, "Two friends roomed with me."

"Part of most college experiences: learning to deal with roommates. Tell us about your two friends." He stopped in front of one of the gun cabinets—assorted antiques, modern assault rifles, and his favorite semi-automatic Saiga shotgun behind glass. Studying his reflection, he squared his shoulders a little more, straightened his spine, smoothed a wrinkle from his camo shirt. "First names are sufficient. I don't want to impinge on anybody's privacy."

"You—" She stopped as if to gather herself.

He slid his canteen a quarter-inch to the left along his web belt so it wasn't so close to the holster. Then he smiled and resumed pacing. She seemed to be biting her tongue, having finally learned not to screw with him. Good—he didn't want to ruin any more gloves on Oscar.

In a calmer tone, she said, "You already know who they are, don't you?"

"Our audience doesn't. Enlighten them."

"Well, uh, my best friend was Susanna. Everybody else called her Suzie or Suze, but I preferred her given name. She was sweet and shy, sort of innocent."

That was a bit of revisionist history. He could've pointed out that Suzie had let him do her anally on only their second date. However, there'd be plenty of time to brag later. "Anything else about her?"

"She had really lousy taste in boys." A pause. Was she hoping to elicit a response? He wasn't sure whether she had some suspicions and was fishing or simply stating a fact and waiting for the next question. With that visual hearing, she could possibly detect a telltale reaction in his voice, something that would betray him, so he remained quiet and let dead air accumulate.

There was nothing that broadcast talent hated worse than lingering silence, the kind that made the audience glance at their devices to see if a glitch had occurred. Sure enough, she jumped in to fill it. "Each one of those guys was a reclamation project, somebody she could rescue and fix. Of course, that never ended well."

He asked, "Where is she now?" After he'd broken up with her, he never gave her another thought—other than that he should've pursued Lori instead.

"I don't know. We lost touch and didn't try reconnecting."

"You said you had two roomies."

"L-L-Lori. She, uh, was the other one."

Bo probably hadn't said the name out loud in twenty-five years. That made two of them, but it was good that she said it first. He checked his chronograph: more than five minutes gone. If they tacked on the extra time from the previous segment, he still had about ten minutes with her.

Not wanting to give her any ammunition, he stayed quiet.

She stammered, "She was the, uh, adventurous one. The first of us to try hard drugs. Never backed down from a beer pong challenge. The one who educated me and Susanna about STDs, carrying protection. Very liberated, very—" Her voice cracked, and more silence built up. "She was her own person."

"Lived life on her own terms?"

Another long pause. Was she choking back tears, or choking down a challenge that could get Oscar hurt even more? Or both? His recording would yield lots more screenshots for the Inspiration Wall.

"Yes," she managed.

"What made you want to live off-campus?"

"Not *what* but *who*. Lori wanted more freedom than the dorms would allow, but she couldn't afford a rental on her own, so she recruited me and Susanna. My parents weren't really in favor—Lori probably reminded them of their reckless hippie days—so they wouldn't help me with the rent. I worked a job on weekends and some weeknights to pay my share."

"That must've put a cramp in your love life." The sarcasm slipped out. Could she see lingering jealousy about her old boyfriend?

"Yeah . . . Nick wasn't a fan. Did you know him?"

Sneaky. The Barracuda still had some fight in her after all. He checked his watch again, resisting the automatic urge to answer her. She'd either spot his lie or follow-up on the truth. No percentage either way, but silence was damning, too, so he said, "All three of you had boyfriends—tell us about them."

Maybe she thought she'd regained some advantage. Her voice became more confident as she talked about Nick Cohen, making it sound like they'd dated casually instead of being deeply into each other—more revisionist history—and Lori's sometime-hookup Tom Brogan, a loser according to Bo. As she critiqued Tom, she kept pausing, as if waiting for him to protest. As if she thought he might, in fact, be Tom. Perfect.

When she finished with those two, she said, "Like I mentioned, Susanna went for the boys in need of saving. There was Cy, a real jerk, and another who called himself Ace and broke her heart—and several others. I remember one named Deacon, which was sadly funny because he was anything but."

He stopped pacing again and lingered outside the Vault, wondering if she had decoyed with her suspicion about Tom and now baited the trap she'd hoped to spring all along.

When he began to switch topics again, she cut him off, saying, "We're almost out of time. Are you through with me or will you be back with us tomorrow?"

Frowning, he checked his chronograph. Damn, the hour had sailed by. "Say my name."

"Um, Oscar?"

"Yes, Bo. I'll be back with you on Wednesday, when we'll talk about this cast of characters you've described. And we'll discuss your role in Lori Lambo's murder."

He disconnected. From his pocket, he withdrew a list: items to pack for a road trip.

# CHAPTER 34

**B**o told herself to inhale. He was stealing everything, including her breath.

The sandbags on her shoulders and neck had doubled in size. *Keep it together. Don't pass out.*

She recovered enough to do the show outro on autopilot while questions echoed in her mind about Oscar's injuries, Candace and her parents hearing about the murder, whether Oscar's kidnapper was also Lori's killer. If so, Bo wondered, was all this about somehow pinning the murder on her?

Even after two days, she still didn't know what he wanted from her or how to free Oscar.

"Murder?" Jeff asked. "What the hell's going on? What's he talking about?"

Pinwheels of alarm that used to be fuchsia now wavered in cinder-gray. She didn't see him doubting her involvement in a killing. As if he'd bought in completely to the accusation and just wanted to hear her side of things.

That hurt even more than the still-distorted shapes and colors.

The shift in focus to Virginia Tech had rung alarm bells, but she'd thought, at worst, the lunatic would charge her with not preventing Lori's death. She'd also counted on having one more night before he broadcast the worst of his delusions to the world. Now she needed to deal with everybody's questions before she was ready.

Past the point of wanting to scream at this mounting madness, she felt her emotions shutting down instead, like circuit breakers tripping. Soon, she'd be dead inside. She had been there before.

Her phone rattled with more incoming texts and calls—smeary grays that should've looked like undulating green coils. No doubt from friends who were also loyal viewers.

At least Gus had stationed himself at the house. The allegation would probably bring out a few more curiosity seekers.

She replied, "You're going to edit this before posting it to our website, right?"

"Sure, but—"

"We've edited shows before. That time the actress gave out her ex-fiancé's social security number, hoping somebody would steal his identity. The drunk Congressman who fell out of this chair."

"Yeah, we can take out anything you want, but—"

Harry unlocked and entered the studio, breathing hard, perspiring, as if he'd sprinted for the first time in thirty years. His big belly had pushed out his dress shirt, untucking it. Between gasps, hands on knees, he said, "Tell . . . me . . . everything."

"There's nothing to tell," she said, feeling the fuzzy gray walls close in. "I wasn't involved in Lori's murder, but I was in the house when it happened. As far as I know, the Blacksburg police never caught the killer. I bet Oscar's kidnapper did it, or knows who did."

"If he did . . . he'd be hiding . . . not going on the air."

"Maybe he's doing this to taunt me for some reason, to rub it in that he's still free."

Jeff asked, "But why put you through days and days of this? Why not just go live on Monday, rub your nose in it, and call it done?" His voice finally betrayed the doubts she'd wanted to see earlier. Unfortunately, he was questioning her logic, not the maniac's claim.

Their tag-teaming made her even more claustrophobic. Pulse pounding in her temples, she staggered to her feet and started to pace. "He's getting off on the attention. Remember how he bragged at the start of today's show about the audience size? He thinks these are his fans now, not ours. If interest grows even more, that'll mean a bigger arena for him tomorrow."

Harry sat, still panting. "But nobody knows who . . . he really is . . . so what does it matter?"

"He knows what he's created. Maybe it's like those art thieves who steal famous paintings they can never sell or show off to anybody. They still get to revel in what they did."

Jeff asked, "What'll happen tomorrow?"

She closed her eyes and ran both hands through her hair, which felt oily with sweat. "If he murdered Lori, I think he'll tell everybody how she died, and he'll try to put some of the blame on me."

Eddie knocked on the unlocked studio door and stuck his head inside. He looked her over. "Did you really, like, kill somebody?"

"No. How could you even—"

"Then you're a total goldmine." He entered, grinning at her. "There're a few reporters here and others are on the phone or sending emails. They all want to talk to you."

"I don't want to talk to them."

Harry said, "I'll give them a statement." He aimed for a reassuring tone, but even with her chromesthesia short-circuiting again, she could tell he was excited by the prospect.

He stood, tucked in his shirt, and patted his thinning hair. Without so much as a nod to her, he preceded Eddie like an actor striding toward center stage to deliver his big soliloquy.

The door closed behind them. Jeff said, "Shit, each new day sucks worse than the last one. What're you going to do until tomorrow's fiasco?"

"Lie low at home. Not open the door to anybody."

"I'm sorry about everything that's happening."

"Why?" she asked. "None of it's your fault."

He held his hands out to indicate his mixing console, computer, and screens. "I've got all these ways to control what comes in here and what goes out to the world, but I can't stop him without hurting Oscar. I just feel so goddamn helpless."

"Welcome to the club."

"Yeah, sorry about that, too. You don't need my gripes on top of your grief."

"I know we can't do anything about what he says while we're live, but we can edit out whatever we don't like for our podcast. Or what if we don't post it at all? Claim a technical problem if the kidnapper or anyone else asks about it."

"That's Harry's call; we're both helpless there. If the dude's going to spend the whole show slandering you tomorrow, I wish we could pretend to be live for his benefit, but no one would hear him except us."

"Which will get Oscar killed when the guy checks afterward. In fact, even editing the show could make it worse for Oscar, so scratch that." Everything she'd tried had backfired; any new gambits would get her husband killed. Weary and sluggish, she loaded her satchel.

Jeff checked one of his screens. "We've, um, got to talk about the calendar. Sometime, I mean—not now, of course—but, uh, even after I reschedule some guests, we'll still have to fill in the blank spots at the end of the month. It might even be a good distraction."

Doing something forward-looking could help her pretend there'd soon be an end to this ordeal, imagine some future that would look like their lives before the kidnapping.

Until she got Oscar home, though, nothing else mattered. There was no future.

"I'll need time off to help him recover," she told him. "How about putting the guests from this week and next into those blank spots and back-fill with 'Best of' shows until then?"

"Okay. You're lucky your director takes such good direction."

"Oscar would be much better off if I did, too. Bye." She left the studio before he could reply. No voices in the office, and Harry's door was closed. Apparently, he was still holding court with the media, or they'd left after speaking with him. Rare good news for her either way.

When she reached the garage, she remembered the problem with assumptions. A man and a woman stood beside her Mercedes, puffing on e-cigarettes and chatting, while two other men looked at their phones nearby. Thanks to the On-Air reserved-parking signs and Jeff's addition of her name to the concrete tire bumper, the reporters knew right where to set their ambush.

The male smoker turned her way as the elevator doors closed behind her. In the movies, he would've shouted, "It's Bo," and they would've descended like hyenas. Instead, he calmly dropped the vape pen in his pocket, switched on his cell, and waited for her to approach.

She glanced at the remote in her hand to make sure she didn't pop the trunk lid or unlock the doors by accident. Wondering what shapes and colors she'd see, she thumbed the alarm button.

# Chapter 35

Boiling storm clouds churned in Bo's mind, appropriately dark but blurry. The reporters scrambled away from her car as if it had come alive. She headed toward the electronic shriek, pain from the alarm forcing her eyes into slits. Two of the men jogged in her direction. Their mouths moved but the blaring alarm overwhelmed their voices. The other man and the woman fast-walked up the ramp, no doubt planning to stop her on the way out.

She told herself to look straight ahead and keep moving as the pair of journalists intercepted her, phones raised. This close to the din, she could barely see them through the thunderheads churning in her mind. She adopted the "church face" her mother used when encountering unlikable fellow parishioners: vacuous smile, crinkly eyes. Cupping a hand to one ear while she shook her head, she pushed past them.

The insulation inside the Mercedes cut the noise level in half. She left the alarm on as she reversed out of the space—forcing them to backpedal—and then raced up the ramp and turned toward the exit.

Sure enough, the other two reporters stepped out to block her path. She swerved left and right to make it look like she was losing control.

The woman mouthed something but gave way, backing between two parked cars as she covered her ears.

Her colleague stood his ground, apparently confident he wouldn't get run over. He raised his phone. Bo hit the high beams to spoil his shot. Just in case, she made a show of covering her eyes with one hand while she steered haphazardly with the other.

Through the gaps between her fingers, she watched him sidestep to safety before she passed him. She thumbed the panic button on the fob again to silence the alarm but beeped her horn a couple times in parting. What should've looked like another explosion of browns and greens appeared as washed-out, gunmetal smears.

She was losing everything.

Her phone vibrated with incoming calls. The dashboard console displayed the names of other friends and their cell numbers, but she let them all go to voicemail—what was there to say? That instead of rescuing her husband, she'd only succeeded in getting his hand mutilated? And maybe something even worse was happening to him now, all because of her?

Trapped in a long line of cars trying to merge onto the interstate, she further punished herself by reliving lowlights from the day's show. She figured she deserved it.

The recording played through the car speakers, starting with the kidnapper's taunts before the program opened. When he launched into more adventure-hero stories—one knotted mosaic of lies after another, but now in hazy monochrome—she skipped all the way to the second segment, during which he solicited information about her life.

Traffic continued to lurch forward, allowing her to focus on the playback. As she saw her recorded voice in blurry gray hues, a realization struck her: every minute she had engaged with him was a minute he wasn't hurting Oscar.

"How could you have been so damn selfish?" she groaned.

She saw it so clearly now: if she'd kept Oscar in mind instead of thinking of herself, she would've tried to talk the psycho into a round-the-clock marathon session, to keep him on the air only as long as needed to inflict the emotional pain and torment he wanted her to suffer. Then he would've been through with her and set Oscar free. Instead of enduring just one long, hellish period, she'd continued to resist and fight back—and helped to create a situation that ensured Oscar's torture over many days.

"I'm so sorry," she whispered. She repeated it as a mantra of contrition while, on the recording, the kidnapper tried to give out her address the first time and Jeff muted him, only to bring the man back on the air a half-minute later, sputtering curses.

The rational part of her argued that he probably wouldn't have gone for a marathon dialog, or maybe Harry would've refused, that there was no way to prevent what had happened. Logic didn't lessen her guilt.

"I'm so sorry. I'm so sor—"

The phone rang again, which paused the recording. This time, the console showed "Oscar" and his cell number.

She stared at the display, not realizing she'd drifted into another driver's path until a horn blared at her. More gunmetal smears. With a jerk of the wheel, she returned to her lane and waved an apology.

Talking to the maniac kept Oscar safe, she reminded herself. Unless the monster had called expressly to torture her husband while forcing her to listen.

Dry-mouthed, she clicked to accept the call. She projected her voice toward the built-in car microphone, sounding raspy as she said, "Y-Yes?"

"Hi, this is Nithya Rajan at the AT&T store in Jacksonville, Florida. To whom am I speaking?"

A fresh jolt of adrenaline made her fingers tingle. She wished she could see Nithya's true voice instead of fuzzy grays. "I'm Bo Riccardi. Do you have my husband Oscar's phone?"

"That's correct. A gentleman brought it in. I was able to bypass the security code. The contacts directory has been deleted, and most of the apps are gone. But I could retrieve the call log, and yours is the last number there."

Oscar had never bothered to put a passcode on his phone, so that must've been his abductor's doing, to prevent this very conversation. "I can't thank you enough for this, Ms. Rajan," she said. "Is the gentleman who found the phone still there? I'd like to thank him, too."

"One moment, please."

A youthful-sounding man introduced himself as "Ensign Martin Albom, serving at Jax Naval Air Station." She asked how he'd found the phone, and he said, "It was in the bed of my pickup, ma'am, wedged behind the tool chest. I never would've seen it if I hadn't cleared everything out when I got back home, to help a friend move into a new place."

"Can you tell me where you were on Monday? It'll help me figure out what happened."

"Yes, ma'am. I was visiting my sister and her family in Florence, Alabama. I set out for Jax in the morning and made two stops along the way, same as I always do: once for lunch and gas in Heflin and then a faster fuel-up in Valdosta before reaching home."

His words, and Nithya's, had both revealed blurry spheres, more like dirty snowballs than pearls: what truth now looked like. This wasn't some elaborate performance by accomplices of the kidnapper, designed to deceive her.

Valdosta, Georgia, was way down near the bottom of the state, four hours away from her home. Plus, she'd seen Oscar's cell heading south *toward* that city. The kidnapper must've planted the phone in Heflin, after the ensign had left his truck to get a meal.

She asked the young man about the location of Heflin, Alabama. It turned out the town wasn't far from the Georgia border—probably two hours or less from Roswell.

Finally, a genuine lead.

"Ensign Albom, I really appreciate you going to all this effort. Where is it in Heflin that you always pull off for gas and lunch?"

"The BP State Line, a big truck stop on I-20."

She thanked him again and then spoke with Nithya about how to get the phone back, unable to keep the rising excitement from her voice.

After she disconnected, her mantra changed from an apology to a plea for Oscar: "Hang on, just hang on."

# Chapter 36

During her drive north on Georgia Highway 400, Bo called Gus. The background color of his voice was now nickel instead of French toast. She began with what happened to Oscar's hand, for which he gave her absolution she didn't feel she deserved. He was equally magnanimous in reassuring her as she explained that the accessory allegation was bogus.

She saved news of the Heflin lead for last.

"An auspicious break," he concluded. "I think we can eliminate the other surrounding states and much of Georgia now. And I have good news as well. Harry authorized me to bring in some help: a telecommunications expert plus additional security."

Feeling a little more upbeat, she chided, "I knew those powernaps weren't enough to keep you going."

He paused, and she thought they'd lost the connection, but he was apparently choosing his words with even more care than usual. "The situation here at your house has deteriorated. We need others to provide around-the-clock coverage, while I seek your husband and his abductor."

Her newfound optimism died a quick, brutal death. Kneading the steering wheel, she asked, "What's happening?"

"Some media people have camped along the street, but they're far outnumbered by spectators. The police are moving anyone who blocks the road or encroaches on your property, but there are too many bystanders to manage effectively. You and your daughter should consider staying with friends tonight, or at a hotel." He paused again and then added, "Also, there has been some vandalism."

"Shit! Broken windows?"

"No, but someone used spray paint on your garage door."

"You mean like a gang tag?"

"No, a word."

She signaled for her exit. "Come on, tell me. I'm a big girl."

"The perpetrator wrote KILLER, preceded by a hashtag. When I drove up, people were taking selfies with it in the background. One of the additional security I've hired is at the hardware store getting paint. I sent him a photo so he can try to match the door color."

"Thanks for handling all that," she murmured. With her anger reignited, she conceded that she hadn't sounded as grateful as she should've. "Seriously, I really appreciate everything you're doing. But why would somebody . . . wait, do you think the man holding Oscar did it? He could be living right around the corner and ran over after the show."

"If he were behind this, instead of a random troll, it's more likely he'd pay an individual to pull this prank. The Heflin clue definitely indicates he's closer to that vicinity than yours."

She realized she'd been driving on autopilot, heading home despite his warning. "Hold on for a sec. I need to pull over and focus."

A gas station was nearby. She parked facing the convenience store. "Okay, so either he has an assistant close by, or it was some random person with a mean streak."

"Alternatively, as I said, he paid someone to pull a prank, to apply additional pressure on you. There are websites where you can find people who'll do quite a lot for a mere five dollars."

"What a screwed-up world." She sighed and kneaded the wheel. "Well, I guess that's another dead end. At least we still have the Heflin connection."

"Agreed. I'll send my telecom guy, Randy Cleator, over there with his Stingray. Hopefully, he can catch the IMSI for one of the phones the kidnapper used. Keep in mind, the IMSI can be spoofed along with the phone number, but it's also possible to intercept voice, text, and data, so maybe we'll get lucky."

A young, well-muscled man emerged from the store. He seemed like the kind of guy Candace perked up around, which reminded Bo that her daughter would be heading home before long. She told Gus, "I need to find a place to stay and tell Candace to meet me there. Then I'll have to sneak into my home after dark to get clothes and toiletries. What about you?"

"I'll stay here until the repainting's finished and the security rotation is set. Then I need to go back through the old tips, and look at the new ones Eddie keeps sending, to see who lives in western Georgia and eastern Alabama. Tell me when you plan to head back to your house so I can alert the person on duty."

"Yeah, that'd be ironic, to get shot by the people hired to protect me." She thanked him more profusely this time before she hung up.

After reviewing lodging options, she booked a room with two beds in a hotel along Holcomb Bridge Road, Roswell's main drag, with restaurants in walking distance. Before heading there, she texted the details to Candace, who fired back another checkmark.

WITHOUT ANY LUGGAGE, "SETTLING IN" to their new digs consisted of kicking off her low heels and dropping the suit jacket over a chair. She sent Candace the room number and started a list of the items they'd need to retrieve from home. Quantities were the big question. Would the craziness die down after tomorrow's show? No way. He'd truthfully said two more days. Besides, her confession of cowardice would only make the firestorm blaze hotter. She had to survive the maniac degrading her through Thursday before he'd be done and let Oscar go.

She eyed her phone with the sounds of torture stored there and poor Oscar's screams and wondered how long he'd need to be in a hospital. She'd want to stay with him 24/7, which meant lots more changes of clothes.

And once the full story of his kidnapping and release leaked out, the media and gawkers would camp near their house in even larger numbers. So, would there be even one day in the next month when they could all be at home, undisturbed? The nightmare could go on and on.

With the list drafted, she noted seventeen more calls she'd neglected and almost thirty texts from friends in the past few hours alone. She responded to them all with a brief note, promising to explain as soon as things calmed down. What she really wanted to tell them was that she wasn't just trying to save her marriage—she was trying to save her man.

Eddie had forwarded thirty-seven more tips to her email along with his analysis of which way the social media winds were blowing. Apparently, the Tuesday program had divided the listenership into Team Bo, Team Bourne, and Team WTF. Team Bo had her back, but they were frustrated about why she'd let some guy hijack her program and accuse her of being involved in a murder. Team Bourne smelled blood in the water and wanted to see The Barracuda get mauled. The last group couldn't figure out whether the drama was serious or scripted. According to Eddie, Team Bo was in the minority and #KILLER was trending, with people starting to photoshop controversial celebrities and politicians posing in front of her garage door. Freaking hell.

She opened the tip emails Eddie had provided and swiped through them. When she reached the last message, she finally saw a name she recognized. The tipster identified himself as "Adam Johnson" and provided a Gmail address. Though she had no idea who Adam was, she knew the man he'd informed on: Tom Brogan.

Lori's sometime-lover had never liked Bo, and the feeling was mutual. He'd used Lori when it suited him, ignored her when he could con someone else into bed, and threw jealous tantrums when she went out with other guys. Susanna had spent the night of Lori's murder with Deacon at his place, clearing that creep, but she'd never heard a decent alibi for Tom.

The clues she'd extracted during the past two days didn't help her confirm he was the kidnapper, because she couldn't recall his background. Googling him gave her current details, including his address in Gadsden, Alabama, less than fifty miles from Heflin and only two-plus hours from home. She found nothing useful about his past, but she knew it had to be him.

Did Tom kill Lori but want to frame her? Or did he blame her for Lori's death? She had no idea. Still, two breaks in one afternoon. Maybe someone was watching out for them after all.

# Chapter 37

Deke sat in the Ops Center, gazing at the new images on his Wall of Inspiration. The On-Air buffoons hadn't posted the podcast of the Tuesday show yet—probably still wringing their hands about the content—so he'd used screenshots of Bo from his own recording to update the collage.

She showed none of the fierceness he'd enjoyed seeing on Monday. Instead, she'd begun to hunker down like a whipped dog and look resigned to a prolonged thrashing. Long periods of closed eyes and a grim set to her mouth: the same as he remembered on his twin's face as Billy braced himself for another night of payback beatings.

He missed the fire in her eyes, the snarl as she retaliated, but this was an unavoidable tradeoff. She'd finally accepted her powerlessness. Only by giving in totally could she save her husband. That message seemed to have sunk in at last.

The photos offered him motivation and comfort as he redressed a small setback in the social media sphere. People who'd become his ardent fans on Monday hated the shift in focus from commando-style adventures to Bo's dull backstory. Since returning from his fieldtrip and updating his Wall, he'd renamed his most popular accounts "The Real Bourne" across numerous platforms and changed his profile image to an action closeup of Matt Damon. Then he revealed to his followers that he was the one crossing swords with Bo—and promised Judgment Day for her:

The Real Bourne @realBourne
Tuesday's show was vital for the op I'm running against Bo. Tune in Wednesday, On-Air Web Radio, 1pm US EST for the climax! #BourneVsBo

The Real Bourne @realBourne
Watch The Barracuda's confession on Wednesday, On-Air
Web Radio, 1pm US EST, and tell your friends! #BourneVsBo

The Real Bourne @realBourne
Bo Riccardi: accessory to murder. She'll admit it & more
on Wednesday, On-Air Web Radio, 1pm US EST. Share &
don't miss it! #BourneVsBo

Convinced the On-Air bozos would claim "technical
difficulties" with their podcast, he posted his recording of the
Tuesday program on YouTube and blasted out the link along
with more promises of a juicy payoff. After a prolonged blitz,
the tide began to turn again in his favor. In fact, lots of people
dropped the "accessory" part and simply started calling Bo a
murderer.

Perfect.

With those flames growing into a firestorm, he retweeted
and shared the #KILLER selfies people were posting. He linked
them with a map pinpointing Bo's address and included her
cell number.

The 21st century lynch mob took the weapons he handed
them and rioted. Within another hour, even some mainstream
media outlets carried stories with headlines like "Web Radio
Star Accused of Murder" and "Virginia Police: New Look at
Cold Case."

Shaping public opinion was playing God, creating interest
where none had existed before and nurturing it into fanatical
attention and devotion. It was addictive—when this ended, he
knew he'd miss the high.

He refreshed a search engine every few minutes to see what
other media had filed stories about Bo. It was a pleasant way
to fill the time as he went about the tedious work of launching
and sustaining denial of service attacks against her personal
website. If any companies still wanted to offer her endorsement

deals, they'd find her closed for business. Also, fans trying to view those pages would get the impression she'd pulled up her drawbridge and gone into hiding.

Her website quickly succumbed, and he scratched that task off his checklist.

Bo's actual home was under siege. Her husband remained a hostage whose freedom depended on her complete submission. And her career lay in shambles. Check, check, and check. In one day, he'd whisked her to the pinnacle of her popularity and then kicked her off that pedestal. What was next on the list?

She probably still had the love and support of her daughter. Another lifeline that needed to be cut.

Thank God for two of the most remarkable phenomena in modern society: the amount of free time people had, during which their obsessions and fetishes could fester and mutate, and the limitless creativity of those who used the dark web to satisfy every hunger.

One enclave of enthusiasts had sold him the software and codes to access various portals in the Darknet and commune with its purveyors. Weeks ago, he'd provided those merchants with the best photos and videos he'd recorded of Candace and Bo during his many months of surveillance. The high-resolution images could be manipulated in a multitude of ways: the girl's virginal face grafted onto a much more experienced body, her voice made to say the most provocative things. A mother-daughter threesome. Orgies, toys, animals—endless possibilities.

Nothing motivated skillful people as fiercely as money combined with mania. The results had been extraordinary. He'd saved them for just this moment.

Spoofing Bo's identity across a variety of accounts he'd created had been easy—anyone could do it. He now used those to send Candace's online friends the best examples. Show them variations they surely hadn't ever considered. "With <3 from Candace's Mom." That done, he gifted the whole collection to

Darknet devotees and encouraged them to share the photos and videos far and wide. And to tag Candace and Bo—as a courtesy, of course.

"It's only fair," he murmured. "Ruin my life, I'll ruin yours."

His hands itched inside his new gloves, as if eager to do more to her.

To distract himself, he considered other checklist items. Time to change Oscar again and add a new layer to the mind fuck.

First, though, he needed On-Air to get back in the game. They had access to a much bigger audience than he did.

The previous week, he had phoned the station one evening to see if anyone would pick up. Sure enough, the On-Air president had routed after-hours calls to his cell. The curse of the entrepreneur who was terrified of missing an opportunity.

Time for another call.

He initiated the voice synthesizer, spoofed Oscar's caller ID and number, and dialed. As the phone rang, he gazed at the images of Bo with her spirit crushed in his grist mill.

"This is Harry Pinzer," the man barked. "Are you the one holding Oscar?"

"I am. Have you heard his pitiful screams?"

"No . . . but I know about your sadism."

His hands continued to itch. He splayed his leather-covered fingers like brown starfish and admired the precise, tiny stitching. "If you don't want to be responsible for more of that, you'll post the podcast of today's show. Unedited and complete."

"Hey, you might have power over one of my employees, but you've got nothing on me. What if I just pull the plug on the show?"

"Then Oscar will die. Horribly. And I'll tell the world it's your fault. As proof, I'll include the recording I'm making of this conversation. You know the stakes—you have no excuses."

The man hesitated, then asked, "How much longer is this shit going to go on?"

"As long as I want. Now post the fucking podcast. If I don't see it on your site in ten minutes, I'll call back with Oscar and my power drill. Maybe you won't answer, but you'll still be responsible for what happens to him. And that'll go on the recording, too."

In the ensuing silence, he indulged an idea he'd toyed with since Monday's interview. "You know, after this week, you'll no longer have a hit show with Bo, and I hear Sean's program is imploding as well. Whereas my star continues to rise. I could help you fill those gaps."

Another pause. Then Pinzer said, "I'm listening."

# CHAPTER 38

Oscar tried so hard not to move his pulverized right hand that the muscles throughout his arm spasmed. This caused his hand to twitch against the metal bedframe and send out fresh bolts of agony, making him scream.

Tears had long since soaked his blindfold. A cold, steady trickle of them drizzled into his ears, forcing him to loll his head to the right and then left to drain them. The saltwater trapped in the cloth irritated his eyes.

His body shuddered as he cried, which jarred his hand further and produced more torment. The perpetual cycle of anguish made him feel like he was going insane.

To distract himself from the pain, he tried to remember the few other times in his life when he'd cried. Guys in his half-Italian, half-black neighborhood in South Philly learned early not to show fear, pain, or weakness. Still, there was the day he wiped out on his bike when he was ten, trying to jump a row of metal trashcans using ramps he and his buddies built from scrap plywood and cinderblocks—he'd ended up with a broken nose, chipped teeth, and seventeen stitches in his scalp. He'd wept like a sonofabitch.

The only other instance he could recall was while holding newborn Candace, who'd cried much less than he had. Everything about Candy had been so small and delicate and perfect. And Bo, despite being a sweaty, exhausted mess, somehow managed to look radiant, victorious, as if she'd just set a world record or won a war. Those had been tears of joy that day. Lots of them.

Now, though, he suffered endlessly. Father Solanki back at St. Joseph's would've counseled that this was but a small taste of the Hell that awaited him if he didn't go to confession and relearn the rosary. Well, fuck those priests and every vicious goddamn nun. This wasn't a minor ache he could pray away. It felt like Jesus-on-the-Holy-Cross kind of torture.

Before this afternoon, he'd sort of looked forward to the kidnapper's periodic visits. Something to break up the monotony, the lack of sensory stimulation. And the kidnapper always arrived with a long drink to fill his empty stomach. Since the bastard had been *forced to make an example* of him, though—apparently because Bo wouldn't say whatever bullshit thing she was supposed to—he was terrified of hearing the lock snap open and feeling the vacuum-seal pop in his ears.

He'd become more aware than ever of his vulnerable state. His left hand stayed balled in a fist, to shelter those as-yet unbroken fingers. He could feel air from the overhead vent on his bare feet, as if to remind him of his unprotected toes, the thinness of the skin stretched across so many fragile bones. And, of course, one tug of the sweatpants would expose him utterly. Crushing, burning, shocking, cutting—so many sick tortures came to mind.

Only Bo could save him, but he couldn't signal her about where he was because he didn't have a clue. She must have police looking. They had no money for PIs, but at least she'd called the cops, right?

His heart thudded like in his marathoner days. Absentmindedly, he tried to close his swollen, heavy right hand.

Molten pain tore him apart all over again. He shrieked, head thrown back, cracked lips stretched wide. Fresh tears flowed into the saturated blindfold.

The deadbolt thudded back, and the door opened. Not wanting to show weakness, Oscar tried to clamp his jaws shut, but a moan forced its way through.

"It's been hours," the man said. "I can't believe you're still screaming like a little girl."

"F-f-fuck you."

"Mm-mm-mm. Such language. You kiss your daughter with that mouth?"

Oscar heard what sounded like the usual bin dropping to the carpet near the cot. Instead of the supplies he'd come to expect—wipes, talc, a fresh diaper, Ensure—he pictured a basket full of rusty tools. Maybe the bastard wanted to try a few amputations, just for fun. And send Bo the videos.

Constrained by the bindings on his wrists and ankles, he shied away as far as possible. A mewling whine came from high in his throat, even as he told himself to man up.

"Hey, dude, relax. I'm not going to hurt you again. Today anyway. Whatever happens tomorrow is up to your wife. She's still not cooperating." He sighed. "I don't get it; she knows what I'll have to do if she's stubborn. It's like she doesn't even care what happens to you."

He gripped the waistband of the sweatpants and slid them down to Oscar's knees, latex-covered knuckles grazing his thighs. The motion was gentle, as if his abductor was taking care not to jar the injured hand.

"I hadn't considered it before," the guy said, "but do you think she's a sadist? Is she getting off on your pain?" He chuckled as he removed the adult diaper and started the usual wiping process. Cool, rubbery fingers manipulated Oscar's genitals only long enough to clean him. "It's none of my business, of course, but I've gotta ask: is she into that dominatrix stuff? Leather, whips, and chains? I can see it: Miss Prim and Proper in public and then Mistress of Torture in the bedroom."

A dusting of talc, a fresh diaper, and then the sweatpants eased back up around Oscar's hips. The man said, "Awfully quiet there, pal. Silence can be an answer, too, you know. It's personal—I get it. Your secret's safe with me, though."

Gritting his teeth against the pain, Oscar tried a Hail Mary pass: "I lied about not having money. We're loaded. By now, Bo has all kinds of people looking for me. Cops, PIs, the feds. Big rewards to the public. Better let me go while you can."

After a long moment of silence, the kidnapper said, "Well, I'm not supposed to tell you about our arrangement, but you're right—your wife does have a stash of money. She's paying me to do all this to you."

"What?"

"Yeah, she wants me to kill you, after she's milked the publicity for all it's worth."

"No way—prove it." The idea was so crazy, he forgot about his hand for a moment.

"It's not like she put anything in writing—she's a smart lady—but I do have souvenir photos of us. My idea, kind of an upfront payment to prove her sincerity and seal the deal."

Oscar felt the right side of his mask lift. He clamped his eye shut until a smooth, rounded edge of plastic tapped his cheek.

"Come on," the guy said. "You won't see my face—in this room or in the picture either."

The light from the phone and an overhead glare made his eye blur with fresh tears. It took a while to focus. Leather fingertips held the screen close. All around its sides, he saw only a gray background that gave no clues about his surroundings. When he forced himself to look at the picture, his chest tightened and heart began to thud. He snarled, "Fuck."

"Actually, that came next, and so did I. She's a talented bitch, that's for sure. Hidden cameras in the room; I've got her from all angles. Want to see more?"

Oscar groaned again. Wanting to forget the image conjured it in even greater detail.

The man pulled the mask back into place. His tone changed to reassurance. "I know it sucks—pardon the pun—finding out this way. Not just cheating on you but also wanting you dead. But hey, her plans could change. Or maybe I'll refuse her final payment and just let you go. I'm starting to like you." He laughed. "It's not like she can sue me."

In a moment, his voice sounded very close to Oscar's ear. "If I do set you free, though, I don't recommend trying to reconcile with her. Truthfully, your wife scares me. She's a nasty piece of work." Without another word, he exited, and the door closed behind him.

Oscar started to cry again. Had he imagined the conversation? Was he delirious?

Could Bo hate him so much that she'd set up the whole thing to boost her precious ratings and score more money for endorsements? He never would've believed it, but that disgusting picture of her. . . . Pictures could be faked, but that one had looked so real.

If he died, she'd probably slant the truth to make herself look like the victim. People would feel even sorrier for her. Throw more money her way. Give her a book and movie deal. A year from now, with Candace away at college, Bo could have a TV show and spend all her free time fucking Hollywood stars. And the only one who'd understand the hypocrisy, know the extent of the joke she played on everybody, would be the guy who had killed him—acting on her orders.

Bullshit . . . or not? It was getting so he couldn't tell the truth from the lies anymore.

# Chapter 39

Bo called Gus about the tip, asking him to redirect his telecom expert, Randy, to Tom Brogan's address in Gadsden. With luck, Randy would find the proof they needed to bring in the cops, the FBI, and the National Guard if necessary. In a matter of hours, Oscar could be freed and Tom imprisoned.

The phone showed countless new texts, mostly from strangers now, with attachments. Tom probably had plastered her cell number across the Internet.

Finally, though, she had some good news for Candace—whenever she finally decided to come to the hotel. Her after-school activities had ended hours ago.

Per the tracker app, Candace had passed by the hotel several times but kept going. For long periods, she paused in shopping center parking lots and then drove on, seemingly without a destination, always looping past the hotel again. She wouldn't answer any calls or texts.

Time to give chase. Candace would be pissed off that she'd been mom-stalked, but the aimless driving was freaking Bo out.

Another call made the cell rattle on the tabletop. The blurred mental image of an undulating, platinum-colored coil accompanied Candace's name and photo on the screen. She never called anymore, only texted.

Tom had spoofed Oscar's ID and number—why not hers, too? If he had kidnapped their daughter and was reaching out to gloat, Bo knew she'd lose what little sanity she had left.

"Hey," she answered, trying to sound casual but braced for the synthesized voice. When she heard no reply, she blurted the first thing that popped into her mind: "Why do you keep driving past here?"

"How could you do this to me?" Candace's voice sounded shrill and tearful, edging toward hysteria. Despite the gray tones and fractured shapes, Bo saw unmistakable spiky hate. Candace had never spoken to her with hatred before. Was Tom there? Had he done something to make her lash out?

Over her daughter's hiccupping sobs, Bo said, "I don't understand. What did I do?"

"The pictures, the videos." Each syllable sounded forced, as if her shoulders shook and chest heaved with the effort. "I mean, they're so dirty and gross."

"What are you seeing? I need details."

"Oh God, I can't—they're too awful. And they're, like, everywhere," she screeched. "Everywhere!"

As possibilities flooded Bo's mind, she took a breath to make sure she didn't start shouting as well. "Watch my voice. I don't know what you're talking about. You can see that's true, right? Tell me the shapes and colors."

"Moss-green pyramid," Candace replied, voice hollow. "With, like, lemon zigzags. You're afraid." Fresh tears, but at least the hate had vanished. "What's happening, Mom?"

No way would she be able to talk like this if Tom were with her. However, Bo had no doubt he was responsible for whatever her daughter had seen. She replied, "I think it's the man holding your father. He did this."

"But they're all from you. How could you be so stupid and let him hack you?"

She flinched at the insult but tried to stay focused. "I haven't sent you anything but texts asking why you keep driving by. Which sites are the messages from?"

Candace rattled off a few, and Bo relaxed a little. "He's pranking you. I don't use those."

"All my friends are getting them and sending them to me with angry emojis," she said between sobs. "I mean, dudes I don't know keep sending me disgusting stuff and putting things online, tagging me. Guys from my classes are sharing them and making sick comments. I had to shut down all my accounts."

"Come to the hotel. We'll figure out how to stop it. Maybe Gus can help us."

"Oh, hell no. He can't see that . . . that porno with my face on it."

With this detail, it wasn't hard to imagine what Tom had released online. She would've given anything to erase those repulsive things from her daughter's memory.

"Okay, no Gus," she said. "Just come here. We'll figure out what to do together."

"I can't. I don't want anybody like, looking at me right now. Especially you."

"Honey, you didn't do anything wrong. I know you're—"

"No, you don't get it, Mom." Her voice had grown hoarse, a precursor to more tears. "You're in a lot of them, too. With me. And sometimes other girls and guys. *Doing things.*"

She heard the revulsion, the horror, but the shapes and colors had become murkier in her mind as despair began to suffocate her own spirit. "I'm sorry he's forced those awful things on you. Lie low at the hotel. You can wait until next week to go back to school."

"God, I can't show my face there ever again." Her crying resumed. "I just want to die."

"Please, no. There's nothing so bad it can't be fixed. Or we can start over somewhere else." In desperation, she promised every crazy thing that came to mind. "We'll get new names. Move to another country. Whatever you want."

Over Candace's wailing, she said, "Look, just meet me somewhere. The diner in front of the hotel—you always liked that place. We'll sit and talk it through and make a plan."

No reply except louder crying. What should've looked like swirling yellow grief had become an indistinct muddle. "Candace?"

Then nothing. No sound, nor image. Her daughter had ended the call.

Attempts to dial her went to voicemail. When Bo checked the tracker app, she sighed with relief: Candace was outside the hotel.

She ran down two flights, the echoes in the stairwell barely registering in her mind, slate bursts on a charcoal backdrop. The hatchback wasn't in the parking lot, but the tracker showed the phone at the same location where Bo now stood. Looking around, she glimpsed a glassy pink reflection: a cellphone left under a blooming azalea.

Surely Tom hadn't snatched her in that brief timespan—it was much more likely that Candace had wanted to prevent anybody from finding her.

Heart pounding, Bo snatched up the phone and hurried back to the hotel room.

First, she tried calling the mothers of Candace's longtime friends, but—if they talked to her at all—they acted frosty. Several of them blasted her for the pictures they said she'd sent their own daughters. Worse, no one would promise to tell her if they heard from Candace later.

Her next call was to 911. She told the operator about the "want to die" comment and provided details about the hatchback for the police. The dispatcher promised to broadcast the description and tried to reassure her. Maybe he was sincere, but she could no longer tell for sure.

Slumped on the bed, giving in to fear and anxiety, she dialed the one person who she knew could help. As she told Gus about Candace, it took all her willpower not to bawl as her daughter had.

He said, "You did the right thing to report it. Hopefully the police will recognize the car."

"Is there any way to get rid of the filth people are spreading about her . . . and about me?"

"All you can do is report the harassment to each web-administrator, but it'll take time for them to respond." He paused, and then asked, "Have you googled your name lately?"

"What now?"

"An increasing number of outlets are carrying stories about the Lori Lambo murder and speculating about your involvement."

She wanted to kick a wall but managed to lie still. "That can't be helped. Where's Randy?"

"I'm tracking his phone; he'll arrive in Gadsden soon."

"If he can get a match on any of the numbers Tom used, what'll happen?"

"We'll turn the information over to the local FBI field office—they have a resident agency there. They'll want to make their own confirmation of the evidence. A task force with state and local police might get involved, because this is an interstate kidnapping. Search warrants could be sought if the special agents don't have enough for an immediate arrest."

It was all too much. She sat up and said, "He could be hurting Oscar again right now. Why can't Randy just kick down Tom's door and rescue my husband?"

"We're not vigilantes. Please, let the professionals do their jobs." He seemed frustrated with her, but she couldn't read the blurred, oyster-gray shapes well enough to be certain.

She hung up without another word and headed for the door.

# Chapter 40

Driving to all the places Candace had lingered earlier yielded nothing. After two hours of trying to find her, Bo's eyes burned from peering at cars through headlight glare, and her neck ached from leaning out the window at stoplights to search other lanes of traffic for the hatchback.

She reassured herself that Candace would come to her soon, after taking some time to calm down. Way back when she was a teenager, those end-of-the-world emotional jags always smoothed out in a few hours.

Back in the hotel room, she gathered what remained of her wits, composed a message, and posted it on each of her social media accounts: "Faked photos/videos of my family were sent from sham accounts. Please ignore them. Sharing bogus items makes the problem worse for everybody."

She tried to post the same to her website, but some problem with the server prevented her from logging on. "Just my luck," she groused.

At least her parents weren't apt to read or hear about her yet. They'd grown weary of the news and had no interest in the online world. With the way things were going, though, one of their golfing buddies would probably tell them all about her as they sauntered around the course.

She considered what to do next. Drive to Gadsden, Alabama, and kick down Tom Brogan's door, like she wanted Randy to do? But armed with what, a heavy satchel? She'd get killed along with Oscar. And then Candace would have to break the news to her grandparents that her mother's stupidity had orphaned her.

*Shit.*

Bo's stomach rumbled with hunger, and she needed a drink. Several of them. Maybe a badass wife would've laid siege to

Tom's house, or a better mother would've held an all-night vigil at the window for her distraught daughter. But she felt lightheaded from not having eaten in more than twelve hours. The need to refuel—and a craving for some eighty-proof stress-relief—pushed her to her feet.

She considered visiting a liquor store for a bottle of Grey Goose, and to stock up on snacks. Two straight nights of drinking on an empty stomach would've meant she wasn't coping too damn well. But the thought of pouring $30 vodka into a cheap plastic cup at the little hotel table while fishing inside a bag of Chex Mix nearly brought her to tears again.

There was the nearby diner she'd suggested to Candace. Maybe her daughter was waiting there or would soon appear. It seemed like the best alternative.

In case Candace came to the hotel instead, Bo placed her daughter's phone atop a note, telling where to find her. Blue suit jacket back on, satchel looped over one shoulder, she hurried to the diner at the other end of the parking lot.

She twice searched the interior dining areas and the patio but couldn't find Candace. Finally, she asked to be seated near the small bar, where she'd have a good view of the entrance.

A waitress approached and took her drink order. In less than ten minutes, she was downing an extra-dirty martini with lots of Spanish olives. She barely tasted it.

When the server came by again, she handed her the empty glass and ordered another and the Mediterranean salad. While waiting for the refill, her thoughts continued to loop while her feelings roiled. *Where's Candace? Is she getting past this? How's Oscar? Can I ever make things right for them . . . and for me?*

*And who were all these people sending me messages?*

She removed the cell from her purse as the waitress approached with the second martini. Even more texts from strangers had come in. Some were interview requests, but most had one-line comments with attachments. In the latest one, some guy had written, "Lemme know if you want a 4th for bridge." Below the inscrutable message was a thumbnail photo she couldn't make out. She tapped it and gasped.

Before the server reached her, she slapped the phone onto her lap and leaned forward to shield it, in case the screen had landed face up. The server must've seen naked skin anyway, because she gave Bo a hard look and plunked the glass down. At the hostess stand, she began talking to two other employees. They glared at Bo as well. *Great.*

To counteract the hot flood of shame, she held aside the spear of olives and took a chilly gulp of vodka, vermouth, and brine. And then another. Using her teeth to draw an olive off the long toothpick, she chewed and peeked down. The cell had gone to sleep. She put it away.

Despite no more than a glimpse, the pornographic threesome had become indelible: her face and Candace's superimposed on other women. "Doing things," as her daughter had said.

No wonder Candace had panicked. They'd both received scores of photos—videos, too.

While Oscar's abduction and torture still ranked as the worst thing Tom Brogan had done to them, targeting her daughter ran a close second. If Tom strolled into the diner, she'd kill the bastard without hesitation.

Before she knew it, the martini glass sat empty with a barren toothpick discarded inside. The waitress approached again, this time with a large salad bowl. Looking past Bo's right shoulder, she asked, "Would you like something different to drink with your meal?" Battleship gray gobs of contempt oozed down with her words. Alcohol normally enhanced the colors and shapes, but even that was being denied her.

"No, make it the same." Her speech sounded a little muddled. She focused on enunciation. "Also, a glass of water. Please."

The server nodded, still without eye contact, and headed for the bar.

She dug into the salad, enjoying the tang of the oily dressing and pungent feta cheese. Somehow, she lost herself in the flavors—when she glanced up, another martini and a glass of ice water sat near the center of the table. She started in on the fresh drink. Her second? No, third. Some of it dripped off her chin and into the salad, but the brine was probably an awesome dressing anyway. Why did they make martini glasses so prone to spilling? So top-heavy?

As she slurped down half the contents to make the architecture more stable—*to reduce its potential energy*, her old mechanical engineering professor might've said—she peered over the wide rim at a boy in his late teens who approached her table with two male friends in tow. Wholesome, clean-cut.

"Hey," the lead dude said, his smile wide and bright, "aren't you Candace's mom?" He wore a Roswell High School Hornets t-shirt, identical to one Candace owned. Something about his voice looked funny, an intent that went beyond the innocent question, but Bo couldn't make out the unfocused, slate-colored shape.

She tried to rise but had a hard time getting out of the chair—must've been the high coefficient of friction between its feet and the terrazzo floor. Forced to set down her glass and lever herself upright with both hands, she asked, "Have you seen her tonight?"

The high schooler looked back at his buddies. They all laughed, though her question wasn't funny. Maybe she hadn't made her tone serious enough? She asked again, much louder, and the leader of the group said, "Whoa, settle down. We don't know where she is. We're just hoping to get a selfie with you."

Again, there was something more in his voice that she tried to grasp, but the novelty of this new reality distracted her. Would she now spend her time fending off reporters and posing with the public? Fame had come at a terrible price, but it wasn't these guys' fault.

Smoothing her pantsuit, she felt an oily smear of salad dressing on one lapel. "Hold on, I need a cocktail napkin or something to clean myself off."

They laughed even harder. The leader told her, "Not sure one will do the job. Though 'cock' and 'tail' are perfect for a MILF and her girl."

She blinked hard as she processed his insult. Heat flooded her cheeks.

He held his phone out to her while they all hooted. The screen displayed another porn photo with Candace's face and hers added.

Indignation turned to fury. Her daughter's schoolmates weren't the best targets, but they were the only ones within reach. She backhanded the cell out of the teen's grip and sent it flying toward the bar. The device smashed through wineglasses that hung upside down and rocketed into shelves of liquor. Bottles fell and shattered on the floor as crystal rained across the bar top.

Everybody in the restaurant, including the boys and the approaching manager, gaped at the destruction.

The back of Bo's right hand throbbed, but Oscar had endured far worse pain for hours. That thought enraged her further. Reversing direction, she slapped the young man as hard as she could. He stumbled back against his dumbstruck comrades.

His jaw blazed with her handprint. "Fucking bitch," he roared.

She'd knocked him out of arm's reach. However, kicking was still an option. She drew back her left foot and slung it forward, leg extended. Wobbly balance affected her aim. She'd targeted his groin with the pointy toe of her shoe, but she nailed his kneecap instead.

He howled and fell across an empty table, scattering flatware and condiments. His wingmen hesitated and then made a reluctant move toward her.

The manager reached them, arms out like a traffic cop. "Enough," he yelled.

Her head felt like it might explode like one of the liquor bottles. She'd bruised the big toe of her left foot, and her right hand hurt all over. If the manager hadn't stepped in, though, she knew she would've gone at the other two with teeth and nails.

Numerous patrons aimed their phones at the melee. If anybody recognized her, the "Barracuda attack" memes would go on forever.

One more wineglass toppled from the overhead rack. It burst into a hundred pieces, sounding louder in the quiet room than everything that had gone on before.

# CHAPTER 41

Fortunately, Bo hadn't maxed out all her credit cards yet. The restaurant manager charged her and the boys $500 apiece, to avoid police involvement. Not surprising for upper-income Roswell, the teenagers all had debit cards and plenty in their accounts. They avoided eye contact with her when the manager forced them to apologize, and exited before she did.

As she hobbled toward the door, left foot throbbing, a few patrons and staff applauded. Word had spread after the bartender found the leader's cellphone among the glass shards and spilled liquor, with the pornographic image still visible. She couldn't tell whether the handclaps were sarcastic because they thought she was a drunken slut trying to defend her soiled honor, or were meant to bolster a wronged woman who'd lashed out in righteous anger at three punks.

Her head buzzed and exhaustion weighed her down now that the adrenaline had worn off. Not only couldn't she interpret their applause, but the colors and shapes of everybody's comments had grown increasingly dark and hazy. She blamed it on all the stress.

Following Lori Lambo's murder, the same thing had happened to her, but the color-hearing had returned shortly thereafter. Assuming she survived the night without her brain imploding from shame, rage, and fear for Candace and Oscar's safety, she expected the grays to become technicolor again, the images once more artful and distinct.

She eyed the dimly lit parking lot that separated the diner from the hotel and thought of the boys she'd humiliated. Even in her befuddled state, she recognized the dangers of an ambush among the many vehicles there.

To get to her flashlight app, she switched on the phone and entered her passcode. Instead of seeing the usual columns of icons, though, she was confronted again by the pornographic photo she'd stupidly opened. Her mostly liquid meal surged up her gullet. Unable to choke it back down, she leaned forward and vomited as far from her shoes as possible.

The stench of stomach acid and brine made her gag again. She spewed out everything leftover from the initial purge. After spitting a few times to clear gunk from her mouth, she used tissues to wipe her lips and chin. She considered returning inside to apologize once more, but the manager would probably charge her card again to pay for the cleanup. The departing diners and staff would just need to watch where they stepped.

She deleted the porn shot and switched on the flashlight. Panning the bright cone before her in a semicircle, she limped to the hotel without incident. Still, the residual alcohol continued to jangle her nerves and feed her fear. She detoured past the elevator—where she supposed the teens could trap her before the doors closed—and took the stairs instead.

Metallic echoes reverberated throughout the stairwell with each footstep, the noises appearing as dark lumps now instead of flowery bursts. The faster she went, the more the sounds amplified, as if a whole gang gave chase. Despite her sore toe, she raced to her room in a panic.

With every lock in place, she leaned against the door to catch her breath. Her phone buzzed with another incoming text, this time from Gus: "Randy confirmed match on cell number pinging at Tom's. Preparing details for Gadsden FBI."

*Thank you, Jesus.* Now they knew where Oscar was being held. But he'd end up enduring more torture while law enforcement created task forces and held meetings and got their shit together.

In about two and a half hours, she could be on Tom's doorstep. "Wait," she murmured, "haven't you gone through that scenario already? Yeah, you and Oscar would be killed, leaving Candace orphaned, stupid."

She knew she needed to sober up before she could put her thinking cap back on.

Slumping on the edge of the bed, she took inventory of her physical woes. Her left foot ached and bruises had begun to appear on her knuckles and the back of her right hand from smacking the jerk's cellphone out of his grip. In the light of the bedside lamp, the purpled patches of skin looked like stigmata, as if she'd begun to exhibit signs of Oscar's wounds. Poetic justice, seeing as how her defiance had gotten his fingers broken and his hand smashed.

If Tom does all that to his left hand next, she wondered, should she bang up hers in sympathy? Probably. How else could she show the world—and herself—she was trying her damnedest to free him, that she cared about his safe return more than anything else?

Well, except for finding Candace. Even Oscar would agree that their daughter's safety was paramount.

She connected the phone to an outlet for charging, dropped her stained suit jacket over a chair, and staggered into the bathroom. Without a toothbrush, all she could do was rinse her mouth and try to ignore the lingering aftertaste of bile. She followed this with a cold, wet washcloth pressed to her face. Chilly water against her cheeks and forehead eased the feverish sensation she'd started to feel.

What to do? At a minimum, she needed to return home and gather clothes, shoes, cosmetics, and toiletries for Candace and herself. Then what? Wait for law enforcement to find and deliver her daughter to the hotel? Go back out on the streets to continue the search—and probably get nailed with a DUI by the same cops who should've been looking for Candace?

Whatever she chose to do, her reward for surviving this night would be to lay herself bare on Wednesday by telling a story she'd never even shared in full with the Blacksburg police, let alone an audience of possibly millions.

Following that, what more could Tom want? Surely he planned to let Oscar go after he pilloried her on tomorrow's program. And Candace wouldn't last long without her creature comforts—unlike those boys, she didn't have a big bank account at her disposal.

"This time tomorrow," she told herself in the mirror, "you could have everybody back. All you need to do is get through one more day."

She soaked the washcloth again and pressed it against her tired eyes. After she recovered her family, she wondered whether any of them would ever be truly whole again. Her stigmata would heal, as would Oscar's hand, eventually, and Candace's humiliation would abate in time, but the mental damage they'd all suffered might never subside.

Fatigue and restlessness warred inside. She blamed the odd combination on too much vodka coupled with the strain of everything that had happened. Maybe both feelings would ease once the liquor had exited in full. Still, she wished she had some of the anti-anxiety medication a doctor had prescribed to her after Lori's murder.

Unable to sit still, she grabbed her phone and satchel and descended in the elevator. In the lobby, she had to pass the check-in desk on her way out. The young man there gave Bo a once-over, his disapproval poorly veiled. She imaged how skanky she looked and smelled to him. A slovenly, middle-aged woman, redolent of vomit and body odor at 11:00 p.m., going out for another round. She was too tired to care.

Before her cautious drive home, she'd texted Gus that she was on the way, so security wouldn't shoot her. Remembering his warning about the circus on her street and the chance that an enterprising journalist might still be on stakeout, she entered the neighborhood one block north and parked along the curb. Because of curves in the road, size differences in the lot layouts, and residual alcohol fogging her brain, she couldn't determine which house backed up to hers. She chose one without a fence and watched for dogs while she crept along the side and rear yard.

Despite her cellphone flashlight, she still stumbled through underbrush and sideswiped a pine tree. Emerging at last onto another property, she saw the vague outline of a house she didn't recognize. However, two lots to the right was the white fence that bordered her backyard.

Her ascent over the pickets tore her blouse, but at least she'd reached home. She scuffed across the patchy lawn and weathered deck. Inside, she turned off the alarm, removed her dirty shoes, and made her way through the first floor and up the stairs in darkness.

She decided to first pack for Candace, whose bedroom was in the back of the house. Still, Bo closed the door to stop light from leaking out. Feeling confident, she flipped the wall switch.

Open dresser drawers tipped downward. The closet door was shoved aside.

Someone had ransacked her daughter's room.

# CHAPTER 42

Bo backed against the door, face throbbing with each heartbeat. The kidnapper must've tortured Oscar for the alarm code. Maybe he or an accomplice really was lying in wait this time.

Before panic completely paralyzed her, more details about Candace's room sunk in. Most of the dresser drawers had been yanked out, but not all of them. Only one of the mirrored closet doors had been pushed back along its track. Her desk remained orderly—laptop, printer, stacks of file folders with schoolwork—and the drawers there were untouched. Either the intruder knew exactly where to look to get what he wanted . . . or Candace had come here after leaving the tracker-tagged phone behind.

It must've been the latter.

The closet carpet showed indentations where her suitcases usually sat. As the one who did everybody's laundry, Bo knew her daughter's wardrobe well. She'd taken a selection of clothes as well as shoes. The drawers she'd left open still held some underwear, t-shirts, and the like. A good sign—at least she hadn't taken everything.

"And if you hadn't indulged in drinks and dinner and mayhem," Bo scolded herself, "you could've been here when she arrived."

Instead, Candace had left this tableau for her to find: Close, Mom, but no cigar.

Bo called Gus and acted as if she hadn't disconnected rudely earlier. "Hey there, what's the latest with Tom and the FBI?"

In his usual polite, friendly tone, he said, "A contact I made in the Gadsden resident agency has my notes and will verify the kidnapper's phone number using their own equipment."

"And then will they hold meetings about convening a task force while Oscar is being tortured to death?"

"Bo, please—" Her color-hearing normally would've made his plea look like brown tadpoles. Instead, she saw black squiggles on a slate background.

"Sorry. It's just so frustrating being only a few hours away but not able to do anything." Ashamed for behaving badly toward him again, she slumped on Candace's bed and stared up at the textured ceiling, cradling her bruised hand.

Small squares of clear tape secured dozens of glow-in-the-dark stars, which looked pale green with the light on. She remembered applying them with Oscar on their daughter's first day of kindergarten, to surprise her that night. Walking atop her mattress, arms overhead, they'd tried to invent constellations, laughing as they kept lurching into each other. For weeks afterward, Candace would connect the stars in various ways to form different animals and wanted them to see each permutation as she did, her little index finger tracing lines in space as she pointed them out. The memories transported Bo. Tears slipped along her temples and into her hair.

In a gentle voice, Gus asked, "Have you received any news about Candace?"

She cleared her throat. "No, nothing. I'm in her room now, but she beat me here. She must have come in through the back like I did, then filled some suitcases, reset the alarm, and left for who-knows-where." Wiping her eyes, she asked, "Is there anybody still on the street out front?"

"A few minutes ago, my sentry reported all but one car has departed—that driver is down the block but maintains a good view of your home. Also, people continue to coast by periodically."

"Great. My bedroom's in the front of the house. Should I pack in the dark?"

"I recommend limiting yourself to a flashlight and avoid shining it toward the front wall of your bedroom. Blinds aren't exactly blackout curtains."

"Okay, good advice." She sighed and forced herself to sit up. "Where are you now?"

"At home in Decatur. I've whittled the tips down to a handful of possibilities in western Georgia and eastern Alabama."

"But we know it's Tom Brogan."

"We don't, in fact. The Adam Johnson who gave us Tom's name hasn't replied to my follow-up inquiry yet; perhaps he's perpetrating a ruse. We should be prepared for that."

"Fine, whatever." She caught her annoyed tone, as if she were afraid he could jinx things by being thorough. "Sorry. I really am grateful—I'm just a little stressed."

"Certainly, don't punish yourself. When should I meet you at your office?"

"I won't get much if any sleep, so I'll be there by 8:00."

"In the interim, I'll let you know if I learn anything new."

She thanked him, ended the call, and struggled to her feet. Weariness had replaced her intoxication.

Before she left the room, she killed the light and peered up at the ceiling. Not a single star shined. It wasn't an omen, she assured herself. They'd been up there a dozen years; no way could they keep glowing, right?

She switched on the flashlight app and went down the hall to the master bedroom, careful to point the beam down. In the gloom, she could make out the dresser. Her jewelry box on top was open, no doubt another of Candace's messages for her. The master bath window overlooked the backyard, so she carried the jewelry box in, shut the door, and turned on the lights above the mirror.

Candace had only taken the quality pieces, items she could hock when she ran out of money; it was further proof that they'd raised a smart girl.

A glint of white gold caught Bo's eye. She lifted out a cheap, unadorned cross on a chain. Mom had worn it for decades, only gifting it to her after arthritis made it too difficult to work the clasp.

The pendant had little monetary worth, but it did carry sentimental value. Because she refused to burden her parents until this disaster ended, it felt good to have this piece of Mom's faith, an essential part of her.

She studied its reflection in the mirror. Maybe it could serve as a sort of religious ambassador, to parlay with the Divine on her unworthy behalf. An act of desperation, giving herself over to magical thinking again, but things were getting worse and worse. At this point, any talisman would do.

With no pockets in her dress slacks—and afraid she'd lose it within the Bermuda Triangle of her satchel—she fastened it around her neck and peered at herself. The only thing that looked okay was Mom's cross. Her face had aged a decade, with deeper creases, more crow's feet, and darker shadows under her eyes than she remembered. Combined with her unkempt hair and torn yellow blouse, she could've passed for an abduction victim. "Maybe you are," she muttered.

Recalling Oscar's screams snapped her out of that pity party.

Time to pack and go. In their walk-in closet, she closed the door and switched on the overhead light.

Oscar's suits and dress clothes hung on one side, unworn in the last few months except for the rare job interview. Bo pushed her face into one of his favorite pinstriped shirts to smell his scent. Instead, she only got a whiff of dry-cleaning chemicals.

She changed into jeans and sneakers and pulled on a Georgia Tech Yellow Jackets jersey. Three work outfits, low-heeled shoes, and a few extra blouses went into the open suitcase at her feet. After a quick trip by flashlight to her dresser, she added an armload of underwear.

With luck, the FBI would rescue Oscar overnight, so these outfits would see her through a few days at an Alabama hospital while he underwent whatever procedures he needed. She'd sit at his bedside, Candace would appear, and they'd have a tearful reunion. Then all she had to do was get everybody through their PTSD, including herself.

When she zipped up the suitcase with a zinging purr, terror seized her.

This time, it wasn't the sudden presence of something awful—instead, the dreadful fear came because of the absence of something she'd come to expect since she was four.

No shapes, no colors accompanied the zipper whirring around the edge of the suitcase. Feeling dizzy, she scrabbled for the pull and reversed its path along the nylon seam. Only sound, nothing more. In her mind, endless black.

Her voice couldn't spark the chromesthesia, so she snapped her fingers beside her ears. Only fleshy pops, no tangerine firecrackers in her head. Not even muted colors or hazy shapes.

She closed her eyes and tried again and again, but she saw nothing.

Her ally, her trusted gift, her only defense had deserted her.

# CHAPTER 43

Frantically, Bo grasped for a logical explanation. She couldn't see her own voice except on a recording, so maybe the color-hearing had just stopped responding to things she did as well as said. To prompt a synesthetic reaction, she took out her phone and played more of that day's interview. No colors or shapes for Tom's voice or hers. Would it at least still work with sounds she wasn't involved in?

To answer this, she needed to escape the echo chamber of the closet and seek out background noises downstairs. Navigating through darkness, she stumbled into the kitchen. The refrigerator compressor hummed, and even the icemaker cooperated by dropping a few more wedges into the plastic box in the freezer. She heard the clatter but saw nothing.

No sounds produced pictures anymore. She'd counted on rebounding quickly, just like after Lori's murder, when the blurred, monochromatic shapes soon snapped back into colorful focus. But the strange wiring responsible for creating her chromesthesia had not only short-circuited this time, it had melted down.

"I'm fucked," she whispered in the black.

A few years ago, she'd read the memoir of a synesthete whose gifts had vanished during a bout of severe depression. They'd returned, but only after a long absence, when his mood began to lift. Well, it wasn't as if she could pretend or trick herself into a stress-free frame of mind. Her family's lives, her whole world, had turned to shit.

Grandma had always insisted their shared talent was a Heaven-sent gift, and now it had abandoned her. Only minutes after putting on Mom's cross, she'd lost the ability she treasured most, the thing that made her so good at what she did, the skill that defined her. Instead of providing comfort, Mom's necklace had brought calamity.

The irony was almost funny. A cosmic joke at her expense.

She tried to remove the cheap jewelry from her neck, but her fingers shook too much to undo the clasp. Just as Mom couldn't work it any longer, now her hands betrayed her as well.

Frustrated, Bo grasped the cross. The white-gold tips jabbed her palm as she yanked down to break the chain. She only succeeded in gouging the back of her neck.

The stinging pain pushed her over the edge.

She screamed. Kicked cabinets. Thrashed blindly around the counter until she found the skillet Oscar had left on the drainboard. She slung it toward the breakfast nook, where it bounced off some chairs. The loud noises only mocked her inability to see them anymore, leaving her even more enraged.

Easy to blame God, but deep down, she knew Tom Brogan was responsible. And she finally understood what he wanted: to create an endless nightmare for her. To squeeze her heart bloodless, to twist her mind beyond repair. He'd stolen everyone and everything. She'd lost them forever.

She rubbed her neck where the chain had dug in, wincing. Who knew such tiny links of metal could be so strong. Probably even sturdy enough to hang herself. Maybe she'd lost control over her life, but at least she could choose her death.

The notion gave her a moment of comfort—and then made her tremble. Though she'd abandoned Lori instead of taking a stand, even at her lowest point after her friend's murder she had never contemplated suicide.

But desperation, the desire for escape, overwhelmed her now. The drinking binges must've been a red flag, a temporary oblivion she wanted to make permanent. She obviously craved an everlasting end to the crushing stresses that had piled on her.

The same impulse that so long ago compelled her to desert Lori—her deepest character flaw—made her consider forsaking Candace and Oscar. Condemning them to whatever fate awaited. They were on their own.

Disgusted by her thoughts, her useless, fucking cowardice, she sank to the tile floor in the dark. Knees drawn up, she hugged them and cried harder than ever before, sounding more like an animal than a person. The noises were raw, wild. She wailed for her daughter, her husband, and her poor, pathetic self.

DESPITE THE BOTTOMLESS WELL OF GRIEF, her eyes eventually ran dry. Her throat hurt from shouting her sorrows, and her body ached from its spasmodic heaving against the cold, hard floor. Misery continued unabated, but she no longer had the ability to express it. That had been stolen from her, too.

She couldn't face the stumbling slog back to her car in the dark, weighed down by suitcases. In a daze, she retreated upstairs, locked her bedroom door, and fell onto the mattress.

Sleep should've hit her like a hammer—she couldn't remember ever feeling more worn out. But she smelled Oscar's lemon and basil scent on his pillow, felt the cold, flat spot where he should've been. She pictured Candace stopping someplace far away. Instead of spending money on a room, their daughter would no doubt save her limited funds, curl up in her car, and maybe lie awake as well, afraid of the night sounds beyond the fogged windows.

A faint glow behind Bo's eyelids made her think her chromesthesia had returned, like it was rebooting or something. Then she opened her eyes and noticed the lit screen on the bedside table. An incoming call.

Her phone rattled against the wood as well, but she'd missed that. She was so used to seeing a sound and interpreting it visually, she had forgotten how to listen with her ears alone.

The screen showed Candace's name and number. Second call of the night—even more terrible news? Or was it indeed Tom Brogan this time, spoofing the ID?

Braced for his sadism, she croaked, "Where are you?"

"Where are *you?*" Candace replied. "You sound super-awful, and I see like, even more fear than before."

Relief competed with a fresh panic attack—thundering heart, hyperventilating—as she re-lived her daughter's disappearance. The worst thing was not being able to see the seafoam background she'd associated with her daughter since the girl's first cries and coos at birth. Bo swallowed and tried to collect herself. "Home. Packing."

"I was so ahead of you on that. Spotted some lurkers out front and snuck in the back."

Though she couldn't picture Candace's voice, it seemed like her daughter sounded more like her old self—the tough-girl shell not entirely back in place but getting there. Thankfully, Candace had inherited her dad's moxie instead of Bo's own weakness.

Bo said, "You're at the hotel? Staying put?"

"Yeah, no, totally. So after I packed, I sort of drove up and down 400 but I mean, I didn't want to go anywhere. No way am I going to hang out at school while everybody looks at that crap on their phones and laughs at me. But I get it that Dad's going through a lot worse." Sniffles and some throat-clearing. "I don't want to make it, you know, even harder for you."

She rubbed her swollen eyes. If she had any tears left, they would've soaked her cheeks. "I'm really proud of you, hon. You're handling things a lot better than I am. I'll be there soon." She swallowed a few times so she wouldn't sound froggy when she told her the most important thing: "I love you."

"You, too, Mom. Thanks for not shitting Frisbees. You're the best."

More like the worst. Worst mother for not protecting her daughter, worst wife for failing her husband, worst interviewer for losing the one thing that set her apart.

However, she wouldn't burden Candace by asking for reassurance. If their daughter could be badass, she would follow her lead and learn to be tough, too. She thanked her, and they hung up.

No longer needing to talk herself into action, she phoned the Roswell police and told them to call off the search, and then texted Gus with the good news. She gathered toiletries in a smaller overnight bag, collected the suitcase, and set the house alarm before crossing the back yard under a cloud-choked moon.

With both hands full, she couldn't use the flashlight app. The trip back to the car required fence-climbing, stumbles through wooded lots, and a painful collision with a giant trampoline. None of that mattered, though.

Her daughter had come back.

# CHAPTER 44

The alarm on Bo's phone startled her awake and then saddened her. No shapes or colors. Her mind stayed as dark as the hotel room.

Even her memories of the images she should've seen were hazy. Her private language of pictures now seemed like the remnants of a dream. She began to wonder whether the ability had existed or only been imaginary. Maybe she was even more delusional than Oscar's kidnapper.

Candace groaned from the other bed. Bo turned off the alarm and told her to go back to sleep. During their reunion six hours earlier, she'd recounted her diner brawl, and they agreed Candace should stay put rather than take any chances at home or school.

No doubt the harassment from bullies and trolls would continue for a long time. Bo needed to call the principal to make arrangements for the rest of her daughter's final semester. Not only was senior prom likely out of the question, she probably wouldn't want to risk walking with her class on graduation day.

At least Candace still had Grandma's synesthetic ability. Several times before they'd gone to sleep, Bo asked what the background color of her voice looked like. Spaghetti sauce, she'd assured Bo, just as it had appeared to her since she was small. Her dad's voice had always resembled creamy peanut butter, which annoyed Oscar no end, because he was the one with Italian roots.

Telling Candace that she was the only one left in the family with the gift would panic her. She probably never thought losing it was a possibility. While Bo couldn't keep that a secret forever, her day would be filled with enough painful revelations without addressing this one, too.

She took her phone and, feeling twice her actual age, shuffled into the bathroom to see if she'd received anything important overnight or just more filth and interview requests. Perched on the toilet, she deleted a ton of new messages from creeps and journalists and saved words of concern and support from friends who would have to be patient awhile longer.

Jeff had sent her the iconic "Hang on, baby" dangling kitten, except he'd replaced its mouth with the toothy snarl of her nickname. She smiled a little, despite her exhaustion and bleak mood.

A long, hot shower inched up her spirits even more, as did the single-cup coffeemaker she brought into the bathroom, where she could use it without waking Candace again.

Last night, in her relief over having her daughter back, she'd forgotten to remove the chain with Mom's cross before sleeping, and now again prior to bathing. She decided to leave the pendant in place, ashamed now about blaming an icon for the loss of her abilities. It weighed almost nothing, and wearing a favorite of her mother's did provide a little comfort.

Her oyster-pink blouse covered it completely. She finished dressing in an olive blazer with a matching knee-length skirt—what she thought of as her lucky outfit. It was the ensemble she had worn when she'd caught the NPR producer's attention so many years ago on the MARTA train. The clothes were too tight now, but she needed any edge she could get.

While she did her makeup, she guzzled a cup of coffee and rehearsed the story she would be forced to tell on-air, assuming the FBI didn't swarm Tom's house and end this ordeal before 1:00 p.m. She needed to pay attention to each word she chose, to avoid incriminating herself, though Tom would cry foul the instant she started to shade the truth about what she'd done on the night of Lori's murder. A cruel irony: she'd lost her ability to detect lies, but he would be able to call her out with ease.

That notion made her bruised hand quiver, so she put away the eyeliner and the rest of her makeup before she did any damage. Deciding 6:32 a.m. was late enough to bug her sworn protector, she called Gus and sat on the toilet lid while listening to the ringtone.

*It used to look like teal spinning tops—hadn't it?*

Their absence felt like a hole in her soul. It made her think of those fantasy stories where someone steals the magic from the special world and everything becomes mundane.

"Bo?" He sounded alert and concerned, but his voice lacked the soothing French toast background she'd associated with him. The colors and shapes used to provide such richness and depth and connected her with the speaker more intensely than a mere voice ever could.

Not wanting to burden him with her latest setback, she forced some cheer into her reply. "Hey, good morning. Any update from the feds?"

"Indeed. The resident agency is talking to a judge this morning about a search warrant. Overnight, they confirmed the same cell signal Randy found. While that's not enough to break down the door and apprehend Tom Brogan, they do think they'll get the warrant and search his place today. Randy will remain on stakeout there, watching the watchers."

She sighed with relief and thanked him. "That's not just good news, it's great. I'm surprised the task force didn't bog everything down."

In a patient tone, he said, "The system can be slow at times, but not because the people involved aren't reasonable, conscientious professionals. Most often, it works. And occasionally faster than you might think."

"Have faith, little grasshopper," she intoned. "Sorry I've been freaking out on you. I appreciate all you're doing, even if I don't always show it."

"I can't imagine your emotional burden. I'm happy to play a small role in relieving some of your load."

"Stop it, you're playing a huge role. I couldn't do this without you. But um, what if I drove to the Gadsden FBI office and remote-in for the interview? Jeff could post a notice that the webcam is down. Assuming, of course, the feds haven't executed the warrant by 1:00."

"That would be noon, Central Time."

She looked at the clock on her phone. "Okay, but even with the usual traffic, I could arrive around 8:00 a.m. their time if I left now. I need to be there when they rescue Oscar. He should see somebody he loves, not just strangers. I want to be with him in the ambulance and stay in his hospital room."

Gus paused so long she thought the call had dropped. He finally said, "I don't want your expectations to get too high. The only reason we've rerouted Randy to Gadsden is because of a tip that named someone you recognized. Perhaps it's a setup by the kidnapper, to add more stressors on you."

She rubbed the back of her neck where the chain had dug in last night. "But we know the phone he used is there."

"Possibly he planted it. This would be a way to expose and punish you for involving law enforcement, to get your hopes up and then dash them. Maybe that would satisfy him for the moment. He'd threatened to murder Oscar if you brought in the cops, but then he'd lose his leverage. You wouldn't speak to him again, and he doesn't want that."

"Right, he hasn't flayed every bit of skin from my body yet." She hung her head. "You really think this whole thing with Tom is a setup?"

"Perhaps not. Most crimes are solved because of tips, and this could be one more. We should have faith and hope—and be ready with a new plan if this one doesn't succeed."

"Faith and hope . . . and love. My parents and the people at their church called it the trinity."

"Indeed."

Love was the reason she was enduring, striving, pursuing every possibility. But for Gus?

She said, "You're going way above and beyond for us. More than any professional would do for just another client. Can I ask—"

"My motivation? That's easy. I lost my wife of forty years to brain cancer a while ago. I did everything I could to comfort her but curing her was beyond my knowledge and capabilities. Now I observe you doing everything you can to rescue Oscar from his tormentor. In this case, I do have some expertise I can lend. Yes, I want to ensure justice is done, the perpetrator punished, but mostly I want to see Candace reunited with her father, and you with your husband."

"I'm sorry about your wife—she must've been a very special person."

"Thank you. She was extraordinary in every respect."

"I wish I'd known her." She took a breath and tried not to feel like a hypocrite as she gave voice to a notion her parents were far more comfortable with. Pressing a finger to her blouse, she traced the shape of Mom's cross. "Okay, faith and hope and love. We have faith we'll bring Oscar home. We hope this tip will be the key. And love is what guides and sustains us, come what may."

# CHAPTER 45

Candace was still asleep in the hotel room when Bo left and drove to work. Despite professing faith, hope, and love as her new mantra, she still felt unsettled by Gus' warning. If Tom wasn't the kidnapper, and was just another of his victims, that brought them back to square one, with no idea where Oscar was or who held him. It had to be Tom. It just had to be.

In the office building garage, Jeff's pickup occupied the parking spot he'd designated for her. Not that she deserved a permanent space, she reminded herself, but she wanted at least one detail in her life to stay normal.

It didn't add up that he'd pull this passive-aggressive move after he'd made the funny kitten image for her only hours earlier. She stopped nearby and checked out Jeff's truck. His tires rested against the concrete parking bumper. The front of the vehicle hid the area where he'd painted "BO RICCARDI: THE BARRACUDA." But she could see the outer edges of the concrete. They now showed random swirls of white, as if hastily spray-painted.

Mindful of her too-tight outfit and the toes of her pumps, she lowered into a pushup position and descended enough to see beneath the chassis. Vandals had sprayed the concrete bumper white and, overtop, painted #KILLER in black, just as they had on her garage door.

Tom was keeping her off-balance every way he could. It made sense that he'd paid somebody to hit her here as well as at home—she should've seen it coming. Dusting grit off her hands, she hoped the overnight security people had been paying attention to their screens.

As she headed to the elevator—hearing cars brake, tires squeal, and alarms engage, all without the palette of colors and jumble of shapes that had accompanied such sounds for decades—she reflected on the positive side of this latest incident. Clearly, Jeff had parked there to prevent anybody, including her, from seeing the libelous hashtag. She'd wanted at least one detail to stay normal, and there it was: Jeff remained a true-blue friend.

On the first floor of the building, she took two wrong turns before she finally found the security office. A pale, tired-looking woman in a rumpled khaki uniform slouched in her seat in front of a huge bank of monitors. She glanced over. "Yes?"

"I want to report some vandalism in the parking garage."

"To your car?"

"Actually, it's to my spot."

"We don't have designated spaces for people, only the tenants they work for." The guard clamped her lips around a straw protruding from a giant cup and sucked up cola.

Bo didn't need her color-hearing to recognize belligerence. However, she'd failed to notice any warning signals about the guard's negative attitude, something the chromesthesia would've flagged instantly.

She felt like a new amputee, still trying to rely on a limb that no longer existed.

Trying to diffuse the woman's combativeness, she chuckled and replied, "Yes, of course, sorry. But a coworker had put my name on the concrete bumper, and—"

"And *that's* vandalism." The guard pulled a pad toward her and snatched a pen from her breast pocket. "What's the name of this coworker?"

"No, he's not the problem. What I'm reporting is that someone spray-painted over that, last night or earlier this morning—"

"On my shift. You're saying I'm not doing my job?"

"I didn't say that. The point is, whoever did it should be identified."

"So, somebody vandalized the vandalism." She clicked her pen. "Let's begin with the coworker who started the trouble."

"I'm telling you, that's not—"

"I'm telling you it is." Her voice became even harder. "What suite do you work in, ma'am?"

Bo backed toward the door. "Hey, just forget it."

"Fine by me."

Fuming, Bo left the office and retraced her steps to the atrium, wondering how she would deal with Tom if she couldn't manage such a simple conversation.

At the elevator bank, a set of doors opened. A suntanned, gray-haired woman in a starched version of the same security uniform stepped out. She gave Bo a professional once-over and a nod as they passed. The woman carried herself in the authoritative way of veteran police officers she'd interviewed. She had wary cop's eyes that seemed to take in everything.

It was 7:58—probably almost quitting time for the graveyard shift. She decided to loiter in a nearby restroom to wait out the handoff to the morning crew and then try again with a simplified story.

Ten minutes later, she returned to the security office and found the older guard now seated at the monitors and jotting on a clipboard. To get a read on her mood, Bo said, "Good morning. Is this where I report a case of vandalism?"

"Yes. How can I help you?" Attentive posture, pleasant tone of voice.

"Somebody spray-painted a defamatory message on one of the On-Air Web Radio parking spaces. It's probably directed at me because I usually park there." She described the hashtag and its location while she watched for reactions. A mild headache began to throb behind her eyes from concentrating on every detail of the guard's face and hands and body language.

"I can imagine how upsetting that must be," the woman said. She stopped making notes on the pad of paper and scrutinized Bo in return.

Worried that she looked to the guard like a deranged #KILLER instead of a distraught victim, she forced herself to blink a few times and relax. "Um, are there any CCTV cameras—"

She broke off when she saw the woman was way ahead of her. The guard had rotated around to consult what looked like a floorplan on another desk. After a moment, she swiveled back and tapped one of the screens on the left. "This one. I'll review the video. What timeframe are we talking about?"

"I left before 3:00 yesterday afternoon, so it happened sometime between then and whenever my coworker parked his pickup there this morning. He usually gets in by 7:00."

"Okay, please give me your name and cell number. I'll call you later this morning."

Bo recited the details, thanked her, and headed up to the On-Air suite. The contrasting conversations reminded her to keep things very simple when she called Candace's school to discuss how her daughter could make up missed homework and tests and graduate on time. The KISS principle would be especially important while relearning how to use her ears alone.

If only she could get away with an abridged story about Lori during the show. Tom, though, would want her to reveal everything in excruciating detail. Unless the FBI got him first.

Before she allowed herself a cup of Jeff's coffee, she washed down some ibuprofen in her cube and dialed the high school.

Her call was forwarded to the principal's secretary, who informed Bo the earliest she could get a meeting would be the beginning of the next week, and Candace's college advisory counselor and other administrators would join them. Despite the woman's butter-wouldn't-melt-in-her-mouth Southern lilt, Bo thought she detected a hostile edge.

She replied, "I'll be there on Monday at 10:30. Is there . . . something else you want to tell me?"

"Honey, I've listened to your podcast every night for years—I *was* a great big fan—so I'll understand if Candace's father has to take your place at the Monday meeting."

The *was* in her statement increased the pressure behind Bo's eyes. "Uh, why do you think I won't be there?"

"Sounds like you might be in jail."

# Chapter 46

M oments after the high school secretary hung up, Jeff stopped by Bo's cube. Faded Space Invaders t-shirt, torn jeans, and boat shoes today, with a Yoda mug in hand. "How are you?" he asked, studying her face.

She wobbled her hand side to side and dropped the phone into her satchel.

"Something new? Or same shit, different day?"

"Newish shit, but it's all related, including the graffiti you tried to hide in the garage. Thanks for that."

He saluted her with Yoda. "Come on, belly up to the bar. I'll buy you a drink."

No leaf-green background when he spoke, no flame tips of passion. However misguided and inappropriate his feelings were, she missed the certainty they'd provided. Not being able to see his voice didn't change what he wanted or the fact that she couldn't give it to him. But there'd been a comfort in *knowing* instead of merely deducing. She'd taken it for granted, but now she had to read between the lines and rely on instinct—and be just as fallible and prone to bias as everybody else.

And in truth, she'd come to count on his unwavering devotion. He had always affirmed her and boosted her confidence on days when Oscar had neglected her or acted spiteful and angry. Jeff appreciated her even when she felt unloved and unlovable.

The tension it caused had even helped creatively, making them challenge each other about interview subjects and approaches. They'd tapped into that undercurrent time and again to power their mutual desire to put together the best program possible. And, more often than not, he had practiced restraint in his behavior. This impressed her, because she'd been able to see the magnitude of what he kept in check.

From the back edge of her desk, she hefted a ceramic Helen, Georgia, Oktoberfest stein he'd bought for her birthday the previous year, on which he'd written in Germanic calligraphy "Die Mutter of All Coffee Cups." Though she normally used it for decoration, today she needed every drop it could hold.

While he brewed a fresh pot to accommodate its volume, she explained the appearance of the same cruel hashtag on her garage door. She didn't bring him totally up to date, purposely failing to mention the faked porn making the rounds. Had she done so, he would've acted outraged on Candace's and her behalf, but she knew prurient curiosity would eventually get the better of him. He was too interested in her already; no point in adding fuel to that.

"So," he said, "are you and Cassie—"

"Candace."

"That's what I meant. Are you guys in hiding now? Or is Gus on your roof with a sniper rifle?"

"We're staying at a hotel. Gus will be here later, hopefully with good news about Oscar's rescue." She poured nearly five cups of coffee into the stein, finding comfort in the fruit-and-nut aroma, and gave him a brief account of the tip, Randy's discovery of Tom's cell signal, and the FBI warrant.

He said, "So, this could all be over before today's show?"

She rapped the countertop. "Knock on wood and fingers crossed. We might finally use that 'Best of Barracuda' you put together earlier." Taking a drink amounted to doing a five-pound wrist curl—the only workout she'd had lately, not counting her brawl.

Jeff looked at his comparatively tiny mug and flexed his arm to make his bicep swell while he drank, as if it weighed a ton. He thumb-wiped his mustache and said, "Too bad I have to stay here to queue it up. I want to be the one who drives you to Alabama to get Oscar, instead of Gus doing the honors."

"Nobody needs to chauffeur me anywhere."

"Hey, I'm just saying I'd like to help. Seems like Gus is getting all the glory lately."

His comments were pressing all the wrong buttons. Anger and frustration, on a constant boil since Monday, welled up again.

Before she could stop herself, she slammed the stein on the counter. "I don't need any man's help. Men are the reason I'm having the single worst week of my entire life. And a man's responsible for what used to hold that record." She stood close enough to smell his strong, woodsy aftershave as she thrust her index finger an inch from his nose. "Men have terrorized my whole family, humiliated me and my daughter, assaulted us and our reputations, and generally ruined our lives. Don't think for one second that I need a guy. For this or anything else."

Jeff stood still throughout her tirade. When she'd run out of steam, he crossed his eyes behind his gold frames to focus on her accusatory finger. It made him look ridiculous.

She stepped back, shaking her head. "Idiot," she said.

He grinned as if she'd bestowed a compliment. "That graffiti upset you more than I thought it would. You know you're innocent, so what's really going on?"

She gulped coffee while she tried to get her feelings under control. Speaking into the depths of the stein, where her voice echoed back, she said, "I lost my color-hearing."

"No shit. That chrome, uh, superpower thing you mentioned during the show? The way you detect lies and stuff?"

She nodded, still looking into the deep well. "It's gone. During the show yesterday, it started to get wonky, but last night it vanished completely."

"So, there's nothing when you hear my voice? Except you getting pissed off, I mean."

"That's right. But you don't always irritate me."

In unison, they said, "Just most of the time."

She topped off her ceramic flagon. "Without that ability, I don't know whether I can do my job anymore. Of course, after this week from hell, I might not have a job to do."

"If we don't hustle to Panzer's office for another meeting, neither of us will have jobs."

He exited. Before she could follow, the phone rang inside her satchel. Thinking Gus might have an update, or Candace needed soothing again, she looked at the screen. It showed the security guard's number.

After Bo answered, the woman said, "This is Officer Williams. I might have something for you."

"You can see who did it?"

"Each camera sweeps across a large area. In the footage I found, it only caught a few seconds of the perp at 1:13 a.m. He looks tall, on the thin side. Only his back's visible, but I'd like you to have a look in case you know him."

"Can you see anything more about him? Is he white? Black? Brown?"

"Hard to say—the camera records in monochrome, and he's wearing long sleeves and pants. Also, he has dark hair covering his neck and blocking the sides of his face."

Bo made a fist with her free hand. "Is there a muscle car parked nearby?"

"Hold on. I'll see what the camera picked up around him."

Jeff scuffed back to the breakroom. "Panzer just fired you for tardiness. Kidding, but he's doing the Sit 'n Spin thing with his coffee mug, so he might be thinking about it."

She held up the finger she'd thrust under his nose earlier and was about to reply when Officer Williams said, "Looks like a Dodge Challenger."

That detail sealed it.

The question was whether the sonofabitch had acted on his own or somehow in concert with the kidnapper. "I'll be able to come down in an hour or so to look at the recording, just to be sure," she said, "but can you please check your gate log in the meantime? See if he used his On-Air keycard. The name is Sean O'Shea."

# Chapter 47

When Bo and Jeff entered the On-Air president's office, he slapped down his mug, stopping its spin. Eddie sat at his left again, swiping his phone screen. This morning, pastry crumbs littered the front of his French *Citizen Kane* t-shirt and the lap of his skinny jeans.

She and her friend once again took the seats facing Harry's desk, their coffees left behind in the breakroom. Harry said to her, "I see the search party found you."

"Sorry, but I was talking to building security. They have a video of Sean spray-painting the killer hashtag on my usual parking space."

Eddie looked up, but addressed Jeff alone. "I sort of wondered why you parked there. Figured your office-marriage was like, heading toward a divorce." He smirked at his joke.

"Dude, that's so not helpful."

"Quiet, you two," Harry said. "Bo, give me the whole story."

She walked him through the identical incidences of vandalism, first to her house and then to the parking bumper. "Maybe Sean's targeting me this way because he's seen the same hashtag on the news or social media. Or he might be working with the kidnapper. Regardless, I reported his earlier behavior to you, and nothing happened to him. Now there's *literally* concrete proof of further harassment today. What are you going to do about it?"

The ruddiness in Harry's face deepened as they stared at each other, but she didn't care about putting him on the spot. In fact, she decided he needed one more nudge. "Remember," she said, "I have that color-hearing—I'll know whether you tell me the truth." Peripherally, she caught Jeff's frown, but he stayed silent about her own lie.

After another moment, Harry said, "When have I ever been dishonest with you?"

"This would be a bad time to start."

"You're not behaving like someone who needs to keep her job so she can save her husband."

"And you're not behaving like someone who wants to stay out of court—and keep his company."

He blinked first. "Okay, I'll call Sean after this meeting and fire him. Will you take my word for that, or do you want to be here while I do it?"

"Your word's fine, thank you." Having won, she needed to throw him a bone. "Also, thanks for financing more security and Gus's telecom guy."

He shrugged, probably afraid she'd spot the insincerity of a "my pleasure" sort of reply. *Not a bad thing, having him intimidated*, she decided. Too bad she'd only begun to use the chromesthesia threat after she'd lost it.

Jeff drawled, "I love the smell of candor in the morning. Smells like authenticity. Hey, boss man, what's on the agenda for this-here meeting?"

"Eddie, tell us the latest."

"So, by every objective measure, we're totally golden. Site visits, time on the pages, downloads of the Tuesday podcast, social media activity: all way, way up, smashing Monday's records across the board. But advertisers are starting to pull out, probably because of the whole murder thing, and the public's comments and tweets are all over the place."

He spoke to Harry and Jeff, but still hadn't even glanced at her. "There's this one dude calling himself The Real Bourne who started a Bourne versus Bo hashtag that's gotten a lot of play. Folks have lined up on both sides, and there's still Team WTF, but he's got the majority. The guy definitely knows how to keep the pot stirred."

Hoping Eddie still didn't know about the kidnapping, she

chose her words with care. "It's the interviewee. He's trying to . . . he's declared war on me for some reason."

He fidgeted with his phone. "Yeah, no, there are these other, darker memes going, too: that hashtag Sean used and, um, lots of photos and videos of you and this younger chick." Still not looking her way, he stammered, "Anyway, her face looks young. Not to say you're old, but—"

"You just keep digging deeper," Jeff said, though he'd perked up at the mention of photos and videos. His hand darted to the phone in his pocket, but she kicked his shin and he froze.

She said, "There are no photos or videos of me or my daughter Candace. The guy I'm interviewing pasted our faces onto a bunch of porn shots. It's all part of his crazy vendetta." To make sure the topic didn't resurface, she added, "Even this discussion about it is making me uncomfortable. If anyone mentions those images to me again, let alone shows them around, that person will be as guilty of harassment as Sean." Harry and Jeff nodded to her, but Eddie continued to focus on his screen. She raised her voice to him, "Got it?"

"Totally. Uh, are we allowed to talk about the murder, or is that off-limits, too?"

Harry said, "Bo, can we discuss damage control?"

"I didn't murder Lori Lambo, and I wasn't an accessory. I'll make that clear today."

"Unless the FBI can—" he halted when she cut her eyes from him to Eddie. "Ah, Eddie, we've got another . . . personnel issue to discuss. Can you give us some privacy?"

Grumbling, the young man left, pushing his chair ahead of him, and slammed the door.

Harry continued, "Gus tells me the FBI's timing might be in *our* favor."

She clenched her fists at "our favor." The only reason he'd paid for Gus and the rest was because he saw this as an attack on his business. He probably wouldn't have done squat for her if her show didn't get high ratings.

"If they get him before airtime," he said, "I want you to make a live statement at 1:00 about what all this was about. It doesn't have to be long, but I want a full explanation out there, so our audience understands. Jeff can fill the rest of the time with a 'Best of' recording."

She shook her head. "We'll tape it this morning. As soon as Oscar's rescued, I won't be hanging around. I'd already be in Gadsden, but Gus said it might all be a setup."

"Fine," he barked.

She didn't want to contradict him on everything, but until he started collaborating instead of issuing orders, he left her no choice. Though she was already on his bad side, she risked adding, "And if I do have to interview the guy again today, I'd appreciate it if we didn't post the podcast. Having me humiliated for posterity on the web is definitely not in our favor."

In a tight voice, he said, "Let's see how it goes. I know you don't always understand or agree with my decisions, but you're not privy to all the facts. Anything else?"

It was an odd response—but one she probably would've understood if her gift hadn't abandoned her. Was pressure being applied behind the scenes?

Maybe Tom Brogan had something on her boss now. Blackmail? Another kidnap victim? If Harry was trapped into obedience like she was, though, why not admit it?

She said, "No, that's all," and he adjourned the meeting.

"Be there in thirty minutes," she told Jeff and then headed for the security office with a side trip to the restroom. The gallon or so of coffee she'd consumed now demanded release.

To her delight, Kathy was washing up as she entered. She definitely needed a dose of the woman's sunshine, even if she could no longer see the kind she craved.

Kathy looked at her in the mirror, murmured a greeting, and refocused on her hands.

"Another staff meeting from hell," Bo groaned, "but that's been my whole week."

"Mm-hmm."

Bo chased more ibuprofen with a palmful of water. "I wish I could tell you about it—hopefully soon—but I really could use one of your awesome pep talks right now."

Kathy yanked out a few paper towels. "You know, you're not the only one dealing with stuff," she snapped. "Most of my department was just let go. I might be next. Where's my pep talk? Huh?" She shook her head as she tossed the used paper in the trash and left.

Bo blinked hard and replayed the encounter. She hadn't used either her ears or eyes to notice Kathy's obvious distress. Apparently, she only cared about her own wants and needs.

Stress was exposing all her flaws, including some she didn't even know she had.

# CHAPTER 48

On the elevator ride to the first floor, Bo thought of various ways to apologize to Kathy. A simple "sorry" would've sounded lame. Unfortunately, every idea to make up for her selfishness would take more time and effort than she could spare until Oscar was safe.

At least the security guard offered good news. Officer Williams showed her the brief segment of black-and-white video during which Sean hunched over the parking bumper. He'd kept his back to the camera, but his flowing black hair was unmistakable, as was the beloved muscle car he'd shown off to the whole staff last year. He'd been smart enough to pay for parking rather than use his keycard, but she didn't need any more proof about the asshole.

Upon her return to the On-Air suite, she strode to Harry's office and knocked on the doorframe. He didn't look up from two-fingered typing on his laptop. More power games, but she wasn't in the mood. Though she wanted to ask whether he'd fired Sean, doing so would put her in a submissive position by requesting information he controlled.

She marched over, set down the screenshots Officer Williams had provided along with the security office's contact information, and left.

Gus waited in her cubicle as he'd done yesterday, but this time he sat in her chair. He wore a suit of charcoal with pinstripes, a lavender dress shirt, gray tie, and shined black wingtips.

She waved for him to stay seated and squeezed past to perch on the edge of her desk. When she told him about Sean, he hung his head instead of congratulating her.

"Hey," she said, "I expected you to be happy I solved at least one mystery."

"I've been late to everything that's happened to you, your family, and your home. Now I'm playing catch-up on the damage that occurred here." He stared down at his huge, empty hands. "I've been a thief, purloining my fee instead of earning it."

"That's not true. Because you put Randy in the field, we're close to getting Oscar back. Without you, I'd be at this maniac's mercy completely." She slid to her feet. "Come here."

He heaved himself upright. In the small cube, this put them nearly toe-to-toe. She closed the narrow gap, leaned against him, and wrapped her arms around his torso. He was so massive, her hands couldn't meet behind him.

Though he deserved a hug, she needed one even more. The big man didn't disappoint—he enveloped her.

She felt like a young girl again, protected by her father's embrace, except Gus' chest was oddly lumpy against her, as were his sides and back. "Is this your body armor," she asked, "or some kind of religious undergarment?"

He patted her and stepped away. "Kevlar is quite useful in many respects, but it's rather forbidding when it comes to non-hostile contact." The gold grillz flashed with his smile. "Thank you for your faith in me, however misplaced it might be."

"Thanks for seeing this through. What's the latest?"

"According to my FBI contact, it'll be noon or a little earlier. Central Time."

"Meaning we could have a live, on-air arrest." Another scenario occurred to her. "What if it turns into a standoff, with him holding Oscar hostage?"

"They're experts at dealing with such situations."

She checked her phone; it was just after 9:00. "I could still get there before they execute the warrant."

"Remember, this might all be for nothing, a snipe hunt for his amusement. And if you're in Alabama, calling from the road, he'll know he can keep supplying false tips to confound you."

Her outlook began to falter. She touched Mom's cross through her blouse again. Faith, hope, and love. *Hang in there.* "Is there anything we can do while we wait?"

"Your conjecture about Sean working in alliance with the kidnapper intrigues me. Does he live close by?"

"Yeah, that jerk once bragged to Eddie how he could walk home after doing his show if he wanted to—except that he picked up even more women with his muscle car."

"Perhaps I could pay him a visit. He might provide some information about our man."

"Do you think he'll tell you anything?"

Gus put on a scowl, crossed his long, thick arms, and flexed. The wool suit jacket didn't split along its seams, but some threads might've snapped. He held the pose a moment, then beamed at her. "Sometimes that act works wonders. If not, I can always display my guns. Time to see Harry about an address." He walked toward the president's office.

She went to the studio and, through the small window, watched Jeff seated behind his monitors and mixer board. The content on one of the screens engrossed him. When she opened the door, he straightened and looked up, face and neck coloring as before.

Had he found some of the fake photos and videos? He knew they weren't real, and she knew he'd never risk her wrath by discussing them. Best not to go to war over it.

She dropped her satchel on the carpet with a *thunk* and shut and locked the door behind her. The current canned program played at low volume overhead. Distinctive sounds she'd heard and seen over a thousand times. Maybe someday she wouldn't miss the associated colors and shapes, but she wasn't there yet.

Summoning the comfort Gus's hug and Mom's cross provided, she still had to fake some enthusiasm as she asked, "Ready to record my monologue?"

"Absolutely. All prepped and raring to go. Just say the word."

She sat behind the microphone and Popper Stopper, no

headphones needed. The thought made her pat her hair. "Uh, do I need to fix anything first? Lip gloss, blush?"

He peered at his other screen and said, "No, you look fine."

She couldn't tell whether he was fibbing. Before despondency could descend again, she squared her shoulders, took a deep breath, and leveled her gaze at the single eye of the webcam.

"I'm Bo Riccardi, host of The Barracuda. I want to start with an apology. Fans of this program are accustomed to a new interview subject every day, with a thoughtful discussion on a wide variety of topics. No doubt you're wondering what's happened to the show. If you just began to watch or listen this week, I'm sure you're equally puzzled about what's been going on over the last few days. You're probably asking yourself whether this show is always so contentious and autobiographical . . . and—frankly—bizarre."

She found her rhythm and relaxed, knowing what she wanted to say next. "I'm sorry for confusing and confounding you. While nothing unprecedented has taken place this week, the events both on and off the show have been unique in my *personal* experience. And they have been deeply, deeply *personal*: an attack against my family and me at every level, from the physical to the psychological and emotional. My husband, the real Oscar, was abducted on Monday morning by a man who disguised his voice and used the threat of violence to force me to interview him. If I refused or pushed back in any way, he said he'd torture Oscar. He told the truth—and my husband has endured horrific pain because of this man. The kidnapper dictated the rules. I had to live by them, or Oscar would die.

"The kidnapper had planned this for some time. His intention was to destroy my reputation, my peace of mind, and my family. The reason? I still have no idea. In March of 1993, I believe he murdered my friend and roommate Lori Lambo in the house we shared. I was the only other person at home that night. Powerless to stop him, I ran to get help, but he escaped.

"All these years later, he devoted himself to waging a war against me and my family. Today, he lost that war. Soon, I'll bring my husband home to recover. I didn't say *heal* because I don't think he, my daughter, or I will ever entirely do this. Since 1993, I've carried scars from the night Lori was murdered. Now, my whole family must cope with this new trauma. We'll stick together, though, and help each other get through this.

"I wish I could leave you with a profound lesson I've learned from this terrible week. Something about the ephemeral nature of safety and security, or the realization that you will do anything—*anything*—to rescue a loved one. Every insight, though, seems trite. The only advice I have is to express your love and gratitude to your family fully, every day. Fight like hell to protect them. And, if necessary, fight even harder to get them back."

# CHAPTER 49

After her signoff, Bo leaned back in the chair, dry-mouthed. "So?"

Jeff twitched his nose and mustache. "Not a bad rehearsal. Want to do another ten takes?"

She threw her shoe at him. It bounced off the fuzzy gray wall behind his head and fell to the carpet.

"Seriously," he said, "I'm surprised you kept Fuckhead's identity a secret. You really think Gus is right about the guy in Alabama being framed?"

"He just doesn't want me to pin *all* my hopes on Tom Brogan, so I decided to play it safe. I don't need to get sued for slander on top of everything else."

"Plus, by keeping it generic, you can reuse the recording if this ever happens again."

Her other pump also missed, but he still groaned and played dead, slumping over his mixer board. She crept behind his table to retrieve her missiles.

The screen that had captivated him before she came in did not show the spread of pornographic images she'd feared. Instead, he'd been clicking through a list of stories posted in the past day about Virginia police reopening Lori's murder case. The search terms he'd used were succinct: "Bo Riccardi accessory murder."

Each article on display included a police spokesman's quote that featured her name and the two other words in bold, always within a single sentence. Taken together, the stories felt like a series of rapid jabs to her stomach.

Eddie and Harry had mentioned the murder and damage control in the staff meeting, but she had no idea how seriously the police and the press were taking the lunatic's on-air comment and his subsequent work on social media. Served her right for not keeping up with her growing notoriety. The nightmare just kept getting worse.

Still stretched across his console, Jeff said, "I know you're innocent. But if the murder weapon had been a high-heeled shoe—"

"The heel isn't that high. Sit up. You're starting to make me feel guilty." She retreated barefoot around the table to give him room.

He straightened. "I think the term *accessory* is demeaning, like you're nothing more than a handbag. If you're going to be charged, you should demand to be the whole outfit, not just an add-on."

"Thanks for trying to make me laugh. You have no idea how much I want to crawl in a hole and feel sorry for myself." Her breakdown the previous night came rushing back. She sat behind the mic and slipped her shoes back on. "Doing that monologue just now didn't exactly help."

"We'll go with the recording as-is if you want, but you'd fooled me. I figured you were going to end with something about the importance of faith."

"Why's that?"

"You're wearing a cross today."

"Damn, it must've slipped out." She hid the pendant beneath her blouse again. "Do you think we should re-record?"

"Up to you." He adjusted his glasses. "I don't remember you ever wearing it before."

"It was my mother's, but she can't work the clasp anymore. I found it last night and wanted to have something of hers close to me today." She touched it through the fabric as she stood. "My mom and dad have no idea what's going on. I didn't want to burden them."

"Maybe you could sport a different religious symbol each day, to be more inclusive."

"Wouldn't that make it look like I don't believe in anything, that I'm just pandering?"

"Do you believe in anything?"

The question stopped her on the way to the door. "Well, I was raised religious."

"Evasive," he said, in a sing-song voice.

"Okay, yes, I believe in God. Do you?"

"Sure, why not? It's a weird, fucked-up world—I like having someone to blame." He spread his arms and bellowed like a stereotypical Deep South evangelist, "Can I get an amen? Praise the Lord! And do you believe, Sister Riccardi, in His deep and abiding love for you?"

Rather than play along, she considered the question seriously. She'd given a lot of thought to it over the years. "More like His deep and abiding disappointment in me."

"Oh." He chuckled uncertainly. "Shit, really? Why?"

"He entrusted me with saving Lori, but I ran. I saved myself instead." She hefted her satchel from the carpet beside the door. "There've been times this week when I felt like I'm being punished for that sin. Mostly though, Oscar and Candace have suffered because of me. So do I blame God for that, or Satan, or just some sonofabitch with a grudge?"

"Maybe all three, just to be sure."

"Funny. The problem is, if I can't bring Oscar home alive—if I fail my husband, and also fail God again—will He ever forgive me? Will Candace? How could she?" Her face burned, and her eyes welled. She didn't want to cry in front of him. "And how could I live with myself?"

She hurried out, her vision blurry and nose damp. In her cubicle, she snatched up a tissue and blotted her face. Belatedly, she noticed two new items on her desk.

Gus had left a note, his lovely cursive in the thick, black ink of his fountain pen: "Sallying forth to terrify your now-former colleague. I hope to return shortly."

At least that cleared up the question of Sean's firing. Beside the note was a medium-sized FedEx box Eddie must've signed for. The label showed her home as the return address, which meant the sender was most likely Tom. Probably something to taunt her, to keep her off-balance.

She shook the box, which weighed only a pound or two, but heard nothing. It couldn't have been a bomb. No point in putting her through the wringer only to blow her up. What then?

Images of severed ears and even worse sprang to mind.

She considered asking Jeff to open the box and look inside to spare her that horror, but what kind of person would she be, to inflict such an awful sight on him?

With a deep breath, she pinched the pull-tab and tore. Pink foam peanuts filled the box. Built-up static made them cling to her hands and everything else as she shoveled a palmful at a time into the trashcan.

Something sharp inside the box pricked the tip of her forefinger. She yanked out her hand, blew away the foam bits, and sucked at the small cut. An old urban legend popped into her mind, about HIV-contaminated boobytraps in coin-return slots.

Angry now, she shook the remaining contents of the box into the trashcan. The pink peanut waterfall yielded a flash of silver and black before more foam nuggets buried the object. With care, she dug it out, realizing when she touched smooth plastic what he'd sent.

A carving knife—*the* carving knife, the weapon with which she could've saved Lori. She flung it onto the desk as if it had burned her. Her cut fingertip continued to ooze. She sucked at the wound again as she considered the cheap, dreadful blade. The maniac had plotted out every other detail, so no doubt he'd planned even this terrible irony: the only blood this knife ever drew was now her own.

Rubber bands held a note to the handle. The computer-printed message stated, in a large, friendly font, "I think you dropped this on your way out."

# CHAPTER 50

Bo had always wondered why the police never questioned her about the knife she'd dropped in the hall, near Lori's bedroom. Now she knew: after murdering her, Tom Brogan had taken it. A souvenir. As if he'd foreseen the opportunity to someday drive her crazy.

Besides Lori and her, he was the only one to enter the house that night. Here at last was proof that Oscar's abductor was not a vengeful relative, nor someone tangentially connected to the case, but the actual killer.

As she'd suspected all along, Tom had murdered his girlfriend.

She didn't want to interrupt Gus's interrogation of Sean with a call, so she texted him about receiving a delivery from the kidnapper.

He sent a reply soon after, "Almost there, with another piece of the puzzle."

While she waited for him, she stared at the knife, willing herself yet again not to relive that night. Regardless, her right hand curled and the nerves in her palm and fingers conjured the sensation of smooth plastic. A cheap item, with most of its weight in the nine-inch blade.

Jab upward? Or reverse grips to stab down?

Those questions had paralyzed her in the gloomy hall, listening to Lori's strangled cries through the bedroom door. Lori had screamed her name, thought Bo would save her.

The carving knife had been the only decent weapon in the house. She'd snatched it from the butcher block at a run. But then what? Though she'd wielded a forty-inch lacrosse stick with ease, had long-ago mastered the complex movements—scoop, catch, cradle, shoot—this simple kitchen tool had stymied her. Jab or stab? Upward or down?

In the months that followed, those questions had popped into her mind whenever she handled knives. The thought always transported her back to that nighttime hall. Finally, she couldn't bring herself to touch them anymore. Even the sight of one in dim lighting could produce a panic attack.

The chime rang when the suite door opened five minutes later. She heard Gus cross the carpet to her cubicle. He said, "Is this something that connects you to the man?"

Grateful for the distraction, she swiveled her seat to face him. "It's not a clue about who he is, but what he did—he's the one who killed Lori Lambo, and he wants me to be sure of it. Have you heard any more from the FBI?"

He shook his head and set his laptop on her desk. "I suspect my contact has shared all he's going to. Professional courtesy only goes so far. But Randy's in place; he'll alert me when the agents arrive."

"What happened with Sean?"

He flashed his gold grillz. "Mr. O'Shea, I quickly ascertained, has a deep-seated fear of males of my race—especially those of us who are double his size. I didn't even need to display my firearms. He confessed to painting the hashtag on your house as well as here in the garage, at the behest of the kidnapper, who'd overheard your conversation with Jeff about Sean swearing at you."

She nodded. "I remember that—we were close to going live again, and he was waiting on Skype. So, he saw the chance to recruit an ally, and somehow got ahold of Sean?"

"He sent Sean a friend request on Facebook—using the profile of a buxom blonde as a honeypot—and soon started messaging with him about ways to get back at you. Finally, the kidnapper called him to finalize the plan."

"You mean Sean heard his real voice?"

"No, the man continued to use the synthesizer. However, with a little persuasion, Sean produced his cellphone, and I copied the number the kidnapper had used." He pulled out his small notebook and read off the ten digits.

She copied them on scrap paper and then scrolled through her own call log. "This doesn't match any of the numbers he's used before, including the one Randy confirmed at Tom Brogan's house."

"Apparently, he has a plethora of burner phones. I texted Randy about this. Minutes ago, he messaged back that he tried his Stingray but didn't get a ping for that number. It's possible the kidnapper destroys at least some of his phones after using them." He paused and gave her a searching look. "Or, with apologies for bringing this up again, we're being led on a snipe hunt."

She turned away, bile burning her throat. "If we go back to square one, I'll go crazy."

"Of course, it's feasible that he'll get what he wants from you today and let Oscar go."

"No, I've got a feel for him now. He wants to crucify me today and then gloat over my mangled body tomorrow." Arms crossed, she hugged her ribs. "He'll probably spend the Thursday show reading tweets and posts and media stories and editorials vilifying me—give voice to the vultures picking at my character."

"You sound resigned to acquiescing to him."

"In English, does that mean giving up?" She rubbed her forehead. "Sorry, that was rude. Look, whenever I've shown serious defiance, he's tortured Oscar. Each time worse than the last. The knife is a reminder that he's twenty moves ahead of anything I could try. He's in complete control. It's a mercy he just wants me to talk instead of . . . doing something else on camera."

"Would you?"

She'd considered the possibility often enough over the past few days that her answer was automatic. "If sacrificing my pride and dignity would free Oscar, absolutely. In a heartbeat. His life's worth so much more than that. Even if he told me to amputate my fingers with this carving knife, I'd certainly try. Anybody who wouldn't doesn't love and cherish their family enough."

He stepped back and looked her up and down. "That strikes me as a little harsh. Most people would fear how much it'd hurt—physically and emotionally. Family might mean everything to them, but they'd be too afraid of the pain."

She pushed out of the chair, challenge accepted. "And maybe they could forgive themselves afterward, rationalize the guilt away. I can't. Remember, I abandoned one person already. Lori will haunt me the rest of my life, and she meant far less to me than Oscar does." She swallowed hard. "If I give up on him, I'll be paying for it long after I'm dead."

Gus closed the gap and embraced her. She welcomed it even more than before. "I understand," he said. His chin nudged the top of her head. "I'll do whatever I can to help."

His cell rang with old-fashioned telephone bells. She sat and collected herself while he answered it. "Randy," he mouthed. After a minute of listening, he asked his telecom expert to hold on. "The local police just arrived," he told her. "They'll assist the agents with serving the warrant. Apparently, the timetable has moved up."

# Chapter 51

Oscar didn't know which would be worse, shock setting in and killing him, or the pain in his right hand driving him crazy. Maybe madness would give him some kind of release.

Every heartbeat made the wounds throb. His two broken fingers felt hot and swollen. The back of his hand, caved-in by the sonofabitch's hammer, pulsed with alternating fire and ice.

Sleep offered the only escape, but the injuries made genuine rest impossible. Instead, he experienced random intervals of falling unconscious and then startling awake again.

All because of Bo?

The idea that she could've orchestrated this whole thing was a sure sign of insanity taking hold.

Brainwashing—the guy wanted to fuck with his mind.

But the closeup picture of her, relishing something she hadn't done for him, to him, in so long. That proved . . . what? Any image could be Photoshopped. Or maybe he'd forced her to do it, at gunpoint, and she'd been too ashamed to confess it. The whole thing could have been staged, a setup.

Unless this was all her idea, to make him suffer every way possible. Bound and tortured, totally emasculated, shown evidence of her enjoying another man. And executed, once she'd gotten the attention she craved, so he couldn't tell anybody. A bullet in his brain, a knife across his throat. Or maybe she wanted his end to be as slow and excruciating as his confinement.

Assuming she was behind this. Which was nuts. Right?

All he had was one man's word—and this was the motherfucker keeping him imprisoned and beating the shit out of him with a hammer.

But his jailer was also the one paying regular visits with water and Ensure and never humiliating or molesting him during cleanups. And the bindings and adult diapers were necessary; had he just been locked in a cell, unconstrained, he'd be too dangerous and unpredictable. It was a sign of respect that he needed to be taped down, out of fear he'd overpower his jailer. The diapers, wipes, and all were courtesies extended to a worthy opponent.

Besides, if the man really wanted to mess with him, what better time to do it than when the sweatpants were pulled down? And yet, the dude always showed him tremendous deference at that most vulnerable point. He was even sympathetic about having to put him in such an unfair, defenseless position. Would a sadist act in such a professional manner, or would somebody paid to do a job behave that way?

The devastating photo of Bo came to mind again. Definitely her face, but did her hands look right? How long ago did she have red fingernails? He should've studied the image for flaws, fakery, but it had hit him like another hammer, and he'd needed to look away.

If she wanted to win his freedom, though, she would've done it by now.

Before the end, did she plan to tell him why her fame needed to grow, literally, over his dead body?

No matter who was behind this, would he be allowed to hear Candace's voice for a final time?

His thoughts circled back around, over and over.

# Chapter 52

The FBI and Gadsden police were going to rescue Oscar any minute now—Bo could feel it. Adrenaline made her legs tremble and her heart race.

Gus said, "I'd like to put Randy on the speaker, so he can describe what's happening for both of us. Is there a private conference room we can use?"

"No, we do our staff meetings in Harry's office. If Jeff's willing to let us use the studio, the soundproofing makes it very private. Do you mind if he listens in?"

"Not at all." He grabbed his laptop from the desk and gestured for her to lead the way.

She opened the studio door and explained to Jeff what was happening. "Can we listen in here?"

"Hell, yes. No way am I going to miss Oscar's rescue. Give me Randy's 411 so we can Skype. That way, he can point his cell at the action, prop it on the dash, and do a hands-free play-by-play."

She and Gus rolled chairs over to Jeff's table, and he turned one of his large monitors to face them. Jeff connected with Randy online, and Bo saw a typical suburban two-story, viewed through Randy's windshield. He'd zoomed in from a few hundred feet away, putting them close enough to see details of Tom Brogan's house: yellow siding, weathered shingles, driveway empty of vehicles. Bland, as if by design, but exactly the sort of place where evil always seemed to live.

Randy addressed them through the ceiling speakers. His gravelly bass voice sounded so low-pitched, it was almost subsonic—she would've loved to see what it looked like. He whispered, "See the patrol car along the street, near the Brogans' mailbox? Two officers inside, still waiting for the Feebies."

Jeff said, "Dude, you're sitting in *your* car, not the cops'. Why are you whispering like a golf commentator?"

Randy spoke louder, "Sorry, it just feels natural on a stakeout."

She pointed at the screen as two white, generic fleet sedans pulled up. "Who's that?"

Gus and Randy spoke as one: "The FBI."

"Showtime." Jeff rubbed his hands together and grinned.

"This isn't a damn movie," she said. "Should Gus and I do this in Harry's office?"

"Hey, Randy's handling play-by-play; I'm doing color."

"It's not a damn sport either. Oscar could be a prisoner in that house." Or worse, he could be dead, but she didn't want to give voice to that fear and make it a reality.

Gus patted the air with his palm. She sighed and said, "Sorry, I'm a little stressed right now—like the ocean's a little deep."

Jeff held out his mug of coffee. "You left yours in the breakroom. Take mine—it's a fresh batch. Doctor's orders."

"Okay. Thanks, doc." She sipped it. Hot and bitter. Perfect. No matter how many times she left muddy footprints on their friendship, he always forgave her. And vice versa.

Two agents exited from each sedan, three men and a woman in total. Randy said, "Here comes the final confab." All of them wore dark suits and moved with purpose. They were joined by a pair of male, uniformed officers at the bottom of the drive. The female agent opened a portfolio and removed some paperwork while all five men eyed the house, hands on hips or against their holsters.

She asked Gus, "Is any of them your contact?"

He pointed at the youngest-looking man, the only non-Anglo. "I surmise that's Agent Martinez. His boss is the agent with the warrant. The other two probably drove over from the Birmingham office."

"Do any of them know Randy's watching?"

"If so, it's not because we told them."

"Professional courtesy only goes so far," she quoted, and he nodded in reply.

According to her cell, it was twenty past noon. Thirty minutes before Tom would call. The feds and cops continued to watch the house as they launched into a discussion.

Anxiety gnawed at her gut. She needed to do something where she was in control, a mindless ritual to calm her nerves.

If she went to fix her hair and face, maybe they'd execute the warrant while she was away. Then she'd hear Gus or Jeff tell her Oscar was safe. If she stayed put, maybe she'd jinx the operation; something bad would happen, or they wouldn't find Oscar after all. More magical thinking, but she couldn't help it.

She stood and told the guys she'd be in the restroom doing her interview makeup, just in case. Jeff added her to the Skype call, and she hurried to the lavatory with cell in hand, speaker activated.

Out of habit, she checked out the stall doors, looking for any that were closed. As if her friend Kathy would always be there when she needed her most, ready to forgive and inspire.

Stupid. She kept setting herself up for disappointment.

From the phone, Jeff said, "Heading up the driveway, widely spaced. Two feds now at the door. Knocking like they're a couple of Mormons— why aren't they kicking it down?"

"FBI policy," Gus said. "They have to knock and announce themselves."

Randy rumbled, "For what it's worth, the driveway was empty when I pulled up at nine. Yesterday, I saw a truck and SUV parked there when I got the initial ping on that phone."

If Tom left, he could've taken Oscar; a second missing vehicle meant he had an accomplice. Hair and makeup became a rush job, with her attention split between those efforts and prodding the guys for faster updates. "What's happening now?"

"No one answered," Gus said, "so an officer and Agent Martinez's boss went around back. She just opened the front door from the inside, and the others are entering. Either they forced a rear door open, or they found one unlocked."

Bo straightened her oyster-pink blouse and olive skirt-suit and returned to the office as fast as her lucky, too-tight outfit would allow.

Stepping into the studio, she asked, "It's been, what, three minutes since they went in? Still nothing?" Her voice echoed from the overhead speaker and created a screeching feedback loop.

Wincing, Jeff disconnected her from the Skype call. "Yeah, but it's a big house."

She dropped her satchel and sat next to Gus. They had fifteen minutes before the kidnapper's call—which hopefully would never come. She kneaded the pleather chair arms while she tried not to hyperventilate.

The guys speculated about what could be happening inside the house. Their voices ran together in a droning hum. She squeezed her eyes shut with such force, pale spots floated behind them. For a second, she thought her chromesthesia had returned.

Maybe the cops had Tom in handcuffs already and were tending to Oscar, with an ambulance summoned. She imagined it darting up the driveway with lights and siren. The front door of the house would swing open. Oscar would emerge, weak but walking on his own, an agent on either side ready to provide support. His right hand would be swathed in makeshift bandages, a brave smile on his haggard, bearded face.

A teeth-rattling explosion blasted her out of the fantasy.

Randy yelled, "What the hell?" as gray and black smoke from the back of the Brogans' house billowed above the rooftop. Neighbors' car alarms shrieked.

It was all a trap.

"Jesus, please, no." Helpless, she could only stare at the screen and repeat her useless entreaty. One hand clamped over the other in a death grip.

She'd just killed Oscar and his rescuers.

# Chapter 53

"No, no, no," Bo continued to whisper until she was gasping for breath. Her heart thudded as if she were racing down a lacrosse field. Instead of sweating, though, she'd never felt so cold in her life. If she hadn't seized on that tip, they all would still be alive.

On the screen, smoke seeped out of the house, and then began to jet from gaps in the windows, front door, and roofline. No one reappeared.

Gus leaned toward the mic on Jeff's desk. "Randy, call 911 and report a fire. Don't identify yourself. Then get out of there and destroy your phone as soon as you can."

"But, but. . . ." The telecom expert sounded shell shocked. "What hap—"

"Do it," Gus shouted. "Now."

"Okay, right." The camera angle swerved crazily as Randy fumbled with his cell. He ended the connection. Jeff's monitor reverted to showing the On-Air account page for Skype.

How could she tell Candace she'd caused her father's death? What would she say to Oscar's family? First, she'd doomed Lori by failing to fight, and now she'd killed Oscar by acting in haste. And maybe a half-dozen agents and officers were dead, too, and—unless Tom had booby-trapped his own house—an innocent family's home was destroyed. All her fault.

Gus and Jeff both tried to talk to her, but she only understood the condemnations looping endlessly through her mind. In a daze, she watched them turn away and exchange comments. Neither would look at her now, as if she frightened them.

Jeff handed Gus a clipboard. For some reason, the big man secured his phone to the board, set it on the floor, and stood with one thick-soled wingtip above the screen. He stomped down with all his considerable weight.

Crunching glass and plastic jolted her out of her fugue. She gasped as his heel continued to jackhammer the device. He turned fragments into even smaller bits. Then he ground much of the shards into powder.

The residue made her think of ashes: what the Brogans' house was turning into, what the agents and cops had become. Maybe Oscar, too. Incinerated, because of her.

Jeff passed a small trashcan to Gus. "Couldn't you just turn it off, or remove that SIM chip or whatever?"

"No, the device's GPS and call logs continue to transmit. Destruction is the only sure way not to be tracked." Gus finger-raked shattered remains back onto the clipboard and used it like a dustpan to tip the debris into the trash. He passed the items back to Jeff with thanks and added, "A wood-chipper is faster, but one has to make do. Randy will need to improvise as well."

"W-w-what's going on?" Bo asked.

Jeff said, "The G-men will be gunning for Gus and Randy."

Her face must've betrayed her ongoing bewilderment, because Gus patted her arm and said in a soothing tone, "We don't know whether anybody was killed, or even injured. Nor do we know Oscar's whereabouts. Maybe he was never there, and all this was planned to inflict more psychological damage on you—as well as compromise anyone you might have reached out to for help."

"I don't understand."

"Look at this from the FBI's perspective: Randy and I spoon-fed them all the details needed to investigate someone who wasn't on their radar about a kidnapping they had no knowledge of. A day later, four of their agents, along with two local police, are caught in an explosion. What about this won't scream *setup* to the Bureau?"

She said, "But somebody vouched for you, right? The agents didn't just take you at your word—you were vetted."

"Correct, and that's what will make their interrogation merely harsh instead of brutal."

Grief and guilt had pounded her into numb immobility, but the image he painted jolted her upright again. "Should Candace and I go into hiding, too?"

"They'll want to talk to you soon enough. In the short term, though, they'll be hunting for Randy and me."

"And you really don't think Oscar or anybody else was hurt?"

"There's always hope. Have faith." He pointed at her neck.

She slipped Mom's cross back inside her blouse again. "How? Everything keeps getting worse and worse. If Tom's innocent, he and his family just lost their house and everything in it. Because of me. Maybe Oscar and the other people aren't dead. But maybe they *are*—because of me."

"Or," Jeff said, "maybe you'll save his life. Why beat yoursel—"

Her cell rang. Windchimes: Oscar's ringtone. The kidnapper continued to spoof his name and number. Fresh panic-sweat dampened her face.

After a couple shaky tries, she managed to start the recording app and tap the speaker function, so Gus and Jeff could hear the call. She cleared her throat and said, "This is Bo."

"You killed him," the synthesized voice bellowed. "You psychotic bitch, you blew up my house and roasted Oscar alive."

The guys looked as stunned as Bo felt. She slumped in her seat as her eyes welled. "What? He—"

"He's dead because of you."

"No, it wasn't my—"

He laughed. "I'm just fucking with you. We're fine. But you obviously know what I'm talking about."

"I-I don't." With her chromesthesia, she never would've fallen for that cruel joke. In seconds, he'd already buffaloed her. She said, "Oscar's still alive, right? I need to hear him."

"He's eager to talk to you, too." A lock clicked, and the door to what he'd called the Vault opened. "Hey, partner, say hello to your wife."

From a distance, the synthesized version of Oscar's voice rasped, "You won't get away with this."

The anguish of the past ten minutes had left her exhausted, but hearing him—as alien and terrible as he sounded—and absorbing his words of defiance helped her rally a little.

*That's right, keep fighting. Hang on and don't give up.*

She gave the encouragement to herself as well.

Faith, hope, and love. Was that all they had left on their side?

She heard the door close and the lock snap back into place. The lunatic said, "So, you claim not to know about Tom Brogan's house?"

"Who?"

"Hold that thought while I visit your husband again. I'll break a rib for each lie you tell."

"No, don't. You made your point. Why did the agents and officers have to die?"

"Smoke grenades can't kill anybody."

Gus and Jeff looked relieved, but she still felt terrible about the plague she'd brought down on the Brogan family. She said, "The house is on fire."

The man snarled, "I counted at least one cop and three FBI-types in their basement. What did I say would happen if you brought in help?"

She heard the lock click open again.

# CHAPTER 54

Deke paused with his gloved fingers on the deadbolt knob. He grinned at Bo's loud, panicked gasp—the sexiest sound in the universe—and hoped she'd start begging again.

The webcam he'd planted in Tom's basement continued to transmit to the tablet computer in his other calfskin glove. Orange flames backlit roiling plumes of black and gray. Smoke grenades were notorious fire-starters, and he'd hidden them in a box packed with an arsonist's wet-dream of kindling and fuel. Brogan deserved it. He'd always been an asshole. Burning down his house was a nice bonus for this op.

Bo had never liked the guy either—she should be thanking him.

Sunlight pierced the murk on the right side of the screen: a door had been opened to the outside. The law enforcement types must've evacuated through the same door he'd lock-picked the day before. They probably sustained nothing worse than a little scare and the need for a shower and a dry cleaner. And they'd have a great story to tell for the rest of their lives—they should thank him, too.

He knew about Augustus Trumbull, who'd emailed the Adam Johnson account about the tip, but Bo obviously had people assisting her in Gadsden, too. That's the only way she would've known so soon about the fire. The one thing that could go wrong now was if the feds seized her when they nabbed Augustus and the other hired help. It was easy to imagine the awesome headlines—"Internet Star Arrested for Pranking FBI"—but sustaining the momentum he'd created was vital to the plan. The public would lose interest if she went off the air for even a few days.

More importantly, being held by the FBI would give her a respite from his attentions. He needed to keep shoving her toward the precipice. It was encouraging that the "you killed him" joke had worked so well—somehow, her special perception didn't catch the lie. Maybe he'd broken her already.

"Remind me," he said. "What did I tell you from the start?"

"No cops or anybody else. I know. But please, take it out on me instead. It's not Oscar's fault." She sniffled, another good sign—she'd look like hell when they went on the air. Guilty and contrite, ready to confess her sins. "You want to punish me?" she asked. "Just tell me where to meet. Let him go, and I'll take his place."

The tablet seemed to glow with the fire that continued to spread through the Brogans' basement. Its light now surpassed even the sunshine through the open door. He laughed again. "No, this is too much fun. Maybe someday, but not anytime soon."

In the background, Jeff muttered, "Three minutes, Fuckhead."

"Thanks, Dickface. Here's the new number to use." He recited it and then softened his tone. "Bo, darling, did you open my gift that arrived today?"

"Um . . . yes."

"Recognize it?"

She replied in a ragged voice, as if fighting harder to hold back tears. "Yes."

"Bring the knife to the studio. I want you to display it for the camera. Perhaps we can figure out a way to put it to better use than you did back in '93. Maybe I'll have you stab Jeff."

He terminated the call and flipped the lock closed again. Oscar probably just breathed a big-ass sigh of relief from his cot. There wasn't enough time to do something creative to him before the show started, but Bo would have to be punished soon for violating several of the rules, from telling Harry to seeking law enforcement help.

Fortunately, there were forty-eight minutes of live programming to torment her, plus the in-between break times. He might take them literally and use Oscar as a piñata.

Onscreen, the fire engulfed the webcam he'd concealed. The transmission ended, and an error message reported the lost connection. Days from now, a forensic team sifting through the wreckage might discover his melted transmission device, along with whatever was left of the phone he'd rigged with smoke grenades and incendiaries, giving "burner" a whole new meaning. But nothing would be traceable to him.

His latest disposable cell rang. He propped his tablet against the wall beside the Vault door and accepted the call. "Hello, Stabbing Victim #1, is that you?"

Jeff grunted in reply. When the fun ended, he needed to send a gift to Bo's sidekick, something from the hipster moron's condo or truck. A little parting shot to haunt his dreams for years to come.

Seriously, the best part of this was the eternal ripple effects, the fact that he'd remain a part of everybody's lives. As with Bo, Candace would act differently from now on, and some of those behaviors and attitudes would get transmitted to her children. And those kids would pass along things to their own kids. On and on, with him as a constant presence in the lives of each generation forever.

He'd ensured his immortality.

Flexing his gloved hands, he began to pace through the basement, past the guns and lawncare equipment and back to the Vault. Even if it all suddenly went to shit somehow, he'd already won, and then some. Not only had he finally become the most important man in Bo's life, he was probably more top-of-mind to Candace now than her father. And for Jeff, Harry, Augustus Trumbull, and that numb-nuts Sean, he'd surely supplanted everybody else at the center of their worlds.

"Thirty seconds," Jeff said. "Sound check, Bo."

No reply.

"Bo?"

Deke asked, "Did you fetch the knife?"

In a hoarse monotone, she replied, "Yes."

No affirmation had ever sounded more dejected. Defeated. "There's her goddamn sound check, Little Jeffy."
Yeah, winning felt fucking great.

# CHAPTER 55

They hadn't even gone live yet and Bo's neck was already cramped and stiff, and her temples throbbed. The headphones seemed to weigh twenty pounds.

She'd set the knife on the carpet near her shoes, so she wouldn't have to look at it. Her hand still tingled from gripping it again. The puncture wound on her fingertip had reopened because she kept rubbing it with her thumb, smearing traces of blood.

"Five . . . four," Jeff said. He counted down the remaining seconds with a raised hand, then pointed at her.

She didn't have enough stamina to fake the enthusiasm her intro was supposed to call for, and she wouldn't be able to sustain it anyway. As she stared at the webcam, all she could muster was the grim tone that reflected her mood.

"This is Bo Riccardi on The Barracuda from On-Air Web Radio. While there might be a handful of first-timers who just happened to stumble across today's program, I'm going to assume you're here either because you're a loyal fan, or you've seen something online that made you curious about what's going on. Unfortunately, I'm not at liberty to explain things yet. I hope to soon, but if you joined us today expecting answers, I'm afraid our guest—who calls himself Oscar and continues to disguise his voice—only wants to deepen the mystery further. Isn't that right?"

"Not at all, Bo. You might remain in the dark as to the purpose of my show today, but my audience will have no doubt about what's happening and why during the next hour."

Despite the electronics, he managed to sound cocky and downright gleeful. Playing to the crowd. He got off on the idea of humiliating her in front of the masses. His audience. His show.

Well, if he'd taken ownership, he could do the work that went along with it. She stayed quiet and merely gazed at the webcam.

"Are you there?" he asked.

*Some uncertainty, maybe a trace of anger? Fear that Jeff had muted him again?*

It was so difficult to interpret nuances with her ears alone. The harder she tried to focus, the less sure she became.

She waited another beat and said, "Yesterday, you made it clear you were in control of this interview. Go ahead. I'm just doing what you wanted."

He hesitated, so she added, "Millions, perhaps, are waiting. They're listening and watching. Judging you." It was the smallest of victories, something she wouldn't even be able to savor once he recovered his wits and started to degrade her. In fact, she was probably worsening her punishment, but she couldn't make this easy for him. She only hoped he would take it out on her, not Oscar.

The madman laughed, though whether he was shrugging off a blow or truly amused, she couldn't tell. He said, "We'll see how they judge *you* at the end of this. Let's talk about 1993."

She wanted to steal his thunder—go right to the murder and expedite the flogging he intended to give her—but he definitely would make Oscar suffer for that. All she could do was keep him off-balance, to lessen the sting of each blow.

"You mean March 13th?" she asked. "It was a Saturday— everybody was celebrating St. Patrick's Day early."

"That's right, the 13th." He sounded disappointed. "You and your roommates were partying with your boyfriends?"

She could see Gus to her left, headphones on, huge hands splayed on either side of his laptop as he watched her. And she saw Jeff staring from behind his mixer board. Their attention reminded her of a recurring dream where she conducted an interview naked. She touched the neckline of her blouse to reassure herself that she still had clothes on, and to confirm Mom's cross remained concealed.

"No," she said, "or at least not all of us. Susanna was. She stayed at Deacon's place that night. Afterward, she told me they'd hit the booze harder than usual and fell asleep early."

"What about you and Nick?" He spat his name.

"We had a very public argument that morning. It was over some dumb comment that I can't remember."

"It started when he asked about your high school romances."

Damn, he was right. She rocked back in her chair as she recalled Nick Cohen sitting across from her that day at Carol Lee Donuts on College Avenue: angular face, intense brown eyes, lips quirked in a perpetual smile. She asked, "How could you know about that?"

"Like you said, it was very public. So, you told him about one boy who broke up with you, and Nick said, 'I would've never let you get away,' and you lost your shit. Apparently, you had a problem with the idea of being held captive. Imagine that."

It was like he knew the details of her life even better than she did. Trying to recover, she said, "Well, I, uh, I sat around sulking at home. Lori was doing a pub crawl. Not that there were many places to crawl to in Blacksburg back then, but she was making the most of it."

"Where was Tom?"

"He'd taken out another girl, so she was on her own."

"You didn't want to be her wing-woman, Barracuda?"

"No. Boys and beer were the last things I wanted to deal with."

"Too bad. If you hadn't been so selfish, you would've changed the course of history that night. Lori Lambo would still be alive."

The thought had never occurred to her. For more than two decades, she'd been consumed with guilt for not acting to rescue Lori. Instead, she could've saved her simply by hanging out with her that night, being her friend. Bo saw the truth clearly: if she hadn't been so wrapped up in her own little drama over Nick, everything could've turned out for the better.

She swallowed and gave Jeff a desperate look. He shook his head with bad news and held up seven fingers. Seven more minutes to endure until the first break.

"Maybe," she conceded, "but her life was literally in your hands, not mine."

"Careful—you're getting ahead of the story. And jumping to conclusions. That can be dangerous *for all concerned*. So, when did Lori come home?"

She settled on a new strategy and channeled every obstinate, difficult interviewee she'd ever faced. Nothing so blatant that he'd retaliate against Oscar, but tactics that would let her SERE, as he'd called it: survive, evade, resist, and maybe even escape. Then do it again after the break. And then twice more. She said, "Half-past eleven? No . . . more like around midnight. Maybe 11:50 or—"

"That's fine. What kind of state was she in?"

"Um, she was . . . intoxicated." She let more silence build.

"And what happened?"

"She kind of stagger-walked past me on the couch while I was watching TV. From what I can recall, she barely said hello at first. But then she joined me for a few minutes, before she decided to go to bed."

"And?"

She tried to say the least amount with the most words possible. "And I stayed up. *Saturday Night Live* was on. Mary J. Blige was the musical guest, and I think John Goodman was hosting. They had a great cast that year: Chris Rock, Dana Carvey—"

"Enough. What happened with Lori?"

"Uh, well, she used the hall bathroom we shared. Susanna had the only private one, because she was in the master bedroom when she wasn't at that Deacon guy's place. I think Lori took care of business after Weekend Update, which has always been one of my favorite seg—"

He growled in frustration. As satisfying as that was, she knew she risked overplaying it. She couldn't put Oscar in any more danger.

Jeff held up three fingers. With her reprieve so close, she said, "What else do you want to know? We only have a few minutes before our first break."

"No breaks," he said. "We're going straight through to the end."

# Chapter 56

Bo was sure her reaction, on full display for the audience, mirrored Jeff's stunned expression behind the webcam. Forbidding their usual breaks seemed ridiculous, as if the madman had declared a repeal of gravity. She said, "You . . . you can't. Advertisers paid a lot for these spots. They make this show possible."

"Harry can send me the damn bill. Quit stalling."

"Remember the millions watching and listening? The breaks are for them, too."

"They don't need a break—everybody takes their phones to the toilet. Get on with it."

She heard rapid pacing at his end. Though she wanted to believe he was losing control, he still had the power of life and death over Oscar. That was all the control he needed.

With the show timing rendered meaningless, she didn't want to string things out anymore. The less interrogation she had to endure, the better. In a rush, she said, "Before the last *SNL* sketch, I went to bed. Then around 2:30 in the morning, a man broke in—"

"Stop. You skipped the most important detail. Somehow Lori ended up in your bed and you went to sleep in hers."

Breath caught in her throat. "No, that's not . . . oh sweet Jesus, you knew the layout of our house, who was sleeping where." She leaned toward the mic, as if she could get in his face that way. "Or at least you thought you did. Your information was old."

"I wasn't there. I'm doing all this for someone whose life you ruined."

Was that a lie? She couldn't tell now, but it must've been. He had made everything so personal. And there was the knife he'd sent.

Many of the pieces fell into place. The nightmare she had lived since 1993 was even worse than she'd believed.

Heart galloping, she stammered, "Y-y-you thought you'd gone into my room. Not hers. You'd targeted me, but you strangled the wrong girl."

A sudden thump on his end, as if the lunatic had punched a wall. He growled, "This isn't about me—you're the one on trial."

"Is that what this is?" Her voice sounded distant in the headphones as she talked through the new picture forming in her mind. "Lori had complained on Friday morning that she hadn't slept well. The city had replaced a nearby streetlight, and it shined through her window blinds all night. My bedroom looked out on the side yard, and it was much darker there. Back then, I could sleep no matter what, so we decided to swap rooms."

"Fuck," he whispered, as if to himself. It sounded like a confession.

Feeling the momentum shift, she pressed her attack. "That's right. Tom came over on Friday night and helped Lori and me move our stuff into each other's room. The way he could be such a nice guy sometimes, and then hook up with some other girl the next day, would drive me bonkers. When Lori was murdered, I figured he must've done it, because he went to her new bedroom. But it was you, in the dark, going to what you thought was my room. Why did you want to kill me?"

He exhaled hard. "Remember what card I hold, what I can do."

"Susanna didn't know we'd changed rooms—she was with Deacon on Friday and all of Saturday. Which meant Deacon didn't know either. And after the murder, Susanna and I both dropped out of school. Maybe Deke never heard the switched-bedroom story from her. And maybe his alibi that Saturday night wasn't so airtight."

The last piece of the puzzle dropped into place, and she finally saw the whole thing.

None of their boyfriends had possessed a key to their place. For years she'd bounced between blaming Lori for leaving the front door unlocked and herself for not double-checking it before going to bed. Ultimately, though, she had always accepted responsibility. It'd never occurred to her that the killer had brought a key.

She said in a rush, "You're Deke Powell. After getting Susanna drunk, you hung around long enough to make sure she was sleeping hard and then you took her house key and left—but made sure you got back to your place before she woke up. You always had a thing for me. I never showed any interest, though, so you . . . what, decided to choke me to death?"

"That's enough." Faint voice, half-hearted protest, as if he'd fallen into his memory as well, and was reliving his crime along with her.

She stared into the unblinking lens, no longer mindful of Jeff or Gus or her strategy. Unable to stop the words from pouring out. "A policewoman shared some of the forensics with me. Bruises all along Lori's back where the man had straddled her from behind. Abrasions on her mouth and cheeks, as if something like a bandana had gagged her. Her own saliva on her chin and neck, because she managed to slip the cloth down and yell my name. That's what woke me. And that's how you learned you'd pinned Lori—not me—face-down on the bed."

"Stop."

She conjured Lori's horrible cry full of fear, panic, and pain: "Bo!" And again. She remembered the scaly pink, splattered purples, an arrow of brick red. The sounds of a victim.

*Action needed*, she had thought. Violence to end violence. The carving knife yanked from the kitchen butcher block. Dimly lit hallway, closed bedroom, standing there in only a sleepshirt and panties. Desperate choking from the other side of the door. Strangled sobs: pus-colored squiggles that blurred into a gray sludge as terror and anxiety made her chromesthesia malfunction.

Jab upward or change her grip to stab down? Paralysis. Then, it was too late. Sudden silence, followed by bedsprings, feet thumping to the floor—gray blobs on an ash background. The door yanked open. A silhouette looming just fifteen feet away.

Now hunched behind the mic, Bo felt tears scorch her eyes and sear her cheeks before they dripped down like hot wax onto the tabletop. "Did you mean to rape me? Not strangle me, but take what I wouldn't give you?"

"I—"

"Well, Deacon Powell, the gag you meant for me ended up around Lori's throat instead. And you used it to silence her, you sonofabitch."

"You could've saved her," he whined. "I opened the bedroom door and turned on my flashlight and there you stood, carving knife in hand, like a fucking statue. Like you'd been there the whole time, listening to every sound, trying to talk yourself into being brave. But you were too afraid to do anything. Then you dropped the knife and ran."

She remembered trying to focus on his face in Lori's doorway, but the flashlight had blinded her. Frightened into motion again, she'd let go of the knife, turned, and raced for the back door. Wrenched the lock open, then down the steps, heading toward the neighbors' homes. Bare feet cut by broken glass, bruised by stones, but she felt none of it. Screams again—this time coming from her. Lamps flicked on from two houses down. Her arms and legs pumped as if she were back on the lacrosse field. The only thing faster in the world was the one word she could yell, which flew ahead of her: "Help!"

The dread, the desperation, all of it rekindled in an instant while she rocked in the studio chair. Her body reacted as it had back then. Frantic heartbeat, panting, face slick with sweat. Her muscles ached, as if she'd dashed around the suite a dozen times. Her right hand prickled with the memory burned into the nerves: a smooth plastic handle gripped tight but impotently.

She wiped her face and saw the knife on the carpet, as if she'd just dropped it again in fright. Her cowardice. Her failure. Now she was failing again, despite her efforts to remain brave this time.

"You were so fast," he murmured. "I knew I couldn't catch you. Besides . . . my hands. They looked all wrong. I kept staring at them in the flashlight beam, one hand, then the other. They'd just killed a girl."

His voice caught, and she heard another thump, as if he'd punched a wall again. He cried, "I never wanted to hurt anybody."

"You brought a gag, you bastard. You planned to hurt *me*."

"I figured you'd be startled at first. After I showed you what I could do, how good I could make you feel, I was going to take it off. Because you would've wanted me then."

The logic of a monster. His twisted reasoning gut-punched her. She couldn't breathe.

"But my hands." He sounded even more pathetic. "I hated the sight of them, then and now. Afraid of what else they want to do. I had to hide them—but everybody wondered about the gloves. The military wouldn't take me. I couldn't keep a job. I had to become self-employed. I couldn't be with nice girls, only whores. All because of you."

He blubbered, "If you'd just stayed where you were supposed to be and done what you were supposed to do, everything would've been fine. We'd be together today. Happy."

"Shut up, you sick fuck." Now she was grateful she couldn't see his voice as well as hear it—his madness had already infected her mind too much. The only way she could relieve the pressure there was to keep screaming at him.

The weakness in his voice, the faltering . . . maybe if she announced what she'd kept bottled up since Monday, he would relent. "You kidnapped my husband, the real Oscar, to force me to interview you. Every day, you've tortured him to keep me in line. Humiliated my daughter and me with fake pictures and videos. Now millions of people know the whole story, Deacon Powell. We're all telling you—begging you—to let Oscar go. Set him free and then run away. Disappear. Nobody will look for you. Just leave us alone."

"No." His tone had become icy calm. Maybe her words had cracked him wide open, but instead of recovering his humanity, it sounded like he'd surrendered to the monster.

"No," he repeated, "you just sealed his fate. Damned him— just like you doomed Lori. We're done for today. On your show tomorrow, he'll die."

# Chapter 57

The call disconnected. Bo looked at Gus and Jeff. Both men were slack-jawed. Poleaxed, just like her.

They were still streaming live, she reminded herself.

She leaned toward the mic. "I . . . um . . . we'll end early. T-t-tomorrow, we won't do a live show. Now that you understand what's been happening and why, we, uh, we don't want to give Deacon Powell the platform he demands anymore. If . . . if he's really going to do something to my husband." She gulped, fighting for control. "We won't let that happen in public. It's bad enough he's destroying my family; he can't be allowed to touch you and yours. I'm not sure when I'll speak to you again. Keep your family close."

Jeff punched a button and pulled off his headset. "The 'Best of' show is playing now. Shit, I'm so damn sorry."

"My fault." She couldn't bear the pity in his eyes, so she dropped the headphones on the tear-stained table and focused on them. "I lost control, just couldn't stand his sadism anymore. If I told the secret to everybody, I thought he'd quit this horrible game. Let Oscar go and slink back to whatever hole he'd crawled out of, you know? Stupid. I heard weakness in his voice, like he was struggling with what he'd become. I thought maybe he'd lost his will to go through with his threats."

Gus said, "Your chromesthesia told you these things?"

"No, that vanished last night—it's just . . . gone." She wiped her face. "The stress, anxiety, depression, I think they built up and sort of killed it. Now I'm like everybody else—well, except Candace. She wouldn't have made the mistakes I did. Wouldn't have misinterpreted. And now her father's going to die, probably in an awful way. Because of me."

Fresh tears swamped her cheeks. Gus held out a crisply folded handkerchief.

Jeff said, "Is there anything else we can do?"

"I don't know what."

Gus gestured at his open laptop. "As soon as you outed him, I started inspecting those databases I can access. I discovered his home address in North Carolina, his LLC—Deacon Powell Enterprises—and his DBAs. He's doing business as seven other companies, from IT and telecom consulting to gun sales."

She sniffed and blotted her eyes. "Find anything else?"

"He was too smart to rent or purchase a location in Alabama or Georgia using his personal data or even his companies. We have no proof of his current whereabouts."

She sagged, her brief hopefulness replaced by the certainty Oscar would never be found alive.

Gus held up his long index finger. "However, his arms and ammo firm owns a gun range in White, Alabama, a little northwest of Heflin, where Oscar's cellphone was placed in Ensign Albom's pickup truck."

"Wait," Jeff said. "Who's that?"

Gus brought him up to speed while she pulled the headset away from the phone and stopped the recording app. She'd received a dozen calls and thirty-seven texts during the abbreviated interview—probably yet more harassment and interview requests, along with words of support and encouragement from friends.

She got her breathing under control. "All of that means there's a chance he's somewhere in the White-Heflin area with Oscar, using an alias. With hundreds or maybe thousands of houses to choose from. And the police have less than twenty-four hours to find him."

Jeff adjusted his glasses. "Um, not to make this even worse, but won't the cops and feds be a lot more interested in coming after you guys after what happened in Gadsden?"

Gus nodded. "He's right. We must look for Oscar on our own. On the plus side, the FBI is not a concern yet. They'll begin their search for us here, while we'll be going to Alabama."

"I know you're the only chance he has," Jeff said, "but there's gotta be a smarter way than just randomly knocking on, or kicking down, doors."

His comment and her experience door-knocking in her neighborhood on Monday produced glimmers of an idea that coalesced as she talked it through. "I'll get Candace to meet up with me, and we're going to find a . . . a realtor listing of the places in that area that were sold or leased in the last, I don't know, maybe six months. Then we'll drop in on their neighbors and see if anybody noticed a single guy in his forties next door."

"I'll join you," Gus said, "and work a third of the grid we devise, but Randy can help, too."

"How, dude? You told him to smash up his phone."

"Every grocery store, gas station, and pharmacy sells burners now. I'll wager he's already acquired one. He won't be able to reach me now, but he has Bo's number."

She scrolled through her call log, looking at the list of missed calls. "What's the area code over there? 205? Are there others?"

Gus went to work on his laptop again. "Also 256 and 938 in the geographic area we've discussed, assuming he bought it in-state."

She read out the only number that contained one of those area codes. "There's a message from that caller—hold on." She pressed Play and the speaker icon.

"It's Randy Cleator." He was whispering again in his deep, raspy voice. "Tell Gus he can reach me at this number now. I'm at a Hampton Inn east of Birmingham." He grunted a laugh. "I figured the Feebies would think I hightailed it back to Atlanta. Instead, I'm not too far from their state HQ. I hope Oscar's okay—I kind of feel responsible for what happened. It makes me want to find the kidnapper even more. I'm standing by, waiting for somebody's callback."

While she saved his number, Jeff said, "That's cool, it's like you're assembling the Magnificent Seven. If Harry didn't need me here, I'd mount up, too, but there's gotta be a way to narrow the search. Maybe something you tricked him into saying earlier this week?"

"No, I didn't . . . wait a sec." She turned to Gus. "Tell me his address in North Carolina."

He read off a road name and house number in some place called Aurora. She used Google Earth to look at Deke's property. Farmland and timber, many acres from anybody else but only a short drive to a major river and the coast. As if he'd wanted isolation, but also some geography in common with his Virginia birthplace.

Deke had told her truthfully on Monday that he wasn't near water now. However, someone who chose to live apart from others in North Carolina probably wouldn't move to a town or the suburbs when he relocated to execute his so-called operation. Also, too many witnesses. "Here's how we can narrow our search," she said, and explained her reasoning.

"That'll help eliminate haystacks as we search for the needle," Gus said. "Good work."

"Unless I just prevented us from ever finding Oscar." Sighing, she glanced down and noticed Mom's cross had escaped her blouse again. "Faith, hope, and love, right?"

Harry unlocked and opened the studio door. Eddie entered behind him. Both looked grim—she was surprised the death threat had affected them so much. The On-Air president said, "I never thought our best week as a business would become our worst week."

"There's no time for a staff meeting," she told him. "Gus and I are leaving."

Harry held up his hands. "Hear us out first. Eddie?"

The young man stepped forward. He held up his phone as if it were Exhibit A in a trial. "All the advertisers have like, pulled out. No one wants to be seen hocking their wares on a show where some dude gets dead."

"Hey," Jeff yelled, "that dude's wife is sitting right there."

"I'm just saying we don't have anybody who wants to pay for a commercial tomorrow, even for a 'Best of' program."

Harry shook his head. "No advertisers, no show. They no longer want to be associated with it—at least until they know the outcome of Oscar's . . . situation. If he gets rescued, everybody's happy. We can probably double our rates again. But if the worst happens, The Barracuda will be radioactive."

His callous economics lesson crystallized her choices. If Oscar survived, some other media company would gladly hire her; she wouldn't need On-Air. If Oscar died, On-Air wouldn't need—or want—her.

She'd resisted the Barracuda moniker at first, but then she had learned to embrace it and even come to love it. Now she had to give it up. Yet another part of her identity to die this week.

Since Monday, she'd suffered countless indignities at work, because losing her job meant Oscar potentially losing his life. The irony was that Deke Powell had just freed her from those chains. She stood, satchel in hand. "We're leaving now and going to find my husband."

Harry said, "I hope you do. Tomorrow's show can be a kind of celebration." He snapped his fingers. "I could interview you and Oscar about what we've all gone through this week."

Gus pushed to his feet. "*We*, Harry? Bo and her family are the ones who have endured everything. *We* have been mere spectators." He towered over the man who paid for his services. "I just emailed you my penultimate bill. You'll get the final one when this is over."

She announced, "It's over now. For me. Here. The Barracuda is dead no matter what happens, because I quit."

Jeff jumped to his feet. "But . . . but—"

She wanted to apologize for abandoning him. To promise she'd stay in touch. She wanted to hug him goodbye.

Unfortunately, they had an audience. She kicked the carving knife toward his desk. "Better keep that," she told her friend. "You might need it around here."

Harry glared up at Gus. "If she's quitting, then what you sent me is your final bill."

"Payment is due in thirty days." The big man left the studio and held the door for her.

Turning to face Harry and Eddie, she said, "Gentlemen, someone who talks for a living should be able to think up a classy exit line, but I'm a little preoccupied. So, please accept my sincerest *fuck you*."

She marched out.

# CHAPTER 58

B o briefed Candace after leaving the On-Air suite. Unsurprisingly, her daughter was gung-ho to join the hunt for her father and Deke, just as Randy was after Gus brought him up to speed. Candace joined Gus and her at The Varsity, a landmark burger joint in midtown Atlanta. They'd meet up with Randy in Heflin, Alabama.

Based on Candace's fear the previous night that Gus might have glimpsed some of the fake photos, Bo figured she would be skittish around him. However, as her daughter leaned against the hand-me-down hatchback, sunglasses blocking the afternoon glare, she seemed totally at ease. One of those benefits of seeing people's intent as they spoke—and something Bo missed dearly about her lost gift.

She asked Candace, "Did you leave your phone back at the hotel?"

"Yeah, like you asked me to."

"That'll keep Deke from being able to track us. Here's your new one." She gave her a cheap substitute loaded with the maximum prepaid hours, along with a car charger.

"Good, my right butt cheek was starting to feel lonely." Candace slipped the phone into the back pocket of her Levis.

The first call Bo had made on the iPhone knockoff she now carried was to Jeff. To his credit, he'd only laid on a little guilt-trip for abandoning him. In return for the promise of a very expensive lunch sometime soon, he agreed to retrieve her cell from the lost-and-found at a grocery store, where she had turned it in and bought the burners and car chargers. Then he would to drive up to the hotel and leave it with the desk clerk. If Deke checked up on her and Candace, it would look like they'd retreated to their hotel room and decided to stay put.

Gus handed slips of paper to both of them. "I lined up a teleconferencing service. Call that number and put in the access code so we can all stay in touch. I briefed Randy and asked him to implement your ideas. He's finding the best list of places that were sold or leased in the last six months in the search zone you defined. Then he'll draw up four grids that focus on rural areas, away from lakes and rivers, where there's a record of a recent sale or rental."

"So like, that helps us how?"

Bo said, "Each of us will have an assigned grid. We'll knock on neighbors' doors to ask if a man in his mid-forties moved next door in the last six months."

"God, that could totally take forever."

"Faith, hope, and love," she replied.

Candace pulled out her car key. "Cool, we've got a family motto now. I mean, after we bring Dad home, we should all get it tattooed on our arms or whatever."

And if they didn't bring him home alive, Bo wondered, what words would be branded on her soul? During the hour-plus drive to Heflin, she figured she would have plenty of time to contemplate the possibilities.

Instead, Gus's conference line kept her gratefully distracted. He set the pace on the interstate in his gigantic black SUV, with Bo tailing him and Candace behind her.

Randy called in and updated them in his usual stakeout-whisper, his voice a low rumble. "I'm working on those real estate maps—fortunately the hotel has a decent printer in their business center. What do we need to talk about?"

Silence on the line. Bo realized they were waiting for her. Though she wanted to rely on Gus to lead this search, she was in charge. He might've naturally taken point on the highway, but he and the others were looking to her for the major decisions. As was the case since the start of this ordeal, they would succeed or fail—and Oscar would live or die—because of her.

She said, "We should rehearse the speech we'll need to give whenever someone opens their door to us."

Candace said, "Yeah, no, totally. We already sort of crashed and burned trying this in our neighborhood on Monday—and some of those people freaking knew us."

"You're right," Gus conceded. "Perhaps something along the lines of, Madam, I'm sorry to bother you this afternoon. However, I'm seeking—"

"Bam," Bo said. "That's the sound of a door slamming. People don't have the attention span for old-fashioned courtesies. I think we only have a few seconds to engage them."

"True that. I mean, how about something like, Hey, this guy kidnapped my dad—did a strange dude move next door lately?"

Randy said, "We don't want to scare anybody off. People avoid trouble; they'll lie to keep from getting involved."

"I can literally spot any lie. Go on, try me."

"Fine," Bo said. "Try your approach. Call them out if they lie and see where that gets you."

"Bam?" Randy asked.

"Exactly." The three of them shifted over one lane as some big rigs merged onto the interstate and then moved back again in unison, as fluid as a snake, once they passed the trucks.

"Well, Mom, you're literally the expert on talking to people. What's your brilliant plan?"

Ignoring her sarcasm, she said, "When you need something from somebody, you have the best chance of getting it by considering what's in it for them. We should couch these conversations as a chance for people to be helpful but not culpable. They have to feel like Good Samaritans who've earned their brownie points for the day, with no chance of blowback."

Gus piped up. "What do you suggest, Bo?"

"We should be the ones who lie our asses off."

# CHAPTER 59

Bo and the others topped off their vehicles at the Heflin truck stop that Ensign Albom had used. As their gas tanks filled, they convened in the center of the island between the pumps.

Gus checked his phone and intoned, "The telecom guru cometh."

A pale man emerged from the restaurant and approached, tapping papers against his denim-clad leg. A t-shirt and tennis shoes complete his ensemble. Based on his deep voice, Bo had pictured a large guy. Maybe not as massive as Gus, but at least someone with a barrel chest. Instead, Randy Cleator was only about five-foot-nine—Candace's height—and of slight build, with a goatee and a shaved head. He was also younger than she'd imagined: late-twenties, tops.

Handshakes and greetings, and then he passed around the pages. They each received a different grayscale map from an online resource that showed the location of every house bought or leased through a realtor in the past six months in that region of Alabama. Over this, Randy had drawn Tetris-like shapes using a straight edge to denote rural areas, so they could focus on canvassing the neighbors of only those homes. Outstanding work in such a short time.

Bo counted twenty-three potential addresses within the zones he assigned her. Many more were grouped outside the demarcation, in and around the adjoining cities of Anniston and Oxford and the smaller nearby towns. Everybody had deferred to her analysis of Deacon's psychology, but Oscar could've just as easily been in one of those population-dense areas. Or he could be somewhere even larger. Birmingham wasn't too far away.

Randy rumbled, "Each of us has to cover hundreds of square miles, but we'll all see a lot more cottonfields and cows than cottages. I didn't include any territory with dense clusters of homes."

The map quivered in Bo's grip as she wondered if she would look at it tomorrow and be able to point to the location where they'd rescued Oscar. Or would that spot haunt her as the house where he'd been murdered because she had led them to search in all the wrong places?

"You okay, Mom?"

"Sure." She was relieved and grateful that the Human Polygraph chose for the first time ever not to make her buzzer sound.

Gus said, "Everybody want to take a restroom break and get some food to go?"

"Download and then upload," Randy quipped. "Not a lot of chances to do the latter out in the country, and the former will have to be done behind a tree or using your car as a shield."

"Oh, gross." Candace tossed her map in her car and stalked toward the restaurant.

The image Randy painted didn't appeal to Bo either, but it forced her think about how vulnerable each of them would be out there. "Something's been nagging at me the whole drive," she told the men. "I didn't want to talk about it around Candace—at least until we have a plan."

Gus asked, "What's on your mind?"

"On the way over, we kept refining the script we're going to use when we knock on somebody's door." Their eyes narrowed, and she quickly added, "It's solid—I don't want to go over it even one more time, promise. But we're all picturing some helpful country person on the other side of that door. We haven't talked yet about what happens if Deke himself answers, because he happened to rent or buy that house directly from the owner, not through a realtor. Long, long odds, I know, but he'll recognize me or Candace on sight. And maybe you, too, Gus. After your visit to Sean this morning, he could've sent Deke a description of you. Regardless, he'll know what's going on after either of you guys start your spiel."

"Granted," Gus said. "But how do we guard against accidentally hitting the jackpot?"

Randy rubbed his shaved head. "Not possible. Hopefully he'll come to *our* attention first, though. I'll have my Stingray on, and I'll check the logs to see if I get a ping that matches any on the list, including the number he used today and the one Gus pried out of Sean." He looked down at his tennis shoes. "I kind of gave myself the smallest territory to search door-to-door, so I can also crisscross each of yours, checking the pings."

"That's a good idea," she said. "But let's say I knock on the jackpot door. Deke opens it, pulls a gun on me, and yanks me inside. None of you will have any idea."

After a moment of staring at the roof high above, Gus said, "Okay, how about a buddy system? Bo and Candace on one team, Randy and me on the other. We stay on the conference line at all times and bring our phones with us to the door." He pantomimed carrying his phone casually at his side. "When one of us drives up to a given address, we recite the road name and house number, and our buddy jots it down. We'll all be able to hear each other's interactions with the locals. If something untoward happens, our buddy will have the address and summon everybody to that spot."

"It's fine to call in the cavalry, but it could be too late for the person who's now a second hostage." She gestured at his suit jacket. "Should we distribute your guns so each of us is armed?"

Randy said, "Might be the first thing he checks for."

"But maybe not—it could literally be the difference between life and death."

Gus patted his hip, where he kept the holstered Glock 19 pistol. "Have you ever fired a gun before?"

"A few times," she said. "After Oscar and I moved in together, my 'paranoid lock fetish,' started to freak him out. We took some handgun classes and were going to buy one, but then

I got pregnant with Candace, and I didn't want a gun and child in the same house."

"Randy?"

"Hunting rifles and shotguns with my dad. He liked target-shooting with pistols, too."

Gus looked past her shoulder. She turned and watched her daughter approach with a sack of takeout food. "No firearms of any kind for her," she said.

"I only have the three in any case. There's the fighting knife in my ankle sheath, though."

Randy scratched at his goatee. "Her jeans taper too much—she could never get it out. Maybe she could carry it in her belt loop and pretend she's Peter Pan."

"This is a truck stop," Bo reminded them. "They're going to sell Swiss Army knives and the like." The thought made her shiver, but she said, "I'll buy one for her. Meet me behind the restaurant, and we'll divvy up the weapons."

She passed Candace and checked the time on her phone as she approached the building. They'd gained an hour crossing into Alabama, so it was still mid-afternoon, and Daylight Savings Time had started the previous week, which meant a later sunset, but she wanted to stop talking and start searching. After nightfall, fewer people would open their doors to strangers.

A glass case near the clerk displayed what for her was a nightmare scenario: two dozen knives. Seated in red velour, they ranged from practical utility and hunting tools to a Marine Corps KA-BAR and what looked like a bayonet. She chose a black tactical folding knife, which would fit easily in Candace's pocket.

They clustered behind the restaurant, which made the weapons distribution feel even more illicit. Bo accepted the small, black Smith & Wesson 360 revolver that Gus removed from his ankle holster. Because she was wearing a skirt, carrying options were few. She settled for tucking his gun in front, where it nestled between blouse and waistband, anchored by her stomach—an unwanted reminder that she hadn't worked out in a while. Also, the gun oil would probably ruin her lucky outfit, but that concern was way down on the give-a-damn list. At least she could get at it quickly.

Randy received Gus's slim Glock 43 pistol in its pocket holster. Even untucked, his t-shirt couldn't hide the slight bulge, just as her suit jacket provided imperfect camouflage. Fortunately, most Southerners, especially out in the country, were accustomed to firearms. She remembered eating in a tiny diner in the North Georgia mountains one time, when a patron joked about concealed-carry permits. More than a dozen people in the place—including the manager, waitress, and fry cook—laughed along as they each revealed a gun under their shirt or in their purse.

She handed over the folding knife to Candace, who rolled her eyes. "Hey, thanks, Mom. Like this is going to do me a lot of good. I mean, why can't I have a gun?"

Gus jumped in. "It's my fault, not your mom's. I only carry three."

"When I turn eighteen, I'm going to buy a ginormous one."

Bo checked the time on her phone again. "We need to get going."

"Everybody teleconference," Gus said. "I briefed Candace about the buddy system."

Randy brought his Jeep around from the side of the restaurant, and their caravan of four lined up at the exit. Bo's assigned area was farthest west, so she brought up the rear this time.

Her phone connected with the conference line. "I'm on," she said.

The other three called out as well, and they merged back onto I-20. She watched Gus's SUV peel off first. Then Randy's Jeep took another exit. Soon Candace signaled and then eased right to go up a ramp. She said, "Good luck, Mom. Bet I find Dad on like, my first try."

"I hope so," she replied, which reminded her of the trinity. "We have complete faith," she added. "Love you."

"Okay." Her daughter sounded embarrassed.

Alone now in a sea of interstate traffic, Ray-Ban aviators on and visor down, Bo sped into the westward sun.

# Chapter 60

After ending the call with Bo, Deke stalked upstairs to his ops center. Dropping into the office chair, he yanked off his gloves and tossed them on the computer keyboard.

He gazed at his pale, waxy hands for a moment. Balled into fists, they itched with the remembered feel of the bandana he'd taken to the house Bo had rented with her Tech roommates.

The edges of the cotton gag had bunched in his palms. Somehow, Lori managed to slip it from her mouth and yell Bo's name twice before his brain had finally rebooted, and he realized he somehow straddled the ass of the wrong girl in the right bedroom.

He had needed to shut her up fast, in case he still had a chance with Bo. With the cloth now around Lori's neck, his fists pulled apart— drawing the fabric tighter and tighter, digging it in deep. She bucked and tried to reach back for his hands but, sloppy drunk as usual, her coordination was shit. Soon, all her energy went into gasping and gurgling. Then silence. Limp and still. Literally dead weight in his hands.

His hands. He hadn't wanted them to kill. They were supposed to bring Bo to ecstasy, make her realize what she'd been missing. Nick the Jock wouldn't understand anything about how to touch a woman, enslave her with a caress. Hands could bring pleasure for hours, make a woman quake endlessly. Each moan would have expressed Bo's gratitude, her growing devotion. And she would've been his forever.

A simple plan, if only she'd cooperated. Instead, she ruined it all. Back then, and again today.

He stood before realizing it. His fingers curved into claws and tore at the Wall of Inspiration. They yanked the printed pictures in one direction and then the other. In no time, his favorites images of Bo lay crumpled on the floor or hung askew, her face in shreds.

Panting, he stared at the destruction and then the causes of it. Left unsheathed, those hands would tear Oscar to pieces as well. Rip the whole world apart.

He calmed himself. *No, not yet.*

Oscar had to die. Bo deserved it, for making him lose control during the program and abandon the script he'd crafted for so long. She'd outed him. Shamed him in front of his fans.

He sat before his computer and pulled on the gloves to assess the damage. The Internet buzzed with talk about Bo and him, using his real name. They'd be forever linked. That would have to provide consolation as he reinvented himself: new ID, new home, new businesses.

Fortunately, he had been a hell of a Boy Scout and was always prepared. First, he moved the remainder of his money through some cutout banks and then to the offshore account he'd set up years ago as a tax shelter. Combined with the bricks of cash he'd brought from North Carolina, those funds would give him a decent stake to begin again. The only domestic account he left was the alias he'd set up to handle the lease of this house and the payment of its utilities.

Everything he needed to take with him could be packed and loaded in his truck in a few hours. The Vault and its macabre contents, along with the perimeter of webcams, would be his gift to the guy he was renting from. Because the bills would continue to be paid, the landlord might not drop by until fall, when it was time to renew.

The thought made him smile, but it was probably too much to ask for Oscar's corpse to remain undiscovered until then. Soundproof didn't mean smell-proof. Even with the air conditioning cranked to the max, the stink would eventually draw the attention of some salesman or Jehovah's Witness who stopped by. Followed by the police.

Scrolling through comments and posts where RealBourne was active, he noted lots of the audience had turned on him—Bo's "sick fuck" comment had become a meme, damn her—but he'd also attracted a slew of new fans from around the world, eager to know more about Oscar's impending execution. Enthusiasts could always smell blood. He would rebuild his team on their shoulders.

First, though, he needed to make sure On-Air cooperated. They hadn't posted the recording yet. With his phone connected to the voice synthesizer, he spoofed Oscar's ID and number so that Harry Pinzer wouldn't need to be convinced about who was calling. He also started to record, in case the man said something useful.

"You again," Pinzer said. "Deacon Powell. Or do you prefer Deke?"

"I'd prefer having your wife in my Vault instead of Oscar. More possibilities for fun. Ol' Maggie has posted a bunch of photos with the grandkids, biking on the Atlanta Beltline. Thursday appears to be their favorite day to do that, and guess what tomorrow is."

"Last time we talked, you pitched some new conspiracy program with you as the host. Promised to let Oscar go in return. Now you threaten me and my family? Go fuck yourself."

Deke laughed. "That's a popular sentiment right now. But don't forget the rest of the conversation we had: Oscar and my power drill, and your name associated with it."

"Nobody will believe I'm involved. You just announced live on-air that you're going to murder him. Threats don't hold water anymore because the secret's out."

Deke flexed his gloved hands and looked at his Wall, at what they could do. "The threats still work with Bo. You'll see tomorrow."

"Wrong again, asshole. There's no more show. She quit."

"What?" No show meant no built-in On-Air audience, no place for his fans to assemble.

"That's right—and she's coming for you, Fuckhead. With a posse. So, why don't you let Oscar go and crawl back under your rock?"

"She'll never find me."

"Don't be so sure. She's got some serious help. Do it—set her husband free."

A helicopter roared overhead. Normally he would've ignored it, but now he tensed and touched the Colt at his hip. Time to switch to his favorite pistol gloves, hard-knuckled and snug, a tacky feel for a solid grip. A little hot to wear all the time, but best to be ready.

He told himself to relax. The notion that she now had air recon was absurd—that chopper was just headed for the St. Clair County Airport. At most, she'd have help from the same idiots that fell for the Tom Brogan tip and got Tom's place burned down. By this time tomorrow, he'd be on the road, having earned everybody's respect, and Bo would be a widow and single mother.

Still, this sonofabitch deserved a parting shot. He recited Pinzer's home address. "Tell Maggie to look for a package on Friday. I'll send y'all a souvenir from Oscar."

He disconnected and ended the worthless recording. Using a phone tracker site, he typed in Bo's cell. Midtown Atlanta. If she was coming for him, she was hunting in the wrong damn state. Even better, she was heading north, in the direction of Roswell. He next checked Candace's phone—Roswell, holed up at a hotel. Pinzer had been bluffing: Bo was joining her, to commiserate and hide out. No more job, soon no more man in their lives. They were awaiting the end of their world together. How sweet.

On the other hand, maybe they had ditched their phones and headed west, suddenly undetectable. No way they could find him, but still . . . best to be prepared.

Options? Put a bullet in Oscar's head and hit the highway. Call Bo just before he shot the man, get him to say some last words. Expeditious, but it would deny him an audience, and it felt too smalltime now. A bunch of people still clamored to be entertained, wanted to pay homage to his prowess. He couldn't disappoint the masses—he might never have this chance on the world stage again.

There was plenty of time to draft a speech about how Bo provoked this finale. As he recited it, the webcam would focus on Oscar. Then his Colt 1911 would come into frame.

In one respect, he hated having to kill her husband. Oscar's bravado had faded since the smashed-hand thing, but the guy still tried to act like a man.

Decision made, he returned to his social media accounts and started to grow his fanbase again, targeting the execution enthusiasts. Yes, he was definitely hosting "the big event" at noon US Central Daylight-Savings Time (GMT-5) on Thursday. Online location? TBD. Check back shortly beforehand. He included a link to his recording of the Wednesday show.

*Share, retweet, and forward this news.*

# Chapter 61

At the seventh address Bo tried, someone finally answered her knock. She pitched her story to an elderly woman about looking for a friend in his mid-forties, but the homeowner had no idea who'd moved in next door.

She trudged back to her car and returned to the road.

"Hey," Candace said on the teleconference line, "at least a lady talked to you. I'm like, zero for infinity on getting people to even come to the door or whatever."

"347 Elkins," Randy said, back in his gruff golf whisper. "I'm going in."

"I copy," Gus replied. "I'm at my next stop, but I'll wait for you."

No traffic in either direction for Bo, so she let off the gas and coasted past a ranch-style house that had been purchased recently and pulled onto the gravel drive of the neighbor on the other side. Before she headed up, she waited for Randy's encounter, hoping he had success.

His brief conversation with a man revealed that the new neighbors were a family of six. Disappointing, but at least the information allowed Randy to cross a property off his list. She hadn't managed to do that yet.

"2344 Vernice," Gus said. He waited as Randy acknowledged this and then gave an all-too-familiar commentary of futility: doorbell, firm knocking, waiting, no reply. Another try, and again nothing, so on to the next neighbor.

She parked at the top of the driveway near a kids' basketball hoop and peered at the log cabin homestead. It looked as inauthentic as the Lincoln Log houses she'd made as a preschooler. "Candace, I'm at 53 Rutherford."

"Woo-hoo, Mom. That's some real progress. The last one was 49."

"I'm bracketing. If this doesn't give me any intel about who's in 51, I'll go to 52 across the road, just like we strategized." Her daughter grunted, sounding just like Oscar, and Bo flipped her map over to review the numerous but wide-ranging addresses Candace had reported. She'd dutifully written them down but hadn't paid enough attention. "Wait, are your targets really far apart? You seem to be all over the place."

"Yeah, no. I'm sort of skipping the Halloween houses."

"The what?"

"Back in the day, didn't they have trick-or-treating in Roanoke?"

"Sure, but what—"

"Don't you remember how it was? I mean, you gotta get, like, as much candy as you can, as fast as you can, because there's literally a curfew. And even before then lots of people turn off their lights and totally pretend they're not home."

Gus said, "How does this apply to our current situation?"

"So, the way you max your haul is to avoid the homes with endless driveways—it takes forever to walk up and back. You can knock off two or three places in the time it would take to do one long-ass driveway. There's lots of those driveways in my zone—it's, like, serious farm country out here—so I'm skipping those Halloween houses. For now. I mean, I get Dad could be next door to any one of them, but I'm maxing my haul before I have to kill tons of time by going down each of those mile-long roads."

"That wasn't the plan," Randy murmured.

"Dude, remind me again of your awesome track record. By the way, I'm at 21 Trinity Lane."

"Go," Bo said, noting the latest stop on her paper. "I'll wait."

Candace didn't bother with the step-by-step monologue Gus always provided. Bo heard knocking and then someone answer. After her daughter's version of their script—searching for her mom's old friend from school—they all learned the new neighbors were a Latino couple. Back to her car and onto the next stop.

Bo told her, "My turn," but her knocking and doorbell ringing at this address received no response. Nor did she have any luck raising someone at house number 52, a quarter-mile down and on the opposite side of the winding rural road.

Behind the wheel again, she circled 51 Rutherford Way on the map to remind herself she still didn't know who lived there and wrote down the addresses where no one answered, so she could revisit them later. Projecting her voice toward the microphone, she asked, "Are we doing this too early? Most people are probably still at work."

Gus said, "If we wait until evening, we'll face the same problem we did in your neighborhood: people don't like to answer their doors after the sun goes down."

"Could we be looking in the wrong place?" She heard the anxiety and desperation in her voice but couldn't help it. "Maybe he's way up in the northeast part of the state or west over in Birmingham. Or south—or maybe he's back in Georgia somewhere, or even Tennessee."

Randy said, "We have two data points locally: the truck stop and his gun range. Three, if you count Tom Brogan's place farther out, because he boobytrapped it."

"Agreed," Gus replied. "This is our best option. I'm at 2791 Vernice."

While he and Randy both struck out yet again, and Candace searched for non-Halloween houses on her grid, she stared at her own map. Randy hadn't drawn any irregular Tetris-shapes past the Coosa River to the west, but plenty of farm country lay beyond that—with recently sold homes there—and the Coosa was a major river. Deke had admitted on Monday that he didn't get to enjoy the water, but he still might've wanted it to be a short drive away, like how some people had to live near forests to feel centered, or the mountains or a desert.

She decided to give it a try. In a few minutes, she'd merged back onto I-20 and headed west again into the sun. Steering left-handed, she logged Candace's stops with her right, the center console an imperfect desk for the crumpled paper.

In short order, she was crossing the Coosa. The wide river boasted tree-covered islands, docks that moored schooners and yachts, pleasure cruisers with fishermen and sun worshippers soaking up the springtime warmth, and speedboats cutting across dark waves that reflected splashes of light. She wanted to buzz down her windows to try to smell the water, but it would ruin the audio for the other three.

"Mom, you there? You've gone like, dead quiet. Are you still at that last place?"

"No, I've gone AWOL. I'm crossing the Coosa River, to check out some of the properties west of my grid area. Sorry, Randy, but I need to try something different."

"No problem," he said.

Candace made her game show-buzzer noise. "Dude, you just earned a detention—that was a total lie. You've got a big-ass problem with her doing this."

"I understand," Bo said and signaled for the next exit ramp. "We agreed on a plan, and now both Riccardi girls have gone rogue. But maybe I'll get lucky and stumble onto something."

At the top of the ramp, she had to pick a direction to turn. Right or left? A glance at the map showed more properties purchased to the north, so she turned right.

The first three stops yielded a couple of no-responses and a grubby, pot-bellied man wearing nothing but pajama bottoms who invited her inside. He promised his trouser snake would make her "forget all about that other feller." One look at Gus's revolver made him rescind his offer.

She accelerated in reverse down his rutted, dirt driveway, arm over the seat as she stared out the back window, and screeched onto the paved road.

All the while, Candace was laughing. "The freakiest thing was that he believed what he was saying, like one hundred percent. I saw it. He's mighty proud of his pecker."

"Yeah, I could see it, too."

She squealed, "He showed it to you?"

"He tried, but I whipped out Gus's revolver first—as modest as it is, it won the *who's bigger* contest." She shuddered as the adrenaline began to subside. "Halloween house indeed."

Gus said, "I'm delighted it came in handy. Perhaps a return to Randy's grid is in order?"

"One more address. If I don't get anything more than silence or a sexual proposition, then I'll turn around. Promise." She consulted the map and tried another road.

As she coasted along the blacktop, searching for the next property in question, she found herself touching Mom's cross and praying silently, though it felt more like pleading:

*Please, God, I haven't bothered You in a long, long time. I haven't felt worthy, and I still don't. But we need to catch a break—for my husband and my daughter, not for me. I'm not asking for a miracle. Nothing dramatic. Just one tiny little bit of good luck. Please.*

# CHAPTER 62

The recently purchased house was set far back from the road, surrounded by trees. Using Candace's strategy, Bo chose the neighbor with the shortest driveway. This led to a well-maintained cottage and a shiny van under a carport. She parked behind the vehicle. "I'm at 6 Monterey Road."

"Got it," Candace said.

A young woman about Randy's age answered her knock, carrying a drowsy baby on one hip. A small boy peered at Bo around his mother's capri pants.

Everything about her and her tidy home felt right, Bo thought, as if she'd been led to this place. More magical thinking, or had God decided her family had suffered enough and needed the break she'd begged for?

When she gave the woman her spiel, the young mother said, "I wasn't never good about guessing ages—specially with men—but the guy that bought the place next door might be forty-something or thereabouts."

"Oh." Bo gazed at her dress shoes and tried to look shy. "Does he, uh, live alone, or does he have someone?"

"Never seen nobody but him. Not that I've seen him very much. I do remember thinking one time that he's not half-bad looking. Were y'all a couple once?"

Bo was glad she'd remembered to remove her wedding ring hours earlier. Still, she covered her left hand with her right; the gold band had left a mark. She used the action to feign more fidgeting. "He liked to think so more than me. But I heard he'd moved back here, and well, I thought maybe I'd give him another chance, you know?" She glanced up, and the woman beamed.

"Spring's in the air." She laughed and jiggled her infant. "Always a good time for romance."

"Here's hoping!" Bo thanked her and, though she wanted to hike her skirt and sprint back to the car, she maintained her poise. They waved to each other before she climbed in.

She'd parked nose-in and made a K-turn on the narrow drive. Then she remembered her white, Peach State-branded license plate: the woman would've expected to see the gold sky, green hills, and blue water of the current Alabama plate. Rather than raise suspicions, hopefully she'd think it was even more romantic for her to have traveled so far to rekindle a love affair.

Too late to worry about it. After she pulled back onto the road, she noticed no one was talking on the conference line. "Did y'all hear that?"

"Totally, Mom. You might be onto something. One sec while I find a spot to pull over." After a moment, she said, "So, what's the address of the place where the mystery dude lives?"

"Uh, 8 Monterey Road. It's one of your Halloween houses, set way back, with woods all around."

Still murmuring, Randy said, "Charles Zonder. That's the name on the deed."

"Fast fingers, Web Whisperer," Candace replied, respect in her voice. "A few with that name on Facebook, LinkedIn, some others. Checking out pictures now . . . whoa. Hey, Mom, was that lady like, legally blind? I mean, I don't see a decent-looking guy in the bunch."

Gus said, "Physical attraction is a subjective matter. Do any appear to be close in age to your mother?"

"One guy definitely. Oops—he's in Portland, Maine today. He posted this totally lame selfie."

As much as Bo wanted to park in the man's driveway and stake out his place, she didn't dare draw attention to herself. She found a side road and pulled onto the weedy shoulder.

Searching online, she reviewed photos of numerous men named Charles Zonder and didn't recognize anybody. "We know Deke wouldn't use his real name to buy or rent. He also created fake personas, with fake photos, for all the social media stunts he pulled. There's no reason 'Charles Zonder' couldn't be an alias, too. What else can we come up with about him?"

Randy said, "Zonder bought the place only six weeks ago. We know Deke's a planner. Is six weeks long enough for him to prep the house to hold Oscar, plus continue to stake out your house and work, nail down everybody's patterns and all? Seems like a lot to do in that time."

"And, yo, do we have any kind of script if it really is the guy holding Dad? You guys could go in from three directions, literally with guns blazing to like, distract him, and I'll sneak up with my puny knife."

"Forget about the script for now," Bo said. "Short of staking out his house and getting his picture so I can see whether it's really Deacon Powell, is there any way to know for sure?"

Gus said, "My apologies for being tardy with this information—my fingers are better suited to keyboards than these touchscreens. I've accessed some of the private databases using the taxpayer ID of our Charles Zonder at 8 Monterey Road. There's quite a long credit history that looks legitimate, and he was born fifty-five years ago. If Deke was to steal somebody's ID, it seems like he'd choose one closer to his own age. Bo, is it possible Deke is ten years older than you?"

"No." She knocked the back of her head against the seat as she shouted, "Shit, shit, shit." Tossing her sunglasses onto the dash, she rubbed her tired eyes. In a quieter voice, she said, "It's not him. I wasted our time because I got impatient. Sorry, y'all. I screwed up big time."

According to the clock, she'd flushed away more than an hour. Maybe the difference between life and death for Oscar.

Had God, in fact, already provided the good luck she'd prayed for—ordained Oscar's rescue if she'd merely stayed the course—but she had just pissed that opportunity away?

She wanted to pound the steering wheel and kick the fenders and tear out her hair for being so impulsive. So fucking stupid. But that would steal even more time from her husband. As it was, he only had nineteen hours to live. And that assumed Deke would wait until tomorrow at the usual show time.

Choking down her self-loathing, she grumbled, "We better all get back to door-knocking. I'm returning to my part of the map. Sorry, honey, I—"

"It's cool, Mom. Faith and hope and love, right? You made us run through like, a fire drill—I mean, we had to figure out all kinds of important stuff on the fly. When it's the real fire next time, we'll totally know what to do."

"I love you," Bo told her, not caring about the men on the line, wishing she could reach through the phone to hug her daughter for such unconditional forgiveness.

"Okay. You, too."

Bo DIDN'T DISCOVER THE REAL FIRE, nor did the others. They all crossed properties off their list as people returned home from work. But when evening came on and then night descended, as Gus had predicted, few answered their doors. They'd generated no substantive leads.

At 10:00 p.m., they limped into the twin cities of Anniston and Oxford. Another of Bo's credit cards barely had enough to cover a room she could share with Candace and to reload the maximum time on their phones.

Her daughter had some funds available on her debit card. She insisted they stow the guns in their rooms, go to the chain restaurant next to the hotel, and get something to eat—her treat.

They slid into a booth, placed drink orders with the waitress, and flipped dispiritedly through the spiralbound menu. Bo stared at the bright colors and bold fonts, not wanting to make eye contact with anybody. A tall cup of water slid into view, but she couldn't summon the energy to drink. Failure felt like a lead blanket draped over her head.

"Earth to Mom, we're ordering. What do you want?"

"I'm not hungry."

"Give us a sec," Candace said to the waitress. She leaned her shoulder into Bo's. "Hey, news flash: if you don't fuel up, you'll be literally useless in the morning when we find Dad."

Randy growled, "Maybe I didn't eat enough beforehand. I've been useless up to now."

Bo looked up from the menu. "What?"

He rubbed his shaved head. "My maps didn't do any good. And my Stingray hasn't helped either. We had one shot at this, and I blew it."

"No," Gus said, "the fault is mine alone. I mistook activity for progress. I should've gone through all the properties on Randy's list the way I did with Charles Zonder's, narrowing the options to a promising handful."

She glanced from one man to the other, slumped side by side and appearing as depressed and exhausted as she felt. At least Candace hadn't joined in the self-flagellation.

These men, her friends, were wrong about failing. As the leader, she deserved the sole blame for this disaster. If she didn't exorcise their guilt, it could haunt them forever.

Fingering Mom's cross, she said, "Faith, hope, and love, right? They're what we started with and they're all we have now. For years—decades really—I thought I'd lost my faith. Not because I stopped believing, but because I stopped feeling that God could believe in me. This week seemed to have used up my reservoir of hope, too. Any little bit of progress has come at a terrible price. Only love—for Candace's father, for her, and for my friends—has kept me going.

"Well," she continued, "I've decided God, the Divine, whatever name you prefer, is more accessible if I have faith in myself. Likewise, hope comes from trust in my abilities, my intellect. If I believe in me, God will, too."

Randy said, "Hope isn't a strategy. And having faith doesn't mean we'll succeed, only that we can deal with whatever happens."

"Maybe so." She held his gaze and added, "But I think our chances for success are much better if we believe we'll do it. And the love that's at the core of this . . . this mission we're on—love for justice, for each other—will give us the inspiration we need to save Oscar."

Candace cleared her throat and announced, "Bathroom break."

She slid out of the booth with one hand tugging Bo, who followed, too tired to resist.

At the sink, Candace turned on her, eyes shining. "So, I bet you think you're like, the greatest actress of all time."

Bo dropped her satchel onto the counter and sighed. "What do you mean?"

"You literally didn't believe a word of anything you just said. All those…convictions, assertions . . . I mean, I saw them as lies coming from you. Manipulations. You were lying to pump them up, restore their morale or whatever. Really, though, you were speaking truths you don't trust yet. What's it going to take for you to see that?"

Bo looked her over, her little girl who'd changed into a self-possessed young woman, coming into her own seemingly overnight. "You know I can't see my own voice," she said.

She still hadn't confessed to her about no longer seeing anyone's. It didn't seem like the time to deliver more bad news.

"You're evading my question."

"When we get your father. When he's safe. That's when I can really believe again."

"And if you need to believe in yourself first, to make that happen?"

Bo touched Candace's beautiful face but couldn't reply.

# Chapter 63

A rattling buzz woke Bo in the dark. Unfamiliar sound, unfamiliar bed, smells, temperature, everything. After another moment of disorientation, she remembered she was in a hotel room in Anniston, Alabama. Or was it in Oxford? Their borders seemed to blend like Roswell and Alpharetta back home. She reached for the burner phone—an incoming call lit its screen. 5:08 a.m. Gus's number. He'd promised to call regardless of the time if anything new developed.

She rolled away from where Candace slept in the other bed and answered, whispering, "What's up?"

"A few matters: Deke is still using the RealBourne persona on social media—he's promising a live, 'monumental' event at noon Central on a streaming service he'll name at the last minute. That means two things, of course."

She dropped her voice even lower but couldn't keep panic out of it. "He's going ahead with murdering Oscar—the whole TBD thing is to make sure he doesn't get preemptively shut down by the site he'll use. He wants an audience."

"Regretfully, I agree. However, it also means we still have almost seven hours."

Tired of whispering, she crossed to the cold tiles of the bathroom, eased the door closed, and flipped on the light. "Right. Faith, hope, and love."

She'd worn the cross to bed again. Her finger that had healed from the knife cut now found one of the sharp corners, and she accidentally pricked the scab. Fingertip to her lips, she tasted blood there, a tiny bead that welled up against her tongue.

Blood on the cross, Oscar dying for her sins—the words and imaged flashes behind her eyes before she could stop them. They hurt much worse than reopening the wound.

Perhaps Gus heard something defeatist in her tone, because he went on in a hurry, as if to distract her. "This also tells us On-Air is not participating. According to their website, your show is no longer on the schedule, not even any 'Best of' segments. A music program is in your slot. And their Barracuda webpage has been taken down; no Wednesday recording was ever posted."

"Why didn't Jeff tell me all this?"

"It's possible he doesn't know. Perhaps Harry made the changes overnight."

"Or Harry fired him—no producer/director is needed if there are no more live shows, thanks to me quitting and getting Sean fired. Maybe Jeff was let go and didn't want to burden me with that right now."

How many lives had she ruined? This latest source of guilt sent chills through her. She draped a thin bath towel around her shoulders and huddled on the toilet seat.

"The other news is about Randy. He's gone."

"Where?"

"I don't know. He's not answering calls or texts. I flipped open the curtain in my room to check the weather, and I noticed his Jeep wasn't parked outside."

They were down to three searchers. Had Oscar's chances of survival dropped by twenty-five percent—or even more, because they also lost the opportunity to pinpoint Deke with Randy's Stingray?

She covered her head with the towel and wished the whole ordeal was over, one way or the other. "So much for my pep talk last night. Guess I shouldn't reinvent myself as a motivational speaker, huh?"

"May I say something that could sound a trifle harsh?"

"Um, go ahead . . . I think."

"In basic training, there was one drill instructor in particular whom I, and everybody else, hated. He had a single tone of voice—full-throated shouting—as well as no respect for personal space and a vocabulary that consisted almost entirely of curse words. In the barracks, after lights out, we'd fantasize aloud about the cruelest ways to torture him to death. However, in the years since then, whenever my spirits plummeted and I felt like quitting, his ugly, screaming face appeared in closeup and . . . motivated me . . . to keep going. And so I did."

Smiling, she pushed the towel back onto her shoulders. "That's the Augustus Trumbull version of harsh?"

"I did say, 'a trifle.'"

"Permission granted to speak plainly, soldier. Tell me to stop feeling so fucking sorry for my shitty self and get my goddamn ass moving so I can save my husband."

"Never."

She heard his gentle smile, his tenderness. "What if I need that kind of thing to motivate me?"

"Sounds like I succeeded without it, General."

They agreed to meet at 6:00 for breakfast, and she readied for the most important day of her life—and her family's—as quietly as possible.

Candace had brought their luggage in her hatchback. Bo had no more "lucky outfits"—not that the skirt-suit had brought her any good fortune—so she went with practical wear: blouse, jeans, and sneakers. The neckline was too low to hide the cross, but maybe its display would help convince a Good Samaritan to assist her when she went door-knocking again in a few hours.

She tapped the center of it and thought about her "believe in yourself" speech to Randy and how Candace had called her out for her hypocrisy. "You can do this," she told herself. "No, you *will* do this."

Her expression didn't match those words, so she imagined Gus's drill instructor shouting at her. She put on her no-nonsense game face: The Barracuda taking charge, ready for action.

The old joke about faking sincerity came to mind. She left the hotel room before she could talk herself into going back to bed and pulling the covers over her head.

Walking down the corridor, she sent Candace a text about meeting Gus for breakfast and then sent Jeff a text, too, reporting the status of their search. By the time she reached the dining area near the lobby, he had replied with the same "Hang on, baby" kitten he'd doctored previously, but, in addition to the Barracuda teeth, he'd added a magnifying glass in one forepaw and, in the other, a sewing needle that emanated bling rays. A deerstalker cap now perched on the cat's head. Nothing about whether her resignation had cost him his job. He would've denied it if she asked, so she replied with a half-dozen thumbs-up emojis.

Gus hulked over a dinette table with their annotated maps fanned out. He wore his rumpled charcoal suit and creased lavender dress shirt from the day before, having no change of clothes at his disposal. Dark bags smudged the skin below his eyes: sacrificing for her family, even though he'd only been in their lives for a few days. He must've been doing it for Oscar and Candace, because she certainly didn't feel worthy.

She said, "You didn't sleep? Not even one of your powernaps?"

His jaws tightened as he stifled a yawn. "I went through the properties we hadn't eliminated yet, cross-referencing the new owners of record with other databases, as I should've done before we started. Those flagged in yellow with the names written beside them are cases where the buyer is a man aged forty to forty-nine years old, in case Deke faked his birth year."

All that while she'd slept—as the leader, she should've been working harder than anybody, not resting. She turned the maps around to face her. Each one bore only a few addresses circled with a fluorescent highlighter. "These are the only potentials?"

"No. As you pointed out, Deke could've dealt with a homeowner directly instead of going through a realtor. However, this is the best we can do with our limited information."

"Thank you." She rounded the table and gave him a long hug from behind. "In three days, you've become a central member of my family."

He patted her arm. "You inspire that in others."

"Not even close." She returned to the other side of the table. "Candace called me a hypocrite last night for only giving lip-service to faith, hope, and love. And Randy saw through me as easily as she did—I guess he didn't want to risk himself anymore for somebody like me."

"Maybe he just couldn't bear the possibility of letting you down."

# Chapter 64

Candace joined them for breakfast, dressed like Bo in jeans and a blouse, hair still damp from the shower. She flipped through the annotated maps and forked up some scrambled eggs. "So, now that we know where he could be, how do we like, find out where he literally is?"

Gus nodded to Bo. She'd told him Candace would go right to the heart of their new dilemma.

She sipped her third cup of coffee. "Before you joined us, we started doing Google and social media searches on these guys."

"Looks like you scratched out, what, only six more so far?"

"Correct. It takes time." Gus gestured at his laptop, face lined with fatigue. "Not everybody uses Facebook, LinkedIn, and the like, let alone posts pictures of themselves."

Candace peered at a map and pulled the burner phone from her back pocket. After a minute of tapping and swiping, she held it out to Bo and asked, "Why'd you X this guy?"

"That selfie looks nothing like Deke. Even with those 200 extra pounds and a mullet, there should be some resemblance."

"So, all this guy did was post one selfie—and that was, like, two years ago. He doesn't have any other shots of himself, and his twenty-seven friends haven't tagged him in any pictures or posts. And twenty-seven, seriously? People in Witness Protection have more than that. You only stay at that low a number if you're, like, trying to fly under the radar. Plus, these people seem random—a bunch of different ages and races and a couple of them totally look like sex workers." She snatched up Gus's fountain pen and circled the owner's address several times on the map. "This could be the guy, hoping we'd fall for his lame-ass disguise."

Bo slugged down more coffee, kicking herself for once again leading them in the wrong direction and wasting more time.

"Better go through the others we crossed off, Sherlock."

While Candace double-checked their work, Gus and Bo resumed their online searches while keeping an eye on the time. 7:41. They had four hours and change to find Oscar. Not only couldn't they afford to have false-negatives—eliminating, as she'd done, someone who could've been Deke—but they also didn't have time to chase down a false-positive, where they were sure they'd identified Deke but turned out to be wrong.

"So, I think you nailed the other five—all of them deserve the X. What now?"

"All done. It's not surprising, but nobody we've seen looks like Deke." Bo had only two possibilities on her map, including Mullet Man.

"Hey, where's the Web Whisperer?"

"Gone."

Gus explained the situation while Bo grabbed two apples from a bowl near the cereal dispensers, wrapped them in napkins, and stowed them in her satchel. Her stomach reminded her that she hadn't eaten sufficiently since Monday. But it didn't seem right to do anything pleasurable in the few hours Oscar had left. He still suffered, so she needed to suffer, too.

When she returned to the table, Candace was saying to Gus, "So, we'll try to get a picture of each dude, to send to Mom's phone?"

"Correct." He gathered his map and Randy's and stood. "Basic surveillance, no risk-taking. If the man matches the photos he's posted, we can eliminate him from further consideration. No need to bother your mother with a verification."

"Mom, any like, distinguishing marks to check out: pointed ears, no chin, or whatever?"

"From what I remember of Deke," she replied, "he was maybe five-foot-ten and had an unremarkable face. His eyes were set close, and his nose was a little on the small side. His hair could be any color or length now, and he could be thin or fat. Not much to go on, sorry."

Gus said, "Still, those details are worth noting. No need to try to get a closeup if the face is too distinctive, or they're too tall or short. We can cross them off the list and move on."

8:03. Less than four hours left. They checked out of the hotel and hurried to their vehicles. As Bo's windshield wipers pushed aside the morning dew, she connected to the conference line, as did Candace and Gus. Soon, their caravan of three returned to I-20 and merged into the steady flow of traffic.

Her zone was nearest, so she exited first; the Google Map directions took her north. The first address in question bordered the Mountain Longleaf National Wildlife Refuge. She followed a winding road through forests and wilderness, with misty blue mountain peaks in the distance.

Fort McClellan was northwest of the Refuge, and the Coosa River wasn't far away, so the place felt perfect for someone like Deke. But she'd learned her lesson yesterday about praying for luck. Better to start believing the advice she'd given Randy, even though it had failed to motivate him. She needed to trust in herself and hope for the best.

"I'm coming up on 85 Wilmette Lane," she reported. "One of those Halloween homes with a long, long driveway. Looks like a ranch house. Beside it, there's a pickup truck under a freestanding carport." She paused at the base of the paved drive and looked for any useful details about the property, including the surrounding fields and woods. This far out in the country, there was a lot of nature to see but nothing distinctive. After a while, her eyes glazed over.

A side door near the carport opened. She jolted back to attention. A trim man exited the house, a ballcap obscuring his face. In each hand, he carried a bloated, dark green garbage bag. With some effort, he heaved one of them and then the other into the bed of his pickup.

Hoping he hadn't noticed her, she accelerated away. None of his neighbors had answered when she knocked yesterday, so she pulled into the nearest driveway, about fifty yards away. The bags had been the heavy-duty lawncare variety. Good for clippings, branches . . . body parts.

*Stop that*, she told herself.

"Mom?"

She projected toward the microphone. "Sorry, I had to move my car. A guy came out. Same compact build I remember Deke having, and he might be the right height—it's hard to tell from so far away. He tossed two big garbage bags into his pickup. Hold on. His truck is coming up to the road."

She lowered her voice the way Randy had done—he'd been right; it felt like the natural thing to do. Scrunching down in the seat and peering over the windowsill, she said, "I'm at a neighbor's. He stopped . . . he's getting out." The truck door opened, and the man hopped down. He turned before she could see his face. "He's reaching into the pickup bed. Okay, got it—he's just putting the bags into the cans beside his mailbox. It's probably trash day."

He glanced up the road at her car. She ducked below the sill and banged her knees against the steering column, but then sat up as she processed the man's face. "It's not Deke. This guy has wide-spaced eyes and a big, squashed nose." She watched the pickup head back toward the ranch house, thinking about yet more time she'd wasted. "Cross another one off the list."

Mullet Man, the only other possibility on her map, lived way south of I-20, near the enormous Talladega National Forest. She put the address into the map webpage and headed that way. While she drove down, Gus and Candace reached their first addresses and settled into stakeout positions.

By 9:00, she'd reached her destination, another of the properties where she'd failed to speak to any of the neighbors yesterday. This house was a McMansion: milk chocolate bricks, copper cupolas, enormous arched windows, and iron fittings everywhere.

As she searched for the best spot to surveil the place, her phone chimed: someone else had joined their conference call.

# CHAPTER 65

The fire in Oscar's hand now blazed through his entire right arm. Infection, gangrene, God knew what.

It had even spread to his dreams. In a recurring one about scuba diving in the Hidden Valley Reef off St. Thomas, where he and Bo had honeymooned, a six-foot fish rocketed out of a hole and seized his hand. He only woke after the monster had chewed its way up his arm, all the way to his shoulder, staring into his face the whole time with Bo's beautiful brown eyes.

Was this part of the plan, to drive him out of his mind with pain? Why not just kill him outright? What had he done to deserve this agony?

The last time he had talked to Bo, that'd been . . . Wednesday? Was it Thursday now? Impossible to know, unless his abductor told him.

If that guy was telling the truth about everything, then he was the one person who could help. Maybe he would.

The man sounded truly sorry for putting him through all this shit. And the blindfold was still in place. That had to mean something.

It seemed like he might come around and let him go based on some professional code. That'd be pretty funny, to come through their front door in Roswell—*Honey, I'm home!*—and see the look on Bo's face. He'd know instantly whether she was delighted . . . or pissed that she'd been thwarted by a kidnapper with ethics.

According to the man, Bo had wanted to be here to personally pull the trigger, slit his throat, or whatever. But she'd decided not to get her hands dirty.

Hard to decipher bullshit from truth when napalm seemed to coat every nerve.

*Think of Candace. Hang on, and you'll get to hug your Candy-girl again.*

The lock snapped open. He tensed—and then groaned as broken bones ground and crunched and fresh magma rippled through his hand.

Boots on carpet as usual, but no thump of the cleaning supplies box. Just silence.

"Hey," Oscar croaked, "wash-up time? Does she want to talk to me again?"

"Neither."

Another beat of throbbing quiet.

Nubs of something touched the sides of his face. Smooth nylon and sticky, textured rubber. Fancy gloves this time, not the usual latex ones. They smelled like that same oil from before—maybe gun oil.

He squeezed his eyes shut as soon as he realized what was happening. Thumbs grazed his temples, slipped under the blindfold. Pulled upward, slid the cloth over his forehead and onto his sweat-plastered hair.

For the first time in days, a light source turned the darkness to a pale gray behind his closed eyelids. Every moment he refused to see anything was another he might survive.

"Don't worry," the man said. "It's not time, yet."

Oscar shook his head.

"Honestly. I just didn't want you to go without having a look around first, to see what you've been missing."

His heart leapt as relief washed over him. He found himself smiling. "*Go?*"

"Sorry—euphemism. I don't mean you get to leave. Not physically, on your own two feet."

"Fuck." His heart continued to hammer, but relief turned to fear. "You mean you're really going to kill me?"

"Not me, remember. *She.* Your wife."

Oscar turned his face to the left, away from the man's voice, and kept his eyes shut. He tried to swallow but couldn't generate any spit. The pain in his hand and arm surged with each heartbeat. "When?"

"A couple hours. I started to feel sorry for you. You're the only person I've seen, except at a grocery store, in four days. And I'm the only person you've heard in all that time. I figured you'd want to get a look at me, check out your accommodations."

"How do I know you won't kill me—or at least hurt me—for opening my eyes?"

"Because I give you my word. Scout's honor."

He kept his right eye closed, in case the guy was lying, and eased his left eye open just a crack. It watered as blue-white fluorescent light flooded in. After a minute or so, his vision cleared. He saw a gray wall—not painted wood but something like carpet. Only a couple feet from his face.

Still turned to the left, he craned his neck to see what was near the top of his head. Nothing but gray, again a few feet away. With his eye rolled upward, he spied where the fuzzy walls joined and connected with an identical ceiling maybe seven feet above him, with small, dark vents pointed down.

He remembered when the guy had paced on the right side of the bedframe, just a few steps in one direction, then the other. The cot lay in the corner of a gray box. A fucking soundproofed coffin. Was this Bo's sick idea of a joke? She had to spend her life interviewing people in such a box, so she'd make him die in one?

Something light and soft dropped over his maimed hand, making him hiss.

"No reason for you to see the damage," the guy said. "I'm sure it's bad enough just feeling it." Oscar refused to reply. Sticky rubber fingers, dimpled like a golf ball, seized his chin and forced his head to swivel right. "Come on, man up. Look me in the eye."

Tears caused by the bright light dribbled across Oscar's face. He blinked a few times and stared at the guy.

A runt, like he remembered. Solidly built . . . but weathered. Prematurely old. His face showed deep lines and grooves, and his short, spiky hair was much grayer than Oscar's own.

The oddest thing about him, though, was his outfit. He dressed like a guy who got off on *Call of Duty* videogames: woodland-patterned camo pants, olive drab tee, the tactical gloves with their leather knuckles, a canteen hooked onto his canvas web belt, and a big, holstered pistol on his right hip.

Not nearly the monster his frightened mind had conjured. Just a guy playing soldier.

Oscar nodded at the camo bandana draped over his ruined, aching right hand and forced some bravado into his voice. "After you snuff me, you gonna join your buddies in the forest for some paintball? Then crack open a cold one and circle-jerk onto a batch of s'mores?"

The man grinned. "I'm going to miss your sense of humor. You cry like a girl, but you're funny as hell."

"For a while, you had me believing you'd let me go. Why the mind-fuck?"

"Up until yesterday afternoon, I planned to. But your wife doubled her offer, even said she'd do me again any way I wanted." He shrugged. "Sorry, I only have so much willpower. Don't worry, though, we'll be streaming live soon, and you can tell the world exactly what you think of her."

"You're going to kill me on-air, like you're some kind of fucking terrorist?"

"No, it'll be tasteful—and painless." He tapped his holster. "You won't feel a thing."

He swallowed hard. "Will I be able to say goodbye to Candace?"

"Absolutely. Maybe you can break your wife's influence over her. She's got the girl doing some freaky things since you've been away." He swiped his phone a few times and swiveled his gloved hand to display the screen.

As with the porn shot of Bo, Oscar couldn't un-see the photo, couldn't erase it from his memory. His only defense was to squeeze his eyes shut so he wouldn't be exposed to any more filthy images of his darling girl. It had to be a fake, right? The only certainty was pain.

"Yeah, it's twisted," the man said, "and that's far from the worst of them. Anyway, you've got some time to think about what you want to say to her. To your wife. You're probably not too happy with me either right now. But don't worry—my next visit will be the last."

# Chapter 66

For a moment, Bo thought Deke had somehow discovered the teleconference number and was calling to scare her. Then, Randy's gruff whisper came through: his stakeout voice. "Sorry I've been AWOL. I got up around 2:00 with an idea and had to check it out. Since then, it's been nothing but driving and fiddling with gear."

"We're pleased to hear your dulcet tones," Gus said. "What was your epiphany?"

"Deke's consulting business is like mine, IT and telecom, but he's almost twenty years older. I started wondering if there was some trick he had from back in the day, to make sure he couldn't be detected with a Stingray. I figured it out."

"Dude, did you find my dad or what? I mean, the suspense is literally killing me."

"I'm not a hundred percent sure—I haven't done triangulation in years. See, I woke up wondering if Deke had built his own 1G network. The FCC would never catch him at it because nobody really uses those frequencies anymore. And maybe, besides the burners, he uses an old analog brick phone, too. You can still get European bricks on the cheap. Those phones don't have an IMSI, so our modern simulators like the Stingray can't detect them. Instead, he uses an IP connection to link with a VOIP from his 1G network."

Bo said, "Let's pretend I understand everything you just said. How did you get a bead on him?"

"My second brainstorm was to use old tech to find old tech: ham radio. Those ancient brick phones aren't encrypted. By scanning the bands with my ham, I actually heard one of his conversations earlier this morning. He was using the voice synthesizer and talking to that guy Sean. Deke was threatening him, demanding a description of Gus."

"Wait," Bo said, "how does Deke know Gus is looking for him?"

"Your boss—former boss—apparently tipped off Deke that you were coming *with a posse*. And then Sean knuckled under and told him about Gus's visit."

While she silently cursed Harry, Gus said, "Also, I emailed the Adam Johnson address, back when we'd thought his Tom Brogan tip might be legitimate, so that made him aware of me in the first place. He'll be on the lookout for us now."

Candace said, "You mentioned like, triangles. What's that all about?"

"Triangulation, direction finding. My dad was a ham radio operator and got me into it when I was a kid. We hung out with a group whose hobby was 'fox hunting': tracking down the source of radio signals. I'm not equipped with everything I need to do it as reliably as they did, but I think I'm close. I ended up south of Pell City, not all that far from the Coosa River."

Bo looked at her map. "That's—"

"Off the reservation, yeah. You had the right instincts yesterday, to try farther out than I'd blocked off. If you'd gone south instead of north after you crossed the river, you might've stumbled on him."

"See, Mom, I told you to believe, even when you thought you were shoveling crap."

"Yes, ma'am." Adrenaline surging, she announced, "Let's all head to Pell City now, and then Randy can give us an address when he's pinpointed it." She set it as her new destination on Google Maps and started her engine.

Oscar had less than three hours, but she liked their chances now more than she had earlier. She squeezed the cross so the points jabbed her fingers and palm, reminders of faith and hope and love.

Randy continued to whisper. "The thing is, it's not like there's this big, flashing radio transmitter beacon I can point to and say, *Ah-ha, I found him*. My skills are rusty, and I don't want to waste more time and finger the wrong guy. How can we know for sure?"

Nobody contributed an immediate suggestion. As Bo drove through the country, she passed a few more homes, all different in their styles and sizes, but each with a mailbox at the roadside and one more thing in common: garbage in cans and bins, ready for pick up. She wondered what Deke could have in his garbage that would act like a beacon. He'd said something back when she could sort the truth from lies. . . .

"It's trash day," she said in a rush. "At least it is in this area—hopefully over there, too. Deke made a snide comment about having lots of Depends and Ensure on hand for Oscar, so he can hold him for a long time. It wasn't just a way to hurt me. I could see he was telling the truth. Randy, are you near a house?"

"I'm on the shoulder of the road, about twenty yards from a driveway. The house is set way back through some trees. I can't even see it."

"Are there trashcans?"

"Yeah, a couple of the old aluminum kind in a wooden rack."

Gus asked, "Can you take a quick look without drawing attention?"

"Okay, hold on." A jostling sound followed, as if he'd tucked his phone in a pocket. "Approaching the cans." The clattering sound of a metal lid being lifted away. "A few bags. I'm opening one. Hmm, microwave meal boxes, plastic water bottles, food scraps. Coffee grounds. I'll try another one. . . . No, just more of the same."

Gus said, "And the second can?"

"Wait—pickup truck coming." Tires on blacktop and engine roaring as the vehicle approached. A country song blared. Then all went quiet again. "Okay, now I'm checking out the second one. Oh my God."

"What?" Bo shouted as she conjured grisly visions of body parts again. She throttled the steering wheel as her heart seemed to stop.

"We hit the jackpot. It's just like you said, Bo. Plus, lots of latex gloves and wipes. Not a pretty sight—or smell."

"Hey, dude, that's my daddy's crap. You treat it like freaking gold."

Bo laughed and cried at the same time. Sniffling, she asked, "What's the address?"

"124 Cottonwood Lane." Lids clattered, followed by heavy breathing as he jogged back to his Jeep. "This property isn't on our maps. Deke must be renting directly from the owner."

She pulled onto the dirt shoulder, entered the new destination into the car navigation system, and noted the ever-advancing clock. 10:09 now.

*We're coming for you, Oscar. Just hold on a little bit longer.*

Candace said, "So, is this where all y'all go in with guns blazing to distract him, and I sneak up with my puny knife?"

"No," Gus replied, "this is where I call Agent Martinez and tell him where to find us."

"What?" Bo's joy turned to panic. "You said they'll be a lot more interested in grabbing you and Randy than setting themselves up for another ambush. Deke will have a front-row seat to watch the FBI haul us all away for questioning."

"They're the professionals, trained to handle hostage situations. If we go in, Oscar's chances—as well as ours—will be negligible. My apologies for such a dire prediction, but this is not the time for cowboying." He disconnected from the conference line.

# CHAPTER 67

"Shit!" Bo pounded the steering wheel and accelerated onto the interstate entrance ramp. By the time she reached the merge lane at the bottom, her speed had jumped to seventy-five.

Randy said, "Is there anything I should do until you get here?"

"Yeah," Candace said. "Make sure that pistol Gus gave you is cocked and locked and ready for me. Mom and I are totally cowgirling this."

Bo outraced a semi and swung into the left lane. In seconds, she flew past the exits for Anniston-Oxford, heading west toward Pell City. "Absolutely not. You're staying with Randy—y'all are our backup."

"*Our* backup? It sort of sounds like Gus left the party. I mean, you can't do this alone."

Two SUVs puttered along ahead. She whipped around them and retook the passing lane, saying, "I can and I will."

A sign along the shoulder provided the miles to reach the Talladega Superspeedway. She would've given anything at that moment to be driving one of those NASCAR rockets instead of a family sedan.

"Whoa. You're like, taking that trust-belief-confidence thing too far, too fast."

"I'm not going fast enough."

It seemed to take forever to reach the Coosa River bridge. Only a few fishermen plied the water. She remembered that Oscar used to love fishing. After his hand healed, maybe they'd rent a boat and spend a lazy week on Lake Lanier. The kind with a cabin, so they could drop anchor whenever they wanted and make love to the rhythm of the waves.

Her phone rang. She recognized Jeff's number on the display. Bad time to chat. She almost let him go to voicemail, but then remembered doing the same with Oscar and all the terrible things that had resulted. Jeff knew what she was doing; he wouldn't waste her time.

"Jeff's calling," she told Candace and Randy. "It has to be important. Back on in a sec." She dropped the conference line and answered, "Hey, can we make this quick? I'm kind of busy."

"You fall for the spoofed ID every time."

It took a moment to recognize Deke Powell's actual voice. No synthesizer—just ragged, deep, and hateful. The vise around her ribs tightened quickly and her muscles locked. She nearly steered into the concrete wall that separated her from a long plunge into the Coosa.

*So close. We came so close, but somehow he's onto us.*

She couldn't hang up and tell Randy to run to Oscar's rescue. Deke would probably kill them both. Barring swift FBI intervention, she needed to be the one to risk everything.

"H-h-how'd you get this number?"

"From my new pal Jeffy."

"There's no way he would've told you. How would you even get ahold of him?"

"The idiot had his personal info on old resumés all over the net. Good thing, because he wasn't at work—ol' Harry fired him late yesterday. Had no need for him after you quit and got Sean fired." He paused, as if to let her absorb the now-real guilt over getting Jeff axed. Then he said, "He traded your new number for a promise that I'll kill Oscar."

As she spluttered a reply, he talked over her. "You can see I'm telling the truth, right? If it's any consolation, this was my idea, not his. Harry warned me about you coming with a posse, and I figured you'd learned from my MO and got some burners."

Cold sweat raked her ribs. "You threatened Jeff, didn't you? Tricked him somehow."

"No need. You've never really understood guys. Yeah, I know, your special voice-reading and all, but that doesn't seem to show you shit about what motivates us. Sean told me how Jeffy panted after you. If you shared your new number with anybody, it'd be with your office husband."

He laughed as these blows rocked her and then continued, "I called him just now and proposed a deal: give me the ten magic digits, and I'd guarantee I would make you a widow. Somebody he could comfort—and one day slip it to—in her time of need."

*Was that all true?* He still thought she would see any lies, so he wouldn't bother bluffing.

Could Jeff be so easy to corrupt? Could she trust anybody now?

Fighting back another meltdown, she snapped, "What do you want?"

Cutting across two lanes, she shot up the ramp for Pell City and turned left, following the verbal map directions Deke could probably hear. Not that he needed those cues; he was undoubtedly tracking her phone.

He said, "I just want to save you gas and time. You're way off-course—Oscar and I aren't even in Alabama. Go home, watch the video with everybody else, and cash in on widowhood. I've even lined up your first date, though I hope you're both into hate-fucking."

"Go to hell, asshole."

"Yeah, I thought you'd say that. Allow me to put Oscar there first." A high-speed power drill whined near his microphone.

Hyperventilating, pulse pounding in her face, she swung into a service station and screeched to a halt. "No, no, stop it." She flung open the car door and lurched out, fighting for breath as the drill continued to howl.

She had ended up near the pumps. People fueling their vehicles looked over as she swayed in place. "Okay, you win," she shouted, and the drill sound died away. "If I head home, will you let him go? Remember," she bluffed, "I'll know if you're lying."

"Well, I did make a promise to Jeffy and my audience. Ethics are important."

A man climbed into his pickup. The engine growled to life, drawing her gaze to the blue palmetto tree and sickle moon of his South Carolina license plate.

She quick-stepped toward the truck. If the driver was headed north and east toward home, she could possibly buy Oscar a little more time. If he headed south in the direction of Pell City, she would quickly doom him. "I'm hanging up and turning around. Track me. When I pass Heflin, promise you'll let him go."

"What if—"

"Your address is 124 Cottonwood Lane. The FBI will be surrounding your house soon. Keeping Oscar alive is your only hope." The driver rolled toward the exit. She ran in pursuit, jeans stretching tight against her legs.

"Stay on. Let's keep talking."

"Never again." She disconnected and underhanded the phone toward the receding truck. It clattered in the bed. The driver made a hard left onto the highway, northbound toward I-20. She realized then that if he turned west on the interstate in the direction of Birmingham, that would condemn Oscar anyway. Even if the driver went east but Deke was determined to kill her husband. . . . Nearly every option ended the same way, now that the maniac was onto them.

*Damn you, Jeff. How could you do this to me? Why wasn't friendship enough for you?*

Angry and fearful thoughts pinballed in her mind as she hightailed it south.

She reached Randy's Jeep at 10:48, parked along a road lined with hardwoods and pines. Twenty yards ahead stood a mailbox and a wooden rack holding battered metal trashcans with the evidence of Oscar's captivity. Deke's drive—a pair of gravel ruts—disappeared among the trees.

Randy exited his Jeep, rubbing his shaved head. "We were worried that something—"

"Deke got my number, long story. My phone's in a truck hopefully going toward South Carolina." She gave him a quick hug. "Thank you. Oscar wouldn't have a prayer without you."

He squared his shoulders as if she'd just pinned a medal to his polo shirt. "It was your doing," he said, keeping his voice soft. "What you said at dinner about your belief in me, even after I'd steered us wrong. It made me try harder."

As he beamed, she felt her face heat up. She'd seen everybody else as contributing much more to giving Oscar a chance. For her part, she could only list her mistakes since Deke's first terrifying call on Monday. If they rescued Oscar, all that guilt should eventually fade away.

If they didn't, though—

He said, "Gus left a message with Agent Martinez but hasn't gotten a call-back."

"There's no time to wait. I told Deke the FBI is on the way, so he'd keep Oscar alive. Even if he knows I was lying, he'll guess that Gus is closing in." She scanned the nearby trees, wondering if Deke had mounted cameras somewhere and already seen them.

Candace came around the bend, followed by Gus, and pulled behind Bo's sedan. They all assembled even farther from the driveway, and Bo updated everybody.

The PI checked his watch. "We still have an hour before Deke's designated showtime."

"Thanks to Harry, Deke knows you're hunting him. We have to find a way in there now."

Candace said, "We're totally getting Dad with you."

"No," she replied. "For the last time, you and Randy are the backups."

Gus touched her arm. "You, too. I'm the only one with experience in these matters."

Candace sounded her lie-detector buzzer, and Bo said, "See? None of us has dealt with this situation. My husband's in danger, so I'm going. You'll have to shoot me to stop me."

"Yeah, no, you'll have to shoot me, too. And Randy." She nudged him. "Right, dude?"

"Uh, sure. If you want to go alone, um, I guess you'll have a bloodbath on your hands."

"I understand. Bo and I will—" His phone rang. He answered and then listened for a full minute. Without replying, he jabbed the disconnect icon. "The FBI's Birmingham office is coming for me. Coming for us all, actually. They have a plethora of strongly worded questions."

Bo gave Candace a hug and a kiss. "Call 911. Give them this address and tell the operator you were walking past and heard gunshots. Lots of them. And screams."

She removed the wood-gripped revolver from her satchel and tossed the bag in her car. *Hang on, Oscar. Deacon, I'm coming for you, too.*

# Chapter 68

Before Bo took two steps toward the twin gravel ruts that disappeared into the woods, Gus interrupted. "A suggestion, if I may?"

"Sure." She waited, fidgeting, the revolver already feeling heavy in her hand.

He tossed his suit jacket on the hood of his SUV, revealing the flat plates of body armor under his lavender dress shirt, and the Glock 19 in its black holster on his left hip. "We shouldn't follow the drive. He has demonstrated technical prowess and a gift for anticipation. At the very least, he could have cameras mounted along there. It's possible he's laid traps on that route as well."

She peered at the dense forest. "We go off-road?"

He displayed his phone screen: a satellite view of the property. The driveway snaked through a quarter-mile of timberland and led to a broad clearing, the green lawn enclosed by trees. From this overhead snapshot, the gray-shingled, rectangular roof was modest in size, so either the house had multiple floors or it was a simple, cabin-like construction. She counted on the former; after the Monday interview, Deke had threatened to kidnap Jeff's family members, saying, "The more the merrier down in my Vault." *Down*—he had a basement.

Gus pointed to the narrowest part of the forest. "If we go back along the road about fifty yards to where it curves in toward the property, we'll be close to the clearing and not walking through a potential shooting gallery or minefield."

"Whatever, let's do it."

"We have time. He's just tweeted again with his RealBourne account, promoting noon for the . . . event, with the link to be posted a few minutes before then."

"But any little thing could make him act sooner. We need to get there now."

Candace had dialed 911 and was vying for a best-actress award as she described the sounds of violence. Randy shook Gus's and Bo's hands and promised to stay connected to the conference line.

Bo pointed out a spot between two pine trees, and they advanced into the underbrush. The litter of fallen branches, clumps of leaves and pine needles, and saplings and bushes pushing up through the loam made each step a challenge. As they trudged deeper into the scrub, the spring canopy shaded everything, including the hazards underfoot. Their steps became even slower because she kept asking Gus to check the time on his phone.

11:10 became 11:14 and then 11:20. At last, they reached the clearing and chose a couple of thick hardwoods to shield them as they peered around the trunks.

Deke's rented house was built into the side of a hill. The twin gravel ruts emerged from the woods well to their left, climbed the slope, and ended at a closed garage door.

They faced the tallest side of the house, with three floors of brick and a few windows on each level shielded by Venetian blinds. The only apparent entrance was a double door set in the bottom. "Down in my Vault," Deke's synthesized voice had said. The basement.

When she pointed this out to Gus, he said, "It would be preferable to survey the entire exterior to determine the best choice of entry. However, time is of the essence, and it's likely we'll be observed. I count two cameras under the eaves. He undoubtedly has them at the other corners as well and possibly near every door."

"Is there a way to get across the clearing without being seen?"

"Not if he's watching the live feed. And thanks to Harry and Jeff, he's likely doing so."

"What if I draw his attention?" She pointed at the garage. "By the time I've run up there, he'll be on the move inside the house, planning how to intercept me. Maybe he won't see you go across the field. You can try the basement doors, or find another way in around back."

"You can't sacrifice yourself that way."

"I'm not planning to—I just want to draw him toward the front of the house."

He leaned against his tree for a moment, seeming to consider her idea. "Admittedly, you're the faster runner, and I have some experience with locks." He unholstered the Glock 19 on his left hip and cocked it. "Do you remember your firearms class? How to aim and shoot?"

"I think so." Aiming at the house, she recited, "See the target. Look through the front sight at it, and then focus on the sight, not the target."

"Excellent. With a revolver, you can thumb back the hammer for a lighter pull. If you just squeeze the trigger, the pull will be heavier. And remember that interior walls are easy to shoot through so, if he starts firing, seek cover behind the thickest thing around. Mere concealment isn't enough; it needs to be able to stop a bullet."

"I wish I had a bulletproof vest, too."

"That term's a misnomer. There are only bullet *resistant* forms of body armor. I'd give you mine, but it won't fit right—and the last thing you need in a dangerous situation is an encumbrance."

She glanced past the tree and plotted her route toward the hilltop. Then she asked for the time again. 11:31. She wanted to stay in this moment forever, with all her goals within reach: Oscar's rescue, the reunion of her family, the exorcism of guilt. Simultaneously, she wanted to wake up an hour from now, with whatever was about to happen already part of her past.

Gus joined the conference line with Candace and Randy. He put them on speaker.

Candace relayed her conversation with the 911 operator, who'd assured that deputies from the sheriff's office would be there soon to check out her "shots fired" story.

Randy said, "No sign of the Feebies or cops yet—not even distant sirens or choppers—so good luck and good shooting."

Only twenty-five minutes left, assuming Deke hadn't acted already. "Thanks," Bo replied. "We'll turn down the speaker volume, so you'll be able to hear us, but we won't hear you. I love you, hon. Don't worry, we'll bring your daddy out soon."

"Kick ass, Gus." After a pause, Candace added, "I love you, Mom."

The words made Bo feel warm all over. "I'm so proud of you." She took a deep breath. "You and Randy look out for each other. Talk to y'all shortly."

As Gus muted the phone speaker, she asked him, "Are you scared?"

"Absolutely. I hope you are, too."

"I'm terrified, but I'm even more frightened of letting Oscar down. And Candace." *And God*, she added to herself, and touched the cross again.

Instead of the surge of confidence she wanted to feel, self-doubt made her legs heavy and fear clouded her mind. Still, it was time. She gripped Gus's hand as if they were about to jump off a cliff together. "Thanks for everything," she told him.

He squeezed back and released her. "I look forward to you introducing me to your husband soon."

With the revolver pointed skyward, she filled her lungs, entered the clearing, and took off running. She didn't run for her life—she ran for Oscar's.

# Chapter 69

Bo sprinted across the yard. Not seeing the Venetian blinds part at any of the side windows, she focused on the under-roof camera at the front left corner.

*Can you see me, you bastard? Do you know what I'm going to do to you?*

The sun had burned away the morning dew and left the grass dry, with good traction. Her breaths puffed out in short gasps. Lungs burned, legs and arms pumped. She heard her sneakers slap the turf and felt the impacts all the way up to her face as she took the hill.

Near the top, closing in on the garage, she expected Deke to emerge at any moment. She banked right and went airborne, legs straight out so she could slide to the bottom floor. Her denim-clad butt hit the earth. She grunted and bounced but managed to hold on to the revolver as she sailed downhill on her backside.

By the time Gus lumbered up, she'd had time to check the solid basement doors. Locked. She leaned against the brick wall, panting, pulse thudding in her throat, and hoped she was out of view of the webcam mounted nearby.

No noises from out front. She couldn't hear anything except their deep breaths. Maybe her decoy plan hadn't worked.

He motioned for her to follow him around the corner to the rear of the house. The hill resumed back here. At the top, uncovered windows bracketed a solid white door with another webcam, and beyond stood a screened porch, which offered a separate entrance.

Gus peered through the nearest windowpane and jerked back beside her. "A broad hallway," he whispered. "No sign of anyone. I'll go back and pick the basement lock. Maintain a watch through this window and tell me if you see him."

Maybe she'd drawn Deke to the front of the house after all and he wasn't checking his camera feeds. She glanced at Gus's phone, which showed 11:45. "We're cutting it too close," she said and scurried around him. She tried the knob. The white door opened without a sound.

He looked alarmed instead of relieved and mouthed something she couldn't make out. She pointed the revolver down the corridor and noted multiple closed doors and branching halls. So many places to be ambushed. One of them, though, would lead to her husband. She choked down the impulse to yell his name.

Before she could enter, Gus pushed past her and swung his Glock two-handed, first one way, then the other. A reminder that their top priority wasn't to find Oscar—it was to keep themselves safe. She now understood his silent word of warning: "Trap."

Of course. Thanks to her, she'd funneled them into an even deadlier shooting gallery than the forest path would've been. And it was too late to retreat.

Her sneakers slid across the smooth hardwood floor. Gus swung into an intersection, whipping his pistol left and then right and stepped forward, surprisingly quiet in his wingtips. His bulk was such that she saw only fragments of the house ahead of him. She couldn't shoot if she needed to.

A noise—a creaking board? Her chromesthesia would've shown her what it was instantly. She tried to identify where it had come from.

Gus's open right hand swung out parallel to the floor. He pivoted around in a sudden turn. His arm swept her behind him as he aimed the Glock left-handed.

Her feet tangled, and she fell onto her tailbone.

A cannon fired. Or that was what the thunderous gunshot sounded like. Something she felt as much as heard.

The explosion of noise blurred everything as her eyes jiggled in their sockets.

Gus crumpled. He'd provided not only concealment but cover—the only reason she'd escaped being hit. Before she could scramble away, though, his crushing mass landed on her.

Air burst from her mouth, but she couldn't hear it or any sound he might've made. Her ears buzzed and rang.

Gus's head lay still on the floor above her immobilized left shoulder, his face turned away. His body smothered all of hers.

Trapped beneath him, her left hand was balled into an aching fist. Her right hand had dropped the revolver and struggled under his folded, elephantine leg. Only her head and neck had avoided being flattened between him and the floor.

She could not feel her friend breathing. Couldn't feel anything really.

With paralysis, though, came an odd stillness in her mind, a sense of being outside herself. Not an acceptance of her circumstances and certainly not peace—she knew she might die shortly—but an objectivity stripped of fear and every other emotion . . . except love.

Love for her husband, still in need of rescue. Love for her daughter, who would've heard everything through the phone. Love for Gus, who had sacrificed his life for her, and for Randy, who'd solved the mystery of Oscar's whereabouts.

And love for herself, at long last. Despite all her mistakes and conceits, her errors of commission and omission, she chose to have faith in her abilities, and to hope that she could still, somehow, make everything right.

The static in her ringing, buzzing ears quieted a bit, and everything seemed to slow down. She could only stare at the plaster ceiling. Pure white except for a stippling of small, rosy spots.

One of those dots dripped and divided in two. Half formed a smaller bead against the ceiling while the other half curled into a perfect sphere of red and descended toward them. As she followed its progress, her field of vision lowered. A trim figure stood at Gus's feet, a matte-black shotgun aimed down at them. The droplet skimmed his olive drab t-shirt at his right pec and skittered down to his flat stomach until it had used itself up in a crimson gash.

Her gaze swung back up to await another fall of blood but stopped when they reached the man's face. Deacon Powell.

He'd aged badly. Spiky hair gone gray beneath his shooter's ear protection, crosshatched lines and furrows cut deep into his face. Stronger-looking, to be sure, wiry as if from a military-style workout regimen—but more haggard than he should've been at forty-five.

Deke stared back at her. She wondered what he saw. Or who. Was he seeing her as she was now, his age and showing signs of her own decay? Or did he see her as she was at twenty, his for the taking at last?

He pointed the black shotgun at her face. "Feeling helpless?" he asked.

Through her plugged-up ears, she could hear his disturbing mix of hatred and lust.

And, in her mind's eye, she saw spikes of mottled brown and red flame tips in front of the plum-colored background—as dark as a bruise—that she remembered from half a lifetime ago.

He smiled, deepening the grooves in his face. "You look like a butterfly pinned to a board."

That was exactly how her body felt. Mentally, though, she saw his signature colors and shapes again and reveled in the return of the chromesthesia, even if the last images she saw were from his voice.

His gloved, leather-knuckled hands dipped down, and he aimed at Gus, which gave her hope her friend was still alive. Deke seemed to deliberate about whether to shoot him again.

"Don't," she said. "Please."

"Yeah, I was just thinking about how I'm leaving all these messes for the owner to clean up. A renter should be more respectful, right?" Golden swirls of amusement, like thin, curly ribbons. He leaned the shotgun against the wall and unholstered the large, nickel-plated pistol from his right hip. The muzzle pointed to her left, at Gus's head. "This will be neater."

"Leave him and Oscar alone. Do whatever you want to me." She swallowed and tasted blood. Either she'd bitten her tongue, or she was bleeding internally from Gus's crushing weight. "I'm all yours. Take me instead."

"No. You'll never be mine. And I never wanted you this way. Not really. I always thought we could be together, as a couple. Even after what happened to Lori. Use that power of yours—you know I'm telling the truth."

The thought of him still harboring such fantasies repulsed her more than if he lusted after her broken body. Somehow, though, maybe she could use that perfect pearl, his delusion.

"Make it quick," she gasped. "If you really do love me, don't let me suffer."

"You mean the way I've suffered? You ruined it all." Grief swirled yellow over the plum background. "I didn't want to kill you, or Oscar, or anybody. You were just supposed to be punished for what you did to me, to my life. I couldn't have a family, so I destroyed yours. That's where it was supposed to end, but now—"

He checked his military-style wristwatch. Then he studied her.

*Buy time, no matter the cost.* She thought about what he'd done to Lori. Squirming, she pleaded with her eyes and elongated her neck.

"But now I have a few minutes to improvise," he said with pulses of blue and gold excitement, "before the big moment in front of my audience."

He holstered the gun, yanked off his gloves, and tossed them aside, along with the ear protection. His pale hands clenched. He stepped forward, boots spread wide around Gus.

Squatting low, he fingered the cross pendant and grazed her skin with damp, cold knuckles. "Looks like you found Christ. You two can hang out and welcome Oscar together."

Deke twisted the chain around in his grip, knuckles under her chin. The links dug into her abraded throat again, but much deeper this time. He curled his wrist, tightened his bicep, and strained upright. The necklace throttled Bo as he slowly pulled her body from beneath Gus, choking the life out of her.

# Chapter 70

Bo strangled on Mom's gift. Her fingers seized Gus's right ankle as she tried to hold herself in place. Heartbeat pounding in her ears, she prayed for the chain to snap. It didn't.

Deke slowly hauled her upward. With his free hand, he touched her hair, her face. His fingers were frigid and waxy against her skin. "Oh," he sighed, red flame tips rising higher, "so soft."

She got stuck under Gus's bulk, and Deke clamped his straining wrist with his other hand. He grunted, teeth clenched, and continued to pull her free.

The crushing pressure around her neck forced her mouth open as she fought for breath. Her vision darkened at the edges and soon narrowed to twin portholes within blackness, focused on his gritted teeth, lips pulled back in a snarl, face now flushed with effort. Sounds ebbed as well, until she only heard the wet crackle bubbling from her throat.

A gunshot penetrated her fogged mind. Muddy browns and greens flared behind her eyes. The noise was so distant, it seemed to have come from outside the back door she'd left open.

"Put her down, fucker." Candace's voice, that glorious seafoam backdrop with crimson thorns bursting from it.

As if looking through the wrong end of binoculars, she glimpsed only a small portion of his rosy cheek and ear as he turned his head. Looking over his right shoulder, he shouted, "You put the gun down. Or I'll kill her."

Her hand had lost its hold on Gus's leg but came away with something narrow and firm, a ring-patterned handle made to be gripped. With her last bit of strength, she swung her arm upward and tried to punch the side of his face with whatever it was.

She missed. Her jab was too low. Instead of pounding the object against his cheekbone, she failed to even reach his jaw. But something warm and wet jetted over her hand, and he shrieked. His alarm looked like fuchsia pinwheels. The noose cutting off her air eased at once.

Her vision expanded as breath returned. Hot, scarlet blood coated her fist. She'd buried Gus's fighting knife into the left side of Deke's neck. Mewling, he flailed at the weapon, which only drove the blade deeper. His cry became a gurgle of pus-colored squiggles.

"Let her go," Candace yelled. Another gunshot, with more bruised colors.

His strength waned as Bo's surged. She continued to dangle in his hands, but the pain now centered near the base of her skull, where the chain cut deepest.

If he released her and she maintained her hold of the knife, she'd fall backward and tear out his throat. By keeping her suspended, Deke was buying time, just as she had.

He weakened, descending until he straddled Gus and loomed over her. As his stamina failed, his right arm straightened. He lowered her slowly, almost gently, back to the floor.

Around the chain, his fingers relaxed and fell open, limp against her neck.

With her chin tilted down, she could make out her mom's cross. *Now my cross.* The gleam of white gold, untouched by blood, lay atop the lines that etched his wax-paper palm. Its shape was stamped into his skin. The hand that had been his instrument of murder, that had wreaked havoc in so many lives, looked as forlorn as a discarded glove.

His eyes rolled as he tried to look at her, but she kept her arm extended, knuckles against his jaw, forcing his face away. The eyes stilled and fixed on a point above her head.

Now she held *him* upright. She shoved her gore-coated fist against his neck but kept her grip on the knife, liking how it felt in her hand. The blade tore free of him with a final spout of blood and a ripping sound that jetted lemon streamers across her mental canvas. Deke's body toppled sideways and slumped beside the wall.

"Gus needs help," she croaked. She wriggled the rest of the way out from under him. "Hurry!" Her voice sounded like she felt.

Coaxing her numb legs into action, she kneeled above her friend. Blood soaked his lavender dress shirt, but she couldn't tell if it was his or Deke's or both. She shook her left hand to wake it up and pressed her fingers to Gus's clammy neck. Maybe a weak pulse. Best to remain hopeful.

When she checked Deke's wrist, she felt nothing. In every respect. Maybe a better Christian would have regretted the need to kill him, and perhaps she'd feel remorse and guilt later. Thinking about what he'd done to her family, though, put her in a wrathful, Old Testament mood.

Candace dashed down the hall, the small pistol Gus had given Randy at her side. She looked at the scene and skidded to a halt. In a little-girl squeak Bo hadn't heard in years, she asked, "Mommy, are you okay?" Cobalt rippled atop seafoam.

"Better than Gus. Do you have your knife?"

Candace set the gun down and patted her jeans pockets. Her chin still trembled. "Yeah, but—" She pointed at the dripping blade.

"I need this in case your dad's tied down. Cut off Gus's shirt and the body armor and press the cloth down hard against any bullet holes."

"Okay, got it." Emotions under control again, her daughter turned her back to Deke's body and went to work with the tactical knife. "Randy's still by the road, so he can direct the cops and everybody. We literally heard everything through Gus's phone, and I guess I sort of kneed his balls so he'd give me the gun."

"I'm glad you got here when you did." Bo staggered upright, sneakers squishing, as sticky with blood as the rest of her. A thousand needles jabbed her thighs and calves as circulation resumed. Her entire body felt like one bone-deep bruise, front and back. A circumference of pain radiated from her gouged neck, but she didn't want to take off her cross. Ever. The pendant had nearly killed her, but ultimately, it had enabled her to survive.

Candace sliced through a seam in the body armor, which bore a large hole in front, and pulled it away. The shotgun slug hadn't penetrated completely, but it'd still caused massive trauma to Gus's chest. Blood welled immediately from the baseball-sized wound. With a gasp, she jammed his wadded dress shirt against it.

"Keep the pressure on it until help arrives." Bo swallowed to ease the pain in her throat. "Thank you for saving my life."

"Thanks for saving Daddy. Go get him."

Bo used the wall to brace herself and hobbled back toward the entrance through which Deke had lured her. At the intersection of halls, she glanced in one direction at a den. The other way led to a room with a long table where he'd put a row of laptop computers and towers of what was probably telecom gear. On the wall and floor behind his setup were scraps of paper. The shreds still taped to the wall appeared to be from photos of her: screen captures from the program. In some instances, the left side of her face had survived, headphone over her ear, one brown eye, half a mouth. Other remnants showed only her right side. It was like looking at herself in the shards of a shattered mirror, like glimpsing Deacon Powell's mind.

Shivering, she limped farther down the corridor and noted one door now ajar instead of flush against the wall. Through the gap, she spotted wooden stairs descending to the basement.

A tablet computer lay on the top step. It displayed a screen split into multiple rectangles, providing the monochrome view from different cameras. One pointed at the gravel ruts that led up to the house. A gray sheriff's car and white ambulance emerged from the forest and jounced along the uneven path, lights flashing but without sirens. Still no sign of the FBI.

Flush with a new adrenaline surge, she hurried down despite the aches from every part of her body. Her jeans felt wet and heavy against her legs, soaked with drying blood. She trotted past gun cabinets on one side of the room and lawn equipment in precise rows on the other, and an alcove holding the water heater and furnace.

Her journey ended at another door. This one was built into the long side of a giant box. Solid wood, like an old-fashioned sea chest.

The Vault.

From Deke's comments, she knew she'd find Oscar alive, but in what condition? Would he wish he were dead? Would it have been something of a blessing—for him, for her, for everybody—if Deke had granted that everlasting relief from his tortures?

She held her breath and flipped open the deadbolt knob left-handed, the grisly knife still gripped in her right. The door made a sucking sound from a rubber seal as she pulled it outward. She squinted in the glare of fluorescent lights overhead. Gray carpet, gray walls, gray ceiling, soundproofed like a tiny version of the On-Air studio.

Peering in, the bottom half of the cot came into view first: bare feet, ankles duct-taped to the bedframe, sweatpants she didn't recognize. The smells hit her as she had to inhale—a miasma of blood and rot, sweat and urine—and brought tears of heartache and revulsion.

*Poor Oscar.*

Before she could say anything or even step into the tiny room, he shouted in a hoarse, hysterical voice, "No, don't do it. You don't have to listen to her. Whatever she's paying you—"

She hurried inside, breathing through her mouth to avoid gagging. "It's okay, it's me."

He lay with his arms taped at his sides, right hand draped with a camo bandana, torso clad in a matching sweatshirt, dark with perspiration. A sleep mask lay atop his black hair, which curled in greased ringlets. His beard had grown thick on his oily face and neck.

Oscar's eyes widened as he stared at her. Then he began to scream.

# Chapter 71

Oscar's wild cries nearly blinded Bo with the same shapes and colors she'd seen when Deke was torturing him—a firestorm of purples, pinks, and brick-red arrows. Now she was the cause—and maybe she had been all along. That thought broke her heart while his terrible stink choked her. The weight of the blood coating her skin and soaked into her clothes made it hard to stay upright.

Deke's final revenge: the bastard had made sure that even if she'd somehow rescued Oscar, he would be lost to her anyway.

She wanted to curl into a ball and give in to her own pain, but he still needed her help, even if he didn't understand that.

His insane shrieks continued. She yanked the door shut so Candace wouldn't hear him, locking the sickening odors in with her.

Over his full-throated uproar, she yelled, "You're safe. He can't hurt you anymore."

"Get away, get away." He thrashed against the duct tape, which made him scream even more pitifully. "Why this? I never did anything to you. Why kill me?"

She wanted to make her voice gentle, but he shouted so loudly, she had to do likewise to make herself heard. "Hold still. I just need to cut you free."

He bucked and keened, like an animal about to be slaughtered. His fear and fury pummeled her like fists.

She tried to imagine herself as he saw her: the fighting knife crusted red, her skin and clothes all bathed in gore. Much more of a monster than Deke had probably ever looked like.

What most frightened *her* was his bandana-covered right hand. The left one clenched in an angry fist, but otherwise it looked fine. Deke must've done all the damage to the right.

Better to release his legs first.

She held down his twitching left foot and sawed through the thick bands of tape at his ankle. The blade performed well despite the blood. Only a few black hairs tore off when she peeled the tape from his olive-toned skin, but he howled with panic anyway.

Before she could start to work on the other ankle, his freed foot lashed out. He kicked her ribs. Not hard—his leg was probably numb—but her bruised body felt tender everywhere, and she yelped.

Gasping for breath, she pivoted along the edge of the cot, out of range. His rant devolved into vile curses. Hot, barbed colors overwhelmed her mental canvas.

He was out of his mind with pain and fright. She told herself this over and over, to block the hatefulness he directed at her.

At last, she cut his right ankle loose and stepped back. Just in time. The foot swung up, and his bare toes barely missed her chin.

He ran out of words and launched into mindless wails, kicking at her with both feet, banging his shoulders and head against the mattress.

She moved alongside his right hand. Her ears, still stuffy from the shotgun blast, rang anew as he continued to bellow. His wild eyes looked like Deke's had when the maniac was dying.

Oscar wouldn't hear any reassurances over his shouts. All she could do was show him tenderness and love to calm his frenzy. So far, it wasn't working.

She nudged aside enough of the camo bandana to see the tape. As she worked with the knife, he writhed even more. The bandana fell away.

Deke had caved in the entire back of Oscar's hand. Black, green, and purple, the wound seeped pus and fresh blood from his frantic movements. Scarlet ringed the area, and darker tendrils colored his tanned skin where the infection had spread from hand to wrist and upward toward his elbow. Crimson flecks peppered everything, including his two smallest fingers, which bent away from the others at sickening angles.

She bit her lips to keep from crying out. Bile rose in her throat, but she managed to choke it down.

His arm shook, and his thumb and unbroken fingers twitched while she sawed through the bond. Afraid he'd punch her despite the horrible injury, she leapt back as soon as the tape split.

Instead of attacking, he rolled away, left arm still secured to the cot, his broad back to her. Sweat had soaked through the heavy shirt and the bare mattress beneath him. He tucked his devastated hand to his chest and curled up his legs like an infant. Wracking sobs, in waves of canary yellow, replaced his shouts.

He probably wouldn't let her near him again. Candace, the paramedics, or the sheriff's deputies would need to finish the job. She returned to the foot of the cot, so she could at least see his profile. The soft, gray walls propped her up.

When she tried to release the blade, it wouldn't fall. Deke's blood had glued her fingers to it. She needed to pry them apart with her left hand and rip the handle from her palm, which was caked with congealed slime. Finally, the weapon dropped onto the carpet. Once freed, her cramped fingers curled again, as if seeking the reassuring, ring-patterned grip.

At least Oscar was safe now. Thank God.

*And thank You for Gus.* She prayed to please let Gus live, too. Without his knife, maybe Deke would've murdered her and everybody else by now.

Her husband trembled and cried, no doubt from the pain and lingering horror. She joined him.

The door scraped open. "Mom?" Candace called. "Ugh, that smell. Wha—" She looked from Bo to Oscar and began to cry as well. Her jeans and blouse were black from the blood they'd soaked up.

She tried to go to her father, but Bo held her in the doorway, scared he would blindly lash out. Through her tears, Candace shouted, "Daddy, it's me. Daddy!"

As she struggled harder, Bo's strength failed. Her daughter broke free and dove for his cot. All Bo could do was yell, "Watch out, he's hurt. It's his right hand."

Spooned behind him, Candace embraced his shoulders and pressed her face to his grime-coated neck. They rocked together that way for what seemed like an hour.

Bo wanted to join them, but she feared Oscar's reaction. All she could do was lean against the wall and hug herself.

Two St. Clair County deputies—an older man and a young woman—clomped down the stairs, followed by a pair of male paramedics with a stretcher between them and medical kits slung across their shoulders. Bo staggered out of Deke's Vault and tried to explain the blood that had shellacked her skin and made her clothes as stiff as cardboard. "Oscar, my husband—"

The senior cop nodded. "We know. Candace told us everything."

She said, "His right hand's a mess, and he's traumatized, so be careful. He seems to be okay with her, but he was violent with me."

Oscar's prison barely held two people, let alone a crowd, so the EMTs set the stretcher down and carried their kits inside. Bo leaned against the alcove entrance, near the female officer. Her male counterpart stood at the threshold of the Vault, blocking it.

Bo asked the junior deputy, "Did Gus make it?"

She said, "I'm not sure. The first crew took him away—he was bad off, so they couldn't get to your husband, too." She hooked her thumbs on her belt. "These guys came—"

Oscar started to yell again. Bo nudged the male officer aside so she could see. Candace had wedged in between the head of the cot and the gray wall. She begged her father to cooperate with the paramedics, who were trying to roll him onto his back.

He pulled himself into an even tighter ball. The men shouted over him that they needed to tend his wounds and cut away the remaining tape.

Candace gripped his sleeve. "I won't leave you, Daddy. I'm here. Let them take care of you. Then we can go home." She glanced up, looking anguished and uncertain.

Bo could only nod encouragement, worried her voice would send Oscar on another rant. What the hell had Deke done to brainwash him?

He continued to face the wall but eased his right arm back toward the paramedics. His nightmarish hand spasmed. Candace shrieked and covered her mouth.

The EMTs gave Oscar a shot, explaining it was for the pain and to calm him. After he became more docile, they packed the wound, bandaged his hand, and splinted his fingers. Hopefully, the hospital doctors would repair his physical injuries. But who could heal his mind?

They cut him free and peeled the tape from his left wrist. Dozens of black hairs tore away as well, but he didn't flinch. At last, he was in a place where his agonies couldn't reach him. The men cleared Bo and the deputies from the doorway, so they could bring the stretcher through.

Upstairs, agents from the FBI announced their arrival.

The deputies returned to the first floor while Oscar was hefted into place. He said in a slow, sleepy voice, "Love you, Candy-girl. Knew you'd save me. Don't do any more photos for your mom, okay?"

Candace turned her face away, cheeks scarlet.

Bo scrambled around the side of Deke's Vault to hide from Oscar as they carried him out. No point in setting him off again. His left hand gripped Candace's right like he never wanted to let go.

Watching them go, Bo wondered whether he'd ever welcome herself again.

# Chapter 72

In downtown Atlanta, Bo strode through the bustling hospital lobby. She headed toward the elevators, heels clicking and skirt brushing her legs. In the two months since Oscar's rescue, the institutional layouts, smells, and sounds of such places had become as familiar as the On-Air Web Radio office and studio once had been.

"Hey, Bo," a man called to her left. "Um, how are you?"

She saw the background, the green of a leaf backlit by the sun. *Jeff.* She identified him even before the sound of his voice really registered. His uneasiness showed itself in flat disks of ice-blue.

Though she was tempted to keep walking, she'd known this moment would come one day. Might as well get it over with. Her right hand curled around the imaginary ringed grip of Gus's fighting knife. A habit she'd found herself doing more and more, whenever she needed to feel empowered.

She turned his way and paused. If she hadn't heard—and seen—his voice, she wouldn't have recognized him.

He approached her with tentative steps, his spine stiff, shoulders back, dressed in what he probably considered formal attire: blue sports coat, starched white dress shirt open at the neck, pressed khakis, and tasseled loafers. He'd shaved off his mustache, which made his pale upper lip appear vulnerable. His other trademark—the gold-framed glasses—had gone as well. He must've switched to contacts.

Without the constant reflections across his eyes, she noticed they were a lustrous hazel. He peered at the scar on her neck, which she had not repaired with plastic surgery, and, below this, took in her cross before meeting her gaze again.

It irritated her that such a disloyal person looked so much better after his betrayal, instead of suffering for it. "I'm fine," she lied. "You?"

"Oh, me, too . . . uh, couldn't be better." A rainbow scarf tangled on itself. Apparently, he was suffering on the inside, which made her feel good—but then she felt bad about that.

He waited until an orderly passed by and closed the gap to a few feet. She caught a subtle, pleasing scent of cologne—no more strong, woodsy aftershave, either.

"Is Oscar better?"

"Physically, somewhat. How'd you know I would be here?"

"Well, you changed your cell number and email, and I didn't want to be weird and show up on your doorstep—though I guess I could've sent a letter."

"So, you've been following me around, learning my routines. Just like Deacon Powell. Nothing weird about that."

"Hey, not for any stalker-y reasons, nothing sinister. I just want to talk to you and . . . I miss you is all."

A flicker of the old flame tips. Not everything about him had improved. She opened her hand so she'd stop thinking about how good that knife would feel, what it could do.

*Forgiveness*, she reminded herself, touching her cross. *You pray for it, you listen to sermons about it. Time to practice it.*

She said, "If you came to apologize, I accept. Your conscience can be clear." He smiled and relaxed his shoulders, so she quickly added, "But we can't be friends anymore. You sold me out to Deke."

As he started to defend himself, she talked over him. "I got my color-hearing back, so be careful what you say."

"Look, I'm really sorry." He touched his temple, as if trying to adjust his old glasses, and then stuffed his hands into his pockets. "Fuckhead caught me at a low point. Panzer had just fired me, and it seemed like, even if you did manage to find Oscar, you were going to get killed along with him. He promised me I could at least save you."

She remembered Deke's remarks about Jeff and his grieving-widow fantasy. "To be precise, you mean you wanted to save me *for you*."

Face and neck reddening, he said, "I wasn't myself, okay? The consequences only sunk in later, when it was too late. I don't want forgiveness; I want to make it up to you."

She saw that he believed everything he told her. "But there's nothing I want or need from you."

"I read about that TV interview-show you'll be doing. You know I'd be perfect as your director. For my penance, I'll waive my salary for the first dozen episodes. If you don't think I'm qualified, there's plenty of time for me to meet with the producers and prove I've got the chops."

"No. I made a mistake at On-Air, discounting the warning signs and even using you to boost my ego and make me feel better about myself. That blurred the line between friendship and something more. I know it must've confused you, and I apologize for *that*."

"We've always been just friends," he said. "And you're bringing other friends on board. I saw y'all hired that lady who worked on our floor, the one you introduced me to a year or so ago."

"Kathryn Robertson. She's a terrific writer and researcher, and she beat out dozens of other candidates without any politicking from me. If she doesn't work out, or if she gives me up to a maniac bent on destroying my family, she'll get the axe."

Jeff put up his hands in surrender. "I never wanted to see your family destroyed. You don't know how happy I was after you saved Oscar and everything."

All true, she noticed—unless he'd suddenly become delusional. Perhaps she owed her former office husband a minor concession, and a confession. "You and I did good work together, and we had fun. I'll miss you."

"You don't have to miss me—I'm right here." He pulled at the cuffs of his dress shirt and squared his shoulders. "Give me another chance?"

She shook her head. "I'm sorry you got all dressed up for nothing."

"Yeah, no, this?" He waved a hand at his ensemble. "I'm, ah, I'm meeting a woman for lunch. It's kind of a date. But about us—"

She mustered a parting smile for him. "Good luck to you, Jeff. And goodbye."

# CHAPTER 73

Bo stepped off the hospital elevator, traded nods with the ICU charge nurse, and headed toward the patient rooms. The encounter with Jeff had not been as horrible as she'd envisioned, and it put her in an expectant mood for her daily visit. Her pilgrimage.

She tapped on the door to number 753 and waited. Most often, she found Gus asleep or only able to talk for a minute. On those days, she would sit vigilantly at his side and leave a note, telling him again of her eternal gratitude.

"Enter." Though his voice was weak, she saw the rich French toast backdrop and navy-blue swirls of anticipation.

Pushing open the door, the odor of rubbing alcohol and other disinfectants greeted her. She tried to suppress the shudder that swept through every time she saw the man who'd nearly died for her. To whom, along with Randy, she and her family owed everything, forever.

Thanks to Deke, Gus was the one trapped in a kind of Vault now—but with tubes and catheters holding him in place instead of duct tape. Rather than sound-absorbing walls, her friend was surrounded by machines on carts and monitors attached to swivel-posts that descended from the ceiling. Even the monotonous, drab color palette of the room—beige instead of gray—seemed to box him in.

His pallor echoed the paint scheme, and the massive hospital bed with footboard and siderails seemed to diminish his physique.

Gus pressed a button to elevate his upper half. That dull rumble and the periodic noises from the machines produced technicolor spatters of shapes that she found hard to filter out.

He said, "You look well." His typical waves of friendly, respectful green and gold.

"And you're looking and sounding much better," she replied and forced a wide grin.

"Were Candace here, she'd make her buzzer sound."

That coaxed a sincere smile. "It was only a slight exaggeration. Please forgive me."

*Please. . . .*

Fingernails pressed into her palms, she commanded herself to stay strong for him.

As if he'd read her body language as clearly as she saw his voice, he said, "You don't need my absolution. Had you not fallen for Deke's trap by going through the unlocked door, he would've allowed me to break into the basement and then shot me from his perch on the stairs. Perhaps the slug would've gone high and removed my head. In the hallway scenario, had I not moved you behind me, his round would have torn through your body and either killed or incapacitated me as well. You're a remarkable person in most respects, Bo, but your physical stature offers scant cover. The present situation is the best of all likely outcomes."

The little speech—so typical of him before—seemed to drain his reserves now. He coughed a few times, groaned, and placed a hand on the covers that overlaid his chest.

She rushed to his bedside. From a table, she fetched his water cup and brought the straw to his chalky lips. She remembered Oscar's stories about Deke doing the same for him.

Thanking her, Gus fell back. He set his jaw and focused straight ahead, like he was trying to gather his strength.

She didn't want to make him self-conscious, so she sat beside the table and inspected her hands. Her nails had stamped half-moons in the skin. Impossible not to think of Deke's wax-paper palm, and the outline of her cross that he'd crushed into it.

A succession of images followed, always the same: a lake of blood, Gus's fighting knife clenched in her hand, Candace hunched over him and pressing on his chest as if trying to dam the gates of Hell, shreds of her face in photos taped to the wall, Oscar insane with fear and pain as he bucked against his restraints in the Vault. Over and over again.

As lucid and painful as the recollections were, they never lasted long. Her prescriptions for depression and anxiety saw to that. The images soon slithered back down their grates in her mind.

Gus continued to stare off. No doubt he had even more effective medicines to keep his suffering and horrors under control. She touched his arm atop the covers. "Rest. I'll sit with you awhile and be back tomorrow, the usual time."

"No, I believe I've rallied," he said, and she could see he meant it. He pointed to her neck. "The TV show . . . they're okay with your determination not to get cosmetic surgery for it?"

"This is who I am now. When I interview survivors, people who've overcome, I won't ask them to hide their own wounds—inside or out."

"Will you miss The Barracuda sobriquet?"

"No need; she'll always be part of me." She gave him another sip of water and set the cup back on the table beside the issue of *Time* she'd brought him earlier in the week with her image on the cover: game-face closeup, scars still raw on her throat, her cross shining in the V of her blouse. Beside her image was the title she'd suggested: "Watch What You Say."

The article, planning the TV show, and her agent's ongoing negotiations for book and movie deals had provided useful distractions from her endless fixation about her family almost being destroyed and nearly losing her own life. Along with having to end Deke's.

Trying to get the focus off herself, she said, "I had lunch with Randy last week. Has he come by lately?"

"Indeed, though his messages of support aren't as eloquent as yours. My lawyer also visited yesterday while I slept and left a note. Harry declared bankruptcy with my invoices still unpaid.

Apparently he's gone to ground, in anticipation of you filing a devastating lawsuit."

"Have your lawyer tell his that I won't file if he covers your invoices and all medical expenses and gives both you and Randy a six-figure bonus. That'll be enough payback for me—though Candace has concocted a range of revenge scenarios she thinks I should try."

"How is she faring?"

"She didn't walk with her class on graduation day, but she did earn her diploma. After working this summer, she'll start at UGA in August."

"My alma mater—go Dawgs. It's a rebellious tradition for the child of Georgia Tech alumni to attend the University of Georgia."

His eyes closed again. She took his hand, amazed as ever that something so big could feel so insubstantial now in her much-smaller grip. He seemed to be made of light and air.

At last, he looked at her. "You haven't mentioned Oscar."

"He's still a mess. The infection is finally gone and the breaks have healed, but he needs more surgeries for his hand. His doctors think they can give him eighty-percent functionality."

"Is he treating you better?" Cobalt ripples of concern over the French toast backdrop.

"Our marriage functions at way below eighty percent. We have a new couples' therapist, and we each see a psychiatrist. The prescriptions regulate our moods. Staying out of each other's way helps, too. His parents and mine have visited, but he hated those *pity parties.*"

"It's not possible that he still blames you."

"No, he's heard the show recordings I made. Agent Martinez even briefed him about what the FBI found on Deke's computers. He knows I did all I could, but everything's worse for him: few job prospects because of his disability, nightmares and panic attacks, fear of strangers, claustrophobia. None of that's my doing, but I'm the reason he was targeted. After we get Candace set up in her dorm in August, he wants a trial separation." She gave him a shrug, mouth quivering. "Turns out, I could save my man but not my marriage."

"Remember the trinity?"

"Of course, but my practice of faith, hope, and love seems to be better suited for hostage rescue than relationship repair." She rested her cheek against his hand. "Oscar's alive, you're alive, and I finally avenged Lori. That's enough."

Relief, acceptance, and forgiveness of herself came with the words she had not given voice to before. She felt guilt's dark hold on her—which had kept her strangling for so long—release its grasp and fade away. Its absence brought a comfort she hadn't known in decades, like she could take in twice as much air.

Gus stroked her hair with gentle fingers until she heard him return to a recuperative sleep.

# CHAPTER 74

The *snick-snick* of the blade against the cutting board produced crimson splashes, while the wet slicing of scallions sent forth mustard-yellow streamers. Dressed in her favorite teal skirt suit, Bo stopped in the kitchen entrance and read Candace's latest snarky text about her UGA dorm. She glanced up. Brassy August-morning sunlight streamed into the room.

In the one shadowed spot, Oscar stood at the counter in his dress shirt, tie, and suit pants. Slimmed down—but mostly because he'd lost interest in eating. Another legacy of the Vault.

Her husband went through the motions of preparing their meal, while she stayed out of his way to avoid a potential conflict. Following the same old patterns, she conceded, even though they'd become different people.

He chopped with awkward, left-handed strokes. His right could only hold the green onions in place, because he still couldn't make a fist long enough to grip anything. At rest, his fingers and thumb tended to splay like a five-legged spider. Months of physical therapy exercises lay ahead. She wouldn't be able to "pester" him with reminders about that if he indeed moved out and they were no longer together.

*Together.* One of those words that sparked images of devotion and romance and sex. As with all words, though, said enough times in repetition it began to sound meaningless, its promises fleeting at best, illusory at worst.

Ever since his trial separation announcement, she'd gone from measuring her time with him in months to days, but she wondered if she now had mere hours.

It was like facing Deke's countdown all over again.

This, she saw, was one of those mornings when the power of mood overwhelmed the genius of pharmaceuticals. The Serenity

Prayer and thoughts of Mom's trinity helped to counter those negative thoughts that the drugs could not. They put her back in a productive frame of mind.

Maybe she could apply lessons from their ordeal that she hadn't considered before. It seemed like she, Candace, Gus, and Randy had only made progress in finding Oscar when they'd tried new strategies.

"Hey," she said, "can I help?"

"I got this—I'm not totally useless yet."

Despite his indignant words, she saw amusement in golden, curly ribbons over his backdrop of apricot. He was in a good mood. Either he was looking forward to his first day back at his old job, thinking about how they'd made love last night to celebrate, or deciding which apartment lease to sign after work. Maybe all three.

Instead of rising to the bait of another potential argument—what he said—she paid attention to what she saw. "Would you teach me? I want to learn."

He looked over. "Really?"

She nodded and set her phone on the counter, screen down.

"Okay." He slid the bamboo board in front of her. "Well, um, cutting veggies is all about knife safety and getting the shapes you want."

He showed her how to tuck her fingertips under her knuckles and set the blade against those ridges, and went through various cutting techniques to achieve different shapes.

"The shape you go with," he said, "affects cooking time and mouth feel."

She minced the rest of the scallions and then began to slice a half-dozen baby bella mushrooms, appreciating the excellent balance between the sharpened steel and the thick wood handle. A fine tool. "Differences in cooking time I get, but tell me more about mouth feel."

"When you take a bite of something that's too chunky or too long, all your focus instantly goes into chewing instead of tasting—because you're trying not to choke. If the shapes are right, though, the chewing becomes automatic and you can enjoy the flavors."

She focused on creating thin planes of brown and white, enjoying the teamwork between hands and blade. "You never look at recipes. How do you know which ingredients to use?"

He snorted, which looked like red sparks dancing. "You sure I'm not doing too much mansplaining?"

"No, I asked."

"This might sound weird, but lots of times I cook by colors as much as flavors—I can tell if I don't have enough sweet green veggies in something, or I'll think that a dish needs more acidic red. That's probably not how anybody else does it, but it seems to work for me."

"So, you're tasting shapes and colors." She grinned. "It's a kind of synesthesia."

"Huh, I never thought of it like that. I'll be damned, you're right." He looked away from her and fanned out the sliced portobellos like tiny, oval playing cards. "All this time in therapy, I kept saying we don't have anything in common. What else have I missed?"

Aquamarine horsetails of apology and regret spread in her mind's eye.

"They told us it's a process. If we do the work, we'll see the results." She bumped him with her hip. "Right now, that means breakfast."

"What can I do?" he asked.

She saw he wasn't talking about kitchen duties. But rather than drag him into yet another deep discussion about their relationship and recovery, she said, "Beat the eggs and heat the pan."

"Yes, ma'am." His smile, such a rare sight since the ordeal, made him look twenty again.

He had mastered cracking eggs with one hand, squeezing the separated shell to slide the yolk and whites into a bowl, but he still had some trouble producing a smooth southpaw rhythm with the whisk. The benefit was that it kept him by her side longer.

She shook her head in wonder. This simple act—making a meal together—had always been available to them. Maybe happiness as a couple wasn't about grand romantic gestures and soaring passion. Perhaps the foundation lay here, in the small activities of everyday life, learning from each other and sharing experiences.

"Bo, are you chopping or what?" The golden ribbons had returned to his voice.

She went to work dicing the Roma tomatoes. The last one she cut spurted pulp and seeds at her. She jumped back belatedly, but Oscar had moved faster. His damaged right hand protected her skirt suit from the spray of juice.

Chuckling, he said, "That was an overripe one. You can always tell because the skin wrinkles when you slice into it. I was saving that lesson for next time."

She tore off a paper towel and dampened it under the faucet while she tried not to overanalyze his implied promise. "Thanks for saving my outfit."

"Can't have you going on camera covered in red. Viewers will think you just freed me again."

He made it a joke, but this was a good reminder of what they'd be dealing with for the rest of their lives. Tamping down the onslaught of memories from the Vault, she took his damaged hand in hers. After she wiped it clean, she maintained her grip on him. "Is . . . is today the day?"

"First day back to work—you know that." He looked into her eyes and then dropped his gaze to their clasped hands.

"I mean the other thing."

"Well, um, I'm not sure. I haven't seen any places I've really liked so far and, you know, things have been nice here lately. Like we've turned a corner?" Expectant azure ripples.

Getting hired back and getting laid on the same day seemed to have been enough for him, but it wasn't sufficient for her, despite the relief she felt.

*Time to stop pretending, stop holding back the words that are long overdue.*

She said, "No, the relationship we had died before it got to that corner."

"Oh." He tried to turn toward the stove, where he'd set the omelet pan, but she held fast, now with both hands.

"We can't revive it," she said, "but we don't need to. We're different people now. That means our relationship will be different. For the last six months, we've tried everything to resurrect our old marriage. It hasn't worked because we both have deep scars—inside and out—that we didn't have back then. But I think we also discovered some good new things we can build on. Resiliency and thankfulness and an appreciation for what we used to take for granted."

"Can I have my hand back, please?"

She shook her head. "Your hand's part of me, just like my wounds are part of you. Maybe that means we're united more than ever before."

"Yeah, but how are we gonna make breakfast like this?"

She smiled and kissed him, slow and deep. When their mouths parted, she saw mica-like glitter. Keeping hold of him, she reached over with her free hand and twisted a knob to ignite the gas flame under the pan. "You tilt, and I'll scrape."

They kissed again while the pan heated. After he lifted the cutting board, she used the knife to slide the tomatoes, scallions, and mushrooms into the spreading puddle of olive oil, creating a sizzle of marmalade-orange pinwheels. He traded the board for a spatula and pushed the food around, still a little awkward left-handed. She swirled the pan in a few rapid circles to help.

Watching the ingredients sauté, he said, "I love this," which showed her silvery bands around a perfect pearl. "What should we call it?"

"With three things in there, we could name it our Trinity Omelet."

"No, I mean *this*." Oscar closed his damaged hand on hers, fingers entwined, and kept it that way, eyes narrowed as he focused. His grip felt tender . . . fragile . . . but seemed like it would last. "I want to cook, shower, do everything three-handed."

"*Our trinity* sounds right for that, too: faith in each other, hope fueling our journey, and love as our goal—and also the way." Bo shook the pan to stir the food. "Ready with those eggs?"

# Special Offer to Readers of *Watch What You Say*

I am eternally grateful to readers of my books. There are so many other ways you could've spent your precious time and money. Your decision to select my work for entertainment and to connect with characters and circumstances that feel real—regardless of how extraordinary they are—never fails to humble me.

Without readers, writers are superfluous. Without readers' feedback, writers can't know whether they've succeeded in their purpose. Moreover, other readers won't have guidance about whether a book is likely to suit their tastes. If you post your review of Watch What You Say on Amazon, Goodreads, Facebook, or elsewhere online, please e-mail me the link to your comments at GeorgeWeinstein@Gmail.com.

I'd love to engage with you about your reactions to this story and also sign you up for my newsletter, with two new essays written each month for readers and for writers, respectively. These will give you a glimpse of how and why authors do what we do and provide insights into the writing life. To read my past essays, please go to my website, GeorgeWeinstein.com, and click the "Author's Notebook" link at the top.

Thank you in advance for sharing your comments with other book lovers and with me. I hope you also will adore the other novels I've written—with the range of genres I cover, there's probably something else you're bound to enjoy as much or more than this one!

# Acknowledgements

Feedback from my critique partners helped me to improve the prose, develop the characters, better define the settings, and (hopefully) correct any errors. It's a privilege and an honor to share my work with such talented writers and insightful readers.

Thanks, too, to the topnotch team at SFK Press: Steve McCondichie, April Ford, and the others who have dedicated themselves to publishing a million tales of "Y'all Means All."

Finally, I want to express my appreciation to the many women and men who have discussed their various forms of synesthesia in person with me, written about it online and in books, and spoken of this phenomenon across other media. The blending of senses of one kind or another is estimated to affect at least five percent of the world's population, according to the National Institutes of Health, but I think we've all experienced some form of this from time to time. Perhaps numerous people do so regularly and never consider mentioning it. They assume everybody assigns a personality to each number, tastes shapes, hears odors, sees color and motion in every sound, or interacts with their world in other ways the rest of us would regard as singular.

We all exist in our own, special reality. I hope Bo Riccardi's felt that way to you.

# ABOUT THE AUTHOR

George Weinstein is fond of telling readers the stories behind the stories, and providing writers with advice he wished he had received when he embarked on his writing career in 2000. Information about his books, novel excerpts, endorsements and reviews, book club questions, and more ephemera than you could conceivably care about is available on his website, GeorgeWeinstein.com.

For the past decade and counting, George has directed the bi-annual Atlanta Writers Conference to give writers access to top acquisitions editors, literary agents, and other industry professionals: AtlantaWritersConference.com. He is also the once-and-current President of the Atlanta Writers Club, AtlantaWritersClub.org.

George lives with his wife—whom he courted with handwritten love letters, naturally—and their furry four-legged children in Roswell, Georgia.

# SHARE YOUR THOUGHTS

Want to help make *Watch What You Say* a best-selling novel? Consider leaving an honest review on Goodreads, your personal author website or blog, and anywhere else readers go for recommendations. It's our priority at SFK Press to publish books for readers to enjoy, and our authors appreciate and value your feedback.

# Our Southern Fried Guarantee

If you wouldn't enthusiastically recommend one of our books with a 4- or 5-star rating to a friend, then the next story is on us. We believe that much in the stories we're telling. Simply email us at pr@sfkmultimedia.com.

# Do You Know About Our Bi-Monthly Zine?

Would you like your unpublished prose, poetry, or visual art featured in *The New Southern Fugitives*? A bi-monthly zine that's free to readers and subscribers and pays contributors:

**$100 for book reviews, essays, short stories**
**$40 for flash/micro fiction**
**$40 for poetry**
**$40 for photography & visual art**

Visit **NewSouthernFugitives.com/Submit** for more information.

# Also by SFK Press